"Exquisitely well-made—not so much written as . . . . est of instruments. Dense blocks of gorgeous prose, ... edge, line and surface reveals the intelligence within. . . . . and thought-provoking meditation on art and creativity . . . .
—Charles Yu, author of *How to Live Safely in a Science F. . . . .*

"A beautiful book about the two most unwieldy kinds of alche. . . . love. The bold intelligence of the voice would have been enough . . . the book, but it also provides all the pleasures of obsessions, rich d. . . . of the sixties world and plot twists."
—Katherine Rundell, *Telegraph* (UK; The Best Books for Summ. . .

"An intelligent examination of creativity, psychology, and a riveting mystery . . . This ambitious novel will haunt the imagination long after the final page." —*The Independent* (London)

"A mark of the elegance and conviction of Wood's writing is that he absorbs the reader entirely in whichever setting he takes you to. . . . Intricate and ambitious, with shades of Kazuo Ishiguro and Eleanor Catton."
—*The Bookseller*

"Here is such an intense evocation of the hell of creativity that one might begin to wonder whether art is even worth it. Well, yes, it is, case in point being the novel itself: whatever debilitating mental toll it must have taken on Benjamin Wood to sustain such vividness and intelligence for its entire length, we can all be grateful for the result. Terrific."
—Ned Beauman, author of *The Teleportation Accident*

"A thrilling novel that combines fine writing with a propulsive plot, *The Ecliptic* will rightly appeal to fans of Patricia Highsmith and Donna Tartt. It confirms Benjamin Wood's place as one of Britain's best young writers."
—Jonathan Lee, author of *High Dive*

ABOUT THE AUTHOR

Benjamin Wood was born in 1981 and grew up in north-west England. His debut novel, *The Bellwether Revivals*, was selected for the Barnes & Noble Discover Great New Writers program, shortlisted for the Costa First Novel Award and the Commonwealth Book Prize in the U.K., and won France's Le Prix du Roman Fnac. He lives with his family in London.

The Ecliptic

BENJAMIN WOOD

PENGUIN BOOKS

PENGUIN BOOKS

An imprint of Penguin Random House LLC
375 Hudson Street
New York, New York 10014
penguin.com

First published in Great Britain by Scribner,
an imprint of Simon & Schuster UK Ltd, 2015
First published in the United States of America by Penguin Press,
an imprint of Penguin Random House LLC, 2016
Published in Penguin Books 2017

ISBN 9781594206863 (hc.)
ISBN 9781101980354 (paperback)

Printed in the United States of America
1   3   5   7   9   10   8   6   4   2

FOR STEPH

History repeats itself, but the special call of an art which has passed away is never reproduced. It is as utterly gone out of the world as the song of a destroyed wild bird.

JOSEPH CONRAD

One of Four

- - - - - - - - - - - -

Habituations

One

He was just seventeen when he came to Portmantle, a runaway like the rest of us, except there was a harrowed quality about this boy that we had not seen before in any of the newcomers. A private torment seemed to clamp the muscles of his face, as though every disappointment in the world had been disclosed to him too young and stunted his expression. We knew him as Fullerton: an ordinary name, a plain one, but not the sort that sinks into the depths of memory without unsettling others.

Our anticipation of him was enough to disrupt our normal routines, setting us off course the way a premature adjustment to the wind can strand a kite. Rarely had we paid so much attention to the refuge gates, or given more than a terse thought to another resident's circumstance. But he was presented to us as a special case, a kindred spirit worthy of our time and interest. So we offered it.

We were conscripted to his cause from the beginning: Quickman, MacKinney, Pettifer and me. The provost himself had called a meeting in his study to explain, over a glass of pomegranate juice, that Portmantle was about to receive its youngest ever resident, and had made a show of outlining how much he would personally appreciate our support. 'You know I'm loath to burden you with this kind of responsibility,' he had told us, 'but the boy's going to need some help finding his feet, and Ender can't manage on his own—his English isn't up to it. I need the four of you to be there for him while I'm gone. You remember what it's like to be gifted at that age—a sympathetic ear can really make a difference.' In truth, we were cajoled into a volunteering mood by the hint of a reward, some luxury that might be procured from the mainland in return for our good deed: Earl Grey tea leaves, smoked bacon, porridge oats; the most banal of pantry items were great delicacies to us, and we wilted at the thought of them.

There was plenty that the provost did not make clear and much that we were not privy to. The details of Fullerton's troubles were as confidential as our own. No doubts were raised as to his temperament. Nothing was discussed as to his reasons for admittance. We only asked for some small insight into the type of work the boy was known for, but getting answers from the provost was like trying to press cider from geraniums. 'You can ask him yourselves in a few days,' he said. 'I wouldn't want to prejudice the boy before he even gets here.'

We awaited his arrival from the mainland for two eventless days, like prisoners expecting mail, and cursed him on the wasted afternoons he did not show. 'Assuming the little sod ever gets here,' Pettifer said, 'he's going to work off every last bit of time he owes me. He can start by polishing my boots. I want a shine so good I can see up my nose.' This after we had given up an entire Saturday morning to assist the caretaker with his preparations.

While Ender and his staff had cleaned and organised the boy's lodging, we had dug the snow from all the footpaths around the mansion, taking turns with the shovel, only for another flume of mothy flakes to come down overnight, leaving just a faint and rutted trail to show for all our grunt work by Sunday lunchtime. Our charity did not extend to shovelling a path twice, which is why the snow was so thick and undisturbed when Fullerton finally appeared.

He came stumbling up the hill with nothing but a canvas bag and the hood of his cagoule cinched tight around his head. MacKinney spotted him in the window of the mess hall—'Hey-o,' she said, 'here comes trouble'—and we abandoned our plates and gathered on the landing to get a better look at him.

It was clear from the simple determination of the boy's strides as he pushed and staggered through the white-dusted pines that he needed the sanctuary of Portmantle as much as we did. From our very first glimpse of him, we understood that he was one of us. He had the rapid footfalls of a fugitive, the grave hurriedness of a soldier who had seen a grenade drop somewhere in the track behind. We could recognise the ghosts that haunted him because they were the same ghosts we had carried through the gates ourselves and were still trying to excise.

'He hasn't even stopped to catch his breath, you know. It's quite impressive,' Quickman said, bothering to lift his pipe out from his teeth for the first time that day. He had run out of tobacco so long ago that the bowl was dry, but he was content just to chew on the mouthpiece—there was residual flavour there, he insisted, that would suffice in lieu of smoke. (He still kept an empty pouch of Golden Harvest in his trouser pocket and would often be found inspecting it, as though in hope the contents had replenished by some miracle.)

MacKinney tilted down her glasses, peering over the lenses. 'What kind of coat is that to be wearing in winter?' she said. The boy was stooped now, battling the slope, both hands folded into his armpits. 'I don't understand why it's so hard to get a man into a proper coat. There's nothing heroic about freezing to death.' She was the most parental of the four of us, being the oldest by a distance, and the only one with daughters of her own out in the world. Her mothering nature often surfaced at mealtimes, lending her the compulsion to cant her head and tell us, too often, that we were drawn or undernourished. She had this very look about her now.

Pettifer gave an amused little snort—his own peculiar laugh. 'No scarf, no hat, no gloves. Stupidity is more like it.' The boy was stumbling over the frosted Mediterranean scrub, into the open space before the boundary wall. When he reached the gates, he fell forwards, gripping the bars, pressing his head to the metal as though in prayer. 'Look at him—he can barely stand up in those silly shoes of his.' And, with this, the boy bent and vomited. The yellowy liquid steamed by his feet. 'Oh dear. There goes breakfast.'

'Don't laugh,' I told them. 'He's got to be exhausted.' It was a mile uphill from the ferry—a draining enough hike in clement weather. And the boy was not even wearing proper boots. No wonder he was retching.

Pettifer grinned. 'How do you know he didn't eat something bad while he was on the mainland? That street offal the Turks love so much. The chopped-up stuff.' He turned to Quickman. 'What's it called again?'

'*Kokoreç*,' Quickman said. 'Sheep's innards.'

'That's it. All very tasty while it's going down, but once it's in your system—' He mouthed a silent explosion, then made the action with his spreading fingers to illustrate it.

I ignored him. 'You'd think someone could've warned the lad.'

'About what?'

'The snow. I'll bet he doesn't have much in that bag of his, either.'

'Nobody warned me about *kokoreç*,' said Pettifer, 'and I survived. He's a teenager, not an eight-year-old.'

MacKinney wiped a circle in the fogging glass. 'Tif's right. You start telling people what to pack, next thing they'll be showing up with their valets.'

'Especially the women,' said Pettifer, winking. 'We can't have them coming here with evening gowns and whatnot.' This sort of provocation was a feature of his company. He was a flirt by reflex and, because the pickings of women at Portmantle were so scant, he quite often directed his affections towards me in the manner of schoolyard teasing. That I harboured no physical attraction for him and made this fact consistently evident was what gave him the confidence to be flirtatious—such was the male tendency, in my experience. He was no more a chauvinist than a fascist, but sometimes he liked to test my temperature for his own entertainment.

MacKinney leaned closer to the pane. 'A bit of snow shouldn't stop anyone who needs this place enough. Man or woman. And, anyway—he seems fine now, look. He's not complaining.'

'Can't be anything left to spit up,' Pettifer said. 'Half his guts are on the ground.'

He took my boot tip in the shin for this. 'I wish you wouldn't revel in it quite so much. When was the last time *you* hiked anywhere?'

'I ran cross-country when I was his age.' He patted his paunch. 'Now I can't get off the toilet in the morning.'

'Jesus,' Quickman said. 'What an image.'

'You're welcome.'

It was difficult now to recall the days when Pettifer and Quickman were strangers to me. They had landed at the refuge a season apart, but they had bonded almost immediately, over a dinnertime discussion of the weather (what better topic was there for two Englishmen to deliberate upon?). Later, when MacKinney and I had been playing backgammon at the shady end of the portico, they had both lurked some distance from our board with glasses of *çay*, making disparaging remarks about our game in whispered voices. 'If you're going to sit there tittering all day,' MacKinney had called to them, 'why don't you come and show us how it's done? We're not exactly playing to the death.' They had apologised for their rudeness and sat down with us. 'Didn't anyone ever tell you,' Quickman had said, 'that all games should be taken seriously? My father used to drill that into me.' I had scowled at him then, uncertain of his meaning. 'Still, once you've seen a grown man break his ankle playing musical chairs, you start to question his advice a bit.' Mac had laughed her big, ingenuous laugh, and that was it—the beginning of our attachment. It did not seem to matter that we had travelled thousands of miles to remove ourselves from the hindrances of life in Britain only to hitch ourselves to each other.

'Has anybody seen Ender? Someone's got to let the boy inside.'

I looked back into the emptying mess hall, where the old care-taker had last been spotted at the back of the line for bluefish stew. A few of the other guests were still finishing their lunches, alone together on the same long table. We had hardly taken the time to learn their names, but we had heard about their projects in various ways and dismissed them as short-termers already— 'transients', Pettifer called them, which was his way of saying 'lesser talents'.

It was our judgement that the duration of a stay at Portmantle was equivalent to the value of the work being done: if you were gone after one season, it was likely because your project could not sustain a greater period of gestation. For example, there was the Spanish poet we had spoken to at lunch, who had proudly an-nounced that he was working on a sequence of minimalist poems that were disdainful of linearity, narrative, and meaning. 'Sounds like an important collection,' Quickman had responded, and turned his head to roll his eyes at us. 'If anything needs to be eradicated from poetry, it's meaning.' The Spaniard had nodded at this, deaf to the sarcasm, and proceeded to discuss the remark-able complexity of his work with Quickman, whose feigned in-terest was admirably upheld throughout.

We gave this poet two seasons, maximum. Any guest who could not wait to talk about the project he was working on was usually a short-termer—that was our evaluation. Anyone who proclaimed his own genius was a fraud, because, as Quickman himself once put it, genius does not have time to stand admiring its reflection; it has too much work to get finished. We never sought out the company of short-termers. We left them to work and find their clarity alone, while we got on with jabbing at our own unwieldy projects. None of us seemed to recognise the fact that our separation from the others was, in fact, a tacit declaration of our own genius—and, thus, it surely followed that we were the biggest frauds of all. We did not even consider that the purest talent at Portmantle was standing at the front gate in a pool of his own vomit.

'No point calling the old man,' said Quickman, eyes on the window. 'Our boy's about to hit the buzzer.' And right on cue, the hallway below us echoed with the sound of it: three long, grating blasts. Quickman set the pipe back in the crease of his mouth. 'Places, everyone,' he said, his voice betraying a little excitement.

The buzzer sounded again.

Ender, the old caretaker, emerged from the mess hall with a napkin stuffed inside his shirt collar. It was streaked with pale stew-stains. He was still holding his spoon. 'It is him?' he said. 'The ringing?'

'Yup,' said Pettifer. 'He's probably got hypothermia by now. Better hop to it.'

'OK. I go. You stay.' Ender tore the napkin from his collar, dabbed his moustache clean, and tucked the spoon into his breast pocket. He went scuttling down the stairs. 'You can wait inside the library, yes?' he called back to us from the bottom step, putting on his coat. 'I bring him.'

From the window, we watched the old man tread across the thick white lawns, making holes in the snowpack. He carried the provost's shotgun with him, as was the customary practice, hinged over his left forearm, unloaded. The fur trim of his parka matched the two-tone grey of his hair. When he got to the gate, he spoke to the boy through the ironwork.

There was a passphrase incoming guests were told to use, which the provost changed every season, though it was usually a line from a poem or some favourite literary reference. MacKinney and I had both been given the same quote to recite: *Eastward we turn and homeward, alone, remembering.* Pettifer had: *To turn, as swimmers into cleanness leaping, glad from a world grown old.* Quickman's had been a translation of a Turkish author, Hüseyin Rahmi Gürpinar, whose work was the provost's academic fetish, though Quickman claimed he could not remember the line in detail. Poor old Ender had to memorise all of these passphrases every season, his spoken English being the most reliable. His mind must have been loaded with enough disordered verse to rival our resident Spaniard. But, in all his time as caretaker, there had been no cause for him to fire a single shot. The system worked too well. Anyone who deigned to buzz the gate at Portmantle had to know the procedure for entry. You would be turned away at gunpoint if you did not.

After Fullerton had spoken his noiseless passphrase, the old man let him in. The boy stepped through, peering up at the window where we stood above the portico. If he saw us staring back at him, he did not let on. He waited patiently for Ender to lock up, and then the two of them slogged across the grounds in single file.

At the front steps, Fullerton stopped to kick the powder off his heels and switched his bag to the other shoulder. He gazed back in the direction he had travelled, pausing there awhile, as though the gate signified a line between the present and the past and he was taking a moment to acknowledge the gravity of his circumstance. We had seen this quirk of behaviour in others. Some time ago, too far back to recall how it felt, we had made the same gesture ourselves.

'We ought to get a move on,' MacKinney said.

We went along the corridor, into the dark library with its classroom smell and its awkward collection of furniture. I opened the curtains and switched on the lamps. Pettifer and Quickman crouched at the hearth, debating the merits of lighting a fire. 'How long are we expected to entertain this lad?' Pettifer asked of nobody in particular. 'I mean, there's only so long I can sustain these airs and graces.'

'Just hurry up and light the thing. He'll be in need of it,' MacKinney told him.

'Seems to me—' Pettifer sighed, reaching for a block of firewood, 'that others are getting the benefit of my exertions a little too often these days.'

Quickman nudged him. 'How about you give us the benefit of your silence then, instead?'

'You're going to wish you hadn't said that.'

Quickman laughed. 'Here—toss this paper on the pile.'

'You should twist it first. Burns better.'

The two of them were still lighting the fire when Ender shuffled in. The boy loomed behind him, shivering on the threshold. He was wrapped up in a blanket, standard issue: scratchy orange wool with a hand-embroidered P.

Ender coughed and said, 'Excuse me, our guest is very cold and tired, so maybe not much of talking for today. Hello, hello, and then we go—OK?' The old man took a step to one side, presenting the boy with an extended arm, as though he were the conclusion of a magic trick. Then he said, 'Fullerton, this is some people who take care of you now, for today, and soon the provoss hisself will be here.' In the old man's unaccustomed tongue, it sounded more like *Foolertinn*. 'They are old but not so bad for talking. You can like them.'

'Crikey.' Pettifer rose, wiping soot on his trousers. 'Impossible to live up to that sort of introduction.'

The boy lifted his chin and forced out a whisper: 'Hey.' He was trembling so much the blanket quivered about his body like a storm sail. Now that his hood was down and he was close enough, we could see the wholeness of his face. His small brown eyes were close together, sunken, drawing attention to the slim pillar of his nose and its bell of soft cartilage. He had a slack lower jaw— what my father used to call a 'lazy mouth'—the tongue nesting behind the bottom row of teeth, giving wetness to his lips. His dark hair parted easily in the middle, like the pages of a Bible, and it was fashioned in that lank teenage style, curtaining his brow, obscuring what appeared to be a birthmark on the left of his forehead. He was probably shorter than most boys his age, though his broad, hod-carrier's shoulders held an arching shape beneath the blanket that made him seem older.

I was the first of us to speak to him. The others hung back, unsure. We had almost forgotten how to talk to anyone but ourselves. 'Hell of a trek, isn't it?' I said. 'Your feet must be aching. Sit down.' For some reason, I did not offer him my hand to shake but gave an odd sort of Sitting Bull wave, palm flat and raised. 'I'm Knell. With a K. Good to meet you.'

He nodded back, shuddering.

'Come on in by the fire. It's going a treat now. Get yourself warm.'

He moved in closer to the hearth. Then, casting off the blanket, he leaned with both arms spread across the mantelpiece, imbibing the heat. From behind, it seemed as though he was holding up the wall itself.

'The two gents to your right are Pettifer and Quickman.' They both waved, but the boy's back was turned to them, and he did not seem to be listening. 'And that's MacKinney there by the window. She and I have been here since, oh, I'm not sure it's polite to say.'

'Not so long as me,' said Ender, still in the doorway. 'I am getting the white hairs.' He combed his moustache with his fingers and crowed.

The boy did not move. 'Please,' he said, so quietly it was almost lost amid the crackle of the flames, 'if I could just have a minute to—' He clutched his stomach. We took a few paces back as a precaution, but nothing came up. The boy sighed and continued: 'Just to thaw out, that's all. I still can't feel my toes.' He turned now, his back to the fire, a radiant outline about his middle. His eyes were shut and he was inhaling through the nose, exhaling through his puckered mouth. 'You can talk . . . I just need to . . . to be quiet for a sec . . .'

'Of course,' I said, sitting down on the couch, making eyes at MacKinney. We shrugged at each other. 'The provost asked us to be your welcoming party. He thought, with the four of us being so used to the place, and speaking the same language, it might help you bed in quicker. A little familiarity goes a long way here. He wanted to give the induction himself, but—'

Fullerton kept on trying to regulate his breathing. I was not sure that he was receiving me.

'He's had to go off-island,' I continued. 'Organising your paperwork, I should think, just in case you decide to stay longer. So we're only substitutes, I'm afraid. But I promise you're getting the same treatment as everyone else.'

Pettifer spoke up then: 'Actually, we've never rolled out the red carpet like this before. For *anyone*.' He cleared his throat, as though the implication of this noise would prompt the boy into a response. But it did not, and Pettifer folded his arms, affronted. 'Well, I'm really feeling the glow of philanthropy right now, I must say.'

'Leave him be,' said MacKinney. 'He's just got here and we're crowding him.'

'It's OK,' the boy said at last. 'I told you . . . I'm just cold.' He opened his eyes then, and stared back at us. 'And I *do* appreciate you all being so friendly. But I didn't come here to make friends. I just want to get out of these clothes and rest, and maybe we can all have dinner sometime later. That's how it works, right? I was told I'd be left alone.'

Quickman bit down on his pipe, smirking. 'That's the long and the short of it. Dinner is any time after the bell goes. There's a rule about taking it in the mess hall, so I suppose we'll save a place for you.' He narrowed his eyes at the boy, checking he was being heard. 'There are other rules, too, of course—but I expect you've been told most of them by now. The rest you can figure out as you go. Or ask the provost when he gets back. When *does* he get back, by the way?'

'Three days,' Ender informed him.

'Well then.'

Fullerton blinked. He tucked the strands of his hair behind his ears.

'Perhaps we should let Ender take him out to his lodging,' I said. And then, flicking my eyes to the boy: 'We were asked to show you how things worked, that's all, answer your questions and such. But I suppose we can leave you alone, if that's what you'd prefer. We'll be around, in case you need anything.'

'You can't miss us,' said MacKinney. 'We're always somewhere.'

'All right, thanks,' the boy said. He bent to retrieve the blanket from the floor and then began to study the shelves above the mantel. 'Are we allowed to take these books?'

'Some of them,' Pettifer said. 'You're not old enough for *Lady Chatterley*, are you?' He tried to engage the rest of us in his amusement but we kept quiet.

'Funny, I don't see that here.' The boy browsed the spines serenely. 'Maybe you could bring it back when the pages are dry.'

Pettifer flushed. 'That's disgusting.'

'OK, OK,' Quickman said, 'let's get back to work.' He made for the door, patting Pettifer on the shoulder as he went past. 'We'll adjourn this for later.'

I stood up, smiling at the boy. 'It's nice to have a young face around.'

He nodded back.

Pettifer waved at the fire. 'You can let that burn out. Or you can get more wood from downstairs. Up to you.'

'Yeah, all right. Thanks.'

We were reluctant to leave him. Not just because we felt guilty for reneging on our promise to the provost, but because we found the boy such a confusing presence. We were not used to having gloomy teenagers about the place. He had a very modern manner that we did not know how to decode. There was something dis-

comfiting about him in the most thrilling sense, the way a familiar room can be changed by a new arrangement of furniture. He
enlivened us, shook us out of our habituations without even trying to. Of course, we could not anticipate how much he would
affect the next period of our lives. It was as though, on that first
afternoon with us, he loosened our connecting bolts quite accidentally, and the slow turn of the days saw to the rest.

On our way out, Quickman stopped, gripping the doorframe.
'Say, Fullerton,' he called. 'You don't happen to have any pipe
tobacco, by any chance? I'll strip down a cigarette, if that's all
you have.'

The boy, for the first time, showed a glimmer of warmth towards us. His jaw hung open and he ran his tongue over his
teeth. Then he reached into the pocket of his jeans and drew
out a packet of cigarettes, a Turkish brand. He threw the whole
crumpled box to Quickman. 'I recognise you,' he said. 'I think I
do, anyway.'

Quickman remained polite. 'Ah well, don't hold it against me.'
He clutched the cigarettes to his heart. 'Thanks for these.' But
the box made no sound when he shook it. He pulled out the foil
lining and scrunched it in his fist. 'I won't lie: that's a blow to
morale.'

And the boy smiled at last.

Two

We were told that Heybeliada lay twelve miles off the coast of Istanbul, the second largest in a constellation of islands the locals knew as Adalar. It was crowned by two steep forested hills to the north and south, and its middle section bowed into a plain of settlements where the natives lived and plied their trades. Much of the work there was seasonal. In the winter, the squat apartment blocks and rangy wooden houses stood vacant and unlit, but when the bright weather came again they filled up with summering Istanbullus, who sat out on their fretwork balconies, sunbathed on the rocky beaches, flocked upon the shining Marmara like gulls, and drank merrily on their roof-decks until dark. The Turkish meaning of its name—Saddlebag Island—evoked its shape at sea level, but, looking down from a higher vantage as we did, the place bore a closer resemblance to a hipbone. It was far up on the south-eastern peak, amidst the dense umbrella pines on the tubercle of the island, that Portmantle was positioned. The only part of it that could be seen from the ferry as you approached was the upper limit of its gabled rooftop, and even this

had been seized by so much moss and grime that it was lightly
camouflaged.

Every guest who came to Portmantle took the same route from
the dock. It required specific information just to find your way.
You could not step off the boat and expect to pick up signs. You
could not stop into any of the cafés or *lokantas* on the waterfront
to ask for directions. The horse-drawn *faytons* would not take
you there. It was too removed from the populated strip for any of
the locals to be concerned with, and those few natives who knew
of the place believed it was a private residence, owned by a reclu-
sive academic who took violently to trespassers. And so the refuge was afforded the same courtesy of disregard as any other
private mansion or holiday villa on the island, which made it a
perfect spot to disappear.

The only way into the refuge was from the east, via Çam Limani Yolu, a dirt road that led up to a spear-top fence, cordoning
off the property. MacKinney always said it might be possible to
circumvent the gates by swimming across the bay from the south-
western point of the island and climbing up the promontory on
the blind side, but we had never seen her theory put to the test.
The phoney warning posters stapled to the fence along the slope
were a good enough deterrent: DIKKAT KÖPEK VAR /BEWARE OF
THE DOG.

It was not known how long Portmantle had existed, but we
understood that many others had sought refuge there before we
ever claimed it: to rescue the depleted minds of artists like us
was the reason it was founded. In the seclusion of the grounds,
artists could work outside the straitjacket of the world and its

pressures. We could tune out those voices that nagged and pecked, forget the doubts that stifled us, dispense with all the mundane tasks, distractions, and responsibilities, detach from the infernal noises of industry—the endless ringing of the telephone, the urging letters that came in logoed envelopes from galleries, publishers, studios, patrons—and work, finally work, without intrusion or the steering influence of another living soul. 'Creative freedom', 'originality', 'true expression'—these terms were spoken like commandments at Portmantle, even if they were scarcely realised, or just phantom ideals to begin with. It was no more than a place for recuperation. A sanatorium of sorts—not for the defeat of any physical affliction, but for the relocation of a lost desire, a mislaid trust in art itself. Clarity, we called it: the one thing we could not live without.

It was a custom at Portmantle to forgo the mention of time except in the barest measurements: the passing of days, the turning of seasons, the position of the sun above the trees. Both Ender and the provost kept pocket watches to ensure the smooth running of things, but there were no clocks in our lodgings, and we were not encouraged to have timepieces or calendars of any kind. It would be wrong to say that we were not *allowed* them, because we were free to do as we pleased, within certain limits. Any of us could have smuggled in a wristwatch or made a sundial with our bodies and a line of chalk, but the idea was acknowledged by everybody as self-defeating. Why should we let our thoughts run clockwise? Why should we live by the laws of a world we were no longer governed by? Art could not be made to fit a timetable. Instead, we used vague descriptors—'tomorrow morning', 'last Wednesday', 'three or four seasons ago', et cetera—and they served us well enough, liberated us from the notion we had that our pulses were countdowns to zero.

That is why I cannot say with complete accuracy how long I had been at Portmantle by the time of Fullerton's admission. The year I arrived was 1962, but since then I had watched so many winters frost the surrounding pines that they had begun to blur into one grey season, as vast and misted as the sea. Early on, I ran out of things to write in my journal, so I could not extrapolate a definite figure from the tally of entries. According to my best calculation, though, I had spent at least ten years at Portmantle along with MacKinney, while Quickman and Pettifer were closing in on eight.

We were given false names because our real ones were too much baggage; some reputations were greater than others, and Portmantle was intended to be a place of parity. It was also believed that our real names fostered complacency and restricted us to established methods, familiar modes of thought. So the provost chose new surnames for us from telephone directories and old ship's manifests (he collected these on his travels and archived them in folders in his study). Our given names took no account of race or ethnicity, which is why MacKinney—the daughter of Russian émigrés—bore the handle of a Celt, and why the place had been home to numerous other oddities: a Lebanese painter called Dubois, an Italian novelist called Howells, a Slav illustrator called Singh, a Norwegian architect who answered only to O'Malley. In a funny way, we became more attached to our false names than the true ones. After a while, they began to suit us better.

I was born Elspeth Conroy in Clydebank, Scotland, on 17th

March 1937. I had always thought my family name quite unremarkable, and my Christian name so formal and girl-pretty. Elspeth Conroy, I felt, was the name of a debutante or a local politician's wife, not a serious painter with vital things to say about the world, but it was my fate and I had to accept it. My parents believed a refined Scottish name like Elspeth would enable me to marry a man of higher class (that is to say, a *rich* man) and, eventually, I managed to prove their theory wrong in every aspect. Still, I always suspected my work was undermined by that label, Elspeth Conroy. Did people exact their judgements upon me in galleries when they noticed my name? Did they see my gender on the wall, my nationality, my class, my type, and fail to connect with the truth of my paintings? It is impossible to know. I made my reputation as an artist with this label attached and it became the thing by which people defined and categorised me. I was a Scottish female painter, and thus I was recorded in the glossary of history. One day, when I felt secure enough to leave Portmantle, I would return to being Elspeth Conroy, take her off the peg like a stiff old coat and see if she still fitted. Until then, I was allowed to be someone different. Knell. Good old *Knell*. Separate and yet the same. Without her, I was nobody.

Of the four of us, it was surely Quickman who valued his detachment most. In the early days, we could not look at him without thinking of the famous photograph on the back cover of his novels—the sunflower lean of him towards the lens, arms crossed defiantly, the brooding London skyline on his shoulders. We had grown up with him on our shelves, that stylish young face squinting at us over bookends, from underneath coffee mugs on our bedside tables. His real name was known in many households, even if it was not part of daily conversation; in literary circles, it was a synonym for greatness, a word that critics added *esque* to in reviews of lesser writers. Every resident at Portmantle—even the provost—had owned, or at least seen, a copy of Quickman's first book, *In Advent of Rain*, published when he was only twenty-one. It was a required text on school curricula in Britain, considered a classic of its time. But the good-natured soul we knew as Quickman was not quite the same person—he was prickly at times, though self-effacing, and stood opposed to all the fuss and fanfare of the literary scene. Now he hungered only for a quiet room to be alone, a basic legal pad, and enough Staedtler HB pencils to fill an old cigar box. His given name suited him perfectly. His speed of thought was exceptional. And he was so unbothered with grooming that his beard spread all across his cheekbones like gorse; it hid the handsome symmetry of his features and gave him the look of a man long shipwrecked.

Pettifer's real name also held some weight out in the world. As an architect, he was rarely in the public eye and, in truth, his stubby face did not register with me at all when I first saw it. If he ever spoke of buildings he was responsible for (it happened, on occasion, when he got maudlin), their shapes could be summoned to mind, but only in the nostalgic way you might recall a favourite chair or a special bottle of wine. His real name was the type brought up at dinner parties and society gatherings, after which people nodded and said, 'Ah yes, I always liked that building. That's one of his, is it?' Now he was so used to being called Pettifer, and its various abbreviations, that he had vowed to adopt it when he left the island. He would establish a whole new practice one day, so he claimed, under the banner of Pettifer &

Associates. We did not know if this was a serious promise, but it would not have surprised us to find such a plan eventuated.

Of course, we assumed that Fullerton's real name must have held some equal notoriety on the mainland—everyone at Portmantle had earned a reputation in their field, which is why great measures were taken to safeguard its location. The fact is, we were too removed from the world to understand the scale of the boy's renown. He was a frequent surprise to us.

He did not show up for dinner on his first evening, and I found myself worrying about him more than I had reason to. What if he had caught the flu, I wondered, or pneumonia? I could not bear the thought of him alone and suffering in his room, having had a bladder infection myself during the summer: there were few things quite as lonely as a summertime fever, with the sunshine spearing in through the shutters as you lay waiting for the provost's medicine to take hold. I believed a winter illness might be the only thing worse. And so the four of us agreed—not entirely unanimously—that we should pass by his lodging after dinner, just to make sure he was in decent health.

Pettifer was curious to see the boy's studio and find out what he was working on. 'He's surely too young to be a painter,' he had suggested at dinner. 'I've known a few good illustrators under twenty, but still—*seventeen*. Awfully young to have any sort of authoritative voice or style. Unless he's one of those ghastly pop artists. He doesn't look the type to me. But then, why would they have given him a studio when there are plenty of free rooms upstairs?'

Fullerton had been allocated the remotest lodging on the

grounds, set fifty yards back from my own, in a closet of pomegranate trees and dwarf oaks, and so many varieties of oleander
in the spring. The refuge comprised ten buildings, spread over
what was said to be nine acres but which felt more like fifteen.
An imperious fin-de-siècle mansion with spindly wrought-iron
cornices loomed at the dead centre; its timber panelling was so
weather-struck that its entire bulk had taken on a dreary, ele-
phantine colour. The provost lived on the top floor. He had decided against repainting as the building's very drabness was its
most effective disguise. In certain places, below the guttering and
such, we could make out the remnants of the original aquama-
rine gloss and could imagine the house as it once was, the majes-
tic thing it was made to be.

At full capacity, the other twelve bedrooms in the mansion
were occupied by artists whose projects demanded little by way of
space or apparatus: the playwrights, the novelists, the poets, the
children's book writers were all sheltered here in humble rooms,
along with Ender and his staff of two: a youngish woman, Gülcan, who cooked, cleaned, and laundered, and an ungainly fellow
called Ardak who saw to the garden and generally fixed things
about the place that did not work (if only he could have fixed us
too). The day room was on the ground floor, the kitchen and
mess hall on the level above. Orbiting the mansion were eight
basic cinderblock huts with flat shingle rooftops that guests
would often sit upon when the weather allowed, watching the
trawl of the sea, examining the stars. These were the studio lodgings for the painters, the architects, the performance makers: any
artist who required a broader plot to work in, or who had materi-

als and equipment to store. (Only one sculptor had been admitted in our time, and she had made such a commotion throughout the workday with her chisels and hammers that there had been great relief when she finally left—no others had been invited since.)

The studio huts had all the grandeur of shoeboxes, but they were spacious enough to feel untrammelled, and had large windows that vented cool air and natural light. Mine served its function as well as any workspace I had ever owned. I had everything I needed: a bed to sleep on, a coke-burning stove to warm my fingers by, regular meals up at the mansion, a place for ablutions and calls of nature, and, above all, a glorious peace I could count on not to be broken.

As we approached Fullerton's lodging, we found his door hanging open. The lamps were on and a stream of yellow light was angling out onto the trodden snow outside. 'I'm quite sure he said to leave him alone,' Quickman warned us. 'He might actually be getting work done in there.'

'Shsshh,' I said. 'Can you hear that?'

There was an odd din emanating from behind the studio. It was not a musical sound as such, though it had a bouncing sort of cadence. 'See, I told you—he's perfectly all right,' Pettifer said. 'We've done our duty. Let's go.'

MacKinney pulled on my elbow.

'I'll fetch the board then, shall I?' Quickman said. 'Pretty sure I had it last.'

'Knell—are you coming?'

'You three go. I won't be long.' I could not settle until I saw the boy again. Quickman's backgammon games sometimes ran late, depending on how well Pettifer fared against him, and I planned to stay up afterwards, working until dawn—I would probably miss breakfast. It seemed cruel to leave Fullerton unchecked for all that time. 'I'm just going to look in the window.'

The others started backpedalling through the snow. Then they paused, waiting in the moon-blue space between the dwarf oaks. They made hurry-up gestures with their hands: 'Go on then!' 'Get on with it!' 'Don't take all night!'

I walked up to the bare front window of Fullerton's lodging. The shutters were folded back and the inner blind was not yet closed. Nobody was inside. His canvas bag lay open on the floor with most of his clothes spilling out. There was a classical guitar leaned against the bedframe. He did not quite have the look of a composer to me, or the swagger of a rock 'n' roll singer, but I thought perhaps he could have written music for the theatre or the folk scene.

It was then that he emerged from around the side of the hut, dragging an oil drum behind him. I had no time to move away. When he saw me, he stood still, but he did not flinch or seem surprised. He carried on hauling the empty drum through the snow, towards a patch of level ground, where he shoved down hard on its edges to stabilise it. 'Knell with a K,' he said, sounding less angry than I expected. 'Are you lost?'

'I just wanted to see how you were feeling.' This came out rather meekly. 'You missed dinner.'

'Wasn't hungry,' he said. 'Mystery solved.'

'Yes, I suppose so.'

He gazed at the ground. A fat bird cawed and streaked the dark above us. Fullerton jerked his head up. 'The crows are all grey here. I can't get used to it.'

'You should see the herons when they come in the spring. They make nests all round the island. It's wonderful.'

The boy gave an uninterested murmur. Then he turned for his lodging and walked straight inside, leaving the door wide open. I was not sure if he was coming back. I waited, hearing the scuff of his footsteps on the floorboards. After a moment, he came out with a stack of what seemed to be pamphlets or magazines, bearing them in his arms like offerings. He did not look at me, just tipped the entire set into the rusty drum, rumbling it. The glossy covers glinted as they dropped into the can. He dusted off his fingers and headed for the door again, stopping only to squint into the trees. 'Your friends are waiting,' he said.

'Will we see you at breakfast?'

'I doubt it.'

I could not understand his hostility, so I did what felt most natural to me: I turned the problem inward, assumed that I had spoken out of turn. 'I'm not usually one for small talk,' I said.

He sighed. 'That makes two of us.'

'Well, I'm trying to make a special effort.'

'That's nice of you,' he said, 'but I don't need it. The whole point of coming here was to be alone. I really don't get on with people much.' And he threw up his hands and carried on into his studio.

'You're much too young to talk that way,' I said, when he came back. Now he was holding a set of ratty papers, banded with a thick elastic. A burgundy passport was on top of the pile, under his thumb.

'I'm old enough to know my limitations.' He dumped everything into the drum. 'Why did *you* come here? For company?'

There was a lot I could have told him then, but I sensed he

would not be glad to hear it. 'There's a difference between privacy and solitude, you know.'

'Uh-huh. I'll take your word for it.' He padded the pockets of his cagoule. Underneath, he had on a coarse wool sweater that could not have been his own, as the round-neck collar was so loose it revealed his bare clavicle. It must have been one of Ender's, or taken from lost property. He was wearing sturdy boots now, too, which gave him extra height. 'Shit,' he said, frisking his torso. 'D'you have any matches?'

'There should be some by your stove.'

He cleared his nose and spat. 'There aren't.'

'Well, I've a full box in my studio. I can fetch it if you like.'

'Nah, don't bother. I'll have to do it the hard way.' With this, the boy dropped to his haunches and began to burrow into the snow and mulch and pine cones. Soon enough, he was bringing up clods of rust-red soil. He tossed an armload into the drum and it rained fatly on the metal.

'What are you doing?'

He did not answer, just kept on digging with his hands and plunking the loose earth inside the can.

'What are you burying?'

It did not seem to bother him that I was watching—there was something tunnel-eyed and frantic about him as he quarried the ground, like a fox hunting rabbits. After a while, the drum was about a quarter full, and he stopped, sitting on the snow with his back against the metal. Strands of his fringe were stuck upon his forehead. He looked so young and afraid.

'Fullerton,' I said—it was a difficult name to speak tenderly. 'Is everything all right?'

He sat there, panting, gazing at nothing.

'Do you want me to go?'

'I couldn't care less what you do,' he said.

The others were still waiting. I saw their huddled shadows and felt glad of them. But Fullerton called after me as I walked away: 'Wait a sec. Hold on.' There was a note of contrition in his voice. I turned.

'It's nothing personal,' he said. 'It's just—look, I haven't sussed this place out yet. There are loads more rules than I thought there'd be.'

It bothered me that he had been admitted without understanding everything. My own sponsor had spent two full days readying me for the prospect of Portmantle, explaining everything that lay ahead. So I went back to the boy and said, 'If you have any questions, just ask.'

He spat again. 'I was told no drinking, no drugs, no phone calls and whatever. But your mate Quickson said there was other stuff, too. I don't know if he meant the ferry tokens, but I bought two of them like they told me—there's one in my bag somewhere. You think that's what he was talking about?'

'It's Quick*man*.' I smiled. 'And, yes, that's part of it.'

'Do you still have yours?'

'I do, but not on me. Somewhere safe. That's more a superstition than a rule.'

'Oh.' He gave another sigh. 'Well, that old bloke went through my bag before. I thought that's what he was after.'

'Ender, you mean?'

'Yeah, he patted me down. It was weird.'

'Ender's OK—just doing his job. If there weren't any rules, this place would fall apart.'

'So everyone gets frisked?'

'Only once. You're no different from the rest of us.'

'It just took me by surprise, that's all.'

'Your sponsor should've warned you.'

Fullerton got up from the snow. He studied my face, as though gauging every pore of it for weaknesses. 'Well, I don't plan on staying here that long anyway. I just need to clear my head and then I'm going back to finish what I started.'

'If I were you, I wouldn't set myself too many restrictions. It'll take as long as it takes.' I wanted to tell him that I had believed the same thing when I came to Portmantle. That I would find my clarity in a matter of days. That I would not need the provost's intervention: the visa documents specially acquired and signed on my behalf. But there was no point in daunting the boy any further. 'You know,' I said instead, 'when I came here, I was lucky. I had someone to help me through the early part, the hard part. You remember MacKinney?'

He nodded.

'She and I were admitted on the same afternoon. We took the same ferry from Kabataş and didn't even know it. If it hadn't been for her, I wouldn't have made it this far.'

'Look, I'm glad it all worked out for you,' said Fullerton. 'But that doesn't mean we're the same. I'm not like that. I can't count on anyone but myself.'

'Well, maybe you should try.' I held my smile this time, until I was sure he had received it. 'We're all loners here. With the right people, you can be alone *and* together—that's something you learn how to do when you get older.'

'I don't see it happening. No offence.'

'It'll happen all on its own.' It was easy to feel sympathy for the boy. Not just because he was sweat-shined and muddied, but because I could remember what it was like to be his age, so wearied by my own guardedness, letting nobody in, too frightened of getting hurt. 'And, in the meantime, Tif and Q can probably help you with—whatever it is you're trying to dispose of there.'

The boy eyed the can and kicked it. 'I can sort it. And besides—' He nodded to the space behind me. 'They've already gone.'

But they were not quite beyond sight. I could still make out their shapes between the trees, heading for my lodging. 'Can you whistle?' I asked. The boy thought about it, then put his grubby fingers behind his teeth and made the cleanest steam-kettle sound. It took a moment for the others to realise we were calling them.

Pettifer was the first to arrive, covering his ears. 'I think they heard you in the Serengeti. What's the big emergency?' He leaned an arm on my shoulder.

'Fullerton needs your advice.'

'Does he now. You hear that, Q?—I'm being asked for *advice*.'

'Goodness,' said Quickman, appearing behind him. 'Whatever next?'

The two of them laughed.

MacKinney noticed the boy's condition. His cheeks were striped with the dull red soil. 'Everything OK here?' she asked.

'Trying to get rid of a few things, that's all.'

He went about explaining his intentions for the oil drum, which caused Pettifer to push out his bottom lip and shake his head. 'No, no, I wouldn't recommend a drumfire unless you have kerosene. You need to build up a little pyre of timber in the centre to direct the flames. Otherwise, things don't burn right, and it can all get out of hand rather quickly.'

The boy stood back. 'Just as well I don't have any matches then.'

'I tried to barbecue a manuscript at my editor's house once,' Quickman said. 'Made a glorious mess of his lawn. There was a lot more ash than I expected. Dangerous thing to do, really.'

Pettifer hummed in agreement. 'Even a small fire can creep up on you if you don't know what you're doing.'

'How d'you know so much about it?' Fullerton asked.

'My father was a scout master.'

'That's cool.'

'He certainly thought so.'

'Mine wouldn't even take me camping,' the boy said. 'I still went, though.'

'I don't blame you.'

'Did he let you have a jack-knife?'

'No. But he kept one for himself.'

MacKinney looked back towards the attic lights of the mansion, yawning. The only lines that did not smooth out of her skin were the furrows round her eyes, which seemed to have the deep-set quality of woodgrain. 'I suppose we should start getting used to all this macho conversation, Knell. They'll be duelling with pistols before we know it.'

'That's an idea,' Quickman said.

'Well, I'm turning in before it gets to that.'

'What about our game?' Tif said.

'I'm not really in the mood. But I hope my money's still good.' She leaned into my ear and mumbled: 'A scoop of French roast on Quickman. Double down if it's two-two.'

I nodded. 'I'll hold on to your winnings.'

She kissed my cheek. 'Night, all.'

'Night, Mac.'

I watched her traipsing off into the dark. It was not unusual for her to retire to bed this early, citing some excuse about the need to work. But she made no mention of her play at all that night, and I assumed that she was suffering again with her insomnia. (MacKinney often joked that she would overcome these bouts of restlessness by reading back through early drafts: 'Even in broad daylight, I can bore myself to sleep.')

'What were you trying to burn, if you don't mind my asking?' Quickman said to the boy. 'Hope it wasn't anything I could smoke.'

'Just a few things I'm not meant to have brought with me. I thought it'd be OK, but the old man said I needed to get rid of them.'

'Ah. Been there,' said Quickman.

'Been there *twice* now,' said Pettifer.

Fullerton grinned, and his face seemed unaccustomed to the strain of it. 'It's not a competition.'

'Funny you should mention that,' Quickman said. 'We were about to start some backgammon. Ever played?'

The boy looked away. 'Once, I think. At school. I'm more interested in poker now.'

'Poker! That's a bit too Hollywood for us, but Tif and I have a regular dice game every Sunday, best of five, and to be frank—'

Quickman screened his mouth to stage-whisper. 'He's hopeless. I wouldn't mind having someone else to beat.'

'All right,' said the boy. 'When?'

'Tonight.'

Pettifer coughed. 'A bit high-stakes for beginners, isn't it?'

'Hardly,' I said, cutting in. It was quite irregular for Quickman to extend an invitation and I wanted to give the boy every chance to accept.

Fullerton looked interested. 'You lot play for money?'

'No. Just trinkets,' I said. 'We don't have much to gamble with.'

'I nearly won that pipe of his once,' said Pettifer. 'Another six and it would've been mine. Imagine the power I could've wielded!'

'It's true,' I said. 'They've played a few epics. No one can beat Q, though.'

'OK, count me in,' said the boy. 'Why not?'

'Super! We'll make it a triangular.' Quickman clasped his palms and rubbed them. 'Go and fetch the board, Tif. It's up in my room.' His voice was sunnier than I had heard it in a while. 'Knell, can we set up at yours again? We'll need a bigger table.'

I saw an eagerness about the boy's eyes then, too, and I realised that it was happening just like I said it would—all on its own.

— — — — — —

Even though the world Fullerton had left was different from the one we knew, altered by a history that had taken place without us, his way into Portmantle was the same as ours. The procedure for admission never changed. First, your sponsor had to seek the authorisation of the provost—no specifics could be shared without this prior consent. It was an inherited knowledge, paid forward by residents of the past to the residents of the present, and if your sponsor could not adequately relay directions, you might never reach the place at all.

Any guest who checked out of the refuge with a clean record—that is to say, without having wilfully contravened any of its rules—was afforded one endorsement to pass on. This could be bestowed upon any artist who it was felt could benefit from the sanctuary of Portmantle. It was stressed by the provost that endorsements should only be offered to artists in the direst need. The cost of a new resident's tenure had to be covered by their sponsor; a fairly meagre sum, paid seasonally, but it could last for an indefinite period—such was the case for MacKinney, Quickman, Pettifer, and me. Sponsors, therefore, had to be sure that the artists they were recommending were truly worth helping, as they could remain beholden to that financial outlay for a permanent duration. The responsibility could not be relinquished or transferred to someone else. Because of this, we stalwarts of the place were looked upon with respect—it was assumed that our sponsors' long-term commitment reflected their valuation of our talents. But there were some who viewed us with a dim-eyed pity, as though we were just shadows of ourselves, washed up and doomed to failure.

Only when the provost had accepted your sponsor's recommendation would you be told where Portmantle was located. Only then could your sponsor offer you precise instructions, and you would be required to commit these details to memory fast, because they could not be spoken again or written down. Only when you had made it to the Gare de Lyon in Paris were you allowed to open your sponsor's envelope with the provost's pass-phrase. Only then could you take the night train to Lausanne, following the Simplon Orient Express line with a second-class ticket your sponsor had paid for under his own name, his real name, through Milan and Belgrade, to the Turkish-Bulgarian border, showing your passport when you arrived at the terminus in Istanbul. Only then could you pay your fee for the entry visa and find the cheap hotel room your sponsor had booked, and burn that passport in the bathtub, dousing it with the shower-hose before it set off the sprinklers (you had to set fire to it early, to stop yourself from turning back later). Only then could you go out into the bright spring sun of the wide-open city and walk along the main road, past the swell of traffic, the taxis with their rolled-down windows and their music blaring, the clattering trams, the towering mosques, until you reached the ferry port at Kabataş.

Only then could you put one dull *jeton* in the turnstile slot, like your sponsor had advised, keeping another to remind you of your homeward trip every time your fingers met it in the folds of your pocket. Only then could you walk through the barrier and wait in the muggy departures terminal with your hat on, your eyes concealed by wayfarers, fanning yourself with the newspaper until the doors were opened to let you step onto the hulking white ship. Only then could you find a seat on the upper deck amongst the gathering hordes, right up close to the railing, to watch the ferry push away and feel the sudden breeze upon your cheek, taste the brackish cool upon your lips, the thrill of it.

Only then could you know the full splendour of the Marmara as it ebbed around you, fathomless, agleam.

And this would be your final chance to lean back and exhale, to listen to the outcry of the seagulls following the stern, the dizzy flocks that clamoured near the deck as though escorting you. Soon, the Turkish men would lean over the railing with *simits* held aloft; the birds would swoop to steal the bread right from their fingers, screeching; and you would come to realise the gulls were not escorts at all, but hustlers and hangers-on, like everyone else you were sailing away from.

Only as you arrived at the first stop in Kadiköy could you undo your watchstrap and remove it, let it slide between the slats of the bench, as though you had forgotten it. Only as you sailed by the first strange island with all its tombstone houses could you glean how far you were from the world you knew, the people you loved, the people you did not. Only when you passed the next of them—one broad and inhabited, another just a sliver of green where nothing seemed to live but herons—could you understand how close you were to what you needed. Only then could you see the khaki hump of Heybeliada rising in the sun-stirred haze and know that you had made it.

Only then could you stand with the giddy tourists on the lower decks as the ferryman threw a withered rope onto the dock, waiting to step off onto a foreign land but somehow feeling you were almost home. Only then could you skirt by the Naval Academy where the uniformed cadets did their parade drills, and head south-east on Çam Limani Yolu, as you had been instructed, until the streets became narrower, emptier, and the space between houses grew so wide that you could see the spreading forest up ahead. Only then could you lose yourself in those dry, slanting pines and sense that you were now released from everything that had weighed on you before. Only then could you see the shoulders of a tarnished mansion surface above the treetops. Only at its gate could you throw down your backpack, push the buzzer, watch a squinting Turk with a grey moustache and a shotgun come up to the bars, asking your name. Only then could you say you were a different person. Only then would the old man enquire about the passphrase, so you could finally release it to the air, the meaning of the words becoming clearer as you spoke them. Only then would the gate unlock and slide back for you in the old man's grip. Only then would you hear him say, '*Portmantle'ye hoşgeldiniz.*'

Three

When the boy demolished Pettifer in the first game of backgammon we all cried beginner's luck, but then they played twice more—each bout a little faster than the one before—and it soon became clear that young Fullerton possessed a startling tactical acuity. He came away with a haul of Pettifer's belongings: a *çay* glass, a wind-up turtle made from camphor-wood, and a woven leather belt; and, because I had backed Tif to sweep the best of five, I was forced to surrender my last remaining pack of cinnamon gum. We assumed that Quickman, a shrewder, more experienced and aggressive player, would prove too wily an opponent for the boy, but it did not transpire that way. Fullerton outmanoeuvred him to the tune of seven points per game. In truth, it was barely a contest. By the time the boy was done, he had won a fountain pen, a Roman coin, and a silver lighter that once belonged to Quickman's father, inscribed with two faded initials. (Tif won back a pair of loafers he had previously lost to Q, and I earned a scoopful of French coffee beans from Mac, though it seemed unfair to claim my winnings in her absence.)

'We've been hustled,' Quickman said, staring at the chequers

that were left on the board. 'That last bump-and-run was tournament stuff. What are you, regional champ? National?'

The boy beamed back at him. 'I swear, I've hardly played
before.'

'You don't fool me.'

'I'm just lucky, that's all. The dice fell kindly.'

'Rubbish. I've never seen so much blockading. That was all
strategy.'

'It's a blocking game all right,' Pettifer added, 'but it's deadly
effective.'

The boy gave nothing away. 'If you say so.'

'I'd better sharpen up my end-game before we play again,'
Quickman said.

'I'm not sure that'll help you much.'

I could not tell if the boy was being earnest or smug. He got up,
took his cagoule from the chair-back, and walked across the studio, pausing before my wall of samples. The room was so bright
with the overhead fluorescents that there was nothing but an arrangement of white patches for him to see, a grid of small canvas
squares that I had pasted to the wall, in a pattern only I could interpret. There were at least a hundred of them, each square containing a smear of white paint, hardly discernible from the canvas
itself. Fullerton took another forward step, trying to read my pencilled notes in the margins. 'What is it you're working on here,
Knell?' he said quite innocently. 'I'm going to take a wild guess
and say it's something white.'

Pettifer tutted. 'You're overstepping.'

'It's all right,' I said.

'No, come on—he needs to be told.'

Quickman called to the boy in a chiding tone: 'We don't intrude on other people's work round here.'

Fullerton held up his hands in surrender. 'Jesus. Sorry. I take it back.'

'They're studies for a mural,' I told him. 'That's as much as I care to explain right now.'

'Anything else would be an imposition,' Quickman said.

The boy was still facing the wall. 'But don't you ever want to run ideas by each other? Just to see the response?'

I was getting used to holding conversations with his back. 'Sometimes,' I said. 'But then I wouldn't really be painting for myself. And that's the only way to paint.'

Quickman was now gathering the backgammon chequers into one hand, stamping down at every piece. It was evident that he was still stinging from defeat, because he said sharply to the boy, 'This isn't a conservatoire. If you've come here for other people's input, you might want to try a different crowd.'

Fullerton turned and pushed up his sleeves. 'It's OK. I'm not the sharing type.' There was still a pale disc of skin on his left wrist where a watch used to be. 'I've got something I need to finish, yes, but I won't bore you with the details.'

'I saw a guitar in your studio,' I said. 'It's been a while since we had a musician here.'

'Oh, I wouldn't call myself a musician.'

'What are you then?'

He backed away from my samples now, eyes slatted. 'Jacqueline du Pré—she's a *proper* musician; Glenn Gould, Miles Davis. I can bash out a folk song when I'm in the mood. But I haven't felt much like it recently.'

Pettifer stood up. 'All sounds rather simple when you put it like that.'

'I'm sure it's more complicated than he's making out,' Quickman said, 'or he wouldn't be here, would he?'

The boy gave a wan little smile. 'Stop me if I'm sharing too much.'

'Well, I always wished I could play an instrument,' I said. 'Somehow I just can't get the knack for it. A bit like backgammon.' As a child, I had often sneaked my mother's squeezebox from its case and tried to draw a tune from it, but all it ever gave me were wheezes of complaint.

'I taught myself from a picture book,' the boy replied. 'It's not that hard.'

Quickman folded up the game board and shoved it under his armpit. 'The last musician we had played the bloody flute all night. It was like having swallows in the loft. I was *this* close to throttling him.'

'Then I should probably keep the noise down.'

'If you know what's good for you.'

The boy did not answer. He stooped to examine the samples again. 'There's something really peaceful about this wall of yours, Knell. Not that you want my opinion.'

'It's a far cry from anything right now,' I said. 'But thank you.' I did not ask him to clarify what he meant by 'peaceful', as he had said the word with such a tone of admiration.

He side-stepped an easel to get to my workbench and started looking through the jumble there, too, picking up a palette knife, examining the crusted blade.

'Oi! Hands to yourself!' Pettifer said.

'Sorry.' The boy put down the knife and moved away.

'We don't mean to be fussy,' I said, 'but we've got used to things being in a certain order.' In truth, it would not have mattered if he had upturned the entire workbench and trampled it. Nothing it held was worth protecting any more, only the kind of effluvium that all painters accrue over the course of a long project: dirty turps in peach cans; oils hardening in tubes; rags and palettes congealed with colour; brushes standing in jars of grey water like forgotten flowers. Such ordinary things had lost all meaning for me. I kept them there because I had nowhere else to store them, and they served as a reminder of my limitations. My real work was in those samples on the wall, and I would have cut off the boy's arm before he touched a single square. But he did not try.

He zipped up his cagoule. The trophies of a hard night's backgammon distended the front pockets. 'Well, I'm going to hit the sack. Thanks for the game,' he said. 'I thought I would've forgotten all my moves by now.'

'I knew it!' Quickman slumped into his chair. 'Hustled!'

'Blimey. How good *are* you, exactly?' Pettifer said.

'I might've played a tournament or two, after hours. You know, backroom games.'

'For money?'

'Don't see the point otherwise.'

Quickman said, 'I've seen those backroom games. They'd never let a kid like you at the table.'

'Well, they don't exactly check your age in the places I'm talking about. Not hard to find a cash game in Green Lanes—all the Cypriots round there. You pick things up if you watch them closely. And they'll talk strategy all night after a few drinks.'

There was something about the way Fullerton spoke—head down and to the side—that did not quite convince me. I just could not imagine him gambling his pocket money in some dismal London pub with a crowd of Cypriots. He was spinning us a story. Quickman must have agreed, because he stroked his beard and said, doubtfully, 'Green Lanes, eh?'

'Yup.' The boy put up the hood of his cagoule, smirking. 'Thanks for the gum, Knell. I'm sure you'll get a chance to win it back.' He yanked at the door. 'Everyone sleep tight.' And off he went.

Quickman waited until the boy's footsteps could no longer be heard, then he stood up and buttoned his coat. 'There's something shifty about that lad,' he said. 'I don't know if it's a good idea to entertain him.'

'You're just sore because he thrashed you,' Pettifer said.

'Well, all right, perhaps that's part of it.' Quickman upturned his collar. The sheepskin was bald and grubby round the neckline. 'There's something a bit off about him, though. Am I being unfair?'

'No—he's definitely unusual,' I said. 'But I thought the same about you once, Q, and it turned out fine in the end.'

It was too soon to claim we had a common understanding, but I could see reflections of my own youth in the way the boy behaved. I was about Fullerton's age when I first started painting—not yet out of my parents' house, with barely enough experience of life to qualify me, in the eyes of society, as an expert on anything besides schoolyard gossip and girls' fashions. But I understood, even then, how much I knew. At sixteen, I had seen enough modern art in picture books to tell a depth from a great hollow. And I reasoned that if so many vapid contributions had been made by artists gone before me, what was there to be frightened of? The precedents of their failure would be my parachute. So I began in this context: without fear, without doubt, without expectation. The year was 1953.

In the last few weeks of school, when other girls were thinking of summer jobs, I stole oil paints from the art-block cupboards at Clydebank High. I prised two window-boards from a derelict outhouse and dragged them home along Kilbowie Road, sawing and sanding them with my father's tools, stowing them behind a coal box. The pleasure of it—the secret purpose—was so bracing I could not rest. That summer, I committed my entire life to painting.

In the gloomy backcourt of our tenement, as far away as I could get from the stinking middens, I leaned my first board against a wall. I was undaunted by the blankness of it. I did not pause to scrutinise the fabric of the thing itself, to wonder if the wood-grain was right, if the whitewash had set evenly, if it would need to be glazed later on. Instead, I walked up to the board as though it were a boy I had decided to kiss and streaked a layer of phthalo blue across the surface with a palette knife, the floppy baking kind my mother owned, making an impulsive shape upon the wood. There was no history standing on my shoulders then, no classical references hanging in my head like dismal weather. I was alone, uninfluenced, free to work the layers of chalky stolen paint with a big lolloping knife, to smudge with my fingers, pad flat with my fist, pinch, thumb, scrape, and scratch. No judgements of technique arose in my mind, because I did not invite them, did not think to. I simply acted, expressed, behaved, made gestures of the knife that seemed unprompted and divined. There was a scene in my head that I tried to reproduce, something from a wartime story of my father's, but I could only paint it the way I imagined, not how it really was.

The hours ghosted by. Soon my hands became so colour-soaked and waxed I could not see the pleats of my knuckles or the rims of my fingernails. The dumbshow of the world—that other place I had forgotten, the outer one—broke into road noise and tenement din. Neighbours were squabbling in the close, coming out into the yard with dustpans of ash, telling young lads with footballs to clear off their landings. An early dark was settling and I heard my mother at the window, already home from work. She was calling me. And so I lifted my head to see what I had finished.

There it was upon the wall, drying: a semi-abstract thing, made in a flurry. The suggestion of a place I had never been to. A spray of rain. A slate-grey ocean spattered by bombs. The remnants of a foundry, dismembered in the sky. A falling road bridge, or perhaps a wall, and so much else I did not recognise, which somehow conveyed more in its obliqueness than I could ever have spoken in words.

When my mother came down into the backcourt and saw what I had done, she must have glimpsed my future in it like bad runes. 'Whitsat?' she said. 'Did *ye* dae that?' She chided me for wasting a full day on a silly picture and told me to clean her good icing knife. There were better uses for my time, plenty of errands I could do for her. But I spent the next day working on another painting, and the next, and the next, and did not care about the punishments that came after.

Whatever happened to this backcourt spirit? When exactly did it leave me?

I had always wanted more than my parents' life and its routineness, but I did not take my education seriously enough, and my Leaving Certificate showed only the barest of passes in English and history, ruining any aspirations I might have had to become a teacher. Still, I could not settle for a job in the Singer factory or the biscuit warehouse, as my father had ordained. The afterglow of painting prodded me awake at night, urged me to submit an application to the Glasgow School of Art, told me I could conquer anything if I just applied myself. At the admissions interview, the registrar studied my portfolio and said, 'Your work is naïve. It leans too much towards abstraction for abstraction's sake. But it has more intensity than one normally finds in a woman's painting, and you are still very young. Of course, you won't be trained in oils until third year—that ought to correct the bad habits you've developed.' A week later, he wrote to offer me a scholarship: *We truly hope you'll accept*, the letter signed off, as though I had other choices.

By October, I found myself in colour theory lectures, attending slideshows on the canon; in drawing classes, idly sketching vegetable arrangements; in cold studios, measuring the proportions of nude models against a 2B pencil. My parents' tenement seemed so far away, and I feared that the 'intensity' of my work was being dulled—normalised—by too much refinement of technique. In fact, this attention I paid to the rudiments of drawing and the methods of the Old Masters only heightened my ap-

petite for painting. I made discoveries in these classes that I did
not expect: how to imply the mood of a body with a sweep of
Conté crayon, how broader narratives could be revealed through
compositional decisions. My backcourt spirit survived in all the
paintings I made in this period, though my early tutors did not
reward it.

It was in the mural department, under the tutelage of Henry
Holden, that I began to thrive. I was inspired by the grand tradi-
tions of mural painting: from the ice-age pictures in the caves of
Lascaux, to the mosaicked churches of Ravenna and Byzantium,
the frescos of Giotto, Tintoretto, Michelangelo, Delacroix, and
the great political gut-shots of Rivera. In Holden's tutorials, I felt
energised and unhindered. He was a rangy old socialist in half-
moon glasses, who gave us curious monthly assignments: *Devise
a scene for the ballroom of the Titanic.* (For this, I painted a ballet
of furnace-room labourers in cloth caps, dancing with wheelbar-
rows of coal, and was marked down for 'discounting context'.)
*Paint a scene depicting a work by Shakespeare as it relates to modern
times.* (For this, I created a swathe of Glasgow tenements with
Juliets waiting at every window, graveyards full of Romeo head-
stones and wounded Mercutios in army uniforms. The picture
was kept for the School's collection, and subsequently lost.)

Holden was the finest teacher I ever had. To 'avoid any earache'
from the external assessor, he steered us away from the influence
of Picasso ('talent like his can neither be taught nor replicated'),
but he allowed us to eschew the mannered ways of easel painting
that were sacrosanct to other tutors: the single-viewpoint rule, the
vanishing point, chiaroscuro. A great mural, he used to say, was
perpetually in conversation with its environment: it should not

retreat into the background or vie for attention, but ought to span 'that invisible line between'. When Holden talked, his words stayed with you. He would twist the tip of his ear while he admired a work-in-progress, as though turning off a valve, and he walked along the building's topmost corridors racketing his cane against the radiators, or whistling Irving Berlin tunes. Sometimes, he came to drink with us at The State Bar, and would cradle the same small measure of whisky in a glass until closing time.

Holden's least prescriptive brief came in the fourth year, prior to our diploma show. *Complete a mural for a platform at Central Station.* There were no limits on theme or materials, he told us. 'It needn't convey anything of the railway per se. But, of course, you should think about how the work will be slanted by its location, and vice versa. I want to see your imaginations taking you places. I also want you focusing them where they ought to be. Understand?'

For weeks, I failed to summon a single idea. I spent full days in the studio, numb and depleted, searching for a hint of something true, but any bright intentions I had soon floundered on the pages of my sketchbook. Anxieties began to overrule my normal instincts: what if the backcourt spirit was not enough to sustain me? What if I was never meant to listen to it in the first place? Then Holden came to rescue me. He edged into my workspace, saw the blankness of the canvas I had stretched upon the frame, and said, 'What's the matter, Ellie? Have you let the fight go out of you?'

That was exactly how I felt, and I told him so.

'Then pick a different battle,' he said. 'Disturb the peace a bit.'

'I don't know how.'

Holden pondered my face, as though seeing it for the first time. 'Remind me again: are you Catholic?'

'My mother is.'

'That wasn't my question.'

'Well, I suppose I still believe in God, but not in what the Bible says.'

'There you are then. Paint what you believe.'

In the moment, his advice seemed so woolly and impractical that I felt even more adrift. *Paint what you believe.* He might as well have said, *Paint the air.* But when I got back to my little room-and-kitchen flat and tried to sleep, his words kept pinching at me, until I relented to their meaning. Holden was not telling me to reach inside myself for some pious motivation; he was inviting me to paint the world as I understood it, to convey my own perspective with conviction. The mural should be the picture I would hope to see if I were standing on that platform with my suitcase, waiting for a train to sidle in and carry me away. It should resonate with its location but also transcend it. It should be both personal and public.

I sketched until the light of early morning, making sense of my initial ideas in ink, and finishing with gouache on paper. The next day, Holden found me in the studio, adding a grid of construction lines to the completed image. 'Ah,' he said, 'you've finally picked a battle,' and I did not see him again until the entire twelve-by-three-foot canvas was completed. At the diploma show, modest crowds formed around it. There was head-scratching and consternation. There was excitement. I felt the shift of my trajectory.

What the crowd saw that night was a depiction of an ordinary station platform. The grey-rendered steam of a locomotive swelled from the lower aspect of the canvas. In parts, I had thinned the whorls of paint to near translucence; in others, it cloyed like molasses, in level spots of oil and glaze that almost shone. Amidst the curls of smoke was a rolling horde of men in rags and bedraggled women holding babies. They were clambering from the west side of the platform, stumbling over each other in a tumult, falling headlong. And in the calm space to the east, where the grey mist was dispersing, a figure stood in a baggy pinstriped suit, his body turned, his face unseen, but slightly peering backwards. His right hand was stigmatised and held a crown of thorns. He was barefoot and his tawny hair was greased and combed. A trail of oats was spilling from the briefcase in his other hand. A Bible rested in his top pocket. Beyond him were sunlit pastures fenced off with barbed wire; ships already leaving port; the distant flatline of the sea. I called it *Deputation*.

The external assessor was so insulted by the picture that he did not deem it worthy of a passing grade. I had sensed that the mural would provoke strong opinions, but I did not expect that it would rouse such ill feeling that the School would deny my graduation. Whilst I was painting *Deputation*, I daydreamed of installing it at Central Station, imagining the railway manager being invited to the show, falling in love with it. I had taken the trouble of designing it so the canvas could be detached from its stretcher frames and affixed to the brickwork with lead paste, as many of the great muralists in America had been known to do. I had thought—vainly hoped—that it would help me acquire more commissions. Instead, the School gave me two options: repeat the fourth year, or leave without a diploma. I preferred the idea of packing sewing-machine needles with my mother.

At the end of term, as the show was being pulled down, I went in to the studio to collect my things. Henry Holden called me to his office. I sat on his paint-smattered banquette while he rummaged the papers on his desk. There was a reek of whisky about him. 'I've spoken again with the School governors,' he said. 'I wish I could say they'd changed their minds.'

'I'm starting to think it's for the best.'

He shook his head. 'Rubbish. You submitted a wonderful painting, and I'm embarrassed those cowards aren't supporting it. When you go off and make your fortune as a painter, they're all going to look rather silly. *Now*—' He lifted up a folder and gave it a cursory glance before tossing it aside. 'You might not have seen this in the newspapers, or heard about it on the wireless, *but*—ah, here we are.' He unfolded what looked like a grocer's receipt, skim-reading it. 'There's a new travelling fellowship you can apply for.'

'I really don't think I'll be—'

'Shssh. Listen. This is *good* news.' He paused, swallowing drily, and I realised that he was very drunk indeed. 'Now, I should warn you, the endowment is not much, but it's been decided, and the committee chairman—namely *me*—will be most upset if you don't accept. In fact, he insists that you do. Here.' He offered me the grocer's receipt. A name was scrawled on the back in pencil—Jim Culvers—with a number and an address. 'An old student of mine in London is looking for an assistant. If he doesn't pay you well enough, give me a ring and I'll lean on him.

It's not the same as a diploma, or even a proper fellowship, I know—but, anyway, those are his details.'

I felt as though I should kiss him. 'You don't have to do this for me, Henry.'

'I'm aware.'

'I don't think I really deserve it.'

'Then give it back, I'll tear it up for you.' He creaked forward on his chair, turning out his palm. I would always remember this moment with Holden, how he looked at me with certainty, knowing I would not release the paper to him. 'Thought not,' he said, and withdrew his hand. 'It'll take Jim a while to notice you're a better painter than he is. When that happens, move on. Until then, I suspect the two of you will get on famously. He's already expecting you.'

If I had chosen differently, and carried out my plan to take a factory job alongside my mother, I might never have painted again. But how much worse off would I have been to live without art than to have it consume me and spit out my bones? There are still days when I count up all the sewing-machine needles I could have packed instead.

Four

There is no doubt that Fullerton's arrival at Portmantle had some influence on my painting, but I cannot credit him for the discovery that mattered most. It was in the springtime—two whole seasons before he was admitted—that I took myself into the deepest woods in search of herons to draw, and found one perching on a rotten tree trunk swathed in mushrooms. I sat and sketched that splendid bird until it suddenly took off. I tried to keep track of it, gazing up through the branches, but it glided out of sight, and by then I was halfway out of the forest and the dinner bell was clanging at the mansion. It was only when I got back to my studio, after dusk, that I realised I had left my sketchbook somewhere in the trees—most of the drawings it contained were not worth saving, but I felt the heron sketches had potential and I did not want to lose them. So I got a torch and went back into the woods.

That night, the dark was full and thick; the firmament of stars was at its clearest. There was a waxing crescent moon and the yellow-white shimmer of the neighbouring islands seemed closer than ever. I hurried through the pines by torchlight, hunting for the spot where I had found the heron, but everything looked different in the dark. My foot caught in the scrub and I tripped over. The torch spat out its batteries as it hit the ground. For a moment, there was terrifying blackness and I thought I had passed out. But then I saw the most unusual thing ahead of me: a spread of pale blue light, like the haze of a gas flame.

I lifted myself up and moved towards the glow. It was coming from a clutch of fallen trees not far away. As I got closer, the blue intensified: a curious shade, vivid yet lucent, like the antiseptic liquid barbers keep their combs in, or the glaucous sheen on a plum. It did not emanate from the trees themselves, but rather from a substance they were covered in: luminescent mushrooms the size of oyster shells. Their caps had pale blue halos that, when packed into dense clusters as they were, gave off a gleam so bright I could make out all the textures of the forest floor, insects crawling in the mulch, my sketchbook lying on the ground—I no longer cared to pick it up. There was a slow, electric crackle in my blood, a feeling I had not known in years. Not quite clarity, just the tingle of it surfacing. An idea. A glimpse of home. The rest, I knew, was up to me.

- - - - - -

By the winter of the boy's appearance, I was still learning the nuances of the pigment, sampling its versatility. Some inconsistencies had to be corrected in the mixture before I could commit to painting with it; the production methods needed more refinement, and I had lingering concerns about permanence and lightfastness. But my excitement for the material could not be dampened. Quickman always said the best ideas 'invade your heart'. This one had become a romance.

It was not a difficult pigment to make, though it required considerable patience and commitment. I established a simple routine: working through the darkness until breakfast, sleeping until lunch, resting until dinner, resuming after dusk. I lived this way throughout the summer, finding respite in the cool of nightfall, hiding from the glare of daylight. I persisted through the muggy autumn evenings, the early rains, the frost, the sudden snow. But when the boy arrived, it knocked me off my rhythm. I allowed his presence to divert me from my purpose much too readily. His sparring with Quickman at the backgammon board was just the first instance of this distraction—their game dragged on much longer than expected and I did not even think to put a stop to it, just let the two of them battle it out, paying no mind to the delay it caused my work. It may have only set me back a fraction, but a fraction was too much.

As soon as they were gone, I went about the drudgery of organising my studio. There was a long night of sampling ahead of me and I had not rested much since lunchtime. I closed my shutters, rolled down my blinds and stapled them to the frame. I brought out the mortar and pestle, the stone muller and the mixing slab, wiping down my workbench and dragging it into position. I prepared another fifty canvas squares. I cleaned my sable brushes. Then I put on my coat and satchel, laced up my boots, and waited for the last few lights to blink off at the mansion. Lanterns glared for a while in the portico until Ender came to snuff them out, and then a perfect darkness settled all about the refuge.

I was mindful not to switch on my torch until I was safely through the apron of the pines. The route had become so familiar that I no longer had to look for the notches I had carved into the tree trunks to get my bearings; but I walked slowly, cautiously, knowing that if I went too far I would emerge onto a rocky escarpment and be confronted by the open sea. (I could not face the sea at night-time because I was afraid of it, ebbing and heaving in the blackness, as though it had some secret mission.)

It seemed I was the only person at the refuge who knew what could be found in its deepest woods at night. I often feared another resident would see me in the trees and make me explain myself, so I went about my work quite furtively. When the air became dank and the ground turned spongy underfoot, I could tell that I was close. I was looking for an enclave where the pines stood at a slant. Another twenty paces and I saw the trunks begin to lean, until I came to a small clearing—a kind of bald patch in the woods—where several trees were rotting sidelong on the mulch. I shut off my torch and let the miracle reveal itself.

Pale blue mushrooms, glimmering like stars.

I had learned, through trial and error, to harvest only what I needed. The fungus was fast-growing and it replenished quickly, but the best fruitheads were the oldest—those big-eared clusters that were left to fatten on the bark. From my satchel, I got out my knife and the tin foil. My joints cricked as I knelt in the dirt, reaching out with the blade. One clean motion of the knife was all it took, running it against the bark until the gleaming fruitheads fell into my palm. Too slow, and the mushrooms would crumble as I sliced them. Too rough, and they would lose their colour. I cut off twelve of the fattest and laid them on a sheet of foil, enfolded them tightly, and stowed the whole lot inside my satchel.

No light could be allowed to creep into my studio while I was sampling, so the first thing I did when I got back was shut the door and seal its frame with duct tape. Next, I extinguished my stove and turned off the overhead fluorescents.

There was a total darkness in the room for half a breath, and then my wall of samples bloomed with light. A stroke of blue appeared on every square of canvas, but no two were alike. Some of the swatches had a strong, unwavering glow—a blue almost as rich as the live fungus itself. Others were dilute and faltering—a Star of Bombay colour. There was dullness where the paint had been applied too thickly or the pigment was too granulated, and glassiness where it had been oiled too heavily. That same blue was now spewing from the joins of my satchel, and I could not afford to let it die.

I had tried so many different variations of the process with changeable results: (i) applying the powdered fungus as an essence to ready-made oil paints; (ii) boiling down the mushrooms, adding gum arabic to the run-off to make briquettes of watercolour; (iii) mixing the ground fungus with glycerine, honey and water, oxgall and dextrin powder, to make a gouache; (iv) breaking egg yolks into the powdered fungus to make tempera, and so on. The facilities at Portmantle were such that I could call upon as many materials as I needed, and if there was anything that Ender could not provide for me from the supply stores, the provost would order it to be shipped from the mainland. In any case, the method that produced the brightest pigment required only the most basic equipment.

To begin with, I brought out the mushrooms from my satchel and placed them on the table. The brightness of their caps was strong enough to work by, though it always took a moment to adjust my eyes. I had discovered that washing the fruitheads only stultified the glow, so I brushed away the dirt with a soft sable and padded off the moisture with a paper towel. Then I chopped each mushroom into even pieces, not too thin, not too narrow, as though preparing them for a salad. In the cold studio, it took no time at all for my fingers to numb, which made the next step particularly difficult.

I took a large sewing needle from my drawer and threaded it with parcel string, spiking every slice of fungus until I had made a garland. Tying off the ends, I carried it to my closet and hung it beside the water boiler to dry with all the others. (It was important not to let the slices shrivel too much, so I checked on them quite regularly.)

One of the other garlands had been drying in there for six days already and was just about ready to be powdered. It was pleasantly warm in my grip as I unhooked it. Picking all the curled-up mushrooms from the line, one by one, I placed them in the mortar, grinding until I had a fine blue soot. I gave the pestle as much force as I could muster and worked it longer than usual, trying to achieve a better granulation. The pigment had a compacted quality that brought to mind volcanic ash. One garland made a cupful of powder, which was enough to make about forty samples.

I emptied a third of the powder onto the granite slab, depressed a groove into the pile with my thumb, and tipped in three-quarters of a fluid ounce of linseed oil from the measuring spoon. With the palette knife, I worked it into a paste. Then I ran the muller over it, circling and sliding, until it had a cream-cheese consistency. This was the point at which the nascent glow of the pigment became a usable material. It collected easily onto a flat-head brush, coating the bristles with little persuasion. I took a swatch of bare canvas and made one slow stroke across it, noting the oil measurements in pencil below, the fruithead sizes and amounts, and, finally, a log number. Then I pinned it to the wall beside the others.

This procedure had to be repeated many times, adding oil to the paint by increments and remixing, until only a smear of blue remained on the slab and my arms were aching from the strain of the muller. The last of the powder was scooped out of the mortar and decanted into an old tobacco tin, which I hid in a recess behind my bathroom cabinet. At the end of it all, I had just enough strength to put fresh coke in the stove and light it, but I was too exhausted after that to wash my hands. I fell upon my couch with my dirty boots on and my fingernails speckled with the glow.

By the time I awoke, the snow was thawing on my rooftop and I could hear the spits of water on the walkway. When I peeled the tape from the door to look outside, the sun was like a mist above the canopy of pines, and I could not tell if it was morning or afternoon. The lawns were green now in patches and the footpaths to the mansion were edged with slush. I could see a couple of short-termers under the portico, drinking coffee: Gluck, a timid fellow who wrote children's stories, and the giant Italian in the white leather coat who made self-portraits from animal photographs. ('I do not like this word, *montage*; it is very concrete,' he had explained to us one mealtime. 'I am concerned with many representations of myself. How I choose to explore my ideas is not the issue. Discussions of process are so boring.' This had caused Pettifer to dab his lips and respond, 'Yes, I lost interest the moment you brought it up,' and the Italian had not spoken to us since.)

I showered and changed and made my way up to the mansion. When I reached the portico, Gluck and his companion were gone, and their coffee cups were left out on the swing-seat. I found Ardak in the lobby, standing high upon a wooden ladder at the heart of the stairwell. He seemed to be fixing a curtain pole; one of the velvet drapes was slung over his shoulder like a lamb for butchering. With the window bared, the room had a gutted feeling. Dust clotted the daylight. Fingerprints deadened the balustrade.

As I stepped by his ankles, Ardak paused and stared down at me.

'What happened here?' I asked, expecting he would not understand.

'Pssshhh,' he said, and mimed the smash of glass. He pointed to the topmost window panel and I saw that the pane had been replaced; the putty was still damp in the frame.

'Lucky we have you to fix these things, eh?'

He gave a vacant nod.

Coming upstairs, I found MacKinney at our regular table in the mess hall, breakfasting alone. She was a fastidious eater on account of an old bowel complaint, and could often be found this way, finishing her muesli long after the kitchen had closed. In fact, we counted on Mac to save our places every morning. The head of the table by the window was known to belong to us; it afforded the best view of the grounds. If we ever encountered other people in our spot, Tif or Q would shoo them away with a few stern words. Sometimes, we really were no different from school bullies, but we had spent so long at Portmantle that we had become protective of the smallest comforts.

I called to MacKinney through the doorway: 'Who broke the window?'

She gestured to the far side of the room. 'He was trying to kill a moth, supposedly.' By the serving pass, Fullerton was standing in an apron and rubber gloves, wiping food-scraps into a dustbin. 'He's been doing chores with Ender all morning to make up for it.' The old man was going from table to table, collecting cutlery and dishes, and he did not seem especially glad of the boy's help.

I sat down with Mac and she slid something towards me. 'That's what did the damage, if you're interested.' It was a *jeton*— a dull brass token with a groove along its middle. 'Ardak found it in the garden. No sign of the moth, by the way. Perhaps it was obliterated.' She did not move her gaze from Fullerton, who was now stacking all the empty dishes in the way Ender disliked, so that the undersides became coated with the grease of eggs and *sucuk* and required extra rinsing. 'Think it's probably best you speak to him. He doesn't seem to like me very much.'

I slipped the *jeton* into my skirt pocket. 'You take some getting used to.'

A forlorn expression came over Mac then, the milk quivering on the spoon as she lifted it to her mouth. 'Well, I've been think-ing a lot more about my own two since he's been here, that's for sure,' she said. 'Not that they're even kids any more. But still . . . It's hard to watch him. How he stands, how he acts. Makes me feel old.'

'We *are* old.'

'Oh, please. I've got decades on you.' Mac prodded at her muesli. 'Think about it—he's basically a schoolboy and he's already jaded enough to need a place like this. What hope does that give the rest of us?'

'Everyone's problems are their own, Mac.'

'Maybe,' she said. 'But mine don't seem to be improving. I've forgotten what the point of it was, anyway.'

'The point of what?'

'This. Being here.' She was going to say more, but there was an almighty clatter of dishes. A stack of plates had toppled from Ender's serving trolley. The old man was standing in the middle of the mess hall, peering down at the debris, as though confounded by the physics of it.

The boy rushed over to help. 'Let me sort that out for you.' He bent to pick up the fragments. 'Do you have a brush?'

'Go!' Ender said. 'This is not your job. I will sweep for myself.'

'I don't mind. Honest.'

'*Çik! Git burdan!*'

There was a very long silence.

Fullerton stood up, wrenching off his gloves, ducking out of his apron. He returned them to the old man with a sarcastic bow. Noticing me at the table, he traipsed over, looking stung and apologetic, but all he said was, 'What's his problem? I didn't even do anything.' He reached for the milk jug in front of Mac and drank straight out of it. The rolling lump in his throat was oddly prominent. He had not shaved and there was a faint moustache above his lip, a dandelion fuzz about his cheeks that I could not help but think a tad pathetic. As he drank, his fringe fell back, revealing a streak of raw pink acne at his hairline. It was possible that he had been awake all night. He seemed fragile, twitchy.

'Didn't you sleep?' I asked.

He wiped his mouth on the sleeve of his sweatshirt. It was baggy and bee-striped. 'Couldn't keep my eyes open,' he said.

'Well, sorry if we kept you up too late. Quickman gets a bit combative.'

'You didn't.' The boy sniffed. He set the jug down so briskly on the table that it wobbled like a bar-skittle. 'It's going to take me all day just to clear my head again now. Sleep is not my friend.'

'Come off it,' said Mac. There was a mound of raisins left in her bowl, which she had managed to sieve out, and now she was swirling them with one finger. 'Try staring at the ceiling every night of your life, *then* tell me sleep isn't good for you. I'll swap places with you any time.'

'No, trust me,' the boy replied in a heavy voice, 'you wouldn't want dreams like mine.' With this, he angled his head until the neck-joints clicked on both sides. His sweatshirt lifted, revealing the waistband of his boxer shorts and the neat balloon-knot of his bellybutton. Then he said evenly, 'Will Quickman be around later, do you reckon?'

Mac glanced at me. As though to give the boy a lesson in patience, she removed her glasses and wiped the lenses. Her whole face took on a sallow hue. 'Quickman, let's see . . . He can be quite hard to predict.'

'That's true,' I said. 'But I'm sure he won't miss lunch.'

'Well, if you see him, tell him I was looking for him.'

'Happy to,' said Mac, slotting her glasses back into place.

The boy gave a lethargic two-fingered wave, as though consenting to a yea-vote at the end of a tedious meeting. 'Bye then,' he said, and walked out, shutting the door behind him.

The weather had been so severe that we had not paid a visit to the mansion roof all winter, knowing the frost and snow would make it perilous. But I could see no other way of consoling MacKinney that afternoon. I insisted that she follow me up the attic stairs, into the rafters, where a bolted hatchway opened to a ledge just wide enough for two or three people to stand on. She was doubtful about the conditions still, but I promised her that we would be safe. 'It's a little wet, that's all,' I said, climbing out onto the shingle. 'There's plenty of grip.'

Mac lumbered out of the hatch and patted the cobwebs from her knees. She took one glimpse of the view and exhaled. She was soothed by it, I thought—restored. For a long moment she stayed quiet, her eyes absorbing the scenery.

There was a brilliant, flooding sunshine. On all sides, ferries were traversing the inky water in slow motion, oblivious to everything except their course between the islands. Most of the snow-scabbed houses and apartment blocks of Heybeliada stood dormant, just a few curls of smoke from a few stubby chimneys far away. At the Naval Academy, the parade ground was vacant of marching cadets, and the restaurants on the promenade had nobody to serve. We could see the clock tower of the Greek Orthodox church from where we were, too, and the outlines of horses in the paddock across the bay; the old theological school, high on its northern summit, was framed by a narrow arc of sunlight that seemed to angle from the clouds like a projector beam. I expected this would remind MacKinney of how privileged we were to be at Portmantle, hovering above the world, subtracted from it. It usually did us good to remember that the clockwork of the world never stopped, that history was already forgetting us. But MacKinney crossed her arms and said, 'I don't know how much longer I can stay here.'

I moved closer to the parapet, looking down at the moss-grown shelf over the portico, the thawing gardens and studio lodgings. It was difficult to judge MacKinney's mood. We had eased one another through gloomy spells so often it had become a kind of running joke between us: 'Will you help me dig a tunnel?' I would ask her sometimes; or if I caught her doodling on a napkin, she might say, 'Planning our escape.' Now she seemed to be stricken with something more than her usual disquiet—a deeper hurt I could not reach—and she was resistant to the normal platitudes. I wondered if it might all be related to the boy somehow. 'There isn't a person here who isn't tired of it, Mac. We have to keep going. Work through it.'

'You think I've been sitting on my hands all this time?'

'No. That isn't what I said.'

'I've tried everything. Nothing fits, nothing feels right. I can't even put down a simple stage direction without questioning myself. Sooner or later, I'm going to have to surrender. It's clear I don't have another play in me. Whatever talent I might have had once—it's long gone.'

'Just write what you believe.'

'*What?* Is that serious advice?'

'I don't know what else to say.'

Ardak came out from the portico beneath us, carrying his ladders back to the outhouse. As he walked, the rungs cast beautiful zoetrope shadows on the sunlit lawns and, for a moment, I lost track of where I was.

'Knell—are you even listening?'

I turned to find Mac squinting at me. 'Of course.'

The intermittent shine had got me thinking of the squeeze-box in the dusty space beneath my mother's bed, the lolloping weight of the instrument in my hands, how the lamplight used to shimmer on the metal when I took it out.

'So you really don't mind? I've lost all my objectivity on it now, but I think it's the only thing worth developing.'

'What is?'

'The scene I've just been telling you about. The monologue. Jesus, Knell, you were nodding along while I was talking. Did you not hear *anything*?'

I apologised, and this seemed to placate her. If I had known how much of the conversation had skipped by me, I would have confessed to it. 'Sorry. It might not have been such a good idea to come up here on an empty stomach.' I felt totally disoriented.

'Let's go down then,' Mac said. 'We'll get some *salep* and go to my room. You can read it there. It won't take long.'

Once I was back through the hatch, I felt better. There was a pleasant sawdust smell about the attic and a satisfying closeness to the walls. 'Wouldn't it be better to ask Q to read it, or one of the other writers? I don't know if it's right, involving me like this. We ought to keeps things as they are.'

Mac put her arm around me. 'Quickman will only bring a certain—how to put this—*intellectualism* to his readings, which isn't what I need right now. I'm looking for a simple emotional response. And I wouldn't trust those short-termers with a single word of mine.' She squeezed my shoulder. 'You're the perfect audience for this—you understand where I'm coming from. I wouldn't ask if I wasn't desperate.'

We stopped outside the mess hall, where Gülcan kept an urn of *salep* constantly warming throughout the day. It was the provost's favourite drink and we had come to share his fondness for it as a winter tonic. Mac filled two cups and we carried them along the corridor to her room, passing the thresholds of other guests, some of whom I could hear working at typewriters. It seemed to me that Mac's corridor was forever rattling with these factory noises—the bright clamour of thoughts being machined—and I had always believed it was a heartening sound until that day. 'Listen to them,' she said, 'typing up. They'll be out of here soon.'

'Isn't that a good thing?'

'For them maybe.'

MacKinney's room was deliberately spartan: a single bed made up with hospital corners, a bureau with the tidiest stack of manuscript pages, an oak wardrobe as solid and imposing as a casket. We were not discouraged from bringing in photographs of loved ones, but if any of us possessed them they were not put on display—I suspected Mac had pictures of her daughters hidden somewhere and spent her evenings tenderly thumbing their faces in private.

On the ottoman by her window was the tan leather suitcase I had seen her carry into Portmantle many seasons ago; she kept it with its lid open and its belly packed with hardbacks, preciously arranged, all of them page-marked with strips of ribbon. What belongings she had were organised like this, aligned to some private schema. Only her camping stove and coffee pot—special items she had requested from the provost—bore the scars of regular use; they were so blackened and spilled-on that she kept them tucked behind the door, covered by a tea towel.

She put down her *salep* on the bureau and slid out the top drawer, carrying the whole thing to her bed. 'On second thought,' she said, rifling through, 'it's probably best if you don't read it while I'm standing here in front of you. That will just be agony for both of us.' The foolscap pages wilted in her hands as she held them out to me. 'It's my only copy. I'd tell you to be careful with it, but I'm quite sure it's headed for the fireplace in the end.'

The papers were a little greasy. Flicking through them, I saw that each page bore Mac's careful handwriting—an upright style that never broke the borders of the rulings, whose letters crouched like tall birds herded into crates. At least a quarter of the text was neatly struck through with black pen, and Mac had redacted most of her own notes in the margins. 'Just, you know—tell me if there's anything there,' she said.

'I will.'

'Think you could get back to me by dinnertime?'

'What's the rush?'

'I told you, I don't know how long I have.'

There had been such wistfulness about the way MacKinney had been talking on the roof that I had mistaken her meaning. I thought that she had been trying to vent her frustrations about Portmantle again, weighing her regrets against her achievements. But I understood now, from the urgency in her voice, from the way she was tap-tapping her foot on the floorboards, that it was something else. She was leaving us—and not by choice. 'Did something happen? Are they trying to kick you out?'

'Shssh. Close the door.'

I pulled it shut. The *salep* taste in my mouth began to sour. Without the echo of the corridor, the room had a very cloistered feeling. It seemed there was no one else alive in the world but the two of us.

Mac said, 'I don't know anything about your sponsor. Tell me about her.'

'What?'

'*Tell me about her.*'

'Him,' I said.

'Really? A man?' She raised her eyebrows. 'I can't say why, but I expected better of you.'

'Well, I didn't exactly choose.'

'Is he older than you?'

'Yes.'

'By how much?'

'A good ten years or so.'

'That's a shame. You better hope he gets plenty of exercise.'

'Oh, he was never much of a sportsman, I don't think.' Then I finally grasped her point. 'Is there something the matter with your sponsor?'

'Not any more there isn't.' She gave a long exhalation—less of a sigh than a test of her lungs. 'But you can't smoke fifty a day and expect to live forever, can you?' Lifting the drawer from the bed, she went to slip it back into the bureau, wobbling it home. 'Seventy-three years old. Not bad in the scheme of things.'

'God, Mac. I'm so sorry.'

'That's OK. I just wish I could've been there for her.' She went extremely quiet. 'I'd still be working in my uncle's bakery if it weren't for her, you know. Boiling bagels for a few shillings an hour. She took me out of that. Always believed in me.'

'And never stopped,' I said.

'I don't know. I always thought she'd be the first person to read my play when it was done, and now she's dead. It feels as though I've let her down.'

'I'm sure she'd tell you that was nonsense.'

'Well, I've got precisely nothing to show for all the time I've spent here. That tells its own story.' Mac combed through her hair with her nails, gathering it at the side. 'Fact is, I don't know how much longer they'll let me stay. Her lawyers have been sending letters to the trustee board, asking what the cheques are for. Can you believe that? Miserable vultures.'

'How long have you known about this?' I said.

'Days. I wasn't supposed to say anything until the provost gets back. That's where he's gone—to speak to the trustees—but I don't like my chances. They're going to boot me out, I know it.'

'It won't come to that.'

'There's always some procedure to follow. You know what the provost's like—he's a bureaucrat to the core. If there's a precedent, he'll find it.'

'God, Mac. I don't know what to say.'

She pointed to the sheaf of papers in my hands, smiling. 'You don't need to say anything. Just read for me. Tell me there's a sentence worth keeping in that lot or I'm better off away from here.'

- - - - -

There were short-termers in the library—five of them, reading in silence—and all but one of their heads lifted as I came in, bothered by the intrusion. Only the Spanish poet, who was sitting cross-legged on the sofa with an encyclopaedia, failed to look in my direction, though he gave a grunting cough as I left.

It proved difficult to find any space in the mansion that was not already possessed: there was another group of short-termers in the lobby, conversing timidly in French, and they turned their backs when I approached, lowering their voices; Gülcan was folding bedsheets in the portico; Ardak was chopping wood by the front steps and tossing the shards into a barrow. Even the sky seemed busy with the flow of birds and the tangled streams of aeroplanes.

And so I headed to my studio with Mac's pages, feeling duty-bound to find potential in them. There was a good reason why the four of us did not share our work with anyone. We had given too many seasons of our lives to Portmantle, invested too much in the pursuit of clarity to ever doubt we would accomplish it, or to wonder if all the solitude and sacrifice would have meaning in the end. We were comfortable in the vacuum we had created, and told ourselves that other people's validation of our efforts was nothing but a crutch. That was why we had come to Portmantle, after all, to rid ourselves of external influence and opinion—to be originals. And so we declined to attend the readings and performances that the provost arranged for departing guests, and took no notice of the workshops and get-togethers that sprung up like crabgrass every summer amongst the residents. Of course, we were curious about each other's projects, and knew just enough to satisfy this interest—Pettifer had his cathedral designs; Quickman his epic novel; MacKinney her great play; and I had my mural commission—but we never enquired too deeply or encroached beyond these limits. Our work-in-progress was the one thing we truly owned, and to release it to the eyes and ears of the world was to corrupt it. When Quickman's book was ready, we would be thrilled to set eyes on it. When Pettifer had built his cathedral, we would all go side by side to wonder at it. Until then, we supported one another just by sharing the same objective.

MacKinney, in her desperation, had now broken this arrangement. I was terrified to look at what she had given me. It was unlikely to be a shambling mess, but what if she had written an equivalent of the pictures in my studio: something competent but lifeless, unexceptional? I lay down on my bed and forced myself to read:

WILLA (*hushed*): No, the problem is I love you more. (*She comes down the last stair to comfort Christopher. He shrugs off her hand as she touches his back.*) Listen to me. I've thought about this. (*Pause—the slightest gesture of interest from Christopher.*) Before I met you, I was alone for so long that I had a system all worked out, you know, a way of turning that aloneness into something good. The only thing I had in my life was painting. Any intimacy I got, that's what it came from—a brush and a canvas and my own imagination. It was like having a husband in a lot of ways. I mean, I was devoted to it, spent all my private time in rooms with it, went to sleep dreaming of it. Having something in your life like that, well, I suppose it stops you from missing what you don't have—can you understand that? Painting was there for me when I had nothing. (*Willa sits down beside Christopher and he does not resist.*) Then I met you . . . (*She nudges her hip against him.*) Once you love a man more than your art, that's it, you lose it forever. You can't get the intimacy back, no matter what you try. It gets replaced by something so much better. (*Responding to Christopher's confused expression.*) This is not about me blaming you—don't look at me like that. I'm just trying to explain what I've been feeling. And what I'm trying to say is that I'll never paint the same way ever again. I'll always feel adrift. (*Willa takes his hand, but Christopher is not responsive.*) When I'm painting, my whole heart has to be invested, and it just isn't any more—it's chosen you instead. It's not big enough to hold all things at once, and I have to cope with that somehow, but I can't. You're always saying that I pine too much for the old days, and you're right, that's part of it. I do. Always. But what I can't figure out is: how can I miss the loneliness of it all? How can I miss the unhappiness? (*Long pause.*) I know this doesn't change anything. I'm not dumb enough to think it will. And maybe it's true what you've been telling me—maybe this is what I've really wanted from the start. But I don't regret falling in love with you, Christopher. How could I? You're the best thing in my life.

Christopher waits, then stands up slowly.

CHRISTOPHER: Well, I regret it enough for the both of us.

There was nothing for me to measure this fragment of a scene against. I had no experience of reading scripts, and could count on one hand the number of serious plays I had watched at the theatre that were not by Shakespeare. I was neither a critic nor a writer. But I felt sympathy for Willa from the outset, and that seemed to be the most important thing Mac could have achieved. Perhaps the dialogue could have been more tidily constructed, perhaps the staging was too static, perhaps it was all too composed, or not composed enough—it was not my right to make those judgements. What mattered most was that Mac's characters seemed real to me, that they raised questions I had not previously considered. I was honestly relieved to find such values in her work.

The afternoon was getting away from me, though, and I had not yet cleaned my studio. All my palette knives were in the sink, unrinsed. The muller and slab were resting on my workbench, encrusted with dried paint. The tables needed wiping down. I could see a few spilled globs of powder on the wood—the pigment was pure white in the daytime, like ordinary flour, but if I didn't wash away the spillages properly, they would sink into the grain and glow weakly in the night. At times like this, I yearned for an assistant.

I found the boy at the front of his lodging, perched on an upturned crate. In his part of the grounds, there was still abundant sunshine, but Fullerton had somehow arranged himself in the smallest patch of shade, at the very corner of the building. He was leaning back against the cinderblocks, knees up, scribbling on a length of narrow paper, the tails of which were hanging over his shins. It was clear that I had caught him in the wake of inspiration but I was too close to turn back.

When I reached his doorway, I held the *jeton* above my head, pinched between two fingers, as though it were a white flag. I intended to say nothing, but he stopped what he was doing and called out: 'What do you want?'

'I have a delivery.'

I flicked the token at him, thinking he would catch it. Instead, it hit the concrete and rolled towards his feet. He stopped it with his boot.

'Next time you get frightened by a butterfly,' I said, 'do me a favour and throw a cushion instead.'

'It was a moth,' he said flatly. 'And I'm not frightened of them.'

I could see now that he was writing on a stack of index cards that had been taped together, end to end. When he stood up, the whole set sprang outwards like the bellows of a concertina. He laid them on the crate. For a second or two, he scrutinised the *jeton*, bearing it to the light. Then he put it on his thumb and catapulted it back to me. 'Thanks, but I've got one already.'

I clutched it from the air. 'It's yours—the one you threw. Ardak found it.'

'Must be someone else's.' The boy reached into his jeans. He drew out another *jeton* and displayed it on his palm: a newer, brighter version of the faded thing I held in mine. 'Believe me now?'

'Well, I don't know who else it could belong to.'

'Try harder.' He moved the crate along half a yard, fussing over its position, until he had it in the right amount of gloom.

Then he gathered up his stack of cards again, flip-booking their edges with his fingers. 'You know, I'm starting to understand why you've been here so long, Knell. You make a lot of friendly house calls, but you don't seem to do much painting.'

I knew that he was trying to deflect me before I got too settled in his presence. It was a tactic I had often used myself with the short-termers. 'I work at night,' I told him.

'Like a moth, you mean.' He attempted a smile. 'Honestly, I'm not scared of them. I just hate the stupid things, the way they move. I hate tipping them out of lampshades. I hate watching them fail. So I put them out of their misery.'

'You're a complicated boy,' I said.

'I know.' He sat down in the same hunched manner as before, unravelling his chain of cards; I could see the yellowed tape on the reverse of them. He resumed his work as though nothing had curtailed it. The motion of his pen seemed automatic as he scrawled away on each card, gliding from edge to edge, top to bottom. When one card was done, he lifted it, bringing up the next part of the link; he filled that, too, and another. Not once did he peer down to check what he was writing. His gaze was fixed upon the hinterland between our lodgings and the bare pomegranate trees. In turn, I could do nothing but marvel at his productivity.

At first, he did not respond to my staring. His pen gathered speed, making a noise like knitting needles. The cards collected themselves into a tidy pack between his feet. Then he said, 'If you're just going to stand there, gawking, you're in for a long afternoon.'

I was used to his forthrightness by now, but he still had the knack of putting me off-kilter. He was a fascinating thing to watch at work, a collision of focus and detachment. 'Don't you need your guitar?' I asked.

He dipped his head towards the ground. When he looked up again, his bottom lip was sucked under his teeth. He blinked once, heavy and protracted. 'OK,' he said, 'now you're definitely annoying me,' and reeled in the line of cards, hand over hand, as though bringing up an anchor. 'It's funny, I was just thinking of my granddad. He used to read the papers and get all worked up about the drug addicts in the articles. He reckoned the best way to solve their problems was to lock them all up in one big house with all the finest heroin and clean needles they could want—no food, no TV, no water, no getting out, just round-the-clock heroin, the good stuff. He reckoned that after a week or so, half of them would overdose—no big loss, according to him—and the rest would get so bored of taking heroin they'd never touch the stuff again. He thought it was the chase they were addicted to, bless him. The lifestyle. Stupid, right?'

'Just a bit.'

'Well, here's what's funny about it: I've been here two days, and I'm starting to think he wasn't all that loony.' The boy took five quick strides towards me, boot soles clapping the cement.

'I don't really see your point.'

He flipped the edges of his cards again. 'I mean, that's the reason we're all here, isn't it? The *making* part is what we're addicted to, the struggle, the day to day. Our drug isn't the actual fix, if you get what I'm saying.'

'Partly,' I said. 'But I don't believe that painting is an addiction. It's always felt more like a survival technique.'

This appeared to have some effect on the boy's opinion of me. He peered down at his stack of cards, nodding, as though some silent plan had been decided upon. Then he offered them to me. 'Go on—have a look if you want. We'll consider it a trade.'

'For what exactly?'

'For being so nice to me. I know it isn't easy.' But just as I was reaching for the cards, he lifted them away, as though withholding ice cream from a child. 'Just messing,' he said with a smirk, lowering his arm again.

There must have been a few hundred cards in total and they had a surprising heft. I skimmed through the entire set while the boy stood at my shoulder, breathing loudly. Barring the last twenty or thirty, which were blank, every card was covered with elusive Japanese characters.

たくさん食べなくてはいけないという訳ではありません。事実、歳を重ねるにつれて身体が必要とする食事の量は減少します。大事なのは様々な種類の良い食品を摂取するということ。例えばバナナを取り上げてみましょう。手に取って、皮を剥いて、そして食べる。満足感も栄養もたっぷりです。

'So?' he said, and made a platform with his hand. 'What's the verdict?'

I placed the cards back on his palm. He had that same affected look of innocence—head down and to the side—that I had seen once before, when he had bragged about gambling with Cypriots. 'Another thing you learned from picture books, I take it.'

'Sort of.' His pulse was visible in his neck, depressing and returning like a switch. There was an oiled quality about his complexion in the shade, too, an awkward teenage lustre. 'It's a pretty difficult language,' he said. 'I don't understand a word of it.'

'You're lying.'

He shook his head. 'I'm really not.'

'Then how do you know what you're writing?'

'I don't. I just scribble it down and ask questions later.' He shrugged, acknowledging his strangeness. 'It looks like it might be real Japanese this time, but I wouldn't bet on it. There's always ten cards of gibberish in my head for every one that makes sense.'

'So where does it all come from?'

He tapped his forehead. 'Certain things just stick with me.'

'Like backgammon.'

'Yeah, in a way.' He must have thought I was trying to challenge him somehow, because he took a step back, and said, 'I've got to get it down on paper while it's still fresh, or it just breaks up into all these little pieces. Then it gets harder to remember. I can't explain it any better than that.'

'You should ask Quickman to translate it for you. He wrote a whole book about—' I stopped, realising that the boy was several moves ahead of me. 'Japan,' I finished pointlessly. 'But you knew that already.'

The boy softened his stance. 'Well, I don't think he'd help me now anyway. Not after last night. I shouldn't have bothered asking you to find him.'

'Oh, don't worry about that—Q doesn't bear a grudge for

long. Even if you did give him a thrashing.' I did not sound very convincing. 'Why don't you sit with us at dinner? You can ask him then. Or I'll do it for you.'

'Maybe,' the boy said. 'I've got a lot to finish here.'

'You can't afford to keep missing meals, you know. It's bad for the brain.'

'I'm fussy when it comes to food.'

'Well, it's Monday, so it's probably *karnıyarık.*'

'I don't even know what that is.'

'Now you're sounding like a proper Englishman,' I said. 'Think aubergine and minced meat. It's always good when Gülcan makes it. Shall I save you a space?'

'OK. But I might have to skip it.'

'I'll lean on Quickman for you in the meantime.'

'Thanks.'

'Just tell me one thing, for my own peace of mind,' I said. 'Are you really a musician?'

The boy snickered. 'I always thought I'd like to be,' he replied, and went back to his crate. 'But, no—it's not why I'm here.' Sitting down, sighing, he unfurled the spine of cards over his knees and blew on the nib of his pen. He glared at me until I moved away.

Five

Quickman loaded his plate with rice and *karnıyarık* and continued along the serving pass. He reached into the bread basket and collected four thick sections, stacking them on his tray like casino chips. He offered me a fifth but I shook my head. 'And what makes the lad think I'm such an expert on it?' he said, adding the slice to his own pile. 'If languages were my speciality, I'd be translating Balzac, not piddling about with my own rubbish. Want some *ayran*?' Again, I shook my head. Quickman was the only one of us who could stand to drink the stuff—a yoghurt gloop with all the flavour and viscosity of a saline drip. 'You don't know what you're missing out on. It's a little brackish, at first, but you get used to it. Great for the digestion.'

'I'll live with the heartburn,' I said. 'Pass the juice.'

He handed me the jug and waited as I filled a glass, peering towards our usual table.

The problem was, I understood the boy's reasons for thinking Quickman could help, but the explanation was not easy to broach with the man himself. An age had passed since I had closed the covers on *In Advent of Rain*. I could still remember the story and its characters in some detail because it was that rare type of novel—disquieting, note-perfect—that settles in your unconscious and becomes hard to disentangle. I knew that a solemn, friendless boy like Fullerton could not have survived his adolescence without reading it, too. But how could I raise the subject of the book with Quickman? For me to have even hinted at its existence would have been to acknowledge his life before Portmantle, to subject him to a reality he had chosen to renounce.

In Advent of Rain tells the story of an unnamed girl whose summer is disturbed by the arrival of a visitor from Japan: an old acquaintance of her father's called Junichiro. It is 1933 and Junichiro, an esteemed mathematician from Nagoya, has come to England to embark on a lecture tour, arranged by the girl's father, in order to propagate an extraordinary claim. The old man believes he has discovered a formula that can predict when rain will fall on any given day, in any given place—knowledge that he believes will be vital to agriculture and the growth of a global economy in the future. He is keen to share the formula with governments across the world, under certain conditions. Junichiro cannot speak much English, so the girl's father—a linguist and a don at an Oxford college—acts as an interpreter. The girl spends her summer holiday following them on the lecture tour, going from one university hall to another, by road, by rail, by sea. At each venue, Junichiro pins up a sheet of predictions for rainfall times and locations that later reveal themselves to be accurate. His claims gather weight and interest from the media. Lecture halls are no longer big enough to hold the audiences, so the tour is extended to theatres in Ireland, France, Germany, and America. But, despite offers of employment and financial reward from private companies, Junichiro refuses to divulge the formula. The press speculates that he is planning to auction off the information to the highest bidder. Junichiro tells the girl's father, however, that he will only reveal the formula if the US government agrees to end its development of atomic weapons. They meet with American officials, who deny that such technology exists. The night before Junichiro is to give a lecture in Munich, he is abducted from his hotel and is never seen again. Just a few months later, the girl's father poisons himself in rather suspicious circumstances, and she is sent to live with her aunt in Devon. She spends the rest of her life—through wartime and peacetime—trying to find out what happened to Junichiro and her father, without success, until one day a photograph of the old man's formula is discovered on an undeveloped roll of negatives, found in the archives of her father's college. Now a teacher of mathematics in her own right, she reads through the old man's workings and finds them irrefutable. But the world has become a different place, bleak and bruised by war. So, instead of publishing the formula or spreading word of Junichiro's accomplishment, she bleaches the negatives and burns the photographs, and—in a final touch of poetry—goes out in the rain to bring in her husband's washing.

Quickman rarely discussed any aspect of his writing with us, and for me to have gone blundering into a conversation about it, unprompted, would have been to risk our friendship. As we carried our dinner trays to the table, I tried to think of some way to introduce the topic of Japan again without expressly mentioning his book. But my thoughts came jabbering out too fast: 'So, let's just imagine, hypothetically, if somebody were to give you a letter from a friend of hers in Japanese, you wouldn't, let's say, be able to determine if it was really Japanese, or Korean, or something similar?'

Quickman walked ahead of me. 'What?'

'I'm saying, I don't think I'd be able to tell the difference between any of those Oriental languages. Never been that far east in my life. All the characters look so complicated, and there must be so many to remember, and I'd probably have to— '

'Stop it, Knell,' he said. 'I can see what you're doing, and I would very much like you to stop it. Immediately.' He placed his tray down beside Pettifer, who was keenly scooping up the dregs of his *karnıyarık* with a crust of bread. The light was faltering outside and the mess hall was moody with candle flames.

I went quiet.

'What's she trying to talk you into?' asked Pettifer, grabbing the tail of our conversation. He looked at me. 'Let me guess: that boy's got in your head again.'

'Keep out of it,' I said.

Quickman tore the cap from his *ayran* and took a gulp. When he lowered the pot, there was a milk-white film on his moustache. 'What I don't quite understand,' he said, padding off the liquid with a napkin, 'is why you feel so obliged to help the lad. He doesn't even have the good grace to show up for dinner. Not to mention the fact that he hustled me out of my father's lighter. I'd quite like that thing back, by the way. But that's not the point. I'm not going to get dragged into someone else's creative problems. I've got enough of my own.'

'He's just a boy,' I said. 'You should have seen him, earlier, scribbling away on his notecards. If you could just let him know if it's actually Japanese, that would be a start.'

Quickman carved up his food. 'Why can't you leave him alone? That seems to be what he wants.'

'Because there's alone and there's *alone*.'

'Ah,' he said. 'Explain to me the difference again.'

Pettifer shifted forwards. 'I know a bit of Japanese myself,' he said.

'The difference, Q, is he's only seventeen, and when you're that age all you really need is someone to—' I was so used to ignoring Tif's interjections that it took a moment for my brain to engage. 'Sorry, did you just say that you speak Japanese?'

Pettifer shrugged his eyebrows. 'Well, sort of. I can read *hiragana*, anyway. I'm not brilliant with *kanji*, but I could probably give him the gist.'

I was so overcome with gladness that I almost leaned over and hugged him. 'Tif, you gorgeous, brilliant thing—I should have known.'

'It's these ravishing good looks, you see. They obscure my intellect.'

'Of course they do.' I blew him a kiss.

At once, Quickman became interested in the conversation. He put his fork down and gave Tif a querying look. '*Doko de nihongo wo narattandai?*' he said.

Pettifer nodded thoughtfully. '*Nihon de shibaraku hataraki-mashita.*'

'*Dākuhōsu dana.*'

'*Chigauyo. Futotta buta dayo.*'

'*Sōdana!*'

It was quite disconcerting to hear another language emerging from the lips of two people I knew so well. 'OK, that settles it,' I said. 'You're *both* going to help him.'

Quickman stabbed at his dinner. 'He'll have to give my lighter back first.'

'I'm sure he'd be happy to trade.'

'My father died with that thing in his hand, you know. I should never have bet with it.'

'You could always try and win it back.'

'I plan to. Just as soon as I've reviewed my strategy.'

'Oi, you two. Get a load of this,' Pettifer said, gesturing to the kitchen pass. 'Mac's talking to those transients again. We should rescue her.' MacKinney did appear to be standing in close counsel with Gluck, which would not have been such a grave misfortune in itself, had the irritating Spaniard not also been with him. 'Is it me, or does she seem to be enjoying their company?'

It was true: she was laughing, and not in the hollow fashion we had come to recognise, but in that wonderful, resounding way that we had not heard for some time. I was glad that she was smiling again, even if I felt resentful of her sudden bonhomie with the short-termers.

'Crikey,' said Quickman. 'This place is going to ruin.'

Mac's face was still flushed by the time she came over to join us at the table a while later. As she sat down, a residue of laughter came out of her nose, like steam releasing. 'Oh Lord, that was seriously funny,' she said. 'Did you know that Lindo did impressions? I haven't laughed so much in ages.'

'Yes, we could hear you cackling from here,' Quickman said.

Pettifer gave his little snort. 'Who's Lindo?'

'The Spanish fellow. He's actually quite lovely. It's a shame we wrote him off so early.'

'You know, she's right,' Quickman said. 'We've been lacking a decent impressionist for a while now.'

'Fine. Be that way.' She nudged up the bridge of her glasses. 'You should hear the one he does of *you*.'

'I'm sure it's wonderfully subversive,' Q said.

Mac huffed. She was sideways on the chair, as though not quite committed to sitting with us. 'Knell, you have to hear the way he takes off Quickman. He does this clever trick with his mouth, as though he's speaking through a pipe. It's hysterical.' Another spitball of laughter came up from her throat.

'Sounds terrific,' I said, the dullness of my voice betraying me.

'Oh, come on, what's wrong with everybody? Can't you stop being so serious about everything for once? A break from all the cynicism might do you some good.' She stood up, reaching for a slice of Quickman's bread, but he moved his plate away from her.

'Get your own,' he said.

Mac lingered at the end of the table, ruminating. 'You know, Lindo says he's getting out of here. He's close to finishing his collection.'

'Bully for him,' Q said. 'That didn't take long.'

'He's having a reading soon. We should all go along and listen. It'll make a nice change to hear something that's actually complete.'

'I don't think so.' Quickman pushed his plate aside. 'Bad poetry is one thing, but bad Spanish poetry? That could push me over the edge.'

'Well,' Mac said, 'it's easy to be critical when your best work is behind you.'

Quickman looked suitably wounded, but he knew better than to rise to provocation. He just drew the pipe from his blazer pocket, tapped it on the tabletop, and bit on the mouthpiece.

At this point, Pettifer leaned into my ear and whispered: 'What *is* she doing?'

'I don't know,' I whispered back, but I knew exactly: MacKinney was letting us go.

After all, it would be so much easier to say goodbye if we resented her. If she attached herself to short-termers like Gluck and Lindo in the time she had left, she could forget them as soon as her feet touched the mainland; but we—the stalwarts who had been together, season after season—we would be harder to miss. She was going to amputate us from her side, one by one, starting with Quickman, because he was the newest and the thinnest joint to hack away. Next, she would come for Pettifer, and then it would be my turn. I decided to intervene before that happened. 'Well, you definitely know how to make a scene, Mac, I'll give you that,' I said.

She glared at me. 'Huh?'

'I suppose when all that drama's in your blood, you never lose it.' I took out the folded pages from my skirt and waved them.

'Oh,' she said. 'You mean . . .'

'What else?'

'Let's go outside a sec. It's too loud in here.'

'Yes, I think that's probably best for everyone.'

We stepped out onto the landing. The noise of the mess hall softened to a drone. There was a thumbnail of a moon that night, framed in the picture window, and the darkness was thickening above the trees. MacKinney turned on a lamp and leaned against the banister. 'Sorry for getting irked in there,' she said. 'It's just that Q can really sound so high and mighty sometimes.'

'I'm amazed you've finally noticed.'

She groaned, sweeping underneath her lenses with her fingers. 'So, tell me: how bad is it?'

I gave her the pages. 'Well, first of all, the Willa character, the painter, she reminds me of someone. Can't think who.'

Mac shrugged. 'That's not exactly a coincidence.'

'Good. I'm glad I wasn't imagining it. People used to see themselves in my paintings all the time and I never had the heart to disappoint them.' I put my hand upon her shoulder. 'The most important thing, as far as you're concerned, is that the characters felt very real to me—in fact, I understood their situation better than you know. I assume that's why you asked me to read it.'

Mac's face bloomed. 'They did?'

'I had the most sympathy for Christopher, of course, though I could understand Willa's dilemma, and I thought she was nicely conflicted. It's strange, I almost never feel for the man in that kind of scenario—usually, it's the woman who has to make all the compromises and do all the forgiving. I found that quite refreshing. It's another kind of infidelity that's breaking them up, isn't it? That's how I read it, anyway. The affair is between Willa and her art . . . I liked that idea. If you'd given me more than a few pages, I could've found out what happens next. Now I'll have to wait and catch it in the West End.'

For a moment, Mac said nothing. I could not tell if she was glad or dispirited. She tightened her fist around the pages, closing her eyes, and when she blinked them open again, they were glassy and mapped with tiny lines. 'You have no idea how much it means to hear that, Knell. Just to know it made you feel something. Thank you. That was all I needed.'

'Wait until you hear my notes on the punctuation.'

She smiled. 'Don't ruin it.'

'Does this mean we can finish our dinner in peace?'

'OK, but Quickman has to tone down the sanctimony. It's getting out of hand.'

'I'll speak to him about that.'

'Good.'

We headed back to the mess hall. 'What kind of name is Lindo, anyway?' I said.

'I don't know. Ask the provost.'

'Hard to take a man seriously with a name like that.'

But Mac had already tuned out. She was hesitating at the threshold, studying her pages. 'You really think there's something worth developing here?'

With my hand on my heart, I said, 'I'd stake my sponsor's life on it.'

'God, it's such a relief. I can't tell you how much better I feel.' She edged away. 'I might just go to my room and dig out the rest of the draft. *Carpe diem* and all that.'

'You're not going to stay and eat with us?'

She started to backpedal. 'No, I've lost my appetite. Give my pudding to Tif.'

'That'll go down well.'

And it was then, as Mac was heading back across the landing, that a surge of footsteps came up the stairway behind us. There was such a frantic energy to the noise, it seemed as though some forest animal had been loosed inside the mansion. But a familiar shape revealed itself—a head of brown hair, a bulky set of shoulders. It was Fullerton. He went dashing up the stairs so fast he could not control his feet. A toecap caught on the very last step, tripping him. His body hurtled forwards, skidding. Knees and elbows slapped the parquet, but he rose quickly to his haunches, stilling his breaths.

'Are you OK?' Mac asked from the corridor.

He seemed to be startled by the sound of her voice, shifting his head in her direction. 'Hello? Who's there?'

'It's MacKinney,' she said. 'I'm right here.'

'Hello? Is someone out there?'

I stepped closer. 'Fullerton, it's *us*. It's Knell and MacKinney. Are you all right?' But when he heard my voice coming from the other side of the room, a greater panic wracked him. He stood gawping at the stained-glass lampshade above his head, as though fearing it would drop. He wiped the spittle from his chin, checking his fingers. 'I think I'm bleeding,' he said. 'I don't have much time. How do I get out?'

'You're fine,' Mac told him.

'*Please*. How do I get out?'

'Calm down there, sunshine. You're not making any sense.' She turned to me, her face bent with concern. 'He must've hit his head or something.'

'Just tell me which stairs to take,' the boy went on. 'Are you there?'

'Fullerton, we're standing right in front of you,' I said. 'Stay still. I'm coming to help you.' Slowly, I moved into his path, not wanting to alarm him.

'You're so faint. Please—how do I get out?' He began to peer at the ceiling, turning in circles.

I was near enough to touch him now, and I held my hand out, hoping he would take it. But, although his eyes were locked wide open, he did not acknowledge me. I waved my arms and, still, he could not see me. 'He's sleepwalking,' I said to Mac. 'Has to be.'

'Tripping, more like,' she said. 'Look at those pupils—he's on something.'

'Hello? Are you there?' the boy called now. 'Tell me where to go. *Please.*'

Mac turned. 'I'm going to get Ender.'

'No, wait.' I spoke very loudly and clearly to the boy. 'Go back to where you started. We'll come and fetch you.'

But the boy just shouted to the ceiling: 'Hello? Please—anyone there?' Then, under his breath, he said, '*Fuck.*' He checked his mouth for blood again, and hurried forwards. I had to step aside to let him past.

The conversations in the mess hall did not quieten and he staggered up to the serving pass. He browsed the leftovers, lifting every dish to check what lay beneath, getting the run-off on his hands. Whatever he was seeing, it was not food. He began to rummage the drinks table behind him, pushing teacups aside and knocking cola cans, until he caught sight of the *ayran* pots and gathered them all in his clutches.

A few of the short-termers noticed him then. One of them said, 'Hey, save some for the rest of us!' Another said, 'Your shoelace is

untied!' They were smirking at each other. But Fullerton took
no notice, or did not receive them. He marched back through the
mess hall, brushing past Mac and me in the doorway. He was
muttering to himself, counting his steps: '. . . fifty-three, fifty-
four, fifty-five, fifty-six . . .' We followed him onto the landing. He scurried off through the ruddy light, down the first
staircase. '. . . seventy-eight, seventy-nine, eighty.' He stopped at
the window and stacked the cardboard *ayran* pots on the ledge in
a single column. 'What is he up to?' Mac said. We watched him
rip the lid off the topmost carton and course down the steps with
another one still in his grip.

For a long moment, we could only hear his presence on the floor
below, the ricochets of him bounding through the house. Then
the last *ayran* pot came spearing up towards the window in a blur.
It clattered straight into the stack and burst against the glass. Great
shocks of liquid sprayed up and sideways, over the curtains, the
wallpaper, pooling on the sill. The radius of the splash was so wide
that it dotted my shoes. There came a whoop of exaltation from
the hallway beneath us.

By the time we reached the lobby, the boy was gone. The front
door was hanging open and there was a sloppy glob of cinnamon
gum pushed into its keyhole. Outside, the night appeared so
empty and permanent. 'Well, I suppose the provost was wrong,'
Mac said, coming up behind me. 'That lad needs more than just
our supervision.'

- - - - - -

I fretted a great deal about Fullerton that night and it took all my
resolve to not pay a visit to his lodging on the way back to my

studio. In the end, I reasoned he was better left alone. I was still convinced that he had been sleeping on his feet throughout the episode, but I could tell that Mac believed otherwise. She did not accuse the boy outright, nor did she raise any suspicions with Ender. Instead, she kept reminding me of how fixed the boy's pupils had been. 'I've seen that spaced-out look before,' she said, as we helped to clean the boy's mess from the windowsill. 'That's all the explanation I need.' But this made very little sense to me.

There was no place drier than Portmantle: we took soluble aspirin for headaches or nothing at all, and even Gülcan's rubbing alcohol was kept in a locked box in the provost's office with all the emergency medicines. It was well understood that artists who relied on substances to pique their creativity were not accepted at the refuge; sponsors were made to vouch for the sobriety and moral character of all the newcomers before they arrived; and every guest was told the same cautionary tale about Whitlock, a fabled resident from the past, who had been caught drinking lawnmower diesel in the outhouse and was immediately ejected from the grounds—no documentation to secure his passage at the border, no help from the provost, not even a farewell handshake. (True or not, the implications of this story echoed long and loud.) Besides, I was sure the boy's possessions had been searched on his very first day, because he had made a point of complaining to me about it, and even his cigarette packet had been empty when he had offered it to Quickman that afternoon in the library. To me, the boy's strangeness was innate, not chemically induced. And I did not believe he would be impetuous enough to jeopardise his place at Portmantle for the sake of a fleeting high.

All of this was on my mind as I went about my nightly preparations in the studio. There was plenty to arrange—blinds to
draw and fix, windowpanes to cover, doorways to seal—and,
while I waited for the fullness of the dark, I could not stop thinking of the boy and his behaviour. As I got changed into my painting clothes, I felt the *jeton* hanging in my skirt pocket like a
curtain weight. It was my duty to keep it safe until someone
came to retrieve it—losing your ferry token for the homeward leg
was as good as a curse—so I took it to the bathroom and stowed
it, for the meantime, with my own keepsakes.

There was a groove in the wall behind the mirrored cabinet, a
cavity in the plaster I had fashioned with a palette knife, just
big enough to hide two things: (i) a tobacco tin that held all
my reserves of special pigment, and (ii) a red jeweller's box. I removed these objects delicately, as though cradling bird's eggs,
and placed them on the lip of the sink. The jeweller's box still
bore the faded insignia of the shop in Paris where it was acquired, and contained a rather ugly opal ring belonging to my
sponsor. Underneath the lining was my own tarnished *jeton*
from the Kabataş ferry port—I could still remember the bottle-
cap tinkle of it dropping on the vendor's counter, the slow quiver
as it settled, the sheer excitement of holding it in my fingers.
How drab and ordinary it seemed now. How purposeless. I
tipped the other *jeton* into the box with it and snapped the lid
shut.

By the time I had replaced the bathroom cabinet on its hinges,
the lights had all gone out in the mansion and the condition
of the night was such that I could make a start on sampling.
The only thing left to do was secure my front door and tape over

the surround. There was a mildness to the air, brought on by the thaw, which made my fingers more compliant. I switched off the studio lights and watched my pigment samples surfacing in the darkness, a medley of colour swelling on the wall, part muted, part luminous. It quickened my heart to see it.

When all my apparatus was in place, I went to the closet. By my reckoning, there were three garlands of mushrooms drying by the boiler, and at least one of those was ready to be powdered. A blue haze eked from the under-edge of the closet door and spread about my ankles.

The glow was unusually strong. My first thought was that the recent batch of mushrooms I had gathered was brighter than average, and this put me in a hopeful mood—perhaps my harvesting techniques were improving, or perhaps the warm afternoon had enhanced the drying process. But when I slid the door back, I found the garlands trodden to a pulp on the dusty concrete. A pair of blue-tinged feet protruded from the space beneath my coats. And there, between the boiler and my rucksack, was Fullerton. He was leaning in the closet like a broom, bare-naked and unconscious.

Instinctively, I turned my eyes away and closed the door on him—a silly, defensive reflex. For a while, my temples pounded with the fright and I could not organise my thoughts. The garlands were ruined and several days of sampling had been lost—I should have been shaking with anger, but I found it very hard to summon anything besides concern for the boy. I hurried off to get a blanket from my bed to cover him.

Sliding the door open again, I parted the clothes on the rail, exposing his pale young body. He did not move. His face was as reposed as I had ever seen it: the eyelids softly clinched, the mouth agape. His stout-ribbed chest was smeared with bluish finger tracks, a kind of luminescent war paint that also streaked his thighs and shins and forearms. I tried to respect his modesty as best as I could, but his awkward position in the closet made it impossible, and I caught a full glimpse of what he had. He was not as puny as the withered models I had drawn at art school, and differently built from the men I had gone to bed with, all of whom were circumcised.

I wrapped him in the blanket, bringing it around one shoulder like a toga, clamping it with a bulldog clip. This buffeted him a fair amount against the wall, but he did not even stir. I switched on all the studio lights and called his name; it made no difference. The only thing to do, it seemed, was douse him a little.

He did not wake up in a jolt, as I thought he might. Instead, he winced and blinked and spat, regaining his awareness gradually. He saw me standing there with the empty jug. 'Oh shit—again?' he said, and huffed the water from his face, pulling the blanket tight around his frame. There was a weariness to his eyes then, a sinking realisation. I had soaked him too well to be certain of it, but I thought he was about to cry. 'How long?' he asked.

'Excuse me?'

'How long've I been here?'

I got the impression he was used to waking up like this, in strange places, in other people's homes. 'At least since dinnertime,' I said. 'You've had a busy night, by all accounts.'

He nodded dolefully.

'Why don't you come out of there? I'll make you some tea.'

'I'm really sorry about this.' He checked the coverage of the blanket. The hem of it just about reached his knees. 'I don't know how I got in, but if I broke anything, I'll fix it, I swear.'

'My fault. The door was unlocked.'

'No, I mean it, Knell. I'm sorry you've got to deal with me like this.' His voice was meek and hoarse. 'Could you get me a towel?'

'There's a stack of clean ones above your head. On the shelf, there.'

He edged forwards, stretching.

I went to light my stove and put on the electric kettle. 'I'm not sure how much you remember,' I called to him from the sink, 'but you left the mansion in a bit of a state. Ender's having to replace the curtains. Hard to get *ayran* out of velvet.'

The boy stepped out of the closet, hair all spiked and tousled. 'Damage tends to follow me around these days.' He stood under the harsh fluorescent lights, sniffing his arms. 'You have mushrooms growing in your cupboard, by the way. Looks like I got most of them.'

'Is that so?' The kindling in the stove began to smoulder. 'It might be getting damp in there. I'll get Ardak to check.'

'Doesn't smell too bad, actually. I've covered myself in worse.' He looked back at the sludge he had left in the closet. 'Still, I feel bad about the mess. And for—you know.' He cleared his throat drily. 'Thanks for the blanket.'

'Should I expect to find your clothes somewhere?'

'Probably.'

'I'll keep an eye out.'

The boy did not respond. He came closer to the stove. His arms were crossed now, his shoulders goose-fleshed.

'We saw you on the landing, Mac and I. You seemed to hear us to begin with, but then you ran off. You kept asking us how to get out.'

'I'm sorry about that.'

'I know you are. It's fine, but—out of where?'

Very slowly, the boy lowered himself to kneel beside the stove. 'I sort of get trapped in my own head.' These words came out in such a freighted tone that his jaw hung slack for a moment after. He warmed his hands by the vents, staring up at me. 'I'm no good at explaining it,' he went on, 'but have you ever been to one of those really giant hotels they have in America? The New York Hilton or somewhere like that. Thousands of locked rooms that all look the same, all those corridors and stairways and lifts going up and down and up and—ugh! Just the scale of it, right? My dad used to take me to places like that. How the hell do they even build them?' His eyes went fat with the thought. 'Now picture that same hotel, but empty. With the lifts all broken and nobody around to fix them and no way of knowing which stair-case takes you where. That's what my head is like most of the time.'

'Well, Mac's convinced you're on drugs,' I said. 'Can't say I blame her.'

He seemed amused by this, but did not answer.

'Please tell me you aren't involved in all that.'

'I don't know,' he said, raking a centre parting in his hair. 'Did it look like I was having any fun to you?'

'No.'

'There's your answer, then. Who wants to take a drug that makes them miserable?' His legs were folded now and he was rubbing at his feet. 'Honestly, I've been wandering in my sleep since I was a little kid. Our next-door neighbours would find me in their basement when I was eight or nine. Sometimes, I'd make it all the way to Hampstead on my bike. Even crawled into a skip once—nearly got crushed by a load of skirting-boards. I see the insides of a lot of cupboards, that's for sure.'

'And are you always in the nude?' I said.

The boy gave his customary snicker. 'That's kind of a recent development. At least I don't wet myself any more, eh?' As he surveyed the room, he must have noticed my workbench, the muller and slab, the canvas swatches that lay in wait for me. 'I interrupted your work, didn't I? I'm sorry. I should go.'

'Stop apologising.'

He moved to get up.

'Sit down. We're having tea. I'll paint later.' There was no use in telling him that the mushrooms he had trampled in the closet *were* my work, or that his roving feet had set my progress back several days.

'Thanks for this, Knell. For not being—' He trailed off. 'You know what I mean. People get angry. They start looking at you funny. They think you can control it, so they end up resenting you. Don't mean to, I suppose, but that's what always happens . . . I had a doctor who said I should tie myself to the bedpost at night. I asked him if he'd chain his own kids up while they were sleeping. He looked at me like I was mad. Anyway, I gave it a try, just to see what happened. Made everything ten times worse. It's not like I *went* anywhere, obviously, but the dreams got more and more intense and I nearly broke my ankles. So that just shows you what doctors know about anything.'

The kettle clicked off. 'What sort of thing do you get up to, then, inside that head of yours?'

'I'm always trying to find my way out, to wake myself up. But it's impossible. Sometimes I'll imagine a new room I've never been in before. Sometimes I'll hear a voice or music in the distance and try to follow that. I'll find some old film playing on mute, or dream up a whole library and sit there, flicking through the books, hoping there might be an instruction to help me escape, a map or something. It's like, every time I go to sleep, I get moved back to the first square on the board—does that make sense? And a few moves in, I realise I've played this game before, you know? I recognise those ladders, and all those snakes look familiar. But the game never finishes.'

It sounded like absolute hell, and I told him so.

'Yeah, but it has its good points, too.' He mused on this for a moment. 'You're going to think it's weird how much I talk about my granddad, but, for some reason, he's been on my mind a lot since I've been here. I used to stay with him on weekends when my parents were away. He had a gammy foot, so he couldn't walk far, and he hardly left the flat. So we used to just stay in and listen to records. Always the same ones. Old ragtime bands, comedy programmes, silly songs, "The Laughing Policeman", stuff like that. His taste was quite narrow. We'd sit there listening to the same records over and over again. I got so bored of them, but there was nothing else to do. He hated modern radio, and he didn't have a garden, and I wasn't allowed to go out on my own. He loved the comfort of it, hearing the same old stuff every day. So I had to sit there with him, listening to it all, pretending to enjoy it. I couldn't wait for my mum to get back and take me home. But then, once it got to the middle of the week, and I was stuck on my own at school again, I'd start wishing I was with my granddad. All those hours I must have spent with him—sitting there, hearing those same records all day—I wouldn't swap them for anything. They made me who I am today. And I suppose I feel the same way now, about my dreams.'

'It must be hard to go to sleep, though,' I said. 'Knowing what might happen.'

He shrugged. 'Feels harder to wake up, believe me.'

The old tea leaves still had some life in them. I swirled the hot water around in the pot. He watched me with slatted eyes. 'It'll be weak, but that's how I like it. I can let it steep, if you prefer.'

'No, weak is fine.'

I rinsed two cups and poured the tea. It was almost colourless. The boy examined it, took a sip and cringed. 'Woah, you weren't joking.'

'My mother's fault. We had to reuse all the tea leaves in our house. Wartime mentality—or maybe just a Scottish one. Now I can't drink it any other way.'

'You don't have much of an accent.'

'Everything gets softer as you get older. Trust me.'

He almost laughed.

'I'm not sure they'd take me back in Clydebank now. It's still in my blood, but I just don't feel part of it any more. And I've never really been drawn to painting it—not like London. It doesn't fascinate me in that way.'

'Yeah,' he said. 'I've seen your work. I know.'

It was uttered so bluntly that it caught me unawares, and all I could do was waft my hand, as though to cleave the very suggestion from the air. 'Come on now, I thought we were having a nice conversation.'

The boy dipped his head. 'I only said that because—' He thought better of it, gulping. Then he got another burst of courage. 'I can't help it if I know who you are. Your stuff was up in the Tate— '

'Please. Let's not do this.'

'I had to copy it once, on a school trip. The teacher made us buy the postcard.'

'Shush, shush, enough now. You're making things worse. Please, let's change the subject.' I frowned into my cup, disregarding him. I was not sure what I was most afraid of: being recognised for who I was, or pitied for who I was not. 'I think I made this too strong. Does it taste a little bitter? I must have swilled it about too much.' I went and dumped the tea in the sink. I stayed there, facing away from him. 'In fact, it's probably time I got some work done. Would you mind going back to your own place now, if you're feeling better?'

I heard him put his cup down and climb to his feet. 'Look, I didn't mean to upset you, OK?' he said. 'I'm sorry.' When I turned, he was already going for the exit. 'I feel really bad— you've been so nice to me and everything.' He had shifted the blanket and tucked it tight around his waist.

'It's all right.'

'Don't be upset with me. I'm not good with people—I tried to tell you.'

'I just need to work, that's all.'

'OK. I get it. OK.' The door was still sealed up and would not open when he pulled it. He questioned it with his eyes, following the line of it around the frame. 'Where'd you get this stuff—supplies? It's pretty strong. I could use something like that.' There was a full roll left on my workbench. I had plenty stashed away, so I told him he could take it, as much to ease my conscience as to please him. 'You're a lifesaver,' he said, spinning it round on his fingers. 'This'll be perfect.' He moved for the door. 'Now, how do I—?'

'Just pull.'

He turned the handle and yanked hard at the door until the tape ripped back and the studio lights spilled onto the path. As he stood halfway into the night, the streaks upon his torso became gently luminescent. 'I don't see my clothes out there. Bad sign.' He shuffled into the darkness, each stride hindered by the blanket. I wanted him to stop, and turn, and tell me he was mistaken, that he did not recognise me at all. But my will could no more influence a boy and his behaviour than it could stop him dreaming.

Six

On an island as exposed as Heybeliada, the rain did not fall, it rioted. The wind carried it across the lawns of Portmantle in shivers, churning up the dirt-soil in the flowerbeds, bullying the pines until their topmost branches cowered. It had strength like no rain I had ever encountered, a swell, a rage, a constancy. And the provost's dog knew better than to go out in it. She lay on the front steps, one paw below her snout, observing the havoc being wreaked upon the grounds—in better weather, she could have been out there, digging and rolling, but instead she was obliged to keep me company on the portico. 'I don't know what you're whimpering about,' I told her. 'We're both waiting.'

The provost had left us, momentarily, to make a phone call in his study. His little cup of *Türk kahvesi* was still steaming on the wicker table and the last bar on the heater was just firing up. He must only have been gone a few minutes, but I could not shake the feeling that the entire morning was draining off into the sluice, and that he would not be coming back to resume our discussion at all. We had hardly begun talking before Ender had arrived in the doorway, mumbling something in Turkish; the provost had checked his pocket watch, holding it close to his good eye, and excused himself. 'Don't go anywhere,' he had said. 'This won't take a moment.'

I knew that he had returned to Portmantle in the night because his dog's unmistakable yapping had awoken me. For such a small animal, she had the shrillest bark, a yelp that rose and dropped away like an aggravated hiccup. I had gone up to the mansion just after dawn to catch the provost on his coffee break. No matter what the season, he always took his coffee outdoors, in that spot of quietude before the guests emerged for breakfast and the day moved into gear. This was the surest way to get his full attention without having to go through the rigmarole of arranging an official appointment.

The sight of the rain had almost kept me in my studio, but I had unfurled the hood from my collar and braved the worst of it. I had gone no further than a few yards before my shoes began to squelch. At the mansion, I had found the provost's wax jacket hanging in the lobby and his green umbrella touch-dry in the stand, so I knew for sure that he was home. Next thing, the old dog had scurried into view, followed by two very ponderous feet descending the staircase. I could not have mistaken those Ottoman slippers or the flimsy bamboo rod as it clacked against the banister posts. 'Is that Knell, up with the lark?' the provost had said, reaching the hallway.

'It is, sir. How was your trip?'

'None too satisfying, I'm afraid.'

He was such a tall man that when he walked under the lampshade it swayed mildly in his wake and the closeness of the light burnished his forehead. He had a bulk of grey-white hair that sat upon his crown, aslant, and two deep runnels flanked his mouth like designs worked into leather. We guessed that he was no younger than sixty, though he had the smooth-skinned hands of someone half that age. He was stone-blind in his left eye and he compensated for this with the use of the cane and the help of Nazar, a mongrel stray that he had trained into an apathetic guide dog. There was an educated air about him that often edged towards the pompous, but he was much too deferent to the residents and their talents to ever be accused of conceitedness. For the sake of formality—and because his name was held back from us—we addressed him as 'Provost' or 'sir', and every time we did, his features twitched a little.

'Step out with me,' he had said. 'Gülcan's bringing my coffee. If I'm lucky, she'll read my grounds and tell me I'm going to live a long and happy life.'

'It's raining quite hard out there.'

'I know. Isn't it perfect?'

We had taken our places on the creaking wicker furniture: he upon the cushioned swing-seat at the east wing of the portico, with his enormous legs awkwardly crossed, and I on a low chair opposite. The dog had circled several times before settling at his heels. 'So—what's on your mind?'

'Who said anything was on my mind?'

He had rubbed the pale dog-hairs from his trousers. 'You only come to see me this early when you've got a bone to pick. That's a good phrase, isn't it? *Bone to pick.*'

'Yes, sir, it is.' I had steeled myself, not wanting to waste time. 'There are a couple of things, actually, that I thought you should know about.'

'Are you listening to this, Nazar?' He had reached to pat the dog. 'Didn't I tell you we should've stayed in bed today? The complaints are coming in already.' He had leaned back, smiling. 'Go on. Let's take them one at a time.'

'First of all, there's Fullerton.'

'Yes, I heard about that.' He had steepled his fingers and pressed them to his lips. Then he had caught sight of Gülcan arriving behind me and his focus had shifted. He had spoken to her in Turkish and she had said something back, laughing as she handed him the dainty white cup and saucer, and by the time they were finished conversing the provost appeared to have forgotten the thread of our discussion. 'I don't know what else you expect me to say.'

'Well, for a start, I think you might have underestimated the amount of supervision he needs. Last night, I found him sleeping in my closet. He was completely nude.'

'This was *after* the incident at dinnertime?'

'Yes, sir.'

'I see.' He had deliberated on this information, rocking in the seat. 'Rest assured, I'll be paying a visit to the boy today. It was always my intention to introduce myself this afternoon. If he has caused you any bother in my absence, I can only offer you my apologies, Knell, and my gratitude. I hope it hasn't been too much of a distraction.'

The provost was known for the stubbornness of his diplomacy, and I had anticipated this type of response. 'It's not that he's a bother. Not in the least. I'm just concerned for him, that's all. He needs more help than I can give him. He's suffering quite badly,

I think, and I don't know if things are working out very well for him here.'

'The boy can judge that for himself.'

'We talked a bit last night, about dreams he was having. Did you know about those?'

'Really, Knell, you mustn't feel it's your job to counsel him. I'm back now, and I'll see to it that he's adequately looked after.'

'But did you know about the dreams?'

'Of course.'

'You should have told us. I mean, if we'd known, we could've made things easier for him.'

'There is nothing you or anyone could have done. I'll be straight with you: I wasn't told how much the dreams affected him, but I am fully in the picture now. I have spoken again, rather seriously, with his sponsor this morning, and I can assure you that we have everything under control. I must say, I'm surprised that you'd expect me to discuss the boy's private information. He may be young, but he's entitled to exactly the same courtesies as everyone else under this roof. Would you like it if I talked to Gluck about your difficulties, or Crozier?'

'Who's Crozier?'

'Our Italian guest.'

'Oh. Him. No, of course not.' In all my time at the refuge, I had never found the provost's even-handedness so deeply aggravating. 'Still, sir, you have to admit that his behaviour is a concern.'

He had glowered at me then. 'I thought if anything would be a *concern*, it would be MacKinney's situation.'

'She's next on my list.'

'I see.' He had bent to ruffle the dog's ears and nuzzle her head. 'Stay in bed, I said. Have a lie-in, I said. But you wouldn't listen, would you, scamp? Now look at the trouble you've got us into.' When he looked up again, his smile had vanished. 'Knell, don't worry. There is nothing the matter with the boy. His dreams are part of his creative process—that's all you need to know. Frankly, I'm only entertaining this conversation because you have his best interests at heart, but you must allow me to handle it beyond this point.' The water had kept on clubbing the roof above our heads, battering the mansion walls. 'Goodness. This rain.' The provost had turned to admire it. 'Doesn't sound like this on the mainland, you know. It has a different kind of music altogether. Makes the heart beat stronger, coming home to rain like this.'

We had sat together quietly, listening to the noise—all those tiny impacts accreting—until Ender had appeared in the doorway to inform the provost about the phone call. '*Telefon*' was the only word that I had been able to interpret from their exchange. The provost had sighed, placed his cup on the table, and stood up. He had told Nazar to stay and guard me. 'Watch out for this one, she bites,' he had said.

Now, the breakfast bell was clanging in the mess hall and even the old dog was getting restless, eyeing the doorway every time she heard a footstep.

And still the provost kept us waiting.

He presided over the refuge the way an auditor haunts an office building, removed from us yet always in our midst. We knew very little about him, in fact, and relied solely on what we had gleaned from our sponsors' explications. They said he was the son of a Turkish envoy, though Quickman claimed he had been told 'ambassador to France', and MacKinney insisted it was 'political attaché'. They said that he had held a number of accountancy positions within firms across Europe (this much was consistent with all our sponsors' stories) and that the role as provost had been bestowed upon him after the death of his wife to a lengthy illness (accounts diverged as to which disease she had suffered from: sickle-cell anaemia or leukaemia). They said that he was schooled in Switzerland, England, and America, and that his grasp of many languages would be clear to us when we arrived (it was). They said he dabbled in essay writing: some papers on English and Turkish literature had been published in journals (this was reasonable, given his tendency towards the poetic). They said he composed accounting textbooks and received significant royalties from them periodically (we had seen no evidence of these texts, but there was no reason to doubt they existed, and he did seem particularly pleased each time Ender retrieved the mail from the post office box in town).

According to our sponsors, the provostship was determined by a board of trustees. The board comprised one retired provost and five former residents, and there was a strict recruitment process, tailored to find a certain type of candidate: childless, unmarried, comfortable with isolation, passionate about the arts, respectful of artists but not creative in his own right. The provost's role demanded resoluteness, fairness, and stoicism. It was his job to maintain regular contact with the trustee board and to uphold responsibility for admissions, departures, budgeting, bookkeeping, as well as the daily oversight of Portmantle's operations and its limited staff. In return for all this, he was afforded the most resplendent view of Heybeliada from his penthouse window, three good meals a day, the company of so-called brilliant minds, and a permanent escape from the demands of mainland living. We were not told how many provosts had gone before him, but Pettifer judged the mansion to be late nineteenth century, and so, by extrapolation, we assumed no more than ten.

And still he kept me waiting.

Pale smoke was spuming now from all the studio flues, clotting the rain. A couple of residents began to appear at their doorways in pyjamas. Another came strolling up the path towards the mansion in a bright yellow poncho. I believed he was a Frenchman, though he may have been a French-speaking Belgian or a Swiss, and his name was either Anderson or Sanderson or neither. He was handsome but incredibly short. (One afternoon last spring, he had forced us all to watch a preview of 'a little work in progress', which had involved him sitting on the lawn, topless, tying blades of grass to his stomach hair to form a kind of umbilical cord, which he then wrapped around his throat. Immediately afterwards, he had distributed pamphlets with three pages of typewritten text explaining the meaning behind the performance and its title: *L'enfance des autres*. Quickman had skimmed through it and remarked, 'I think this is one of those works that is better viewed posthumously.')

As the poncho neared the front steps, Nazar began to spasm; she reared her head and bayed. The poncho halted. The rain slapped its big yellow hood. Nazar got on all fours, yapping, yapping, yapping, and the poncho waved its arms and called to me: 'Hey, why don't you do something about this dog, uh? Crazy animal!' I was about to get up, but then the provost strode into

the portico, clattering his cane on the floorboards, and he took
the dog by her collar, hauling her back. 'Calm down, Nazar,
you'll give yourself a stroke, carrying on like that.' She quietened.
'There's a good girl. Save your energy.'

The poncho hurried up the steps and into the house, thanking
the provost on his way past: *'Merci, Monsieur. Je ne sais pas pour-
quoi votre chien me déteste autant. Mais je suis content que vous
soyez de retour.'*

'Le jaune la rend de mauvaise humeur,' said the provost. He resumed his position on the swing-seat. 'Sorry to keep you. It never
fails to astound me how much work piles up at this place in my
absence. So many things to attend to.' Dredging his coffee in one
gulp, he turned the cup over on the saucer and watched the dark
grounds oozing out. 'You were asking about MacKinney?'

'No, sir, I was still talking about the boy.'

'Then I recommend you move on swiftly.' He prodded the upturned cup with his finger. 'Don't test me on this.'

I paused, heeding his tone. 'Did you manage to resolve anything with Mac's situation?'

'No, things are rather bleak on that front, I'm sad to report.
I can't discuss specifics—don't ask me to get into details, because
I'm already well outside my remit—but I've had several meetings
regarding MacKinney in the past few days. The upshot is that
she will be leaving us.'

I had been prepared for this outcome, of course, but I had not
expected the numbness I would feel when I heard it confirmed.
'When?'

'First thing tomorrow.'

'You know she isn't anywhere near finished. If you make her

leave now, her whole stay has been for nothing. You *do* see that, don't you?'

'Yes, I understand. And it's regrettable.' He lifted the cup, leaving a knoll of coffee grounds on the saucer. For a good few moments, he studied the streaky remnants on the inside rim. 'I argued her case strongly with the trustee board. A bit too strongly—they weren't pleased with me at all. The trouble is, there have been precedents. Not in my time as provost—I had to look them up in the archives—but they're precedents nonetheless, and everyone must be treated the same. I don't like to enforce protocol, as MacKinney well knows, but I have no option in her case.' He thrust the cup in my direction. 'What does that look like to you, some kind of battleship?' His finger was pointed at a few dark rivulets on the porcelain, but I could see no shapes, no auguries in them at all, just the trickledown mess of spilled coffee. 'Don't worry. I'll ask Gülcan.'

'There's really nothing you can do?' I said.

'I've done everything in my power as provost. It's a great shame to force her out, but my duty is to Portmantle. This place will still be here—God willing—long after MacKinney or the two of us are in the ground. That's what I have to consider.'

'But it won't be the same,' I said.

'She'll be missed, of course. But you'll get used to it.'

'No, sir, I mean this whole place is going to change. For everyone.'

'I don't follow.'

'You're putting a cap on how long we can be here. If our sponsors die, that's it, time's up. Doesn't matter if we're finished or not, doesn't matter if we're still struggling. It's going to change the way we work. You might as well start putting clocks up on the walls.'

He looked at me, his good eye half on the rain. 'I said I wouldn't discuss specifics.' He rose quickly, carrying his cup. 'Come on, Naz.' The dog stayed where she was.

'Word gets around this place, you know.'

'MacKinney's case is an anomaly. That's all I can tell you.' He slapped the side of his shoe with his cane. 'Nazar, come on now. Breakfast.' The dog followed. 'Please make an appointment next time,' he told me.

- - - - - -

Customarily, a notice was pinned to the bulletin board outside the mess hall to announce a resident's departure. The provost would often include a quote to inflect the notice with a degree of sentiment (something like, 'His high endeavours are an inward light that makes the path before him always bright') but some guests left without any such kindnesses.

DEPARTURE OF TENGALLON

ON THURSDAY WE MUST SAY FAREWELL TO THE POET, TENGALLON, WHO HAS COMPLETED HIS PROJECT AND RETURNS TO THE MAINLAND WITH OUR BEST WISHES. A POETRY READING IN THE LOUNGE WILL FOLLOW THIS EVENING'S DINNER. CONGRATULATIONS, TENGALLON!

—PROVOST

The four of us paid no attention to arrivals, but departures were a different matter. It could be depressing to watch guests leaving while our own work remained unfinished. So we took a particular interest in the provost's notices when they sprang up, because they kept us attuned to the prospect (however distant) of our own departures. We imagined how our announcements might be worded when the time finally came:

[. . .] SHE LEAVES HAVING DEDICATED HER LONG TENURE TO PERFECTING A WORK OF RESONANCE AND PROFUNDITY. THAT SHE OVERCAME A DEVASTATING CRISIS OF FAITH TO ACHIEVE THIS IS A TESTAMENT TO HER RESOLVE AND INDUSTRY. IF, AS RUSKIN SAID, 'ALL GREAT AND BEAUTIFUL WORK HAS COME OF FIRST GAZING WITHOUT SHRINKING INTO THE DARKNESS,' THEN SHE HAS GAZED LONG ENOUGH AND NEED GAZE NO MORE. A FIREWORKS DISPLAY WILL FOLLOW THIS EVENING'S DINNER.

—PROVOST

We held these dreamed-up notices in our minds, tinkered with the phrasing daily, sharing them in moments of self-doubt. Like our *jetons*, they were gestures to the future. They kept us striving, grafting, exploring, when no end was in sight. We worked hard every day to ensure that the truth would reflect our fantasies by the time we came to leave. So finding MacKinney's actual notice on the bulletin board that morning felt like sabotage.

DEPARTURE OF MACKINNEY

IT IS WITH GREAT JOY THAT I ANNOUNCE THE DEPARTURE OF A TRUE FRIEND OF PORTMANTLE: THE PLAYWRIGHT MACKINNEY. SHE LEAVES US FOR THE MAINLAND TOMORROW, HAVING BROUGHT TO TERM HER NEW STAGE PLAY: 'ALL THINGS AT ONCE'. MACKINNEY HAS OPTED TO FORGO HER READING IN THE LOUNGE THIS EVENING, BUT I LOOK FORWARD TO SEEING YOU ALL AT DINNER TO WISH HER BON VOYAGE. 'SINCE FATE INSISTS ON SECRECY, I HAVE NO ARGUMENTS TO BRING—I QUARREL NOT WITH DESTINY . . .' CONGRATULATIONS, MACKINNEY!

—PROVOST

A few of the short-termers were huddled around it, in discussion. I nudged them aside to get a closer look. I read it four times, stunned by the phrasing of it at first, then nauseated by it. I thought of the provost in his study, winding the paper into his typewriter, arching his fingers to punch out every last untruthful letter. There was no mention of Mac's sponsor, no hint of anything irregular.

'Is it Matthew Arnold?' said Gluck, behind me.

'What?'

'The quote. I think it's Matthew Arnold.'

'Great. That makes everything so much better. Excuse me—'
I pushed past him.

'It's going to be strange for you,' he said as I went by. 'You're
the only woman left. There's Gülcan, I suppose, but she doesn't
really count. And Nazar.' He tried to grab my arm, or I thought
he did—I swung round to glare at him, but he was only reaching
inside his sleeve for a handkerchief. 'What's the matter?' he said,
wiping his nose.

'Gülcan's been here longer than most of us. Watch your tone.'

'Yes, of course. I didn't mean any disrespect.'

'Then you should try speaking less.'

He blenched, mopping his brow.

Everything was normal about the mess hall except for the fact
that MacKinney was not there. Our table by the window was
empty. The foil was still wrapped around the milk jug spout. The
cutlery lay unmoved. Ender was preparing the juices near the
serving pass. I asked if he had seen her but he stroked his moustache and shook his head. 'I don't think she has come yet. See,
nobody touches the muesli.'

I went back out to the landing. Gluck was still there, studying
the provost's note. He did not apologise for his earlier remark.
'I've been thinking more about this quote. Not Matthew Arnold.
I think it's part of an old villanelle, but I can't recall the author.
I'll look it up for you.'

'Don't bother,' I said.

'It's no trouble.'

'If you really want to help me, tear it down.' I could not stand the thought of Quickman and Pettifer discovering the news on a bulletin board—no warning, no context. The shock of it would play hell with Tif's old heart. And the more I was forced to stare at it, the more it had the look of some crass letter of eviction.

'I can't,' said Gluck. 'That wouldn't be right.'

'Then get out of the way.'

I ripped the message from the board and hurried off along the corridor.

'But how will I check the quote!' Gluck called after me. 'I haven't written it down!'

Mac's door was either stuck or locked when I got to her room. At first, she did not respond to my knocking, but soon her voice came through, muffled by the oak: 'Who is it?'

'It's Knell. Open up.'

'I'm sleeping. Come back tomorrow.'

'You'll be gone by then. Let me in.' I slid the provost's notice under the door and waited.

Footsteps approached. I heard the locks turn and the door hinged back. MacKinney peered out at me. Without her glasses, her face seemed flatter, older, and there was an abraded quality to the skin about her eyes and cheeks, a dull red tension. There was a cigarette fuming in her mouth, and the ashy scent of it was wondrous. It belonged to faraway places: the front steps of buildings in Paddington, the grandstand at Kempton, the snug at The State Bar, my parents' bedroom—everywhere I had known in my life beyond Portmantle. She blew the smoke brazenly through the doorway. 'I know what you're thinking,' she said. 'Did I save any for Quickman, right? Well, let's just see how well he behaves today.' She moved her hair to show a couple more tucked behind her ears on each side. 'He's going to wet himself.'

'How long've you been sitting on those?'

'Ages,' she said, dragging, exhaling. 'I was waiting for a special occasion, but there's not much point in that now, is there? They're a bit stale.' She bent to pick up the notice, scanned it for an instant, then stepped aside, holding the door open. 'I wish he hadn't mentioned the title of the play. I'm still undecided. What do you think of it? *All Things at Once.*'

'It's fine.'

'No, really—be honest.' She locked us in.

'I said it was fine.'

Her room was shadowed and airless. The curtains were shut, the bed unmade. Her wardrobe was gutted and her suitcase packed. On the bureau, her typewriter was stowed in its brown leather box with the label: PROPERTY OF PORTMANTLE. 'Oh, I get it,' she said. 'You're mad at me for not being mad.' She perched tiredly on the foot of the bed. 'Well, I thought it was quite sweet, what he wrote about me.'

'Even if it isn't true.'

'There are some true bits. And what did you expect? A ten-page explanation?' She drew on her cigarette, rubbing her finger-tips. 'At least he's sending me off with some poetry. *I quarrel not with destiny.* Rather poignant, I'd say.'

I could not understand her cheerfulness. 'We can fight this, you know. The four of us.'

'Oh, sure. A few cartons of *ayran* to the face ought to do it. You go for Ender, I'll take out the provost. Q and Tif can dig our foxholes.'

'I'm serious.'

She laughed and wagged her hand dismissively. As she got up, a line of ash fell onto the front of her gown and she just smudged it into the fabric. 'It's funny to think I'm not going to be Mac-Kinney any longer. I've been sorting out her last will and testament. Would you like your inheritance now, or do you want to wait until I'm out of here?'

'I'm not letting you talk that way. You might've given up on this place but I don't have to be happy about it.'

She ignored me. At the bureau, she dumped her cigarette in a cup and reorganised a stack of books, choosing one from near the bottom. 'No, I think I'd better give it to you now . . . Chances are, you've read it, but you definitely won't have this edition—it's as rare as they come.'

It was a clothbound copy of *Captains Courageous* by Rudyard Kipling. The fading blue cover was wrapped in polythene. 'Sadly for you, I inscribed it,' she said. 'That might knock a few quid off the value when you come to sell it.' On the inside cover, she had written:

> *To Knell, who was someone else before I knew her, and will be when I'm gone. Your great friend, MacKinney xx*

I felt the urge to cry. It rose through my whole body, starting at my toes. 'I can't accept this,' I said.

'Just say thank you. That's all you have to do. And think of me when you look at it.'

'There has to be a way out of this mess.'

She came towards me, shaking her head. 'I'm afraid our time is up, old girl. It's really happening.'

'We just need to lean on the provost, that's all, put the pressure on.'

'Accept it, Knell. I've been expelled.' She tried to make me smile with this, but I could not. The provost's note was in her hand, and she pushed it into mine, closing my fist over it. 'Look, do you know how many plays I've written in my life? Thirty-six. Know how many of those were actually any good? One. *One!* If I had a market stall, I'd be in penury by now. But it's amazing how far one decent effort can carry you, if you let it—it's taken me further than I had any right to go. I'm tired of retracing my own footsteps for a hint of who I used to be. It's undignified.'

She released my hand and went back to the bed, neatening the covers. 'Fact is, I just can't stick around here any more, pretending that number thirty-seven is going to magically surpass what I've achieved before, because, deep down, I know it won't. How could it? I've already written the best play I'll ever write. I was twenty-three years old and utterly miserable when I wrote it, but that was easily my brightest moment. You never saw it, did you? I wish you had—that production was the most exciting thing I've ever been involved in.' She stopped for a moment, tightening the cord on her gown. 'It wasn't even about anything, not really. Just a family going about their days. A few flawed people in a household, making mistakes with each other. No grand ideas, just ordinary life. My childhood, I suppose. It was quite a special thing. But that's the problem, isn't it? Once your best story's told, it can't be told again. It makes you, then it ruins you.'

The bedclothes were now smooth as a tabletop. She started on the pillows, plumping them, one at a time. 'Well, at least now I can stop trying to be original. And I can see my girls again. That'll be nice. I've neglected them horribly.'

'You weren't meant to be a housewife, Mac,' I said.

'Maybe not. But if I had thirty-six children instead, I'd be a whole lot happier.' She dropped her gown and hooked it on the bedpost. The skin about her clavicle was freckled and pinched, but her body was so slender under her nightdress, and she stood there with the easy poise of a much younger woman, confident of her beauty, or at least oblivious to it. 'Go and put that thing back on the board, would you? If you're worried about Q and Tif, don't be. It's better they think I'm going off with a finished play—for their own sake.' She went into her bathroom and I heard the taps running.

'Then why aren't you giving a reading?'

'I don't want to humiliate myself,' she called.

'You could just do a few scenes. I could play Willa. Q could be Christopher.' The idea made me uncomfortable, but I would have done anything for MacKinney at that time. And I thought it would give the four of us a chance to spend her final day rehearsing together, instead of being stuck alone in our lodgings, contending with our projects. 'You deserve a proper send-off like the others. I'm not letting you leave without one.'

She came to the threshold, a towel around her middle. 'I'd prefer to just go quietly into the night, if it's all the same to you.'

'Definitely not.'

The shower continued to run. Rafts of steam began to flood the space behind her. 'Q would never do it, anyway,' she said.

'Of course he would. You've got cigarettes, remember. We could even give Tif a role.'

'But I've already told the provost no.'

I looked at the rumpled notice in my hand. 'I'll amend it. Or write an appendix. See, you're thinking about it. That means you want to.'

'I suppose it wouldn't be too awful.' She went off again into the bathroom. 'There are one or two scenes we could make something out of, with a bit of rehearsing.' Craning her head around the door, she said, 'Tif's got the wrong kind of voice for it, though. He'll only ham it up, and I don't want to look stupid.' She closed the door. I heard the shower curtain skittering on its rail.

'What about Fullerton?' I shouted, but she did not receive me. 'Mac?'

Once the notion was in my mind, I could not get rid of it. I put the Kipling on the bed and went to the bureau to unpack the typewriter. But I could find no blank paper in the drawers. The room was so dingy, in fact, that the innards of the desk seemed cavernous.

When I turned on the lamp, the bulb popped, startled me. I went to open the curtains. They were the same heavy velvet drapes that adorned the windows all over the mansion, hung on brass loops that were difficult to shift—there was a knack to it, a sideways whipping action. As they parted, the teeming of the rain became louder, more encompassing. And perhaps it was something about this noise and the splatter of Mac's shower, along with the sudden adjustment to the light, that made me lose my senses for an instant; but as I looked out through the misted panes, I saw an enormous stretch of open water where the grounds of Portmantle should have been, a swaying sea that reached up to the sides of the mansion, as though the house itself were an island and MacKinney's windows were the coastline.

It was only there for a blink and then it was gone. Everything returned at once: the lawns, the trees, the lodgings, the surrounding sights of Heybeliada. I rubbed my temples, scrutinised the pattern on the wallpaper. Black spots waned in my vision. I had not eaten breakfast yet and felt a little faint. It was tiredness, a touch of vertigo—nothing more.

There was just enough daylight to help me find what I needed in Mac's bureau. A box of goldenrod paper was buried in the bottom drawer, beneath a heap of manila folders. I spooled one sheet into the typewriter. It was not difficult to replicate the provost's formal tone, though my typing was very unpractised. I was so slow that the page was still scrolled in the machine when Mac came out of the bathroom, towelling her hair. 'What are you writing?' she said.

'An advertisement.' I hit the last full stop and lifted out the paper, handing it to her. 'Leave it to me. We'll start rehearsals after lunch.'

<u>ADDENDUM TO PREVIOUS</u>

I AM PLEASED TO CONFIRM THAT, SUBSEQUENT TO FURTHER DISCUSSION

WITH MACKINNEY, A STAGED READING
FROM HER NEW PLAY WILL NOW FOLLOW
THIS EVENING'S DINNER. PLEASE
ASSEMBLE QUIETLY IN THE LOUNGE.
FRESH SALEP WILL BE SERVED.

—PROVOST

Seven

Quickman had a very particular way of eating a pomegranate. He would slice an opening into its base with a sharp knife, score its rind into eight simple sections, then wrestle the whole fruit over a bowl, working out every wine-dark seed with his fingers, until all that remained was a limp carcass. The complete procedure took less time than it took the rest of us to peel an orange. And when pomegranate season came round each summer, I would sit and watch him honing this technique every morning, aware that I was gleaning something of the workings of his brain. It occurred to me that he approached conversations the same way: nimbly separating all the vital pips and casting aside the worthless dregs while you were speaking.

He took in the news of MacKinney's departure with an attitude of calm, leaning on his fists as he read the provost's notice. The mess hall was nearly full, the rain's attack upon the windows like the crackle of a phonograph. He did not question the facts of the message, just thanked me for showing it to him. Then he said, 'She kept that pretty quiet. I had no idea she was so close to

finishing.' I told him that I had known about it for a few days;
I was not sure that he believed me. 'The provost's quote is a bit
puzzling, though,' he said. 'Not his usual syrupy fare, is it?' He
gave the note back to me. 'Still, it accounts for her gruffness
lately. All that buddying up to the Spaniard. Hah. The whole
thing's starting to make sense.' He grazed his fingernails across
his cheeks. 'Well, no point feeling sorry for ourselves, I suppose.
I'm proud of her. She's bloody well earned it.'

'This place without Mac, though,' I said. 'Doesn't seem right.'

'Best to focus on the positives.'

'I'm trying. It's not easy.'

'Does Tif know yet?'

'He's still in his studio.'

'We ought to wake him up. He won't want to hear this from
someone else. Let me finish eating and we'll go.'

I decided I should have something in my stomach, too, given
my odd vision in Mac's room. I sat and drank two glasses of
whole milk while Q ate the last of his eggs. When I explained my
plan to stage a reading, he was surprisingly enthusiastic; I did not
even have to tell him about the cigarettes. 'Count me in,' he said,
'provided I can stay in my chair for the duration. Proper acting is
beyond me, but I think I can handle reading aloud.'

'I thought I'd have to bully you into it.'

'You know I'd give Mac a kidney if I had to. And besides, I'm
dying to see what she's been working on. Are we going to give Tif
a part?'

'I think she had someone quieter in mind.'

'Shame. He'll be keen.'

'That's sort of the problem.'

'Oh, let him try at least. Exuberance is no bad thing. It's Mac's farewell—he'll want to be involved.'

'I suppose.'

'Come on then. Drink up.'

We borrowed the provost's umbrella. Quickman and I were of similar height, and although the lime-green canopy covered us evenly, the puddles on the path were almost ankle-deep and our trousers were soon drenched.

Pettifer's lodging stood some fifty or sixty yards from mine, behind the southernmost face of the mansion, in a clutch of slightly larger studio huts the provost reserved for architects and print-makers. Only two of these studios were presently occupied (Crozier had the other), and Pettifer's was on the downward slope towards the boundary fence, which made for a slippery descent. The jutting roots of lindens nearly tripped us twice. The waist-high scrub nicked our hands as we brushed through it. By the time we reached Pettifer's walkway, we were in the foulest mood.

Quickman thudded his fist on the door and it swung back. He called, 'Tif, you big lump, we're coming in! We're soaked!' and went right inside, collapsing the umbrella and tossing it to the floor. He marched through the studio with the self-assurance of a man in his own household, going straight up to the dresser to fetch me a towel. I took off my shoes, wrung out my socks, rolled up the hems of my trousers. He did the same, then went to put more coke in the stove—it appeared to have been quite recently ignited. There was a very welcome warmth about the studio, in fact: lamps were glowing in every corner, the walls were covered in sketches and charts, and the spread of unwashed clothes about the room was so profuse that I felt completely enveloped.

Pettifer was just a snoring shape under the blankets. He slept on his front, as though strapped to a knife-thrower's wheel, his arms stretched out, his feet hooked over the mattress. The rise and fall of his breaths was both pacific and unpleasant. Quickman went to bring him round, slapping his toes. 'Rise and shine. We've got some news for you.'

I put my shoes and socks beside the stove.

Pettifer groaned. 'This better be an emergency. Can't you see I'm working?'

His drafting table was set up under the window but there was nothing on it. I assumed that he had placed it there so he could take inspiration from the view into the woods. He always said that it was the job of an architect to absorb and reinterpret nature. 'The truest measure of a building,' he once told me, 'is how quietly it recedes into the past. And nothing is quieter than a tree, or a mountain, or a mulberry bush, or—you get the point.' The adjacent wall was loosely collaged with pencil drawings. All of them depicted a doorway of some kind. There were too many shapes and sizes to count; some were basic, some more orna-mented; there was one, drawn deftly on a slip of elephant paper, that looked like a portcullis, and another, rendered in ink, that showed two squat pillars with the structure of pine cones. I rarely called on Pettifer at his lodging because the extent of his produc-tivity always left me feeling insecure. But I could see now that most of the drawings on the wall had been there a very long time. The only project that had developed since my last visit was the model ship he had started building last winter. It was now a fully formed vessel with balsa masts and fabric sails and even a tiny crow's nest. He kept it dry-docked on the top of his plan chest on a precarious wooden stand, which led me to suspect the drawers below were not in use.

'You'd work all day if we let you,' Quickman said.

Pettifer did not open his eyes. He spoke into the pillow: 'Go away.'

'MacKinney's leaving tomorrow.'

'Piss off, Q. I need my sleep.'

'Did you hear what I said? Mac is *leaving*.'

'I heard you. Ha bloody ha.'

'Tell him, Knell.'

The coke was crackling nicely in the stove. I warmed my feet against the grate. 'He's not kidding. She's taking the ferry, first thing.'

Pettifer was quiet. After a moment, he levered himself upright, yawning. 'If I find out this is a joke, I'll skin the bloody pair of you.'

I brought over the provost's notice and he snatched at it, screwing up his face as he read. He lay on his side, still holding the message. 'Well, isn't this just a perfect way to start the day.'

'Be happy for her,' Quickman said. 'It's a huge achievement.'

'I'm elated.'

'Clearly.'

'I'm so elated I'm distraught.'

I went and sat on the bed. 'Chin up, Tif, you're not the only one who's going to miss her. We're putting on a reading tonight. I was hoping you'd help out.'

Pettifer dropped the note and rolled onto his front. 'That's a terrible idea.'

'Why?'

'Have you ever seen me act? Mac would look foolish, and I would look foolish, and everything would turn out badly for all concerned.' He turned his head away. 'You two do what you like. Just keep me out of it.'

'It isn't acting, it's reading,' I said. 'Don't be a pain. We're going to need a few copies of the script typed up—at least help us with that.'

Quickman made a throat-cutting gesture, but it was too late.

'I'm a woeful typist,' said Pettifer. 'If you want the truth, I'm useless in every respect. But especially—most spectacularly—in the field of architecture, which is a bit of a handicap for an architect, I think you'll agree.' He took the pillow out from under his cheek and covered his whole head with it. 'My God. I can't believe Mac's actually finished. You realise this means she's better than us, don't you? We're never getting out of here. I'm going to be working on this stupid building till they put me in a box.'

'That's the spirit,' Quickman said. 'I knew you'd see the bright side.'

'Go away.'

'It could be worse,' I said. 'You'd have seen it up on the bulletin board if we hadn't told you.'

'Go. Away.'

Quickman retrieved his shoes, stepping into them barefooted. 'Come on, Knell. This was a mistake.' He draped his wet socks on the back of a chair and collected the umbrella. 'Let him stew in his self-pity for a while. We'll try again at lunchtime.'

Pettifer lifted his arm. 'Finally, some sense.'

It was easy to forgive his selfishness. The end of Tif's project was so far off that every departure bruised his confidence, brought on a panic that made him thorny and humourless for days. We had never had to say farewell to anyone as consequential as MacKinney before, so I could not blame him for wanting to stay in bed. If there had not been the consolation of knowing Mac's project was unfinished, I might well have behaved the same way. Looking about his studio now, I could see the remains of so much labour, so much pursuit, but no coherence. How many sketches of doorways could a man draw before he settled on the perfect form? How long could he keep on prospecting the same dry patch of land before it collapsed beneath him?

I knew that Pettifer worked harder at his craft than any of us. From his very first day at Portmantle—when Mac and I had watched him lumbering through the gate with a plan-tube strapped across his chest—he had been toiling at the same project. He had told us all about it on his second night. 'They're building a new cathedral in Manchester,' he had said. 'I'm sorting out the drawings.' What we came to understand later, over the course of so many seasons in his company, was that he had already won the commission. There had been an exhausting competition between him and four other architects and his initial concept had impressed the Archbishop most. It had been a thrilling time in his career—'the very pinnacle'. But, a week before construction was due to start, Pettifer had noticed a serious flaw in the design.

The way he explained it to us, the problem was not a structural error, more of an aesthetic lapse—he would never qualify exactly what this meant, but he often talked of 'light imbalance'. The issue did not concern the engineers, who were eager to break ground; the Archbishop had no reservations; even the partners at Pettifer's firm were confounded by the delay. But Tif believed the fault in the design to be so fundamental that he withdrew from the project altogether, taking back every last plan, elevation, and section he had submitted. He returned his fee to the Archbishop and vowed to pursue other commissions. Still, the issue with the cathedral hounded him, day after day. He told us it had felt like a test of his passion. Competition deadlines came and went. Further commissions were declined or not sought at all. He found that he was no longer interested in anything except fixing the deficiencies of his cathedral—a process that took him so deep into the fog of creation that he began to question everything he knew about architecture. He rejected his own mannered style of drawing and found a different way to express his ideas, contrary to his training. When this new style did not work, he tried another, and another, ad infinitum. He told us that he changed his personal philosophy so often that his mind became a soup. He no longer trusted his own decisions. He lost all sense of proportion, fixating on the tiniest details. His cathedral was stripped down like an engine and reassembled; it was minimised, exploded, modernised, pared back, reshaped. He started anew, and anew, and anew, and anew, until every day became an exercise in undermining the epiphanies of the day before. Soon enough, his colleagues ran out of patience and dissolved their partnership. They left him at his drafting board one afternoon, steeped in his own sweat and sour breath. He carried on without them in an empty office, a solo practice with no clients and one resigned commission to sustain him, until an old friend intervened. The friend (his eventual sponsor) saw the depth of Pettifer's troubles and decided he should be told about Portmantle. The only thing Pettifer had said in reply was, 'How soon can I get there?'

Or so his story went. I did not know if his cathedral was any nearer to perfection than it had been when he arrived, because I had never deigned to open his plan chest to see what lay inside the drawers. Part of me was afraid to. But I had no doubt that Pettifer would achieve it, given time. His doggedness, his principles, his courage in defeat—all of these things made me proud to know him, even if his attitude was sometimes hard to tolerate.

The rain was still hurtling down outside and I feared that lightning was not far off. Quickman and I huddled back under the umbrella and trudged up the slope. 'He took it rather well, I thought,' Q said. 'What now?'

'Let's ask the boy.'

'I had a feeling you'd say that.'

We carved our way through the trees, considering every step, and made it to level ground. The distant sky was misty, dull as iron, and the mansion chimneys puffed out brooks of smoke that seemed solid enough to climb on. As we came round the west side of the building, we found the provost's dog sitting upright in the middle of the path. The rain had made a ragged chamois of her fur and water streamed from her muzzle, but she sat there patiently, shivering. Her nostrils steamed. It was as though she had been waiting there especially for us. She did not bay, just eyed us as we approached. Quickman stooped to pet her. 'Not the smartest of mutts, are we?' he said, wiping the rain from her face. He told me to hold the umbrella and reached into his coat, brought out a dried fig. She was not interested. 'Suit yourself.' When he got up again, she stood right at his heels.

'She must think you're the provost,' I said.

He ate the fig himself. 'Don't know if it's much of a compliment.'

As we moved off towards Fullerton's lodging, the dog followed
closely. I could feel the thump of her tail against my calves.

'I guess we're stuck with her,' Q said.

The pine needles sagged under the deluge. All around the boy's
hut there was a drear daylight. Rain struck the sides of the oil
drum that was still out on the grass, playing a dud calypso tune.
The windows were shuttered and the flue was smokeless. 'If he
agrees to this,' Q said, 'I might just let him keep that lighter.'

'You're more sentimental than you look.'

We stepped up to the walkway and I knocked hard on the
shutters. Nazar went to the door and sniffed around the threshold. She began to scratch at the wood, shadow-boxing. 'Come
away,' Quickman said, nudging her aside with his ankle. He
rapped his knuckles on the door. The dog slipped by him, scratch-
ing again, and then she began to howl and bark.

When I bent down to quiet her, I noticed what she had already seen: water was coursing from the underside of the door. It
was not just a backwash from the rain, but a leak all of its own.
It was gushing like a wellspring over the concrete, merging with
the runnels on the path. My shoes were too sodden to feel it.
'Quickman—look,' I said.

He tried the handle but nothing budged. 'That's a bit off,' he
said.

I knocked again on the door, calling the boy's name. Quickman banged and banged. We folded back the shutters but all I
could see was our reflected faces and the lime-green halo of our
umbrella. Nazar kept on barking.

'Go and find Ardak,' Q said. He must have spotted something I had not. There was a hardness to his voice. 'Go!' He pushed the umbrella into my hand and backed away, hauling off his sheepskin. The rain devoured him. His beard hung down in clumps. The dog was scrabbling and yapping.

'What is it?' I said.

Quickman wound his coat around his arm. 'I said *get help.*' But I could not move. He cursed me under his breath, making for the window. 'Take the dog then,' he said, 'or it's going to get hurt. Hurry up!' I grabbed Nazar's collar and, although she bucked against me, barking even more, I managed to drag her off the walkway.

Quickman punched the corner of the pane and the glass fractured into webs. Before he could strike it again, the whole window shattered, falling down over his shoes. He kicked away the shards from the frame and jumped inside.

However long that moment lasted (I was crouched there on the grass for some time, with Nazar fighting to get loose and nothing to see except the roller-blind flapping in the window cavity), everything happened too slowly to comprehend. I could tell the dog was barking wildly, and yet the noise was somehow inscrutable, subdued. Every sound diminished. I thought I could taste my own blood.

Then the front door swung open. Quickman was shouting at me. I let the dog go and she bolted towards him. 'Help me lift him!' I could hear him now. 'Help me lift him!' He retreated into the gloom.

I went running after.

Inside, the studio floor seemed to sway. A shallow of clear

water rushed over it, like the stream of a hose on a patio deck. The bathroom light was on and Quickman was waiting there with the dog rounding his feet. He had turned off the taps, but the bathtub was still overflowing. Fullerton was slumped inside it, face down. A leather belt was tied around his neck, fixed to the base of the tap. Bands of duct tape ran all round his head. His hair eddied on the surface. 'Hurry up, take his feet,' Quickman said, untangling the belt. 'I can't lift him on my own.'

I held the boy's ankles and Quickman dragged him up from the armpits. We heaved him out of the water and fell back against the tiles with his body pale and slick between us. The duct tape was wound over his mouth and nose, puckering his skin. Quickman tried to free it. There was another clump of it inside the bathtub, covering the plughole.

'Help me,' Quickman said. 'Come on!'

I needed this—a direction, a firm hand—because I was unable to think forwards. My mind had seized and I could hear the blood skulking inside me. The boy's eyes were thick and swollen. I picked away the tape until I saw the whites of his teeth. Quickman started to press at the boy's sternum, blowing air into his mouth. The dog yapped right in his ear and he batted her away. I buckled against the wall. I was voiceless and afraid and crying. 'Do something!' Q said. 'Run and get someone!' He pumped at the boy's ribs and kissed him. The dog would not be quiet. I staggered to my feet, quivering and weak with fright. I was sick all down my front. I was sick again on the walkway. But once I started running, I did not stop until I reached the mansion and found Ardak in the lobby. '*Ne oldu?*' he said. I rushed into his arms and he held me close. '*Neyin var?*'

Rooms from Memory

One

Anything I did not know about Jim Culvers before I arrived in London, I learned within a month of working for him. His reputation was founded on a conventional style of portraiture: straightforward paintings of angry young Teds and Soho brothel-workers in various stages of undress, which the critic in my borrowed copy of *The Burlington Magazine* had described as 'formally impressive and profoundly unspectacular'. By 1957, when I became his assistant, Jim had already begun to withdraw from this traditional approach and was trying to perfect a credible method for removing the subjects from his portraits altogether. A typical Culvers picture, in those days, would depict an empty room (usually some dim view of his studio), rendered in thick strokes of muted colours, at the heart of which would be a vacant armchair or a single lip-smirched water glass. He invited models to pose for long durations, painting nothing until they were gone. To collectors, he claimed the new portraits showed the characteristics of the sitter in the barest terms, through revealing the shape of their absence. 'Any space,' he liked to postulate, 'is altered when a person leaves it: so I paint *that*.' Their response would be to ask him what he thought of Edward Hopper, and this would rile him so much that he would raise his asking price unreasonably.

Jim had a two-room studio on the ground floor of a mews house in St John's Wood. His gallery, the Eversholt, afforded him a monthly allowance for rent, materials, and what they called 'subsistence' (in Jim's case, this amounted to little except whisky and greyhound stakes). Out of this money, he paid me six pounds a week in wages, and I was given free lodging in his attic. It was a damp and charmless space up there, little more than a storage loft. The ceiling bellied when it rained. Pigeons flew in through the dormers in summertime. A burning-coal smell emanated from the neighbourhood chimneys. But there was a straight as-pect to the roof that I could set a canvas underneath, and, if I craned my head out of the window, I could see all the way to Regent's Park. I considered myself fortunate to have my own workspace and to be amidst the London art scene, albeit periph-erally.

In those first few months with Jim, I was no more than an errand-runner. I procured new paints for him from a backstreet dealer in Covent Garden and took his pictures to the framers' on Marylebone High Street, going back and forth on the bus with his suggested amendments, until he was content. I delivered bags of his dirty clothes to the launderette and made his lunch each day—always the same Cheddar cheese and pickle sandwich on wholemeal bread with the crusts removed and two thick circles of cucumber in each triangular half.

It did not take me long to realise that I could fit my own work around these artless tasks. While I waited for a pair of Jim's shoes to be repaired, for example, I would sit by the canal in Little Venice with a flask of tea, sketching people in the mist, making studies of the bridges and the skittering London traffic. I would save all the brown bags that Jim's whisky bottles came in, storing them inside my purse to use as drawing paper. I pinned my hair up with pencils, cross-boned, like an Oriental lady, so I would always have them to hand.

I discovered I could achieve more in a few stolen moments than Jim Culvers could muster in a fortnight. He would arrive at the studio at eight o'clock every morning, looking pink-eyed and dejected, and I doubt he ever gave much thought to my whereabouts in the hours before he got there, in the same way a restaurant patron is oblivious to the manoeuvres of the kitchen staff. He never saw me wandering about Regent's Park just after dawn, when the grass was still etched with frost and the lake had no corrugations, drawing the birdlife and the skyline and the strange pollarded trees: details I would reconstitute in paintings, late at night. There was something about the gathering light of Paddington in the small hours that made its bombed-out spaces seem so vital and romantic, as though each ruin was an untold story. Some mornings, I set up on a wall in Brindley Street, sketching things that were not there, ghosts that lived inside the cavities. Other times, I wandered along the canal and drew the vagrants sleeping on the roofs of empty barges. As long as I made it back to the studio by eight o'clock to greet Jim with fresh currant buns, those precious hours were mine to enjoy.

Before long, I was involved more closely in Jim's practice. He had failed to convince Max Eversholt, his only benefactor, that the empty-room paintings ('absence portraits', as he called them) were worthy of a solo exhibition, and so had backtracked into more familiar territory. I would find subjects for him by taking photographs of people on the street: skiffle groups rehearsing outside coffee bars, bus conductors walking home, rayon-clad girls in cinema queues, boys playing dice on the kerb. If Jim liked the look of someone in these pictures—a particular smile, a dour pout, whichever small quirk captured his imagination—he would pay me a few shillings for the photograph and spend the day copying it in oils. On top of this, I organised his charcoal studies into sketchbooks and dated each drawing so he could track the development of his ideas—he liked to tell me I was keeping a record of his downfall, and I liked to tell him to stop being so bloody miserable.

My time as his assistant lasted nine months. If anyone had deigned to suggest that I was falling in love with James Graham Culvers during that period, I would have protested. Back then, Jim was quite determined to conceal what handsomeness he had with lax grooming and booze. He could go for days without bathing and refused to wash his hair when he was working on a painting. There were times when his sour body odour infused the studio to such a degree that it overwhelmed even the turpentine. After a new work was finished, he would give his hair a close trim with the clippers and saunter in with shaving foam still caught in his ear-folds.

Idle chatter, as a rule, was wasted on Jim. If models began conversations about their holidays, he would purse his lips and nod, letting them trail off into monologue. But he would consider his reflection in the windows as I prepared his easel in the mornings. His eyes were too fat, so he said ('like a sheep's'); his front teeth too far apart, his chin too big, his nose protuberant ('like a bloody outboard motor'). It was true that the constituents of his face were quite unusual, but there was still a pleasant balance to them in assembly. After a while, I came to understand that his complaints spoke more of connoisseurship than of vanity. He was intrigued by imperfections, could wonder for hours at the tessellated cracks in a china plate, at brush-hairs preserved in the gloss of a doorframe, at silly misprints in the newspaper. He believed that if something was flawless, it was artificial and suspicious. 'All these people you've been taking pictures of are much too pretty,' he would say. 'Next time, bring me something else. I want ratty hair and scars and bad tattoos. This lot look like they've dropped out of a magazine. Even the bus conductor's got long eyelashes. I'll have to paint him ten times uglier.'

I came to learn things about Jim that only a wife should have been privy to. I knew the rumbles of his gut, the corns on his feet, the tunes he whistled in the lavatory and the sections of the paper he was partial to. I found out that he had allergies—to peanuts, rhubarb, peaches, crab—and could tell when he had partaken of these foods, even if he swore to me that he had not (the husky throat and rheumy eyes gave him away). He had a joke about Whistler's mother that I must have heard a hundred times, and there was an anecdote he told about his childhood that always included the same phrase: 'My old man, you see, was Anglican, and he wanted me to go into the ministry . . .'

He was not the sort of man for whom you felt an immediate attraction. The first sight of him did not steal your breath or weaken your knees—and, quite frankly, women of my generation knew better than to expect such things. Instead, over time, he quietly detuned the strings of your heart, until his peculiar key became so familiar that you believed it was the only one. And if my life as a painter had begun in the backcourt of my parents' tenement, then I owed the rest of my career to Jim Culvers. Being his assistant gave me the chance to develop my own work in privacy, and, without him, those paintings might never have been seen at all. I did not recognise the depth of my affection for him until I no longer had a duty to include myself in his routines.

It was on one of those routine days in January—cold and grey and mizzling—that I heard the bell of the studio ring and went out to let Jim in. I expected he had forgotten his keys again, but when I opened the door I found him standing with three burlap sacks about his ankles. 'Help us with this stuff,' he said, and carried two of the sacks in with him, leaving me to manage the fullest. It was crammed with several tins of what I thought was ordinary house paint. The worn white labels said:

RIPOLIN

I hauled them into the studio and Jim made me stack them in a pyramid near the window. 'If it's good enough for Pablo,' he said, 'then it'll do for me. Go on, open one up. I want to see what state it's in.'

I did as I was asked, setting a can on the floor, prising the lid off with a spoon. An ammoniac scent rushed out. The oil varnish had separated from the pigment and made an oozing brown lake on the surface. 'What *is* this stuff?' I said.

He crouched before it, sizing up the swirl of chemicals before him. 'Magic in a can,' he said. 'Everyone used it before the war—we used to joke about Picasso spreading it on toast—but then they had to shut the factory down and you couldn't find it anywhere. Doesn't look too bad, this, considering. And I got the job lot for nothing!' I was about to stir it, but Jim slapped my hand away: '*Ttt-ttt-ttt.* Hang about.' He stood up. 'We need to test it. See if it's still usable. It's been standing around in a basement for the past twenty years. The pigment will be fine, I reckon, but that binder looks a bit mustardy; we'll have to siphon it off somehow, or try mixing it in with the tubes we have here.' He went and unhooked his coat from behind the door, putting it back on.

'You're leaving?'

'Well, I carried that lot all the way from Drury Lane. It's worn me right out.' He frisked his pockets for his wallet. 'Thought I'd just nip home and sleep it off.'

I knew Jim well enough by then to know that 'sleep it off' meant 'pass out drunk'. It was not yet ten o'clock, and there was no reason to assume that he would return before dark.

'While I'm gone,' he said, 'do us a favour and try the stuff out a bit, eh? Have a play with it and see what it can do. Use as many canvases as you like, but don't waste the paint—for all I know, they're the last ten pots of it in London.'

I spent that entire day in the thrall of Ripolin, experimenting with its qualities. It was a vexing, stubborn material that had to be coaxed into obedience. I tried a number of methods with limited results, draining one of the tins, until I found the perfect balance in the mixture: two parts oil paint, two parts turpentine, one part Ripolin, thoroughly stirred. This produced dense blocks of colour in its own right, but the trick was to undercoat the canvas with a lot of white gesso. When I did this, the paint became more opaque and also more fluid. It enabled me to hide the brushstrokes and, at the same time, allowed for subtleties of gesture that gave each image a fuller character. Every colour had resonance, a kind of visual hum.

Jim showed up the next morning, headsore and bedraggled. He did not appear to remember asking me to test the Ripolin— or even that he had acquired it—because he just went about his typical routine. It was only after he finished his coffee that he noticed the pyramid of cans and saw the canvas leaned against the wall, turned inwards. 'Did you manage to get to grips with that stuff then?' he asked, as though it had been there in his studio for weeks.

'You were right,' I told him. 'It's magic.' I brought the canvas over.

Jim's eyelids unclenched. The picture I had made was built from memory: a portrait of him in a grey raincoat, striding along a hidden pavement. There was a sense of movement to his body, created by the Ripolin and my own rather hurried technique, as well as an unnerving stillness to the backdrop, a screen of buildings I had assembled from part-remembered walks around the city. Most of the canvas was taken up by this patchy architecture, and, because I had been aiming to check how the paint responded to different applications, the landscape it created was loosely connected: doomy red fire escapes here, watery grey brickwork there;

glutinous pink railings, white-leafed trees, and strange yellow windows. And yet the disparate elements of the painting some-how coalesced. All the little experiments, seen as one, made some-thing original. There was Jim, a concentrated figure wandering across the bottom of the image, with London shimmering, falter-ing, transforming in his wake. It was one of the most arresting pieces I ever made.

All Jim said was, 'Blimey,' which I took as a strong affirma-tion. He must have looked at that painting for a good forty minutes, asking me how I had achieved certain effects, wanting to know about the mix ratios I had tried with the Ripolin. He particularly liked the sense of animation it gave to the human figure—it was not clear if he recognised his own likeness in it—and I spent some time explaining and demonstrating how to handle the paint to get this result. After a while, Jim took the canvas and put it back against the wall, leaning inwards, as be-fore. I did not know if he would let me keep it, given that I had made it with *his* materials, *his* brushes, and the longer it stayed in the unlit corner of his studio, the more I resented the fact that he had left it there to gather dust. For the next fortnight or so, the canvas remained unchecked, unmoved, while Jim went about compiling his own works in Ripolin: the same old faces copied from photographs, only brighter, punchier, more effervescent.

Then, one evening, as I was reading in my attic room, I heard the rumble of a motorbike engine in the avenue below. I looked down from the dormer to see a squat man in a tight leather jacket removing his crash helmet. He shook his head as though to free some lengthy mane of curls, though all he had was a cres-cent of sad white hair that hung around his baldness like a shower curtain. Stepping out of the sidecar was Jim Culvers, who, judging by the indelicacy of his voice when he called out 'Oi, Max! I forgot the key!' was at least seven whiskies into a stupor. The bell rang—one long, urgent trill.

I put on my clothes and went down to let them in. Vernon Glasser, the American sculptor from the upstairs studio, was out on the landing in his vest. 'He's lucky I was only sleeping in there,' he said. 'Tell him, this happens again, I'll bring out the bolt-cutters. You tell him Vern Glasser said that.' He trundled away, covering his ears.

At the door, Max Eversholt was courteous enough to introduce himself. 'Very sorry about the hour,' he said, his accent prim and pleasant. 'We shan't keep you long.' He appeared embarrassed by Jim's inebriation, and kept talking to Jim as though he were a dog: 'Come on now, James. There you go. Watch your head there. Good chap.'

Jim groped around for the studio lights. 'Max has come to check up on me. Haven't you, Max?'

'I believe I was invited,' said Eversholt, zipping off his jacket. He hooked it with one finger and slung it over his shoulder.

'Pssh. Don't listen. He's a crook.' Suddenly, Jim looked panicked. 'Ellie—what did you do with those sketchbooks?'

'They're in the trunk with the blankets.'

While Jim went to rummage for them, Eversholt inspected an assortment of canvases near the doorway. He examined each painting for no more than a few seconds, tilting his head to one side, tilting it back again. 'These are certainly better,' he said. 'I can see a style emerging.'

'Emerging?' Jim said. He had the sketchbooks now and

dumped them on the floor. 'Don't come in here using words like that. *Emerging*. I'm not forcing them out of my arse.'

Eversholt rubbed a daub of wet paint from his fingers. 'Careful, James. Ladies present.'

'You can say anything in front of her,' Jim said. 'She's heard it all.'

'How many has he had?' I asked Eversholt.

'Oh, this is nothing. I've seen him a lot worse than this.' He waved Jim over. 'Come on, old chap, let's have a look at those sketches.'

Jim slurred back at him, 'Nah, I've changed my mind. They're no bloody good. I can't even draw straight.'

'Don't be a fool now. Pick them up.'

Grudgingly, Jim stooped to gather them. He took so long about it, wobbling on his haunches, that I went over to help him. 'Which one is the best?' he whispered to me, and I whispered back: '*That* one.'

Jim collapsed onto his rear, clawing at the floorboards. I gave Eversholt the sketchbook and he just nodded, skimming through it. After a moment, he said, 'You're getting there, Jim, getting there. I must say, it's nice to see you drawing again—I can tell you're really honing something here. It's attractive work. But it needs more time. I'll come back in a month or two, and then we can review things.'

'Wait, wait, wait,' Jim said. 'There's more. Loads of it. Show him, Ellie.'

I was not sure what he was referring to. His best work had already been dismissed.

'Let him see the On High pile,' he explained. 'Go on.'

I looked at him, unsure.

'Go on. Show him.'

Eversholt followed me to the furthest aspect of the studio, where Jim liked to store all the paintings he had lost the motivation to complete. He called them the On Highs, as in 'on hiatus'.

Eversholt went through them with a void expression—it was such a complete look of dispassion that he must have practised it each night in the bathroom mirror, smoothing out the tell-tale wrinkles. He was wearing the oddest plum-coloured brogues and their thick heels stayed planted as he browsed the paintings. 'I fear there's a long way to go with these, Jim,' he called, and started putting on his jacket. 'Very glad to see the work, though, as always. I shall tell everyone you've been hard at it.'

'Christ, don't start spreading that around,' Jim called back.

Then, as Eversholt was heading through into the main room to say his farewells, he stopped, sighting the back of my Ripolin canvas against the other wall. 'No, that's not for sale—I mean, that's not really anything,' I muttered, as he went to turn the picture round. Eversholt did not listen. He rolled his eyes over the image, plain-faced. It must have been that he stood there looking at it for some time, because Jim staggered in and leaned against the architrave. 'Ah,' he said. 'Thought you'd all gone quiet in here.'

Eversholt circled his hand about the picture. 'Tell me what's happening with this. What's the thinking?'

'Long story, that,' Jim said.

'Self-portraits are indulgent. Difficult to sell.'

Jim sniffed. He looked at me sorrowfully. 'That's just an experiment.'

I wanted to interject and explain, but I also wanted to give Jim the chance to speak up for me.

'Always thought that was a lot of guff, myself,' said Eversholt. 'This is giving me the shivers. Ditch everything else, is my advice. Give me another ten or twelve of these little experiments, if that's what you're calling them. Then you can have your show. I'm thinking, end of August. September at a push.'

'Ah, Max. So many imperatives. I love the way you talk.' Jim grinned, turning back for the main room. 'I'm sorry, old pal, but you seem to be mistaking art for press-ups. I can't just drop and give you twenty. I'm a painter. The inspiration comes, the inspiration goes.' He raised his arms. 'Are you hearing this, Ellie? This is what you can expect. It's all a lot of dancing for the organ-grinder from now on.'

'If you need another show of my good faith, that's fine. How much?' Eversholt reached into his jacket and pulled out a cheque-book. I watched the whole thing happening without saying a word.

'I'm not interested in your money,' Jim said. 'But you can make one of those out to someone else, if you don't mind. Last name's Conroy. First name's Elspeth. Don't ask me to spell it, 'cause I'm pissed, but I reckon fifty pounds'll be fair enough to begin with.'

Eversholt started writing the cheque. 'Who the bloody hell is Elspeth Conroy?'

'*She* is,' Jim said, pointing at me. 'Artist-in-residence.'

Eversholt slowly pivoted his neck. 'You did this?'

I hardly knew what to say. The blood rushed out of my head. My palms went very cool. 'Yes. Well, it just sort of came together really. Bit of a fluke.'

'Rubbish,' Jim said. 'She has more of them. Upstairs. Tons of them. They're loads better than anything you'll find in this dump.'

Eversholt tore off the cheque and shut the book. 'Show me.'

'More directives,' Jim said. 'You should really learn some manners.'

'You're right. Let me try that again.' Until then, Eversholt had regarded me with the passing interest he might otherwise have afforded a chambermaid or a stable boy. Now I had his full attention. 'Miss Conroy, *darling*,' he said, 'if you'd let me take a quick look at your work, I'd be delighted. In the meantime—' He came forward, offering the cheque. 'Call this a down-payment on what I've seen so far.'

Within a few months, Max had organised a show at the Eversholt Gallery, in which a small selection of my canvases was presented in a hallway before the main exhibition. The headline attraction was Bernard Cale, a welterweight boxer turned artist, who had forged a good career making ink-and-gouache drawings of the fights. He was popular with male collectors at the time, as his pictures were brutal and unflinching, and there was a certain macho prestige to be gained from hanging a Bernie Cale in your study, all those exploding lips and broken noses to discuss over brandy and cigars. I respected the earnest themes of Cale's pictures and admired the skill of their construction, so I was pleased to see my work displayed as an accompaniment to his. No one who attended the show arrived with the intention of seeing my gloomy bombsite paintings, but plenty stopped to look at them.

Jim turned up at the private viewing, mercifully sober. He stood smoking in the hallway with Bernie Cale himself, examining my favourite piece in the collection: *Stage Ghost Rehearsal, 1958*. It showed the shell of an old theatre in Kennington, upon which I had overlaid a new façade in thinned-out tones of grey; behind the pale windows, I had delicately painted the wraith of a man holding a straight-blade razor, his cheeks lathered in foam, and scratched the reflection of a young girl into his shaving mirror. 'Bernie likes this one best,' Jim said. 'He thinks it's menacing. I think it's sad. Come and settle the argument.'

Cale nodded. 'I want to know what that bloke is thinking. Can't help but worry for the little 'un, I must say.' He moved closer to the painting, blinking at it. 'They all sort of do that, in their way—I was just telling Jim: they all make you feel something— but this one puts me on edge. It's hard to do that with a picture.'

'Thank you, Bernie. That's kind of you.'

'What're you thanking me for? I didn't paint the bloody thing.'

'Don't leave us hanging,' Jim said to me, stubbing out his cigarette. 'Are we supposed to feel sad, frightened—what?'

I said, 'It depends on who's looking.'

'Hear that, Bernie? It's a draw.'

'I want a refund,' said Cale, smirking.

At the end of the evening, I found Jim waiting on the pavement outside. 'Thought someone should walk you home,' he said. 'Unless you've got a limo coming.'

I was still living rent-free in the attic room in St John's Wood, and I had given no thought to the prospect of finding my own studio. At Max's urging, I was no longer 'cheapening myself' by working as an assistant, so I did not have the modest wages to sustain me. Instead, I withdrew funds daily from Max's 'down-payment', half of which I had sent to my parents in Clydebank the moment his cheque cleared in my account. I felt, in that strange period, as though I was caught like a feather on a draught. It was clear that the course of my life depended on the outcome of the entrance hall show, but I could not tell in which direction it was going to propel me. 'I was going to take the bus,' I said.

We walked down Cork Street together. It was a windless night but the cold still pinched and I had not brought a coat. Jim saw that I was shivering and said, 'A gentleman would probably offer you his blazer.'

'He would.'

'But then you'd know he'd burned his shirt twice with the iron. What the heck—' He removed his jacket and I stopped so he could cast it round my shoulders. And, turning, he showed me the singe-marks on his back: two light brown impressions at the spine.

'You had the heat too high.'

'Well, I know that *now*.'

'I appreciate the effort. You look very smart.'

He shrugged. 'Warmer yet?'

'A bit.'

We were at Baker Street before he said a word about the show. It was expressed almost in resignation. 'That painting Bernie liked—the one with the bloke shaving—you've got something there. If I tried to paint a scene like that, I'd get the composition wrong. But you know exactly how much of the little girl's face to show in the mirror. It's got emotions in it most of us would shy away from.'

I found it hard to walk and feel such gladness all at once. 'Thank you. It really means a lot to hear that, Jim.'

'Look, I'm not saying they were *all* great. Don't start leaping in the air.' He swiped at his nose a few times with the crook of his wrist. 'If the whole show was that good, I wouldn't have stuck it out all night.' He walked me halfway across the road, his hand on the small of my back. 'Now you'd better hope nobody buys it, eh?' A car slowed down for us and blinked its headlights. 'At last, a decent citizen.' He gave a thumbs-up to the driver as we passed by the bonnet.

'What's that supposed to mean?' I said.

He was a few strides ahead of me now and had to stop. 'Don't stand about, I'm freezing,' he said.

'What did you mean by that?'

Traffic shone against his back. He blew into his fists. 'Come to the pub with me,' he said. 'I'll show you.'

'No, I've already had too much to drink.'

'I know. Two glasses is your limit. Just—wait a mo.' And hanging an arm out into the road, he was able to flag an approaching cab. It pulled over with its window down. 'Maida Vale, mate,' Jim told the driver. 'The Prince Alfred.' He opened the door for me. 'Come on then, or you won't get your answer.'

When we reached the pub, he did not go straight up to the bar to get a whisky, as I expected him to. He steered me to the far end of the room instead, and called out to the landlord on his way: 'I'll start with a double, Ron. Leave it there for me.'

'Who's this with you?' said the landlord.

'Mind your own.'

'A bit too nice for this place, ain't she? You want to take her somewhere proper.'

'Oh, she won't be here for long, don't worry.'

He took me to a quiet table in the corner: a bench-seat upholstered in tartan. 'This is where I do my best thinking,' he said. 'Grab a pew.'

I pulled out a stool and sat down. He took the bench opposite and looked at me, amused at some private thought. 'Other way,' he said.

'Huh?'

'Swivel round. You need to face the other way.'

I did as I was told.

There was a picture on the wall I realised was Jim's—a portrait, done in oils, of a soldier in a beret, the fumes of a cigarette coiling up around his face. It was a small, uncomplicated painting. The soldier's grinning features were remarkably well made. Jim had captured an attitude in the brushstrokes: helpless but defiant. 'You've got to hold on to the best ones,' he said. 'Keep something for yourself, that's all I mean. I could've sold that for a fortune once, but I chose not to. Best decision of my life.'

I stood up to get a closer view. 'Why not hang it in your flat, or at the studio?'

'I like it here where folks can see it. And, you know me, I tend to stop in for a drink occasionally.'

'What if it gets stolen?'

'Ron keeps a lookout. And someone had to elevate the decor in this place. They had some stupid cartoon of a horse up there before I got to it.' He came to stand beside me. I could smell the linseed on him. When I moved to glance up at his face, I found that he was staring only at the portrait. His eyes were glossed and bright. 'Honestly, I wish I could've sent it to the lad after I painted it, but I did it from a sketch. He died before we left Dunkirk. Wouldn't know it from that grin, though, would you? Poor sod didn't know what he was in for.' Jim coughed abruptly. 'Anyway, that's all I wanted to show you.' He nudged his shoulder into mine. 'Don't tell anyone you nearly saw me cry. I have a reputation to uphold.'

We stayed at the Prince Alfred long enough to have one drink, and then he walked me home. Coming through the frosted avenues of Little Venice, we were both trembling and tired, and I thought that he might put his arm around me then, in solidarity if nothing else. But he kept his hands inside his pockets all the way to St John's Wood. We talked only of domestic matters: which place on the high street should he take his shirts to now for laundering? Which bakery was it that made the loaf he liked? He was readying himself for life without me. As we headed down the mews, he kicked at the cobbles and said, 'I'll probably just kip on the studio floor tonight then.' I could not tell if he was being candid or suggestive, and we reached the front door before I could respond. 'Well, it's no bother,' he said. 'I'm used to it by now.' He let us inside and unlocked the studio. Turning on the lights, he loitered in the threshold, thumbing the latch. He seemed to have something else to say to me besides 'Goodnight', but that was all he offered. I was left to carry his blazer up the dingy stairs, alone.

Perhaps the deflation of this moment was what made me take

my consolations elsewhere. I felt so heartened by the sight of every title crossed out on the gallery's price list at the end of my show's run: all ten of the canvases were sold within a week. I allowed myself to absorb the compliments that Max passed on from collectors, strangers whose attentions would otherwise have meant nothing. More than this, I saw my name up in gilt letters outside the Eversholt, like the sign of a department store, and mistook it for accomplishment.

After that entrance hall show, I did not need to worry about stealing time to sketch, though I still got up at six every morning to go out with my pencils. Max arranged a studio for me in Kilburn, with an adjoining flat, and I was promised the same monthly stipend that Jim received for materials and subsistence. I felt glad of these developments, but sorry to vacate my tiny attic room, whose limitations had somehow influenced the paintings themselves, compacting each landscape, hunching every figure, cropping off so many heads and bodies, distorting all the viewpoints. Above all, I did not want to leave Jim. I had grown so reliant on our closeness, so used to the sound of his downtrodden voice, and even to the scent of him. But I could not be the kind of woman who allowed her aspirations to be stalled by sentiments like these, especially when they were yet to be requited. Jim Culvers would go on surviving, whether I was there to set up his easel every morning or not, and I expected him to stay exactly where he was forever, so I might call on him each week and he might miss me between visits.

On the day I moved out of the mews house, he stood in the doorway of his studio, watching me drag my suitcase down the stairs. He did not offer to help, just waited there, saying nothing, while I heaved the case from step to step. When I reached the bottom, he said, 'You'll have to get used to this, won't you? Lugging your gold bars around.'

I leaned on the balustrade, catching my breath. 'It's just a few library books.'

'I think you're meant to give those back.'

'Ah, but then I'd have to pay the fines.'

The suitcase burst open and a few of the hardbacks tumbled down the stairs. Finally, Jim came to assist me, collecting them. '*The Sea-Wolf. The Reef. Billy Budd* . . . Never had you pegged as a mariner.'

'Well, they happen to be classics.'

'I'll take your word for it. Here.' He gave them back, and I stuffed them in the case.

I had made an effort to read widely during my time at art school, in the hope that engaging with the right books might stimulate ideas for paintings (and if they broadened my vocabulary along the way, I thought, so much the better). Our exuberant headmistress back at Clydebank High had encouraged all the girls to read Jane Austen and the Brontës—'And, for heaven's sake, read *Middlemarch*,' she had announced one day, while teaching our domestic science class; 'if you never do another sensible thing for the rest of your lives, read *Middlemarch*!' I found these books worthwhile and interesting, but perhaps not quite as formative as I expected, like visiting important landmarks I had spent too long imagining. The painter in me was drawn to other voices: to Melville's artfulness and detail, to Conrad's gloomy landscapes, to Stevenson's thrill and adventure. These were the writers whose works I kept returning to. In fact, I reread *Moby-Dick* and

Nostromo so often in those early days with Jim that I found their language mirrored in my journal entries; sometimes, in ordinary letters to my parents, I would copy lines from *An Inland Voyage* ('To equip so short a letter with a preface is, I am half afraid, to sin against proportion!') and felt a slight displeasure when they failed to comment on it.

'How will you get all this on the bus?' Jim asked.

'I won't. Max organised a van. Should be here any minute.'

'Good old Max, eh? Where would we be without Max?'

'Don't start that again.'

He carried the case to the kerb. The sky was cement-grey and the air was sharpening for hailstones.

'We'll not be far from each other,' I said. 'I'll come and visit.'

'No, you'll have work to do.'

'I'll still have my evenings and weekends.'

'Ha, right,' Jim said. He glanced back to the house. 'Is there more to come down?'

'Just a box or two.'

'I'm sure you can manage those on your own.' He would not look at me. 'Let's just shake hands and say cheerio, shall we? No point turning this into a ceremony.' The skin of his palm was as dry as a dog's paw, his fingers ridged and calloused.

'What about this Saturday? I'll bring you some bagels from the good Jewish bakery. We can have a cup of tea and— '

'What? Catch up? Talk about the Arsenal?'

'I was going to say we could look through the racing pages. I don't mind putting your bets on, still. At the weekend, anyway.'

Jim nodded. His whole face tightened. 'I think you're forget-ting how Max does things. He'll have an agenda worked out for

you—mark my words. He'll be getting you in with the Roxborough crowd straight away, and God knows who else. You're going
to be divvied up: a stake in you here, a stake in you there. It's
going to mean deadlines, long hours in the studio. Real work.
Why d'you think I needed an assistant in the first place? It wasn't
to keep my attic warm.' He squinted at the sky. 'No, you're not
going to be sitting here, eating bagels, reading me the form guide,
that's for sure. And, quite frankly, if that's how you choose to
spend your time from now on, I'll bloody murder you.' He sniffed.
A white van was approaching now from the high street. 'I'd do it
quickly, mind—quick snap of the neck—you wouldn't even feel
it. That's how much I respect you.' Patting my arm, he said, 'All
right then, Miss Conroy. Work hard, keep your nose clean. Forget anything I might've accidentally taught you and you'll be
right as rain. Come and say hello to me at your next soirée and
make me look important. Off you go.' He trudged back to his
studio, peering at the ground. And that was the last conversation
I would have with Jim Culvers for a very long time.

Two

- - - - - -

Though all artists strive for recognition, they cannot foresee how it will come to them or how much they will compromise to maintain success. All they can do is cling to the reins and try to weather the changes of their circumstance without altering their course. But no woman can improve her station in life without sacrificing a little of her identity. I was an ordinary girl from Clydebank who had somehow established herself as a prospect on the London art scene: was I really expected to remain unchanged by these experiences? Even my father, who had returned from the frontlines of war apparently untouched by its horrors, was not averse to smoothing out his accent when speaking to the council on the telephone. So how was I supposed to sign away my life to Roxborough Fine Art and still be that same girl who once painted in her parents' yard? I tried so hard to preserve the Clydebank in me that I soon realised I was forcing it. Perhaps if there had been some grounding presence in my life at that time— a good man like Jim Culvers who could have given me a shake when I needed it—I might have been able to retain a semblance of my old self. But on the preview night for my first solo exhibition at the Roxborough in 1960, I did not have a genuine friend in the room.

Instead, I was surrounded by interested parties and loathsome hangers-on. People like Max Eversholt, who paraded around the gallery as though he had painted every canvas himself, tour-guiding young women in cocktail dresses from landscape to landscape with a delicate grip on their elbows. He brought other artists over to speak with me, one fashionable face at a time, and presumed we were already acquainted ('You know Frank, of course . . . You know Michael . . . You know Timothy . . .') because surely all the painters in London were the best of friends? I stood, awkwardly pattering with them, as I might have talked to distant relations at a wake.

Occasions such as these were geared for Max Eversholt and his type. For him, the gallery floor on a preview night was the one place he felt alive. He dialled up his enthusiasm to the point of theatre, revelling in the glory of his involvement in my work, kissing cheeks, patting backs, savouring the thrum of conversations that ensued. I never understood why all this glitz and pageantry was required to sell a picture—it certainly had nothing to do with art. Every painter I respected worked alone in a quiet room, and the images they made were intended for solemn reflection, not to provide the scenery for obnoxious gatherings of nabobs and batty collectors wearing too much perfume. After a while, the company of such people became the norm, and I was expected not only to enchant them with my work, but also to fascinate them with my personality. If I baulked at placating these strangers, it merely served to enthral them even more.

I hovered in the corner with Bernie Cale for much of that

private viewing, and we talked for a while about Jim, wondering aloud where he had gone to, if we had seen the last of him. Bernie had heard all the rumours and was not convinced by any of them. 'I just don't see a bloke like Jim lasting ten minutes in New York,' he said. 'Too many windbags and clever Dicks. Too much competition. And you know how he feels about American whisky. Single malt's so dear over there, he'd never make it.'

I laughed at this, recalling the strength of Jim's feelings on the matter. He had declined to share a drink with his neighbour, Vern Glasser, on so many occasions that, one day, I had asked him why he could not try to be more accommodating. After all, I had to share a bathroom with Vern, and their festering resentment for each other was making the atmosphere in our mews house rather fraught. But Jim said, 'I've nothing against Vernon in particular. It's just that all he has to drink is that awful stuff from Kentucky, and, frankly, I'd prefer to swig from his toilet.' How I missed being Jim's assistant. The simplicity of our life together. That everyday affiliation we used to have. The longer I went without hearing from him, the more I thought of those days in St John's Wood and yearned to restore them.

'More to the point,' Bernie Cale went on, 'if he's in the States, wouldn't somebody have bumped into him by now? I mean, it's not like you can hide in New York, is it? Not if you're trying to make a name for yourself. It's a very big scene over there, but it's all a bit—what's the word—incestuous.' I had never been to New York so was not qualified to pass judgement.

The rumours about Jim's whereabouts were founded on a scarcity of facts, with the gaps coloured in by guesswork. According to received opinion, he had gone to New York to live with his sister. This theory hinged upon a drunken conversation that Jim was supposed to have had with two regulars at the Prince Alfred pub, who had told Max Eversholt that they had held Jim's ticket for the boat in their very own hands (they also claimed that Jim had begged the barmaid for a lift to Southampton). The problem with verifying this story was that nobody knew if Jim really had a sister. His drinking pals could not remember what her name was, where she might have worked, or what part of the city she lived in. They did not even know if she was older or younger. Eversholt believed their word was reliable, even if the details rang false when I called the shipping companies: they had no recent record of a passenger named James Culvers. All in all, the New York theory was quite unsound, but we had no other clues to follow up on.

Jim had abandoned his studio just a few weeks after I moved out of his attic. 'A midnight flit,' was how Eversholt put it. 'Ditched everything but his sketchbooks.' He had shown me the eerie state that Jim had left the space in: all his oil tubes thrown into a box, his easels folded down and stacked, the On Highs painted over with white gesso, leaned up by the window. 'If you want some extra room, it's yours,' Eversholt had said. 'You can work it out between yourselves when Jim gets back. Assuming he's not lying dead in a gutter somewhere.' I was revolted by his glibness, and he quickly apologised. 'Sorry. That was in poor taste, even for me.' The prospect of a stranger moving in to Jim's studio was so dismaying that I agreed to take it on in his absence. I used it mostly to store overflow materials, though sometimes I would go and stand in those empty rooms when I needed separation from a particularly mulish piece of work. At first, it helped me to surround myself with the remnants of Jim's thoughts, to pace in his old circles. But each time I tried to work there, I felt that I was painting over memories of him, changing the meaning of the space, so I stopped going.

Max was good enough to keep on covering the rent for Jim's flat in Maida Vale. The landlady was thrilled to tell me all about the dirty pots that had been left to moulder in Jim's sink, how his bins had not been put out for collection, and how she needed to let herself in with the master key when the smell became insufferable. She had promised to put Jim's things in a storage locker for me if I paid her twelve shillings a month—I was sure that she would only dump everything and pocket the money, so instead I arranged for someone to pack up Jim's possessions and kept the boxes in his studio, guessing he would thank me for it some day. But fortnights passed and still no hospital could account for Jim's admittance when I called around, no duty officer could identify him in the drunk tank, no long-lost friends emerged to claim him as their lodger. I waited months for a letter to arrive, a postcard from America, anything. My heart flinched every time the phone rang, tempering when all I heard was the voice of Max ('Darling, I'm headed your way. Any chance I might swing by with some friends? They're itching to see what you're working on'), or another gentle enquiry from Dulcie Fenton, the director of the Roxborough Gallery, who checked on my progress more frequently than I believed was necessary: 'Anything you need from this end, just say the word.' It took me a full year to accumulate the pieces for the show. Through that long, intensive period of work, I attuned myself to the idea that Jim would not be there to see the paintings when they were finished. In fact, I began to wonder if he would ever see another work of mine again. I accepted my aloneness, embraced it as my fate.

'Paris is a decent bet, I reckon,' Bernie Cale said, pushing out his lip. He picked off a handful of canapés from the server's tray as it went by. 'He used to go on about Giacometti and that crowd all the time.'

'It's possible,' I said, doubting it.

'Wasn't he there for a bit, after the war?'

'I don't know. He didn't talk about it much.'

'He'd like the lifestyle, I reckon. And the racing's not bad either. You might want to put the feelers out, just in case.'

'Paris is a mystery to me. I don't have any feelers. I don't even know if I'm pronouncing it correctly. Par-iss. Pa-*ree*? Which is it?'

'Not a clue.' He looked for somewhere to put his used cocktail sticks, settling for the floor under his boot. 'I'll start asking round, if you want. I know a few people.'

'Sweet of you, Bernie. Thanks.' I smiled at him, truly meaning it. 'I was thinking St Ives might be worth looking into—Dulcie says a lot of painters have been moving down to Cornwall lately. I know Jim always loved the city, but he grew up on that part of the coast.'

'Why'd I always think he was a northerner?'

'I'm not sure. You must've been punched in the head too often.'

'That'd explain it.' He stuffed a finger in his ear and waggled it, studying the damp, waxy deposit under his nail. Another server went by with a tray, but this time he let her pass. 'Well, wherever he's gone and buggered off to, I'm sure he's doing all right. Always thought Jim could handle himself, if he needed to.'

Coming from a boxer, this was oddly reassuring. 'I hope you're right.'

'Course I am.' Bernie stared at me. There was a slothful quality about his features that made him seem permanently on the edge of passing out. But he seemed to take a particular interest in my face that night, appraising it in long, heavy gazes that I tried to ignore. 'So,' he said, 'I hear this lot are taking you to Wheeler's after.' He nodded in the general direction of the crowd, but it was clear to whom he was referring: Dulcie Fenton and her two fawning assistants.

'I'd rather go straight home to bed, to be honest with you.'

Bernie hung a stare on me. 'If the gallery's paying, you should have the number two oysters.'

'I might just do that.'

'You won't find better in London. It's a proper old place is Wheeler's. They do a cracking dressed crab to start with—make sure you get that. And the turbot, if you've room.' He must have noticed my attention was wandering. 'Or I could drive you back to Kilburn, if you like. I'm going that way anyway.'

'I can't just leave. It's rude.'

'Go on, duck out with me. Who's going to notice?'

'It's *my* show, Bernie. I can't.'

He scanned the room, deflated. 'All right. But no one's here to look at your paintings, you know. They're here to be *seen* looking at your paintings. I thought you were clever enough to know that already.'

'I'm trying to stay open-minded.'

'Waste of time. Jim'd back me up on that, if he was here.'

I did not take kindly to this summoning of Jim's name just to unsettle me. 'So that's why you came tonight, is it, Bernie? To make the society page?'

He shrugged. 'I won't lie. When Max tells me to be somewhere, I show up nice and punctual. It's a lucky bonus if I like the paintings.'

'And how do you feel about these ones?'

'Still making my mind up on that.'

'Well, no rush. Send me a telegram when you decide.'

This seemed to injure him more than I expected. 'Actually, I like your other pieces better. Nothing's really moved me tonight,' he said.

'Did you see the diptych yet?'

'Yeah, that was my favourite. But it didn't frighten me like the older stuff.'

I could not pretend to Bernie Cale or anyone else that I was satisfied with the work that had been chosen for the show. Only three days before, I had been installing the pieces with Dulcie and had been overcome with such a sense of anti-climax that it took a great deal of resolve not to run out onto Bond Street and hail a taxi home. We had themed and organised the paintings on the walls, rearranged them in every possible configuration before agreeing on the final hanging. The technician had tacked the title cards into place, and Dulcie had said, 'Wonderful. I think we've finally cracked it.' I had expected this moment to be joyous—the culmination of so much dreaming and endeavour—but I did not feel that way at all. Of the nine canvases that appeared in the show, seven had been worked on steadily, over months, and the labour that underpinned them was much too obvious. I had wanted to include six different pieces: older paintings I had made in a bloodrush late one night in Jim's attic. These works, I knew, were not as technically refined, but there was an exciting tension in their rawness. Dulcie made me second-guess them: 'I'm just not sure I understand what you see in them. I mean, they're certainly striking, and I think they'd be fine in a retrospective further down the line, but we're looking to establish a genuine presence for you here—you understand that's the point of this whole exercise, don't you? It's a staggered process. It's fine for the men to go straight for the jugular with their first big show. We have to tantalise a little. Play hard to get. You know what I'm saying. Show the bolder stuff next time, once you have a captive audience.'

Dulcie had a way of turning every dialogue into a soliloquy. She had risen up the echelons at the Roxborough, starting as a secretary to the gallery's owners, proving her acuity by managing the diaries of artists on the books. Soon, they asked her to stand in as assistant to the director, and, when his tenure ended due to illness, she was made director in her own right. There was no more respected woman on the London art scene at that time. She had established a reputation for intuiting trends in the market and had helped to launch the careers of many artists I admired. Max Eversholt deferred to her instincts on most matters, and I was swayed by her opinions because I thought they were born of an experience greater than my own. When she said that my newest paintings were the most sophisticated, I had to listen. Every time the word 'collectable' escaped her lips, it stung my heart and then recoiled into the ether like a wasp to die. Perhaps I would have felt that sting much harder if Jim had been there. Perhaps. Too many perhapses.

As it turned out, the only painting that did not sell at the private viewing was the work I was most proud of: a diptych that Dulcie had agreed to include in the show by way of a compromise. I had called it *Godfearing*. The left-hand panel was six feet wide and four feet tall, depicting a layered mountainscape in dark grey oils that I had dragged through repeatedly with the edge of a plasterer's trowel, dulling the paint in sections with the heels of my hands (you could see the grain of my skin impressed in some of them). Across one corner of this image, a dazzle of blurred white stripes was roughly scraped on a diagonal. These stripes flowed into a right-hand panel of the same height and half the width. This smaller canvas showed the hollow profile of a baby. It was a ghostly figure that touched the edges of the space, as though enwombed by the frame; a faceless shape, hiding behind a gauze of pallid streaks. Its arching back was pressed against the left side of the canvas and seemed to hold up the landscape behind it. From afar, the baby appeared to be damming an avalanche with its shoulders, and, in turn, the jagged rocks seemed to keep the baby from toppling backwards. I had mounted the two panels a quarter of an inch apart, hoping to imply a sense of conjunction between them. It was the point of much discussion over dinner at Wheeler's that night.

'I'm surprised nobody took it, given the others went so quickly,' Max Eversholt said. He offered to fill my glass with Chablis and I shook my head. 'Still, I have to say it looked a tad incongruous. The title alone was a challenge for some people. Ted Seger's wife didn't even want to stand near it—and we all know who controls the chequebook in that particular household.'

'The Segers haven't bought a piece from us in years,' was Dulcie's response. 'I only invited Ted because he's a handy chap to have in my pocket in certain situations: tax season looming and all that. Besides, the diptych will find a home eventually. You know what they say in Egypt . . .' This caused both of her assistants to chuckle, and Max threw me a helpless look. I could only blink back at him.

'We seem to have walked into a private joke,' he said. 'How unfortunate.'

Dulcie straightened her face. Her assistants went quiet. 'Just something we were talking about on the way over here. In Egypt, when you come to the end of a good meal, it's respectful to leave a small amount of food on your plate.'

'I see. Respectful to whom?'

'To the cook.'

'Well, terrific. Thank heavens you invited so many Egyptians tonight—oh, no, *wait*,' Max said, beaming.

'Not for the first time, old love, you're rather missing the point.' Dulcie shucked an oyster, barely gulping. 'If we'd sold all nine pieces already, what would I tell collectors once the reviews start coming in?' She made a telephone of her thumb and pinkie: *'Yes, that's right, sir, only one left, I'm afraid—oh, by far the most progressive piece in the show, yes, sir—it would take someone with a particular insight just to see its—pardon me? The price? Well, hold on a sec, and let me check the book for you. I'm not sure the artist really wants to part with it . . .'* Dulcie retracted her fingers. 'Don't you know anything about the market, Max? I thought this was your game.'

'You're forgetting who brought Ellie to your attention in the first place. I didn't hear you patronising me then.' He gestured at the waiter. 'Another round of number twos over here, please!'

Dulcie laughed. 'I do wish they'd call them something else.'

'Never. It's half the fun of eating here.'

I had become accustomed to this sort of discussion—the type in which I sat as an observer, hearing my own work being spoken about without being invited to contribute an opinion. I was passed around between people like the head on a coin, regarded only when questions needed a quick answer or small points required clarification.

At least I was not the only person who was adrift from the conversation that night. The young man in the seat opposite had not said a word since ordering his green salad, which he had proceeded to nudge around his plate with a lot of indifferent forkwork. He had told me his name on the pavement outside the gallery, but I had misheard it in the drawl of passing traffic and been too embarrassed to ask for it again. It had sounded like 'Wilfredson'.

He had a smooth, slender face and an attractive way of smoking with one arm slung over his chair-back, as though entirely bored by everything Max and Dulcie had to say. The jacket he was wearing had neat cross-stitching around the lapel in yellow thread, and he kept more pens in his breast pocket than I suspected he required. His blond hair was thickly pomaded, but it flicked into a strip of tight dry curls above his brow, giving his head a curious lopsidedness. 'If I might ask something about the diptych,' he said, gazing at me. 'Unrelated to the pounds-and-pence of things. I don't want to make you uncomfortable.'

'Why would she be uncomfortable?' Dulcie cut in.

'Sometimes it's difficult for artists to explain their work.'

'This is just a friendly dinner, not an interview—I thought I'd made that clear.'

Wilfredson tapped his cigarette. He seemed irritated by the interruption, resetting his gaze on the table before addressing me again. 'For what it's worth, I thought it was the only thing in the show of any substance. Which is probably why nobody paid it the least bit of notice all evening. And why no one bought it. Sorry if that's a bit forthright. It's only my opinion.'

I was about to say thank you, but Max got his words out first: 'Dulcie just said the very same thing.'

'I doubt that,' said Wilfredson. 'Though I admit I wasn't hanging on her every word like you were.'

'Well, I'm telling you she did. Progressive—that's what she called it.'

'Really. Gosh. That's even more egregious.'

Dulcie wafted the smoke from her face. 'They warned me you had an attitude. I can see I needn't have worried.'

Wilfredson gave a flickering smile. 'I'm just wondering who decided to shunt the best work to the back end of the room tonight. Can't think it was the artist's choice. I mean, I know the Roxborough's a commercial gallery, but do *all* the hangings have to look like they've been thought out by an Avon lady?'

'Steady on,' said Max. 'No need for that.'

Dulcie's two assistants blushed on her behalf. But she would not be distracted from her plate of oysters. She picked up another shell and tipped its glistering flesh right down her throat. 'Please, go on. I'm not one to stand between a man and a good tirade.'

She reached for her wine glass. 'Just keep in mind: we only show the work, we don't make it. So if you're going to attack the gallery or its staff in print, don't be surprised to get uninvited to our shows.' Dulcie tidied the sides of her grey bob and sat back, awaiting a response.

'Oh, you've nothing to fear in that regard. I don't mention the names of incidental people in my reviews.' Wilfredson let ash fall upon his meal. His arm was still slung around the chair. 'Enough old faces in the room tonight, I noticed. You'll get your flatter-pieces in the broadsheets, no question. How much do you have to pay those good old boys, by the way, Dulcie? They must charge by the adverb, from what I've seen.'

'Tread carefully now. I'm losing my good humour.'

He grinned. 'I just thought I'd take the opportunity to let Miss Conroy know what I truly think of her work. Before those other critics go parroting your press release and fill her head with applause. If that's OK by you.'

'I'm sure Elspeth can stand to hear an opinion,' Dulcie said. 'Even an ignorant one.'

They both looked at me.

'Actually, I wouldn't mind knowing what he thought,' I said.

'Then I suggest we move our discussion elsewhere,' Wilfredson replied. 'I refuse to discuss art in a place like this. Let's go and have a cocktail.'

Dulcie quaffed her wine. 'You had me fooled for a moment there. If all you wanted was a quiet drink with Elspeth, you should've just said so.'

'Can't bear the sight of oysters, that's all.'

'I'm not really much of a drinker,' I said.

Wilfredson paused. 'Thing is, people tend to resent me for having an opinion, even when they've asked for it. So if I buy them the best daiquiri in London first—well, who could possibly resent a man after that? I take it you've never had cocktails at the Connaught.'

'No.'

'There you are then. A whole new world of happiness awaits.' He stood up and threw on his coat. 'I'll be outside.'

'Stay where you are,' Dulcie said. 'He isn't worth the trouble.'

Wilfredson turned up his collar. 'So she's heard, anyway.'

When he was gone, there was a momentary hush. Max stroked breadcrumbs from the tablecloth. 'Phew, he's a bold fellow, isn't he? What's his name again?'

'Wilfred Searle,' Dulcie said.

'Searle. He wouldn't be related to Lord Searle by any chance?'

'Nephew.'

'Blimey.'

'They just gave him Phil Leonard's column at the *Statesman*.'

'Blimey.'

'Yes, do keep saying that, Max. It's helping.'

'But—wait a minute. What happened to Phil Leonard?'

'Early retirement.'

'Damn. Poor bugger. Always liked Phil.' He tossed his napkin to the table. 'That's a fair readership, you know. More than a drop in a bucket.'

'Which is why I invited him to join us tonight. I was told that he loved oysters.'

'Remarkably poor research on someone's part.'

'Quite.' Dulcie did not glare at her assistants, but they slumped into their chairs at the mere implication.

Then one of them said, 'It's not right what he was saying, though. About the diptych. We had some firm enquiries.'

'Yes, the Levins asked me if the panels could be sold separately,' Max added. 'Just the mountains, not the baby. I told them, "How much would I have to pay to separate the two of you?" They seemed to think I was joking . . .'

Dulcie ignored him. She reached across the table to pat the back of my hand. 'On reflection, darling, there's never a bad time for a daiquiri. And you might enjoy hearing his views. Couldn't hurt to keep him company.'

'Is he really that important?' I said.

'Not right now. But he will be eventually.' She patted my hand again, as though we were sisters in church. 'I was watching him all night—he kept sneaking glimpses at you through the crowd. They're all the same. Critics. Men. Can't ever separate the woman from the art.' She nodded to the glass façade of the restaurant where he was waiting. 'They don't make very good friends, I'm afraid, but we wouldn't want them as enemies. I don't think he knows which one he wants to be yet.'

My mother had raised me to be wary of good-looking men. But even she—a woman so disheartened by the chores of marriage that she was impervious to romance—would have softened in the presence of Wilfred Searle. He was refreshingly decisive about life's small details: instructing the cabbie to drive us to the Connaught and directing him as to the fastest route to Mayfair, taking my coat in the lobby and delivering it to the cloak-room, ordering our drinks as he escorted me to a table: 'Two daiquiris, please. And stick to the recipe. We'll have that table in the corner.' He was just as commanding on the subject of art, and somehow made his disapproval of my work sound charming, as though he felt I was capable of greatness but was allowing my potential to be squandered by other people. When he talked, I had to look across the room, at the bar, at the monograms on the carpet. I hoped my aloofness would help me seem invulnerable to criticism.

'There's an undertone of something in the rest of them,' Wilfred said, 'but it's hard to say what—you've buried the meaning too deeply in the paint. Your approach to abstraction is rather cumbrous. I don't know if that's what you've been encouraged towards in art school, but it's all so oddly constrained. You make one or two leaps of expression here and there—not enough for my liking. I don't blame you. It's a symptom of the bad advice you're getting. You have considerable talent—there's no doubt about that. But your show tonight was so competent it bored me. I mean, it was perfectly—oh, here we are. Thank you.' The barman arrived with our cocktails. He lifted them from a silver tray and set each one down on a crisp paper coaster. 'Look, if you want the absolute truth, I know there's a lot more to come from you. They're not awful paintings, on the whole, they're just painfully unmoving. But then you pull that diptych out of your sleeve, that completely spectacular diptych—come on now, dig in.' He handed me a glass and clinked it with his own. 'If it had been the only piece in the show, I would've gone home and written my review right away, the kind that'd make old Dulcie's knees knock together. But then I suppose we wouldn't be having this little moment together, would we? How's that daiquiri treating you?'

I sipped at the dainty drink and made the favourable noises I thought he was waiting for.

'Not very hard to make one of these, you know,' he said. 'Just white rum and lime, a bit of crushed ice, that's all there is to it. Staggering how often people mess it up.'

'It'll do,' I said, and turned to look at the night. There was a row of stately red-brick houses across the street from the hotel. Under the lamplight at the side of the road, a man was unfurling the tarpaulin on his sports car. For a moment, I felt an urge to be out there with him. I imagined going with him all the way to Southampton.

'The thing about Dulcie, as much as I detest her company,' Wilfred went on, 'is that her instincts are usually sound. She can tell when an artist has longevity. That's why she let you show the diptych. She's no fool.'

'She didn't *let* me. I insisted.'

'If you say so.'

'That's how it was.'

'In any case, her style of management isn't for everyone. It's too early to say how you're going to fare with her, but you shouldn't get complacent. I know she didn't think much of your friend Culvers, or his work for that matter. I always thought he had some promise.'

'You know Jim?' I asked.

'Only by reputation.'

'That's how most people know him. He's a good man, really.'

'I don't doubt it. Someone told me he'd dropped off the map.'

'Well, Jim was never really on the same map as the rest of us.'

'Yes, I could tell that from his paintings.' Wilfred smiled. 'It's a shame he lost his way. I liked his early stuff. Before he started with those Hopper pastiches.'

There was a time when I might have taken exception to this remark, but I had come to view Jim's old 'absence portraits' as nothing more than portents of his disappearance—great flashing signs that I had failed to see. 'I don't want to talk about Jim tonight,' I said.

'Good, because I don't have much else to say on that score.'

The daiquiri was strong and, after a few long sips, the rum began to bite the back of my throat. Outside, the man turned the ignition of his sports car and it gave a rusty, disappointing sound underneath the bar's piano music. 'He's been trying to start that bloody thing for ages,' Wilfred said. 'There's a point at which perseverance becomes denial. I think we're about four weeks past it with this chap.'

'I suppose you must come here often,' I said, which only showed him my naïvety.

'You mean, do I bring all my women here?'

'*All?* That implies a fair number.'

'I can't deny it's a popular place.' He thinned his eyes at me. 'You have an unusual way of talking, you know that?'

'I grew up near Glasgow.'

'It's not how you speak, it's what you say. Your accent's very gentle.'

'Don't you ever stop criticising?'

'No. It's a permanent vocation.'

'Well, frankly, the way I speak is none of your concern.'

'It just seems to me that you're very careful with your words, very measured. Makes me wonder if you approach painting the same way. It would explain a lot about the show tonight.'

'Your ice is melting,' I said.

He looked down at his drink, as though remembering it was in his hand. 'I like to let the lime settle a bit first. Tastes better.'

'I wonder what that says about you.'

He simpered, putting the glass down on the table, twisting its stem so the coaster spun beneath it. 'Look, obviously I'm not going to get to know you in the course of one evening, Ellie, so I'm having to make a few assumptions—is it all right if I call you that?'

I nodded.

'Not that there's anything wrong with the name Elspeth, of course.'

'That was nearly a compliment.'

'Close enough.' The glass came to rest in his fingers. 'I probably shouldn't say this, but when you got in the cab tonight, I thought you were going to be like all the rest of them.'

'The rest of who?'

'You know— '

'I'm afraid I don't.'

He blinked. 'There's a certain pliability about the women Dulcie takes on at the gallery, if you get what I mean.'

'You make it sound like a bordello.'

'That wasn't my intention. Really,' he said, tidying the cuffs of his blazer. 'I was only trying to say that you're not the average

Dulcie Fenton sort of artist. I thought I'd buy you a drink, tell you a few cold truths, and you'd cry on my shoulder and I'd say, *There, there, darling, your work will get better, I know you have it in you*. But I can tell you prefer to keep people at a distance.'

'Not everyone.'

'Just me then. Why? Because my opinion is important?'

'Actually, you have a very high opinion of your own opinion. It could just be that I don't like you very much.'

'Ha. Maybe so.' Wilfred moistened his lips. He sat forward, bringing a cigarette case from his breast pocket, flipping it open. There was only one left. He held it out for me to take but I declined. 'What I know for sure,' he said, drawing out the cigarette, tapping it on the back of the case, 'is you haven't come here for praise.'

'That's lucky.'

He smirked, taking the hotel matchbook from the ashtray and tearing off a strip. 'It's confirmation you want, isn't it?'

'I don't know what you mean.'

'I think you do.' He angled his head. The matchflame illumined his face like a Halloween pumpkin. 'It's not that you need me to explain why the diptych is so good. You already know that. It's authentication you're looking for. You're here to make sure I understand how good you are.'

For the first time all night, I looked directly into his eyes. They were not quite the colour I had thought they were—a murky, gutter-moss green. 'Honestly, I couldn't care less what you write about me in your magazine. Where I'm from, people who sit around criticising other people's work all day instead of doing their own get a very bad name for themselves. I happen to like men with strong opinions. I find them interesting to talk to. But don't fool yourself—it's not your approval I'm after.'

'Then what?'

'Nothing. Just a chance to have a proper conversation about art. I haven't had a genuine discussion about painting since— '

'When?'

'A long time ago. Since I moved to Kilburn. It's difficult to be taken seriously when you look like me.'

'I have a similar problem.'

'You're a woman too, are you?'

'No, but I look younger than I am, which puts me at a certain disadvantage.'

'Oh, please. Don't even try to compare.'

'Well, all right—we're getting off topic.' As he inhaled and savoured the smoke, his arm succumbed to its old habit, drooping over the chair-back. 'You *should* care what I think, because I care what you paint. That's how it works. Our interests are aligned.'

'You presume an awful lot.'

'I do, I know.' He edged forward, shifting his legs. 'Give me a moment and I'll explain.'

'It's past midnight already.'

'Five more minutes.'

I leaned back. 'Three.'

'I'll start with the diptych then,' he said. 'A quintessential Elspeth Conroy painting, if ever there was one.'

I laughed. 'And how would *you* know?'

'Easy. I don't read press releases. They go straight in the dustbin. I just look for the piece that resonates most. I could tell that painting came from a different place than all the others.'

'So you haven't even seen my other work? That's hardly fair.'

'Context is overrated. It wouldn't have mattered if the diptych were the first work of yours I'd seen or the last. I'm no artist, but I can tell when one is fully in tune with herself, not just trying to fake it for the sake of an exhibition. You can feign a lot of things in modern art, but emotion isn't one of them. It has to be there in the paint, not tagged on after. And it's probably the most important thing a reviewer can convey, that distinction. Not everyone can spot the difference, so they leave it up to people like me. And whether I print it in the *Statesman* or stand up on a soapbox in the park and shout it out loud—doesn't matter. Real artists come along so rarely nowadays that modern art is hard to justify. Most people can't tell pitch dark from blindness any more, and that's what makes our interests so aligned. I need artists like you to make great art so I have something to shine a light on. And you need critics like me, or nobody will notice what you paint. That's the nature of the game we're in.' He slugged the whole of his daiquiri, blinking away the sourness. 'Can I buy you another?'

'I should really be getting home.'

He twisted round and made a circling gesture to the barman anyway. 'You're still not convinced,' he said.

I shook my head. 'I'm not like you. I don't see art as a game.'

'All right. Let's try it another way.' He picked something from his tongue—a tiny node of lime-flesh—and flicked it to the carpet. 'I'll bet when you painted the diptych you weren't even thinking of painting, were you? You didn't have a purpose in mind, not even a theme, you were just trying to express a feeling—you let your arm go wherever it wanted until you ended up with mountains. Am I warm?'

'I'm still listening,' I said.

He wet his lips again. 'Something felt wrong after that, I'll bet—I don't mean erroneous. *Less than whole* would probably be more like it. Anyway, let's say you stepped back from the painting at this point—exhausted most likely, sweating a lot and ready to give up working on it altogether—but then—and you don't know exactly *where* it came from—you saw another form leaning against that panel: not completely *there*, in the same frame, just set off against it somehow, almost joined but not quite. It just dropped into your mind. And that's how you painted the baby on the right—from nowhere. You didn't copy from a photograph—not your style. You just painted it straight out of your imagination, didn't you? From memory. It just sort of *felt right* to paint it, so you carried on. And, I don't know, maybe you were afraid of what you were painting as you were doing it, mountains and babies not being your normal kind of subject matter, but you had to see where it all led. Because it *felt* right. In fact, it probably seemed as though the entire thing was somehow predetermined. Like it was happening *to* you. What was that old line Michelangelo had about his sculptures waiting for him in the marble? *That*. I'll bet you made the whole painting so quickly you didn't even stop to eat or sleep. And that's why you begged for it to be in the show. Because you composed all the others yourself, thought about them very deliberately, but that diptych was pure inspiration.' With this, he sat back, returning his cigarette case to its frayed little pocket. 'See, that's the kind of thing you need someone like me to communicate. Your average person can't just intuit it when they walk in off the street.'

Our corner of the bar now seemed more private. The gentle

piano music had become an unmelodious ripple, as frustrating as a dial tone that never engaged. 'You might have a bit more understanding than I gave you credit for,' I said, and took a last sip of daiquiri, just to steady myself. His level of insight had disarmed me. 'I suppose you'd like me to cross your palm with silver now.'

'We'll consider it a freebie,' he said. 'There's no magic involved. Anyone who's ever created anything remotely original will explain his process in the same way. As if he had no control, just influence. Channelling—that's the word that seems to get used.'

'And I take it you're more cynical than that.'

He shrugged. 'I told you, I'm no artist. I don't know for certain. But I prefer to think that great work is made through talent and sheer hard work. If some can channel greatness and the rest of us can't even get an outside line, it's a very unfair system.'

'Says the nephew of a lord.'

'That's irrelevant. I'm talking about art. Creativity.' His face began to twitch. 'You know, my uncle can't stand the sight of me. It's fine. The feeling's mutual. I just wish people would stop lumping us together.'

'I was only pointing out the unfairness of the world.'

'I'm still right about creativity, though. Science is going to prove it one day. Just remember who it was that told you so.' He smiled, allowing a silence to gather. 'What time is it? We ought to see about that cab.'

'Past one, I think.'

'Come on, I'll fetch your coat. Hope I haven't lost that ticket she gave me.' He stood, calling the barman over.

'Yes, sir?'

'Would you have someone bring my drink up to the room, please?'

'Of course, sir.' The barman went away.

'Hate to drink alone in public,' Wilfred said, 'and it seems a shame to waste it.'

'You're staying here?' I asked.

'For now. I've rather fallen out of love with London lately. I'm still working out where I want to go next.' He made it sound so unrehearsed. Patting his blazer pockets, he mumbled: 'Where's that ticket she gave me? It must have got into the lining.'

I had been to bed with two men in my life before that night— enough to keep my expectations low. But I let myself believe that sleeping with Wilfred Searle would at least be an improvement on those shy and muddling art school students who had preceded him, the first of whom had been too conscious of the act's significance to finish what he started, the second of whom had curtly wiped his mess from my thighs with his shirtsleeve before rolling off me.

It was in this generous spirit that I allowed Wilfred to stoop and kiss me in the hotel corridor, forgiving his clumsy lips and their lingering bitterness. I tried not to be disheartened when he insisted I undress myself in the bright lights of his room, or sigh when his dry fingers worked my breasts like sacks of oats he was trying to prise open. Even as he lay on top of me, lodging his elbows by my head so that his chest-hair tickled my chin, I stared up at the ceiling and politely stroked his back, thinking there would surely be a moment when I would feel connected to him.

I let him thrust away with all the stolid purpose of a derrick bobbing in a field, and held on to the fading hope that he would
notice the disappointment in my eyes and try to make amends—
but he did not even have the good grace to pull out of me. A few
minutes later, he fell off me, panting, and I lay tangled in the
soggy hotel linen, wishing I had never met him.

I got up and put my slip on.

'Where are you going?' he asked. 'Lie here with me. We need
to make wedding plans.'

'Very funny.'

'I'm serious. What's a good time for you? My Thursdays are
free until August.'

'I suppose you'll have to organise that with Dulcie,' I said.
'She's in charge of my calendar now.'

'Ah yes, I forgot—the Roxborough owns you.' He sat up
against the headboard. 'Do you think if I call downstairs they'd
bring me up some Dunhills?'

'I doubt it. Have you seen the time?'

'Well, I'm going for it anyway.' He reached for the phone, patting the empty space beside him on the bed as he dialled. 'Yes,
reception, hi. I was wondering if it would be possible for the concierge to do me a small favour . . .'

I stopped dressing and got back into bed, keeping what I
thought was an appropriate distance between his hip and mine.

'Cigarettes, actually . . . Yes, I know, it's awfully late, but perhaps there's a machine somewhere near by? It's Mr Searle, or did
I mention that already?'

Pulling the sheets over my chest only exposed my feet and ankles, and I became aware of Wilfred staring down at them while he bartered with the concierge.

'Excellent, thank you. Dunhills, yes—two packets, if you don't mind.' He covered the mouthpiece and asked me, 'Anything for you?' I shook my head. 'No, that's it, thank you. That'll be everything.' He put the phone down, exhaling. Then he turned to slide an arm across my stomach. I felt his wiry belly hair against my back, needling the silk of my slip. 'Ten minutes,' he murmured, kissing my ear. 'I don't think I've ever had to wait so long for a smoke afterwards.'

'We could make love again twice in that time.' I assumed he would take this as a good-natured gibe, the kind that we had spent most of the night aiming at each other. But, instead, he planted a palm between my shoulder blades and shoved me forwards, and I almost hit my forehead on the bedside cabinet. 'What the bloody hell was that for?'

He was already on his feet, walking naked to the bathroom. 'If you're so dissatisfied, you might as well go home,' he said.

'I was teasing you, that's all. I thought you'd laugh.'

He flicked a switch and stood there in the bathroom light, his body taut and wan. 'Well, I don't find that sort of thing amusing.'

'You needn't take it so personally.'

'I happen to have some pride in the way I—oh, forget it. I don't have to explain myself.' He was scrubbing his hands firmly with soap now, from fingertips to elbow. 'Perhaps you would've enjoyed it more if you hadn't just lain there looking so horrified. It felt like I was hammering a skirting board.'

I gathered my clothes. 'Now you're starting to disgust me.'

'Just hurry up and leave, would you? I have an early train.' He shut the bathroom door and locked it. I heard him clattering about in there while I stepped into my dress and found my coat. Then the door flashed open and he came bounding towards the bed. He was wearing a fresh hotel gown, and every stride he took gave off a strange crunching sound, like spare buttons rattling in a box. 'Still here, I see,' he said, removing a bottle of pills from the front pocket. 'Another one who can't take a hint.' He dry-gulped a clutch of tablets.

The concierge came knocking then: two discreet pips on the wood, barely audible.

'Thanks for a horrible evening,' I said, and showed myself out.

The concierge stepped aside to let me through. 'Madam, your scarf is trailing,' he called after me as I made my way along the hall. 'Madam—your *scarf*.' I unravelled it from my sleeve and let it drop onto the carpet. Ahead of me, the lift doors opened but nobody stepped out.

- - - - - -

Our Next Great Female Painter?

by Wilfred Searle | *New Statesman* | 20th February, 1960

One can hardly blame young Scottish artist, Elspeth Con-roy, for being a woman. Nor can one admonish the Rox-borough Gallery on Bond Street for championing her work so ardently. In this modern art world, dominated by men of soaring talent, the claims of promising female painters are too rarely recognised. But what makes the first solo exhibition by Glasgow Schooled Conroy such a fizzling disappointment is the heightened expectation one carries into the gallery. The Roxborough's advance publicity material is the main contributor: Miss Conroy is proclaimed to be 'Britain's next great female painter' before the oil on her work is even dry. It would be tough for any living artist, with the exception of Picasso, to match the hysteria of such a promotional campaign, so what chance this young lassie?

Well, although there is plenty to admire in the technical proficiency of all nine paintings on display, one is presented with the same niggling doubts at every turn of her debut show: Is this really the work of a true original? Or does one's heart simply plead for it because the painter is a woman?

As yet, no practising female painter has been able to replicate the trembling excitement we encounter in the work of Bacon or Sutherland. The fine sculptures of Barbara Hepworth have brought us close, but even this exceptional artist still struggles to elude the shadow of her male contemporaries. There is no doubt that our next great female painter will appear when she is ready, but I am sad to report that this show offers little evidence of Conroy being our girl. Her landscape paintings are so consciously mannered that they only succeed in aggravating, the way a child who finishes all her homework before bedtime invites suspicion from her father. In short: they try too hard to be appreciated.

Conroy has a tendency to overstate each minor brushstroke, resulting in a suite of tepid, unconvincing images: London canal scenes with crooked, wispy figures whose obliqueness is much too premeditated. The careful abstraction of these scenes, though rendered deftly, is a transplant from another (male) artist's heart: Picasso has lent his influence to everything Conroy paints. This might well be a habit that afflicts too many of our current painters, regardless of their gender, but it is a particularly bewildering trait in the work of a young woman from the banks of the Clyde.

There is just one faint glimmer of promise in this otherwise cheerless show: *Godfearing* is a striking diptych in which Conroy attempts to loosen her stylistic restraints to tackle themes of motherhood. Still, dragged down by the weight of so much pre-show expectancy, even this well-realised work seems meek and insubstantial. One departs the gallery wishing the artist had chosen to express more of what it means to be a woman in the modern age.

Three

The talk in the first-class lounge was all about 'this business'. Five men in dark flannel suits, whose faces were so similarly tapered I expected they were brothers, were constellated on the club chairs near by, turning through *The Ocean Times* and debating the articles of the day. Their wives were elsewhere on the ship (I heard mention of a bridge game somewhere on the promenade deck, a concert happening in the cocktail bar) and the five of them, it seemed, were damned if they were going to pass up the opportunity to converse about men's matters over afternoon Tom Collinses.

First, there was the bantering about 'this business with the Pioneer satellite' and how it proved that the American space programme would be nowhere without the help of British engineering. Then it was 'this business with the train crash' and how, in their glib assessment of the tragedy, such accidents ought hardly to be possible in a place as vast as California, where surely there was enough land for rail and road to never intersect. I could not decide what bothered me more: the ignorance of these men or their total lack of courtesy towards other passengers. Even the drone of the ship's engines—that incessant rumble I had still not learned the skill of tuning out —was preferable to their chirruping and complaining: 'You'd think they'd have laid on something better than the Archie West Trio, wouldn't you?' one of them said. 'We heard all the same acts last year,' said another. 'Getting a bit tired of the Verandah, too.' 'That whole place is looking tired.' 'Oh, absolutely.' 'I wish they'd stop trying to foist that onion soup on us at breakfast, as if it's such a bloody wonder of creation.' 'Oh, good heavens, yes.' 'Probably the same batch they've been feeding us since '55!' 'Certainly tastes like it.' 'Ha-ha-ha.'

I hoped the purser or a steward might come along to quiet them, but the lounge was fairly empty and the crew were otherwise engaged. It was easier to move to a different spot. There were plenty of other rooms where I could sit and finish my book. And if I could not find the peace to lose myself in reading, I had a brochure's worth of 'on-board facilities' to distract me from my troubles: swimming pools and restaurants and a cinema showing *Gidget*, all of which I would have traded for a single hour of painting in my dingy Kilburn studio.

I had already tried the smoking room: too much chatter in there, and not much oxygen. The library had suited me just fine, until the pitching of the ship began to make the books slide fore and aft along the shelves, giving me a dose of seasickness. I had gone to ward it off in the salon before the crew manager arrived to direct the preparations for the evening's cabaret dance and everything got noisy again. The ship was over a thousand feet long—'a floating city', according to Dulcie. It had thirteen decks and enough cargo space to hold the luggage of two thousand passengers. So how was it that I could not find a single place on board where I felt comfortable?

It did not help that Dulcie had arranged a suite for me, when I had asked for a much simpler room in cabin class. We were sailing to New York because she was terrified of aircraft ('A hangover from the Blitz,' she said) and I agreed to go with her because I did not trust myself to fly alone. The gallery was covering our expenses. Dulcie claimed that she would only sail first-class on someone else's shilling, so she booked two of the dearest rooms the *Queen Elizabeth* had available. Thanks to her, I was committed to spending the entire voyage in the company of wealthy cruisers I would never have spoken to by choice: tiresome New Yorkers returning from family weddings in 'charming little towns'; well-dressed London couples with an appetite for exaggerating the splendours of the ship's decoration ('We haven't seen another tapestry quite like it—and so many exotic woods! We've been bowled over!'); obnoxious men of industry who slurped their gimlets and left shrimp-tails on the tabletops. Everywhere I turned, I saw haughtiness and self-absorption, and heard the sneering tones of people who reminded me of Wilfred Searle.

I had found no respite at all since leaving Southampton. My suite was the only place on board where I had total privacy, but this presented its own problems. The room was dwarfing and elaborate—so grand that the bedcovers were made of a fabric more decorous than the evening gowns Dulcie had loaned me for the trip—and, although I slept well enough each night, I could not settle there in the daytime. It was not that I pined to be down in tourist class where I belonged, because sailing the Atlantic was a much less poetic experience than Melville had led me to believe, and I was very glad to be away from the cramped quarters of the lower decks. In fact, the suite afforded so much shelter from the goings-on about the ship that it made me jittery, vulnerable to my own thoughts.

If I could not see the movements of the other passengers, or sense the quiet workings of the crew around me, it was hard to maintain perspective. Alone, my problems smothered me and I grew so dismayed with myself that I could not pass my own reflection in the mirror without wanting to destroy it. I drank cups of pennyroyal tea with honey, and soaked for hours in a bathtub that never quite got hot enough, silently composing telegrams I did not have the courage to wire back to England:

```
WILFRED:  GREETINGS  FROM  RMS  QE.
HALFWAY  TO  NYC  ALREADY.  HATING  YOU
MORE  BY  THE  NAUTICAL  MILE.  5  WKS
PREGNANT  AND  COUNTING.  ELSPETH.
```

Leaving the men to scrutinise *The Ocean Times*, I went out to stretch my legs awhile, going up and down the promenade deck until I got weary. It proved difficult to go ten yards without having to side-step a meandering old lady, or skirt around a steward undertaking some fresh errand. I stopped at the guardrail for a moment to breathe in the air. The grey Atlantic swathed the hull. The soft seam of the horizon was too vast to comprehend. It occurred to me that I was as far from Clydebank as I had ever been in my life, that I was sailing first-class on a ship my own father had helped to build in the John Brown & Company yard. He would have smiled at the thought of me now, being kept afloat by joints he and his friends had caulked, but I did not feel proud. I wanted the ocean to swallow me whole.

A part of me believed I would find Jim Culvers hiding in New York. I tried to tell myself that I would have made this trip regardless, and that any dreams I had of chancing upon Jim and his sister in Washington Square Park were not a factor in my decision. When people on board asked my reasons for travelling, I said that I was going to meet the owners of the art gallery that represented me. Invariably, this would lead to the question of how much money my paintings sold for, as though it were the defining credential of any real artist. Dulcie would often interject at this point; but, in her absence, I would say, 'Enough to travel first-class,' and this would prompt them to confess they were embarrassed not to know my name. People would have been less enamoured of the truth, I suspect, which is why I never told it. The fact was, I had not finished a single piece of work since that awful night I spent with Wilfred at the Connaught, and had felt so anxious about painting since his *Statesman* piece was published; therefore, an exhibition of new work—be it in London or the depths of Siberia—was a very distant prospect.

I had only made the trip on Dulcie's insistence. 'You need a change of scenery,' she had told me. 'Go and travel round Europe for a month, see some things, take a few pictures, meet a few men. Get that imbecile out of your mind. Or better still—' One of the founders of the Roxborough, Leonard Hines, was looking at potential sites for a sister gallery in Manhattan. 'Len's got some ridiculous idea that I should run the place for him. I keep saying I don't have time to gallivant across Midtown, sizing up locations, but he's been getting rather adamant lately. We should go together—I need a good sailing companion, and he needs to get better acquainted with your face. It'll do us both some good.' I would not have considered going anywhere with her except New York; the faint hope that Jim was lurking in its midst had never left me. And I knew that seeing him was the only thing that could rid my heart of Wilfred's strangle-marks.

Desperate now for peace and quiet, I took the stairs up to the sun deck. It was a warm day and the cheerful wives of first-class were out on the terrace. As I scouted for a table, passing sunhats and bare shoulders, I realised there was no comfort to be found amongst these women either. I could not sit listening to their appraisal of the entertainments bulletin: 'Gordon Cane and his Orchestra—quarter to four in the lounge. I'm game for it if you are, Lucy. Unless you've other plans?' I did not even interrupt my stride, just walked a perfect loop around the terrace, back down-stairs, gripping my damp copy of *Below the Salt*.

There was nothing left to do but head up to the racquet court. For the past three afternoons, Dulcie had been competing in the ship's squash tournament. She was an avid player—a fact she had surprised me with early in the voyage, when she had come to my door wearing a bright white tracksuit with a towel tucked inside the collar. She claimed that everyone had to have a reliable form of exercise unless they wanted 'to stroke out in their fifties', and explained that squash was 'sort of an art form in itself—the only one I'm any good at, anyway'. The standard of the competition on board was low by all accounts, and Dulcie had advanced through the early rounds with ease, giving me a shot-by-shot re-port of every set she played in the Verandah Grill at dinnertime. Today's match, however, was a tricky semi-final (her words) against a woman she knew from her old racquet club in Mayfair. 'Amanda Yail'—she had announced the name with a slight tremor. 'Beat me last year at the Open, second round, then got smashed off court by Heather McKay in the next. I must have missed her on the passenger list. It's going to be a long old match.' I had never heard Dulcie sound so unconfident, which led me to suspect that she did not want me there to cheer her on.

As I went up the steps to the viewing gallery, I could hear the rhythmic pop of rubber against walls, the skid of sports shoes. I had never seen a squash match in my life and did not understand how one was played, or how to follow it as a spectator. When Dulcie used phrases like 'the nick' and 'counter drop' and 'short line' in her summaries, I would nod as if I knew exactly what she meant. She had a certain skill for describing the to-and-fro of her matches and it seemed rude to interrupt her. I envied this gift of Dulcie's, in fact—she could find enthusiasm for the most tedious of things and bestow it unto others through sheer force of will.

The viewing gallery was empty, but for one man standing at the railing with his son. I was going to ask for the score, but then it struck me that the proper etiquette might be to wait for a break in play, so I held back. 'Daddy,' the child said, staring at me. 'Do we have to move our things now?' He was not quite tall enough to see over the top rail—a boy of seven or thereabouts, all buttoned up in a stiff Oxford shirt and trousers pulled too high over his waist. The balcony was smeared with his handprints; he was in the throes of driving his Dinky cars over the glass in slow figures-of-eight. His father hummed. 'Huh, what?'

'For the lady. She wants to sit down.'

'Which lady?'

The man turned. He was what Dulcie liked to call 'a studious fellow', meaning he was bearded and bespectacled and not especially handsome. He had hair that thinned on top and greyed around the edges. His jacket was slung over his left arm like a waiter's cloth. It had not been apparent right away, but now I could see that his attention was on something other than the court. He was wiping a leaky fountain pen with a handkerchief. Blue ink marred the fabric of his shirt—a jagged island right below his nipple. 'Sorry,' he said, 'just a moment.' He finished cleaning off the pen and carried it to the chairs behind me.

I told him not to worry. 'Really, I'm better off standing.' But he seemed intent on clearing his belongings, as though they were in some way humiliating. There was a briefcase full of dog-eared folders and a few of the child's toys were scattered on the seat— plastic soldiers, horses and artillery; a tin rocket with chipped-off paint. The man snapped the case shut and began to collect the toys rather hurriedly. 'Come and help,' he told the boy. 'Put them in your pockets.'

'It's fine,' I said. 'Don't move anything on my account.'

'No, no, we shouldn't be acting like we own the place.' He carried on gathering the soldiers. 'Jonathan—come here! Excuse all this,' he said. 'My wife hates it when I do paperwork on holiday. Have to steal these moments when I can.' His son just drove his little car along the glass, ignoring him. 'Don't pretend you didn't hear me, son. Do you want that cream soda we talked about or not?'

The boy came trudging over. Before he could reach his father, though, a cry rose up from the court. Dulcie was stretched out on her side, having lunged to reach a dropping ball, and her opponent was exalting in the glory of a shot well hit. Dulcie kept slapping the floor with her palm. The man rushed back to the railing. 'What happened? Did you see?'

'I think she might have lost that one.'

'Who?'

'Dulcie.'

'Well, thank God for that!' he said.

'Are they finished?'

'No. It's two all. They'll have to play a final set.'

'Oh. Exciting,' I said, half-heartedly. 'And really good news for your paperwork.'

He smiled. 'Well, it would be if all my pens weren't broken. I don't suppose you have one, do you?'

'No, sorry.'

'I'll have to fetch another from downstairs. What's that you're reading?'

I showed him the cover of my book.

'Any good?' he said.

'I don't know—it depends how much you like the Plantagenets. I'm finding it difficult to care about them.'

'Then why are you still reading it?'

'Because I didn't bring anything else.'

'Ah. I used to make that same mistake. Now I don't have time for novels at all—makes packing a lot easier.' He offered me his ink-stained hand. 'Victor Yail. Pleased to meet you.'

His shake was very gentle.

'Elspeth Conroy,' I said.

On court, Dulcie was adjusting her headband, walking back to make a serve. She glanced up and saw me on the balcony, giving a little gesture with her racquet. 'Are you much of a squash fan?' said Victor. 'Don't really have a choice in my house. Amanda has four brothers and all of them play for their county. I've married into the faith.'

'Well, I'm just here for moral support.'

'You don't play yourself?'

'No. You?'

'Once upon a time.' He flexed his arm. 'Bad elbow.'

The two women were hitting the ball at such a speed that I could barely follow the blur from wall to wall. Each shot gave a whipcrack. Their feet thudded the planks as they hustled back and forth. 'Christ,' I said. 'They're really smashing it. I never knew Dulcie had that kind of strength.'

'Yes. Her game's all power.'

'Is that good?'

'Can be, I suppose.' Victor chuckled. 'I prefer to see a bit of grace in the lady's game, that's all, a nonchalant slice and nimble footwork—you know what I mean. Élan.'

'They both seem to be whacking it quite hard.'

He shook his head. 'It's apples and oranges down there. Apples and oranges.'

'Well, Dulcie's not sweating as much as your wife is. I'm no expert, but that has to be an indication of something.'

'Only that Amanda hasn't changed her shirt yet.'

I grinned. 'A pound says she loses.'

'A pound? Phew, that's steep.' He eyed the motions of his wife on court. 'Frankly, I can't trust Mandy to maintain this pace. She only plays well after an argument. Tried to pick one with me this morning, but I wasn't having it.'

'How selfish of you.'

'Yes, that's just what *she* said.'

Victor was an easy man to talk to. There was a serene quality about his face that appealed to me: his eyes soft-lidded, his mouth all thick and pursy. Perhaps I just found him unthreatening. He seemed like a person who would be incapable of tempting me away from the life I should have had.

'Daddy, is it OK if I lie on the floor with this?' The boy came rushing to his father's kneecaps, holding up a comic.

'As long as you stay on the carpet, I don't see why not.'

'Ye*sssss*.' He dropped immediately and crawled into the space between the chairs.

'And Jonathan?'

'Uh-huh?'

'Please read it in your head this time.'

'OK.'

Victor rolled his eyes at me.

'Sweet boy,' I said.

'He's a gifted actor, that's what he is. You should see the hell he gives his mother. Are you on B Deck?'

'No.'

'Then you'll have missed all the screaming last night. Lucky you.' As if it were not clear enough that he was joking, he gave a little wink to underline it. Then he craned his neck to say to the boy, 'Nearly had to throw you overboard last night, didn't we, son? See if you could swim all the way to America?'

'Shshhh,' said the boy, 'I'm reading.'

'Oh, pardon *me*.' Victor leaned close to my shoulder. 'We mustn't interfere with Superman and his adventures.'

'Who?'

He waved this away. 'Doesn't matter.'

Dulcie was flagging now on court. She seemed to be stuck in a pattern of sending the ball back in the same direction—three times she hit it to the far left corner, and three times it came back, with added spin. I did not understand the point of having an opponent when the purpose of the game was to stand there striking the same shot repeatedly. 'It's getting a bit attritional down there,' Victor said. 'I might just finish that paperwork, after all. Do you mind if I—?' He thumbed towards the chairs.

'Feel free.'

He went to get his briefcase, but stopped partway, clicking his fingers. 'Damn,' he said. 'Pen.' For a long moment, he stood there looking from his son to me, his son to me, apparently caught in the same futile rhythm as Dulcie's squash game. 'Is there a chance you'd do me a huge favour and watch the pipsqueak here?'

'Oh, I'm really not qualified for that . . .' The boy was ensconced in the reading of his comic. He was flat on his belly, kicking his heels together. 'But I suppose he doesn't look like too much trouble.'

'You're very kind.' Victor patted his son's head. 'Be good for Miss Conroy. I'll be back in ten.' And so the boy and I were left alone.

I kept him at the edge of my vision, not wanting to seem overbearing, and tried to involve myself in what was taking place on court. The frantic squeal of shoes continued, as Dulcie scampered from one wall to the other like a captive rat, and Amanda Yail dodged around her. It was a claustrophobic sport, lacking in variety—the kind of game I could never imagine myself taking seriously—but it was obvious that Dulcie and the boy's mother were deeply invested in the task of beating each other. They refused to concede a single ball that had the smallest chance of being redeemed, panting and wheezing between shots. It was quite an inelegant thing to watch. I tried to absorb myself again in *Below the Salt*, but could not focus on the words. Then I remembered I was supposed to be looking after Jonathan.

He was still on the carpet, flipping through the pages of his comic. I went over and sat down on the chairs near by. 'Do you understand this game?' I asked.

The boy twisted round to glance at me. He shook his head and turned away again.

'Perhaps there's something I'm missing. I don't know about you, but if someone told me to go and run around inside a box for a few hours with a stick of wood, I'd say they were mad.' He was not listening. 'I suppose grown-ups can be funny, though, can't they?' The boy began to wriggle on his stomach then, as though irritated by my voice or the chafe of his trousers. 'You know, I don't mind if you want to read out loud. I've never heard of this super man before. What's so super about him anyway?'

Jonathan climbed to his knees.

'I mean, does he do his own washing and ironing?'

'No!' he said, aghast. 'That's silly!'

'Does he look into your eyes when he's talking to you?'

'No, but lasers come out of them.'

'Ah. Sounds dangerous.' I smiled at him. He was gawping at me now, gauging my sincerity. 'Well, he must open doors for ladies, then. Buy them flowers on their birthday, that kind of thing.'

'No, no, no—he's not super like *that*.' His face was alight. 'Look,' he said, 'I'll show you.' He came and sat in the empty club chair beside me, laying the comic across the armrest. The front cover had a masthead that said SUPERMAN in stocky 3-D lettering. A muscly blond wrestler in a blue-and-red uniform was swinging an identical man (but for his dark hair) into a telephone pole. The caption read: A GREAT 3-PART NOVEL: THE SUPER-OUTLAW FROM KRYPTON! 'The one with the black hair is the *real* Superman. The other one is just pretending.'

'He can't be all that super if he's being smashed through a pole,' I said.

'It's because Kull-Ex is strong, too. That's Kull-Ex—' He prodded the blond man's face. 'You think he's Superman to begin with and that he's turned bad, smashing up all these buildings and things, and everyone's upset with Superman for a long time, but then he takes off his mask and you see it's really Kull-Ex and he's from Kandor on Superman's home planet. And he's trying to get revenge on Superman because Superman's dad stole *his* dad's invention. But that turns out to be a lie, anyway.' Jonathan gulped. 'Want me to show you the bit where he finds out it's a lie?'

'Of course I do. I'm hooked.'

He shifted closer. I could smell the lavender of ship-issue soap in his hair. There were dry flakes about his crown. I wondered what it might be like to comb that floppy fringe into a nice side parting, if it would make him look more like his father. Keenly, he set about unravelling the convolutions of his comic book story, conducting the flow of action from panel to panel with his finger, calling out the speech that jutted from characters' mouths in white balloons. He did not have any trouble reading—even the longer words, like 'confession' or 'solitude', and the stranger ones, like 'Zenium'—though I sensed he might have memorised the script in places. 'And look, this is the bit when Supergirl goes into the Fortress of Sollichood and tries to pull him out with tweezers! It's silly, but I like it. I like that she can see things that are really really really small. And I think on the next page is where Super-man comes up with his plan to save them. Or is it on—no wait—*there* it is.' He went on breathlessly for minutes, rifling through the pages, until his father came back up the steps and we had to curtail things.

'Managed to scrounge one off a steward in the lift,' Victor said, flashing a silver pen at me. 'I promised to get it back to him, but let's just see how well it writes first, eh? This could be the pen of my dreams.' He saw that Jonathan had been showing me the comic. 'Oh God, sorry about him. Has he been boring you with Dr Telex and his Fortress of Whatever It Is?'

'I believe it's Kull-Ex,' I said, 'son of Zell-Ex.'

'Right!' the boy cried. 'See, Daddy. I told you it was interesting.'

Victor crossed his arms. 'Oh, thanks for nothing, Miss Con-roy. I leave you alone for one minute and you start colluding with the enemy.' He strode to the balcony and gazed into the court. 'What's happening down there? Any idea?'

'I'm afraid we got a bit sidetracked.' I leaned back in the chair. 'And, I have to tell you, this super outlaw from Krypton is much more riveting than any squash game. Isn't that right, Jonathan?'

'Yup,' said the boy, sliding the pages. 'Loads better.'

His father spun round, looking half amused, half agitated. 'They're still playing. From the looks of it, Dulcie's got the beat-ing of her.'

'That's what Kull-Ex thought on the mountaintop,' I said, 'but it didn't turn out too rosily in the end.'

Victor stared at me, eyes bulging behind his spectacles. 'Wow, he's really done a job on you. I wasn't even gone that long.'

I reached to ruffle the boy's hair as a show of unity, then thought better of it, patting his shoulder instead. Standing up, I said, 'He's impeccably behaved. A real credit to you both.'

This seemed to resonate with Victor more than I anticipated. 'Oh—well, yes,' he said, 'thank you for that. I mean, *we've* always liked him.'

The crack of rubber on walls grew louder. I glanced down at the match: Amanda's shirt was now so wet I could see the straps of her bra through it, and Dulcie's knee was trickling blood. I was not sure how much longer the two of them would survive if they kept up this intensity of play. Their arms were shining, their faces burning red, like two old fighters in a Bernard Cale drawing.

'To tell you the truth, I don't really see enough of the boy these days,' Victor went on. 'That's mostly what this trip is about. I thought, if work's going to drag me to New York again, then we'll *all* go this time—make a holiday of it. He's never been further than Hunstanton before.' His voice was quieter now but more intense. 'Maybe that's why he's so fixated on the planet Krypton, I don't know. Mandy is convinced the comics are stunting him socially.'

'And what do you think?' I said, peering back at the boy. He seemed content, even composed.

'I think they definitely stimulate his imagination—no bad thing—but I worry how much they're occluding his perspective on the world.'

'I don't follow.'

'I'm saying, if he fixates too much on the land of superheroes, there's a danger that reality will always seem disappointing. That can lead to genuine behavioural problems in the long run. I've seen it in a lot of my patients. Not with comics, in their case, but science fiction novels, television. The research suggests we ought to be wary.'

'You're a doctor?' I said.

'Yes—a psychiatrist. Did I not mention that?'

'No.'

'Well, I try not to lead off with that leg, you know. Sets people against me before I've had a chance to lobotomise them.' He coughed awkwardly. 'That was a joke. An old one. Anyway—' He sniffed and steered his eyes down to the court again. 'You haven't told me what you do. How'd you know an old tyrant like Dulcie?'

'Her gallery represents me. I'm a painter.'

'Oh, wow. Forgive me. That *is* exciting.' He lifted his brow to edge up his glasses. 'I suppose that means *she* works for *you* then, doesn't it?'

'That's not quite how I'd put it. But she's very good at what she does.'

'No doubt she's tenacious,' Victor conceded. 'What sort of pictures are we talking about here? Portraits?'

'Now and then. I usually paint from memory. Things I've seen or imagined. But I'm not sure there's much of a future in it.'

'Why not?'

I shrugged. 'The research suggests I ought to be wary.'

'Ah, very good,' he said, nodding. 'Still, research can be flawed. There are charlatans and scoundrels in every walk of life.'

'Yes, I suppose I've got to stop doubting myself and just paint. But I've got so many voices in my head at the moment. I thought I might be able to outrun a few of them out here.'

'Well—' He surveyed the limits of the viewing gallery. 'If you can find any relief aboard this heap of metal, good luck to you. Failing that, I know a very good person in New York who you could talk to. I have his number somewhere.'

'A professional, you mean?'

'Yes, he really is terrific.' He squinted at me, tapping his chin. 'What are you? Five foot five, twenty-odd years of age. I wouldn't think he'd charge you any more than thirty dollars an hour.'

This seemed to be another of his jokes.

'Look,' he said, evening his face, 'you don't have to talk to anyone if you don't want to. But this chap is a friend of mine, and he's helped a lot of people get their muses back. Can't move for struggling artists in the Village these days.' He reached into his pocket, as though to retrieve a business card, but came out with a scrap of paper. 'In case you want to look him up while you're in town . . .'

Victor had such a placid temperament, such an innocuous way of inducing conversation that I almost felt obliged to explain myself to him right there in the viewing gallery. 'Oh, I don't know,' I said. 'I've never really believed much in the powers of psychiatry. No disrespect to you. The only thing that's ever helped me feel any better is painting. And now—well, now I suppose I'll have to take up squash.'

'Perhaps you will.' He unscrewed the cap on the steward's pen and scribbled a line on the paper, holding it to the rail. Then, folding it up, he said, 'That's the number, anyway. He's just a block from Union Square.'

'Thank you.' I put the paper inside my book without even glancing at it.

'Funny, I don't think I've ever known Jonathan to stay this quiet before,' Victor said, pocketing the pen. 'How on earth did you manage it?'

'Kryptonite.'

'Please. You'd be amazed how often I hear that.'

Almost in unison, we moved to check on the boy. He was crumpled in the chair, asleep, with the comic still open at his chest.

'He seems to be out for the count,' Victor said. 'Hang on. Don't say anything—you'll jinx it.' He walked over to Jonathan and took the comic gently from his clutches. Then he laid his jacket across the boy, sat down on the chair beside him, and skimmed the pages with a face of consternation.

The match trudged on below us. I could hear Dulcie grunting like a bull, her thudding footwork, and Amanda's helpless cries. The ship began to pitch again, and I felt a quiver in my knees, a rising nausea. I gripped the railing, and must have looked unstable on my feet, because Victor called out in a hushed voice: 'Everything all right?'

'Just a little seasick,' I said.

'There are medicines for that, you know.'

'Yes, I'm taking pennyroyal and honey. Dulcie swears by it.'

'Crikey. That won't do. You might as well take salt and pepper.' He stood up, stooping to lift the boy, jacket and all. 'A little

Dramamine is all you need. Hand me that briefcase, would you? I have to get this one downstairs before he wets the upholstery.' The boy's legs hung and swayed like wind chimes in his father's arms. 'He doesn't sleep much, but when he does, the bladder goes with him.' Victor reached to take the case from me; I hooked it over his fingers. 'Thank you.'

'Will I see you at dinner?'

Victor inhaled, considering my question; his answer came rushing out in one breath. 'Depends.'

'On what?'

'The result,' he said, nodding at the court. 'Mandy hates to lose.'

When I got back to my suite, I found my telephone had been replaced with a much fancier unit: it had a carved jade handset and a golden stand, like something Fabergé could have crafted. I had asked the crew manager to remove the original phone that morning, as the ability to call London from my room at any moment was too great a temptation. But he had clearly mistaken this request for a complaint about the furnishings and had supplied me with an item several times more alluring.

'*Connecting now,*' said the girl at the switchboard. The engaged tone sounded again, and the girl's voice came back: '*I'm sorry. It seems to be busy. Should I try it one more time?*'

'Yes, if you don't mind.'

'*Not at all. Connecting now.*'

The warble of the dial tone went on and on, and then: '*Hello. Connaught Hotel.*' The line was surprisingly clear.

'Oh, good. It's been hard to get through. Are you closed?'

'*My apologies, madam. I'm the only one at the desk at the moment and the phones haven't stopped.*'

I had forgotten there was a time lag between London and the mid-Atlantic, and I must have been calling in their peak hour. Now what was I supposed to say? 'Well, I think I left a scarf somewhere in your hotel. About five weeks ago.'

'*I see. And where exactly did you lose it?*'

'In the corridor. I think it might have been handed in by one of your guests.'

'*Do you know the guest's name?*'

'It's Searle, Wilfred Searle.'

'*Ah yes, of course. Mr Searle. I'm afraid he's no longer staying at the hotel, but if you describe the scarf I'll see if I can—*'

'Did he leave a forwarding address? It's just that, well, I'd really like to thank him for his kindness.'

'*I'll check that for you, madam. Please hold.*' I could hear nothing for a moment but my own huffing in the earpiece. Then: '*I'm sorry, he didn't say where he was moving on to this time. But we do have his billing address. So if you'd like to write to him care of the hotel, we'll make sure the letter reaches him.*'

'Thank you. I'll do that.'

'*Now perhaps you could describe—*'

There were three little knocks on my door. 'Excuse me for a moment,' I said. 'Have to let someone in.'

'*Of course, madam.*'

I set the phone down on the table and went to answer, expecting to be met by a stewardess with a silver trolley and a little dish of English honey for my tea. Instead, I found Dulcie standing crookedly in the corridor. She was listing to the right, as though missing a crutch, with her tracksuit top buttoned all the way up. 'I've completely wrecked my shoulder,' she said, nudging her way past me. 'Have you got any aspirin?'

'Yes. Somewhere, I think.'

She smelled a little tarry. Her hair was wet and combed, clipped oddly at one side. 'Sorry, were you in the middle of something?' she said, noticing the phone was off the hook.

'Oh, don't mind that. Just calling my mother.' I went and put the ugly thing back on its perch.

'Well, that's no way to treat her, is it?' Dulcie said. 'Poor woman.' She fixed herself a glass of tonic water at the bar, one-armed, and sat down on the couch. 'Anyway, aren't you going to ask me the score?'

'It was two all when I left. I assume you didn't lose.'

'Of course I bloody didn't!' She downed half the tonic, then rolled her arm about in its socket, wincing. 'Actually, I thought she was getting on top of me in the last, but then I started to clear a little bit faster to the T, and she didn't have the energy to keep up.'

'What happened to your shoulder?' I said.

'Not sure. It's just muscular, I think. A good massage ought to fix it.'

'I'll get you that aspirin.'

'You're a darling. Thanks.'

I went to the bathroom and dug out a bottle from my vanity case. There were only two pills left. Coming back into the sitting room, I found Dulcie lying on the couch with my fancy phone clutched to her ear and her dusty squash shoes on the cushions. 'Mm-hm. All right, then we'll just have to take what's available,' she was saying. 'Very good of you to fit us in. Thank you.' Hanging up, she reached out for the aspirin bottle. 'Is this all you've got?'

'Yes, sorry, I thought I had more.'

'They'll do for now, I suppose.' She tipped the pills straight into her mouth and swallowed, chasing them with tonic. 'There's a dispensary aboard somewhere. Let me know if you need anything.'

'Have you ever taken Dramamine?' I said.

'No, and I don't think I want to.'

'I'm still getting the queasiness, that's all.' My hands dropped to my belly.

'Always takes a while to find your sea legs, first time round. We're not far off land now, anyway.' She gave a timid burp into her fist. 'Ugh. Sorry. Your tonic's awfully warm.'

'Who was that on the phone?'

'The Turkish baths,' she said. 'I've booked us in for quarter past.'

'You're not dragging *me* down there with you.'

'Well, I can't go on my own again,' Dulcie said. She got up, kneading her shoulder. 'You never quite know who's lurking in those cubicles, and, yesterday, I got saddled with the most dreadful Chicago woman. Please don't be difficult about this. I'm in agony.'

– – – – – –

As we headed down the corridor in our dressing gowns and slippers, Dulcie paused by a room marked ELECTRIC THERAPY. 'I've always wondered what goes on in there,' she said, trying to see in through the keyhole. Narrow strips of ultraviolet light tinged the edges of the doorframe, brightening her face, showing all its downy hairs. 'I don't see any electrodes or wires. Perhaps I'll give it a go.' She straightened up, clutching her shoulder as though plugging a bullet wound. We moved past the locker rooms towards a line of cubicles screened off with drapes. At the reception desk, an attendant in a white uniform greeted us and ticked our names in his ledger. 'Mrs Fenton, if you'd like to follow Katarina, she'll soon have those kinks worked out of you,' he said, then set his big wet eyes on me. 'Miss Conroy, is there a particular treatment you're interested in today? I'm afraid the jet-showers are currently out of order, but everything else is more than ship-shape.'

'I'd rather go with Dulcie,' I said, 'if that's all right.'

The attendant went quiet. He knitted his lips and brought his hands together. 'Well, there's only space for one in the massage room—it's fully booked.'

'You can wait for me in the baths, darling. I shan't be long.' Dulcie headed off with her masseuse, calling back to me, 'Raymond will take care of you, won't you, Raymond?'

'She'll have nothing but the best,' the attendant said. He turned to me, presenting the empty corridor. 'Let me show you to the hot rooms, madam.' He walked on, reeling off a very practised script about the levels of pampering that were available to me, and I trailed behind, pretending to be tempted by all his talk of 'alcohol rubs' and varieties of soap. The further we went, the drier the air became, and my forehead began to mist over. I could not tell if I felt more or less seasick, but I was building up a serious thirst. 'Tell me, madam, how much heat do you favour?'

I thought it was a very strange question and did not know how to reply.

The attendant smiled, as though familiar with this type of silence, as though it were the lifeblood of his working week. 'If I might make a suggestion?' He paused here, quite dramatically. 'Most of our female guests prefer the caldarium—we keep that running at a hundred and seventy-five, Fahrenheit, that is. But if you like it a bit warmer, we have the laconicum.'

'And how hot is that?'

'Well, we'd never let you cook all the way through,' he said, tittering. 'We keep it around two hundred degrees. As I say, most of the female guests prefer— '

'The caldarium,' I said. 'That will be fine.'

'Lovely. You'll find towels as you go in. It's just this door to your right, madam.'

- - - - - -

Nobody will teach you this at art school, but there are many ways to paint a room from memory. You can construct it from delinquent parts: take a fixture from the ceiling of your childhood bedroom, a fall of light from the refectory of a hospital you once attended with your mother, a carpet borrowed from a rented flat in Maida Vale, and assemble them like scraps. You can add flesh to a skeleton of facts: keep the magnolia tiles you know for sure were there and colour them in grey; thicken the mist with candle wax; steal the women from the first-class poolside, paint them lounging chest-down on those tiles in swimming costumes, shine their hair, fatten their legs, shade their backs a different pink. With enough thought and industry, you can paint a room that has no visible joins, which reveals more truth than any photograph could capture, because who could ever dispute what you have seen with your own eyes? Only by painting it this way—grinding it to powder and rebuilding it, particle by particle—can you fully understand what a room means to you. But, sometimes, all this does is reconstitute a whole that would be better left in fragments, like fixing up a shredded letter just to read your old bad news. If you construct a room in paint, you haunt it. Your life rests in every stroke. So paint only the rooms that you can bear to occupy forever. Or paint the stars instead.

- - - - - -

Sitting down to lean my head against the tiles, the tension in my breast began to ease, and I could feel the heat drawing the dirt of London from my body the way that sunshine teases oil out of tarmac. The caldarium was almost empty. On the tiled shelf that skirted the far wall, two women lay frontwise with their arms bent out, their heads a yard apart, just close enough to talk without raising their voices. I could not see their faces, only the scoured pinkness of their backs, the long wet knots of hair that fell over their shoulders. There was a soothing scent of rosewater, a kindness to the light. And it occurred to me that I had found the one space on the ship where I could be at peace: a priestly kind of sanctum between decks, not quite silent, not quite vacant. So what if it was hot enough inside to raise a soufflé?

I spread a towel upon the shelf and lowered myself onto it. The air was thick as plaster and I had to concentrate on breathing. Ten-second inhalations through the nose, out through the mouth. As the rhythm of my heart slowed down, so did my mind. I shut my eyes, surrendered to the heat. It was as if my thoughts started to pearl and separate, like a paint that rests too long inside a can. Everything relaxed: my limbs, my tongue, my neck. And soon I was envisioning things in the bleary heat. I was outdoors, walking in a field beneath the high noon sun. There were fairground rides in the distance. A rag-and-bone man was ambling up the grassy slope towards me, his horse beleaguered, nostrils steaming. It was pulling a cart with a pile of old rocking chairs and balusters. And then I heard the women stirring near by, and this picture fell away.

My pulse felt like a dripping tap, and I was strangely cool inside. The ship's engines were juddering the shelf I lay upon. And the attendant was calling over a loudspeaker: '*Would you describe it as an aggravating scarf, madam? Is it meek and insubstantial?*' The tiles looked greyer when I opened my eyes.

Such heat.

In through the nose, out through the—

My body was laced in sweat—strangely cool—but mostly it was underneath me, in the creases of my thighs. I tried to sit up, and I felt the bones lurch out of me, slip right through my skin— '*Let me show you the On Highs, madam. We'll soon have those kinks worked out of you*'—or perhaps I had just skidded off the shelf and dropped onto the carpet—'*There, there*'—because, when I glanced up—strangely cool—Dulcie was standing right over me, wrapped in a towel, squeezing my hand—'*Don't you ever stop criticising? No, it's a permanent vocation*'—and she was patting my forehead with a cold flannel, and saying, 'I'll wait with her. You go.'

The sweat between my legs was heavy, cloying, cold. I thought I gave an answer: 'No, it's just a cheap thing from the market, not even real silk,' but I must not have got the words out. I must only have murmured something meaningless. And she shushed me—'*There, there, darling, your work will get better*'—and patted my brow and squeezed my hand tighter. Then, reaching down, I felt my belly sink and spill.

'Ellie, don't move now, you hear?' Dulcie said, and she tore off the towel from around herself and pushed it on my thighs. I did not understand. What difference did it make? I was not seasick any more. 'Just lie still,' said Dulcie. 'The doctor's coming.' She was a scrawny, chicken-boned woman, old Dulcie, but she had a lot of strength—'*No doubt she's tenacious*'—and she stopped me touching what was all over my calves and ankles. I thought I answered her again: 'She never even used that icing knife, you know.' But I did not hear the noise come out of me, and the next face I saw belonged to some man I did not recognise. He said, 'Miss Conroy, I'm just going to slip these off you now, all right?' Then I felt him cut the sides of my swimming costume briefs and watched as he slung them, red and heavy, like the tresses of a butcher's mop, onto the rolling floor that held us.

- - - - - -

Another room, a different ceiling. The ship was full of them. I woke up in the hospital bay with the doctor and a po-faced nurse about my feet. My mouth was parched, my lips felt raw. It took effort just to hold my eyelids open. I was curtained off in blue. A tube was in my arm, feeding me what looked like seawater, and the quiet consultation of the voices at the end of my bed was giving me the sense that I had not yet fully come to.

'Miss Conroy, good evening,' the doctor said. He stepped onto my starboard side and strapped me with a blood pressure cuff. 'You've had a bit of an ordeal, my dear, but everything will be fine now.' He told me his name—Dr Randall—and explained that he was making his very first voyage as the ship's physician. 'I thought it would be easier than joining the Navy,' he joked. 'I was wrong.' Smiling, he pumped at the rubber bulb inside his fist until there was a tightness in my arm and the flesh beneath my elbow seemed as numbstruck as the rest of me. He waited, nodded slightly at the reading on the dial, and hummed. 'That's looking better.' The pressure released, tingling my fingers. 'You know, if you'd made someone aware of your condition,' he went on, all the good humour fading from his voice, 'they could have warned you against the Turkish baths. It's such a shame this had to happen to you.'

I did not want to disagree with him, and my tongue was too dried up to speak anyway.

'Would you like some water?' said Randall, watching my attempts to quench my palate. The nurse filled up a beaker for me. She left it on the table, just within reach.

It tasted like metal, but I glugged it all down.

Randall stood there, fiddling with his tie. 'Do you understand what's happened to you, Miss Conroy?' he said. When I did not answer, he cornered his eyes at the nurse.

'Do you know where you are, dear?' she said.

'I think so.'

'Where?' The little watch on her uniform was hanging upside down, confusing me.

'On the *QE*,' I said. 'The hospital.'

This seemed to come as a relief to them. 'Good,' said Randall. 'That's good.' He was fidgeting so much with his tie that the knot was getting smaller, tighter. 'I don't think you'll require surgery. You've passed a lot of blood and tissue on your own. But we'll keep you in overnight just to be sure. It should be fine to disembark tomorrow with the rest of the passengers—but I won't rush you out of here, if your fluids are still down.'

'Where's Dulcie?' I said.

'I don't know who that is, I'm sorry.'

'Mrs Fenton,' said the nurse.

'Ah, yes. I believe she went up to her room to change. I can have somebody reach her, if you like.'

I nodded. 'We're supposed to have meetings in New York tomorrow night.'

'Well, I'm sure you can postpone. It's no small thing you've been through here.' He gave me a kindly look, tapping my feet. 'Bed rest for a few days, I should think.' Then he backed out through the curtain.

The nurse refilled my beaker. She checked the steady drip of fluid in my tube. 'Don't you worry, my love,' she said, rocking my shoulder. 'My sister lost hers at seven months. It's just about the worst thing that can happen, it really is, but she's had two since then, and never had no trouble. So don't you worry about anything like that. You're going to be fine. Here you are—drink this—let's keep those liquids up. We can't have you stuck on this old boat forever now, can we?'

- - - - -

Dulcie felt so guilty about her part in things that she withdrew from the final of her squash tournament and came visiting me in the hospital bay twice that evening, and once more the day after. I would have preferred to be left alone. I did not blame her, or anyone else, for what had happened, but she was insistent on claiming responsibility ('I should never have made you go for that drink with him . . . We should probably have flown . . . I should never have forced you to come down to the baths. What was I thinking?'). Honestly, I could not abide this type of self-involvement, as though the entire balance of the world hinged on the probity of one person's actions. I was grateful for her sympathy, of course, and for the way she had looked after me in the caldarium. But the longer I spent in Dulcie's company, the harder it became to ignore the blankness of her personality, and I wanted—more than anything—to stay friends.

So I let her sit at my bedside, chuntering on about the gall of Wilfred Searle, and how she was going to personally see to it that he never set foot in the Roxborough again: 'I don't care *who* his uncle is—it's about time someone taught him how a real man should behave.' That evening, she brought in copies of *Life* magazine and read aloud the captions from the photo essays for me, speaking in superior tones about the people in them. She made no mention of the blood and tissue that had spilled out of me just a few hours before, the human thing that I had lost and could not reconcile my feelings for. It was not her fault, of course. Even if she had tried to broach the matter, I would not have wanted to listen. Because I was not yet sure what I needed to be consoled for—the life I had evacuated, or the one I was forced to continue. And so, to prompt her into leaving, I pretended to fall asleep on each of the occasions that she visited. I could not bring myself to answer any of her questions, and spent long moments gazing into space.

'You really mustn't worry,' Dulcie said. 'I know we all keep telling you that—and it probably sounds like a lot of mollycoddling—but, really, you *will* get over this. Things will get back to normal. Elspeth, darling, are you listening? Please. I can't bear to see you in this state.'

Evacuated. That was the word the physician had used. A horribly clinical term—compassionless—and yet it captured how I felt about myself for so long afterwards: as though I were a danger that required escaping. I wondered if it was truly possible to feel bereft of something I had never wanted. Part of me had hoped to be rid of Wilfred's burden, and I had speculated, once or twice, if I possessed the wherewithal to throw myself down a flight of stairs to make it happen. Of course, these instincts had been overruled by that other part of me, the one that had pathetic notions of bringing the child to term, of loving it, raising it to be a fine member of society just to spite its father. But there was no denying the fact that I had *chosen* to lie down in the heat of that caldarium—it was no accident or oversight—and perhaps that is why I was overcome by such torpor that I could barely lift my head from the pillow. I could not blame Wilfred Searle any more for my misfortunes. I had *chosen* to put myself where I was, and there was no forgiving it.

Dulcie must have said something to Amanda Yail about my being in the hospital bay, or else the news must have found its way to Victor by some other means. Because, not long after breakfast on the last day of the voyage, he appeared at the fringes of my cubicle with his briefcase. 'Present for you,' he said, setting an envelope on my table. The flap was not stuck down and I could already tell what was inside. 'You don't have to open it now,' he said, but I did.

It was a home-made card with GET WELL SOON! scribbled in dark blue crayon. There was a muddy picture of what looked like Kull-Ex flying over a New York skyscraper. And, on the reverse, in adult writing, it said: *Your super friend, Jonathan.*

'Thanks,' I said. 'That's very sweet of you.'

'Not my idea,' said Victor. 'Actually, I thought you might find it a little insensitive. I wasn't sure if I should bring it or not.'

'I'm glad you did.'

'Well, the lad wouldn't take no for an answer. Mandy's taken him down to the pool to keep him occupied—he was begging to come with me, but I thought I'd spare you that, at least.'

In fact, the thought of talking to the boy again about his comics was as close as I had felt to happiness in days. 'I really wouldn't have minded,' I said.

'He'll be very glad you liked the card. Took him ages to draw. May I—?' He gestured at the empty chair beside the bed and did not wait for my approval, sitting with his briefcase on his lap. 'I hope you don't mind me visiting you like this, but I heard you weren't in the best of spirits, and I just—well, I wanted to make sure you were OK. Only natural to get depressed, considering.'

'I appreciate the thought,' I said, and looked away—anywhere but into those sympathetic eyes. I did not deserve them.

'Look,' Victor said cagily, 'you can tell me if I'm overstepping the mark here, but something's been nagging me all afternoon.'

I did not respond, just rolled my head in his direction.

'You were taking pennyroyal,' he said, with a querying tone. 'For the seasickness.'

'Yes,' I said.

'Hmm.' He drummed his briefcase. 'And how much of that were you taking?'

'God, I don't know, Victor. What does it matter?' I hoped to sound just the right amount offended.

'It's been known to have certain side effects, that's all, in large doses.' His fingers pushed at the leather, rippling it. 'I wondered if Dulcie was aware of that when she recommended it.'

'I'm sure she wasn't.'

'No, of course not. I wasn't suggesting—never mind.' He looked around the hospital bay, studying the decor. 'This place seems very well equipped.'

'It's a hospital. They're all the same.'

'Oh, not true. You should see some of the wards I had to train in.' We were completely alone in the room. Victor was the only person I had seen besides Dulcie, the physician, and the nurse for the past twelve hours or so, and I suspected he knew it.

'Look, if you don't mind, Victor, I'm getting rather tired.'

But he would not be hurried or distracted. 'It's an abortifacient, that's my point. Well, supposedly it is. No medical proof for it, as such, but, anyway—there you are.' Pushing up his glasses with his little finger, he stood, and lingered by my bedside for so long I thought he was about to kiss my forehead. 'Like I said, it's been nagging me all day. Why would you be taking pennyroyal? I should have spotted it sooner.' And he gave a disbelieving chuckle. 'That number I gave you,' he said. 'Throw it out. The chap I recommended won't be right for you. Too Freudian.'

'What?'

'I'm serious.' He set down his briefcase on the foot of my bed, unclipped it, and began rummaging underneath the files. 'I want you to come and see me once you get back to London. It might take a bit of time, but I think I can help you.'

'With what?'

'Your anxiety depression.' He glanced up from his case. 'I don't mean what happened yesterday—I mean what came before. Those are the issues you need to confront, or you'll never come to terms with what you've lost. And I won't just stand aside and watch that happen to you.' He went back to rooting for whatever he was searching for. It was as though I was still on the grubby banquette in Henry Holden's office.

'I told you, I don't need a psychiatrist,' I said. 'I have painting.'

'Is that so?'

'I'm sorry if that puts you out of a job, but it's how I've always dealt with things.'

'And how would you say that's been working for you so far?'

'Don't patronise me, Victor.'

He gave a surrendering nod. 'It's just, I heard you didn't really *do* much painting these days, or finish anything, at least. Isn't that what you told me?' At last, he gave up rummaging in his briefcase and shut the lid. 'Look, I'm afraid I've run out of cards. So this'll have to do—' He tore off the top page of a white prescription pad and handed it to me. 'I really hope you'll take me seriously.'

DR VICTOR YAIL, M.D., F.R.C.L., D.P.M.

'Can't trust a man with letters after his name,' I said. 'That's what my father used to say.'

'I tell you what—' Victor clipped his case shut. 'If you can make it through the next few days without leaping off any sky-scrapers, I'll let you know what they all stand for. Now, can I bank on you to make an appointment?'

Four

At the factory, my mother punched her timecard every morning, then counted down the hours before she got to punch it out again. From the year she left school into her middle fifties, she kept exactly the same job, and if the amount a person complains about her work is an adequate barometer of her satisfaction, then she must have found great joy in it.

At the John Brown & Company yard, my father scorched the skin right off his knuckles daily, caulking ships with men he looked upon as brothers, some of whom he brought back home to share our dinner, some of whom he lent our rainy-day money. He wore down every rung of cartilage in his spine, broke several ribs, developed shin splints, and laboured through the agony, one shift at a time, for measly pay and no assurance of a future.

I admired the doggedness of my parents more than I was ever able to express to them. They grafted to accomplish things for other people, knowing all their hard work would go unseen. My father never felt what it was like to cross the ocean on a vessel he constructed with his friends, nor did he really care to—in his mind, every ship died when it left the yard. My mother never walked the aisles of the department stores that stocked her sewing machines, though she brought home boxes of the reject needles to stitch our curtains and communion dresses for the neighbours' children.

I cannot say how much of their resolve I managed to inherit. Some days, it felt as though I had been gifted with my father's vim, and I could stand up at my easel for long periods, forgetting where I was. Other times, I was steeled by my mother's uncomplaining attitude, and would not let a good idea escape my grasp, even if it took me several weeks to tame it.

But doggedness in art is no substitute for inspiration. The thrill of painting turns so quickly to bewilderment if you let it, and nobody can help you to regain your bearings afterwards. Talent sinks into the lightless depths like so much rope unless you keep a firm hold on it, but squeeze too tight and it will just as surely drag you under.

By the summer of 1960, I was unable to determine a clear reason to continue making pictures, aside from the dim hopefulness that kept lifting me from bed at 6 a.m. to try again. The only way to shake off failure, I thought, was by perseverance and hard work, and if I did not rise to paint each morning at my usual hour then I was denying myself another chance to succeed. And so I carried on through the soreness, as my father would have done, without protest, even though my hands no longer had the skill to translate what I asked of them. I approached each canvas as I always did—with no preconceived ideas, just a willingness to paint—and proceeded to get nowhere.

It is a painter's job to give shape to things unseeable, to convey emotion in the accumulation of gestures, the instinctive, the considered, the unplanned. There is both randomness and pre-destination to the act of painting, a measurement and a chaos, and the moment you allow the mind to implicate itself too much in the business of the heart, the work will falter. It is not something you can control. You might toil long and hard, bullying the paint until it agrees to do your bidding, but you will only beat the life right out of it. And when you reach the stage where you are not expressing feeling in your work but engineering it, you might as well become a forger, or present yourself at a museum and donate your skills to the conservation of its masterpieces. Otherwise, you will be tempted to hang your feeble efforts on the wall and say, 'Good enough,' seeing pound signs where there should be meaning. You must resist this temptation with every fibre of your being.

I tried everything I could to remain true to such convictions during the New York trip and afterwards. I stayed each day in my hotel room on Sixth Avenue, staring out at the gridded puzzle of the city from my thirty-fifth-floor window, drawing the patterns of its dense, dissembling streets and the polished deadness of its architecture. I filled both of the sketchbooks I had brought with me, then used up the hotel notepaper, until all I had left to draw on were a few blank pages at the end of *Below the Salt*. Of course, I had some yearning to go out into the city and experience it on foot, to understand it the same way that I had learned to appreciate the mysteries of London, but something kept me cooped up in the hotel all week—an anxiety that tensed my throat when I stood at the bathroom mirror putting on my make-up, a shame that wetted my eyes. The first morning, I got up and dressed but could not get beyond the threshold. The next,

I reached the midpoint of the hallway and panicked; I heard the voices of other guests approaching in the corridor, got very shallow-breathed and wobbly, then paced back to my room, groping the walls. It did not feel right to be amongst people yet, and the city was teeming with strangers.

During the cab ride from the harbour with Dulcie, I had felt the kerbside energy of the place so intensely it had stunned me into silence. It was as though we had arrived at the very terminus of possibility, the patch of land where everything I cherished most about the world—art, imagination, freedom of expression— existed in the shade of everything I feared: corporations, brinkmanship, the preying of dogs on dogs. It was obvious to me that Jim could never have endured a town so hustling and kinetic, so pitiless and upward-facing, and this robbed me of the only scrap of purpose I had left. I had no interest in a New York City without Jim Culvers in it. So, when the hotel porter showed me to my room, I tipped him a dollar, sent him on his way, and locked the door. I was supposed to join Dulcie and Leonard Hines that night for dinner at Delmonico's, but I cried off, and twice more in the days that followed. Eventually, a breakfast meeting was arranged for us in the hotel restaurant, and we sat clumsily discussing things, not mentioning my sweats or the trembling of my hands upon the teapot. Leonard Hines introduced himself by saying, 'Dee-Dee tells me you're her girl most likely. Hope that's true. I've seen a little of your work, it's—well, it's interesting. I wonder, though, where are you taking things right now? I mean, in what direction are you headed?'

I just dabbed at the table with my napkin and told him, 'I'm not sure yet. Somewhere good, I hope.' And I turned to Dulcie, saying, 'I've been thinking: would you mind if I flew back to-morrow instead?'

'If that's what you want. She didn't have the best time on the ship with me,' Dulcie said, by way of explanation to Leonard, who was squinting at her for assurance. Nothing was said about my brief stint in the hospital bay or what had put me there, bloody evacuations on the high seas not being the anecdote one prefers to tell during business hours.

'Ah,' he said. 'Well, I'm sure my secretary can look into that for you. We have a very good arrangement with Pan Am.'

'I suppose I'll be sailing home alone then,' Dulcie said. 'Ter-rific.'

I thanked them both and went back to picking at my pan-cakes. We exchanged the lightest talk about Leonard's youngest daughter—she had just been admitted into the art history pro-gramme at Radcliffe, a feat that made him 'just incredibly proud'. Had I realised that this was a prestigious women's college at the time, I might have feigned some admiration for her achieve-ments, and not mistaken Leonard's constant use of the phrase 'Seven Sisters' for the area of North London where I once went to buy a second-hand gramophone from a woman with no teeth. He was obviously unimpressed by me, and this exasperated Dul-cie, who sat across the table making reproachful faces at my lack of discourse. 'Don't ever embarrass me like that again,' she said, as we went back up in the lift. 'You could've at least *tried* to look interested.' It was a painful and disastrous meeting, but I had no regrets about it.

As soon as I got back to Kilburn, I cleared my studio and primed a stack of canvases taller and wider than I had ever worked upon before. The New York sketches I had made were pinned up on the Anaglypta near my bed so I could glean some inspiration from them. I ordered a few boxes of oil paints to be delivered to my door and bought in powdered milk and biscuits, tinned vegetables, corned beef, and mushroom soup from the corner grocery—enough to last me several weeks. The urge to paint was rife in me again, and I did my best to seize upon it.

I exchanged the sanctuary of my hotel room for the shelter of my studio, leaving only to collect my mail from the vestibule. I saw nobody except my downstairs neighbours: a kind old theatre director and her husband. The sun rose and set behind my curtains (I stapled them to the frame, preferring to paint in the softness of lamplight, as it helped me focus on the work). I lived sleeplessly in one room with just the kitchen window open, letting out the turps fumes and the fusty stench of my own body (I bathed nightly, of course, but sweated so much in between that my clothes were stiff and yellowed). My hair kept swinging into my eyes, so I cut it with the kitchen scissors.

What did I paint? All I know are the intentions I set out with, and where I ended up.

I hoped to reveal some sense of the caldarium in abstract, to work out how I truly felt about what happened there. But the figures I implanted in the scene looked manufactured, much too literal, so I scraped them off and tried again, only to find myself painting the exact same faces without the pleasing darkness of the originals. I scraped them off and gessoed over them. The more I tried to paint the figures, the more they seemed to signify a falsehood: I had not seen the caldarium from that dislocated viewpoint, hovering over my own body like a vulture; I had seen it mostly from the floor. So I put in a skewed doorway and built up the foreground with an impression of tiles, and then—over-thinking it—I merged it with a sunny field, a Ferris wheel, and a rag-and-bone man's horse. Nothing cohered. The whole scene was contrived and ill-defined, but I continued with it, extending the idea just to see if it would stumble to fruition nonetheless. I ignored my instincts, guiding the paint too consciously, and lost my feeling for the work.

Week after week, I painted like this, with no end result. I re-constructed every picture I began, scrubbing it clean, scraping off and undercoating, layering and layering and layering. The can-vases were laden with so much material that they warped and fell on their faces. I used up every tube of paint I owned. At one stage, I got bored with all my brushes, so I dumped them in the bin and used a butter knife instead, slathering and smoothing anything still left to spread or yet to dry. My furniture got slowly caked in paint. I had to pull up the carpet in my bedroom to save the parts of it I had not ruined, and soon every floorboard was scumbled with a gunge of linseed oil and wax. Dingy liquids quivered in soup cans all about the studio. My clothes looked like a combat uniform. But still the work did not reveal a single speck of what I hoped it would. And, worse, I felt no thrill in making it.

Then, one night—so late the wireless in my room had reached the end of programming—Dulcie called to say that she was com-ing to the flat. She was concerned that she had not heard from me since getting back to London, and wondered if I had given any further thought to her proposal. I could not recall any pro-posal being put to me, so I stalled on my answer, and told her she could visit me on Saturday. In truth, I had no clue what day it was, and she said, 'Darling, it *is* Saturday.'

I was greatly dissatisfied with the work and felt ashamed to show it, even to Dulcie. But I could not let her think that I had locked myself away for the past few weeks without creating anything. So when she buzzed, I let her in, and heard her feet come clipping up the stairs. I glimpsed her through the spyhole: she was wearing a fur shawl, though it was springtime and the weather had been mild, according to the radio. As I opened the door, she took a backwards stride, as though moving with the draught. But it must have been the sight of me that rocked her on her heels. 'Crikey,' she said. 'This *is* a situation, isn't it?'

'Kettle's on,' I said, standing aside to let her through.

'Nothing for me, thanks. On my way to a party and the cab's still on the meter.' She had already removed her evening gloves outside the door, but, seeing the condition of my flat, she slipped them on again. 'Is everything all right with you?' she asked, rolling her eyes over me. 'You're looking skinny. I presume you've been hard at it.'

'That's one way of putting it,' I said. The kettle began to wheeze and I went off to tend to it.

'Would've been good if you'd picked up the phone once or twice,' Dulcie called, 'just to clue me in on what you're up to. You know I like to let you have your space, but it's been a few months now . . . God, this is an awful lot of soup for one person. Is this all you've been eating? A girl can't live on Heinz alone, you know.'

I busied myself in the kitchen. 'It's hardly been that long.' The tea had not been strained properly and leaves floated in the mug. I put three spoons of powdered milk in anyway.

'No, darling. It's the end of June. I've not heard from you since March.' There was a pause. 'I won't bother asking about your hair. But you might want to think about opening a window. It's like a reptile house in here.'

I was so tired of the timbre of Dulcie's voice, and wearier still of the way she spoke to me.

'So,' she announced, as I came back in to face her, 'where is it all?'

I sipped at my tea. It was gritty and foul, more punishment than comfort. 'All of what?'

'Don't play dumb. The *work*.' She waved towards the jumble of the studio, the speckled walls, the debris. 'I see plenty of wood over there but no paintings. Where are you hiding them?'

'I've been keeping them at Jim's,' I said. 'For extra room.'

'Uh-huh.' She pinched her nostrils for a second, blinking. 'Thought Max would've rented that place out by now.' Her attention caught on something else behind me. 'Well, you must've been churning them out at a fair old rate. Is there *anything* here I could look at? What about the sketches you've got taped up over there?'

'They're nothing,' I said. 'Not yet, anyway.'

'All right. I get the message.' She stared at me. 'And what about January, do we still think that's feasible? I've got from the fourteenth blocked out for you, but I can let someone else take the slot if it's going to be a problem.'

'Whatever you decide.' I had forgotten about the date we had set.

'You're being strange,' she said.

'Am I?'

'Yes. You're never this accommodating.'

'Well, perhaps you'd like to go outside again and I'll leave you on the doorstep.'

She smiled. 'That's *much* more like it.' Stepping over a row of huddled soup cans, she went to inspect the empty stretcher frames on the far side of the room. I knew that she would be too sharp-eyed not to notice the ragged strips of canvas that remained along the borders of each frame, the verges of the images I had carved out. 'You cut them off the stretchers?' she said. 'Why?'

'Had to get them on the bus,' I told her.

She was an astute woman, old Dulcie, and she was not easily persuaded to take your word on things, even if you had not given her much cause to doubt it. That is what made her such a fine director of galleries and such a capricious friend. 'Elspeth darling, I want you to listen to me very carefully,' she said, turning to me with a mothering expression. 'Don't let all this get out of hand, OK?' She made a little circle in the air. 'I know an awful thing happened to you on that ship—and I will personally feel guilty about that for as long as I live—but you can't afford to lose the plot here, do you understand me? I don't want to see you throw away your talent over the first good-looking idiot that comes along.'

'I'm not following you, Dee-Dee,' I said. It was the only time I ever called her by that name and she clearly did not welcome it.

'Then I'll be blunt.' She steepled her fingers. 'I don't mind you locking yourself away like this to work. In fact, I applaud it. But if you're not happy with the stuff you're making, put it aside.

We'll archive it. Don't dig yourself into a hole you can't get out of—understand? If you just want to take a break from painting, be my guest—I'll even sort you out with a little per diem while you're off on your tour of Van Gogh's house, or wherever it is you choose to go. But, for God's sake, don't start cutting things off frames and acting stupid about it, thinking I'm some sort of moron by association. Because it might seem as though you're protecting yourself doing that, upholding the integrity of your art or however you want to put it, but—trust me on this, darling— you're only letting it go to waste. It's for your own sake that I'm saying this.' And she smiled again, as though to soothe me. 'You're young. There's so much ahead of you. Don't start worrying about being the greatest painter in the world for the time being, eh? It's a long career, and not everyone is bound for greatness. Just be you, and you'll do fine.'

It is the unsolicited advice that stays with you, the things that people say under the pretence of kindness. I listened to Dulcie that night when I should have plugged my ears, because I was still too fragile and naïve to argue with her. In London at that time, a word from Dulcie Fenton could just as surely leave an artist snubbed and penniless as it could get them noticed, and I knew I was not strong enough to keep on painting without the cushion of the Roxborough's money. My studio was all I had, and I was too afraid of losing it. I could not stand to fret again about how I would pay for materials, food, gas, water, rent, all the banal concerns that populate the head and stifle the imagi- nation.

'And why do you believe it was such bad advice she gave you?' said Victor Yail. 'Sounds like she was trying to take the pressure off.' He was posed in a suede chair with his legs crossed, readying his pen to jot my answer down. Whenever I trailed off in conversation, he always followed up with pointed questions such as this, inviting me to qualify what should already have been obvious through inference. That was the difference between his world and mine: in art, it was better to remain oblique and let the viewer decide your meaning; in rational therapy, things had to be spelled out in the plainest terms. It took me the first few sessions with Victor to get used to that incongruity.

'Because,' I replied, 'it's important to strive. If you don't have the ambition to be the very best at what you do, then what's the point? If you aim for greatness but keep missing—fine. At least you had the guts to aim. There's honour in failing that way. But there's nothing honourable about settling for mediocrity. It's the same in any profession: if I were a dentist I'd try to be the best bloody dentist in the world, and wouldn't stop until I'd proved it to myself.'

'That's really how you see it?' Victor said.

'I believe I just said so, didn't I?'

Victor gave his customary sigh of forbearance. 'You said *to yourself*—until you'd proved it *to yourself.*'

'Yes.'

'That's an interesting distinction, don't you think?'

'No. Not really.'

He scribbled something down.

'Please stop moving around so much,' I told him, lifting my

brush from the sketchbook paper. 'Every time you make a note like that, the angle of your head changes. And so does the light.'

'I'll try to hold still,' he said.

'Good. Or you're going to look very odd when this is finished.'

'I always do.' He straightened his face. 'Would you say there's something particular you need to prove to yourself, then, when you're painting?'

'I'm not sure.'

'Try to qualify it for me, if you can.'

'Well, I don't know. It really depends on the painting.'

'That sounds like an evasion.'

'Yes, I'm glad you cottoned on to that, Victor.'

For once, he let my glibness go unchecked. 'OK, we'll come back to it.' He scribbled again. 'How do you feel now, about this painting you're doing?'

I stabbed my brush into the gummy square of cad red. '*This silly thing?*' The tone needed lightening with a small dab of water. I mixed it to a suitable pallor on the inside of the paintbox. 'It's difficult to say.'

'Please, try to qualify it.'

I did not lift my head up from the paper. With the cad red, I dimpled the fabric of the strangely patterned wall-hanging beyond Victor's head, adding some reflected colour in the window-panes and the glass-topped surface of his desk. 'Honestly, this has to be the dullest picture I've ever made in my life, and I would very much like to set the thing on fire before I leave so nobody will have to look at it.'

'Right,' Victor said, scribbling. Then he folded his arms. 'I asked you how you were feeling and you've come back at me with a volley of opinion. If you're not going to be sincere about this, we might as well call time on it now.'

'Stop moving around. You're ruining my composition.'

He cleared his throat. 'Ellie—come on—time to be serious.'

I dumped the sketchbook on the floor. 'All right.' The page was not quite dry and some of the colour bled with the impact: tiny veins streaking the paper from the centre outwards. 'As far as feeling anxious goes: *no*, I don't feel anything, not with this kind of work. I could make little pictures like this all day because that's all it is: picture-making. There's no emotional connection with this process whatsoever. I mean, no offence to you, Victor, but doing a quick portrait of you in watercolours isn't any sort of challenge. This whole exercise is meaningless.'

'Ah, but you're painting,' he said. 'That isn't meaningless.'

'I see what you're trying to do. I get it. But, really, this is just like all the stuff I've been knocking out for Dulcie in the last few months—I can finish it, and you can hang it on your wall and say I painted it if you want to, but there's nothing of me in it. It's not art, just decoration.'

'Can I see it?' he said.

I shrugged.

He got up from his chair, flexing his legs, then stooped to gather the portrait I had made. It had taken me just under twenty minutes. Sliding his glasses along his nose to appraise it, he made no sound, tilting it to the afternoon light, as though it were some lost relic he was trying to authenticate. Then he said, 'If that's just decoration, then I mustn't know much about art. May I keep this?'

'All yours.' I held my hand out. 'A couple of hundred ought to cover it.'

'Payment in services rendered.'

'Cheapskate,' I said, and he permitted himself a laugh.

He sat down again with the picture on his knees, admiring it for a moment before swivelling it round for me to look at. 'Why did you paint it this way, if you don't mind my asking?'

'I can't do faces very well,' I said.

'Ellie—serious now—please.'

I had been seeing Victor for the past six months. It had taken an enormous effort just to dial his number to organise an appointment, and an even greater determination to present myself at his office for the first time. But I had done it in the hope of salvaging some aspect of my old self, and Dulcie had been only too delighted to foot the bill. When I had suggested that I might see a therapist instead of taking a break from painting, she had responded with all the enthusiasm I had expected: 'Oh, absolutely— that sounds like a very fine idea to me. Did you have anyone in mind?' I had told her Victor Yail would be the only person I would feel comfortable with. 'Well, if that's something you think you need,' she had said. Then: 'Does that mean January is still a possibility?' I reasoned that if I was going to relax my principles just to appease the Roxborough, then I might as well get something useful out of it, and Victor had been so confident that he could help me overcome my problems.

His practice was on the third floor of a Georgian townhouse in Harley Street. It was a rather clerical environment: just an oak-panelled waiting area with an array of mismatched chairs, and then, through a doorway behind the receptionist's desk, Victor's imperious consulting room, where all my issues were laid bare for him and picked apart. This was a space I knew he took great pride in. Burgundy carpet, mahogany bureau (obscuring most of the good light from the picture window), blocky suede furniture arranged in a perfect L. Between the couch and Victor's armchair was an ankle-height coffee table that held a chessboard, its ornate marble pieces uniformly placed, and the bookshelves were replete with dimly titled volumes and obscure foreign artefacts. Drab lithographs of birds and trees were hung on the walls beside two mystifying Aboriginal tapestries and the many foiled certificates of Victor's education. I had included all these details in the portrait, knowing how much he valued them.

At the beginning of the session, he had given me a rudimentary box of paints, a brush, and a pot of water. 'We're going to try something new today, if that's all right with you.' He had invited me to spend the full hour painting his portrait whilst we conducted our usual discussion. 'I'll just sit in my normal spot, as still as I can, while you talk and paint. Let's see what we end up with.'

Now, he was sitting with the results of my endeavour on his lap, asking me to give the rationale behind it. I did not know where to begin. Therapy seemed to be such an inexact procedure, like wetting your finger and circling it around the rim of a glass, again and again, until it finally rang a note you could define as music. 'The striking thing,' he said, 'is that I'm not in this picture at all. Why is that?'

It was true that I had quite deliberately left Victor out of the image. I had noticed that the watercolour box contained a pot of masking fluid, so I had blanked out the shape of him with this invisible solution and then painted in everything else around him. The fullness of his office was rendered in blotchy detail, right down to the outlying rooftops in the window behind his back, the snowy trail of Harley Street, but Victor was just a white void on the paper, a frame without substance. 'You can still tell it's you, though,' I said.

'Is this how you see me, Ellie?' he asked. 'An empty shell? Not really there?'

'*No.* Don't be ridiculous. I just painted it that way because—' And I trailed off. I could not explain why the notion had come to me. When I tried to, the words came out so unpersuasively: 'I don't know, I thought it would make for a more interesting picture, that's all. Obviously, I see you as a person. Bloody hell. I see *everyone* as a person.'

'Do you see any connection between this picture and your life in general? Absences and what have you?'

'Yes. Fine. You caught me out. I was thinking of Jim, OK, not you.'

'That wasn't quite my point.'

'I know what you were getting at. And I'm still not comfortable discussing it.'

'All right. We'll move past that for now.'

I huffed. 'It's just me trying to be less ordinary. I don't want to be so literal with everything I paint—that was Jim's problem. He had good ideas but he stopped himself exploring them.'

'We aren't here to talk about Jim's problems.'

'Well, it hardly matters. I'm still not abstract enough for some.'

'Who's said that about you—not abstract enough?'

'It wasn't *said*, necessarily. Just implied.'

'By whom?'

I tried to look unfazed by the memory of it. 'There was an important show a few months ago, at the RBA. *Situation*, it was called. You probably heard.'

Victor shook his head. 'I don't get out much. And when I do, it's only to the squash club.'

'Well, Dulcie was pushing to include one of my pieces, a diptych I made last year. But they wouldn't have it in the show.'

'Why not?'

'I have my suspicions.'

'Such as?'

'Doesn't matter. They liked the scale of it, but seemed to think it was too figurative. They said my references to mountains and what have you were a bit too clear and they were after something different.'

'What *were* they looking for?'

'Pure abstraction, I think. No obvious representations of reality, just gesture.'

'I see.' Victor was still holding the portrait up in both hands, but he nodded at me in such a way that I expected he was itching to scribble something down. 'And that made you feel bad, did it?'

'At first, yes. No one likes rejection.' I smoothed the creases from my skirt and gazed into the window. The snow was skeltering down the pane. 'It's really picking up out there again.'

'But now you feel differently about it?' Victor said. His professionalism could be so irritating at times—I was never allowed to deflect from a sore subject while we were in session.

'Yes. Now I feel much worse.' I smiled. 'Look, they didn't take Nicholson's or Lanyon's work either, and a lot of others they should have, in my opinion. So I got over the rejection side of things quickly enough—it happens and you have to deal with it. But then I went to see the show.'

'Ah. Not very impressive?'

I just stared at him. 'Sometimes, Victor, you're so far off the pace it worries me.'

He set my sketchbook on the armrest and glanced down at his watch. 'You're saying the show *was* good, but it left you deflated in some way.'

'In every way.' I threw up my hands. 'I mean, there I was, surrounded by all of this outstanding work—stuff that really pushes at the limits of what painting can do—and the only thing I could think about was the pile of rubbish I'd left back in my studio. I felt ashamed, if you really want to know. That these artists were so brave, and I was so desperate to be ordinary.'

'That word again,' Victor said. 'You use it a lot.'

'Would you prefer average? Middling? Mediocre?'

He gave a small sigh of indifference. 'Let's talk about your pieces for the January show. You've been going through the motions with those, you said.'

'Yes. God. How many times do I have to repeat myself?'

He ignored me, thumbing towards the sketchbook. 'And that's how you approached the portrait here, too?'

'*Yes.*'

'But you're not being truthful about that, Ellie. You told me— hang on, I'd hate to misquote you—' He leaned to flick back through the pages of his notebook, one-handed. '*That's just me trying to be less ordinary. Not be so literal.* Isn't that what you just said?'

'Well, I didn't think you'd be transcribing every last bloody word when I was saying it. Is this a courtroom now?'

With this, he eased off, reclining in his chair, softening his stance. 'My point is, what you've made for me here is by no means ordinary. I'm not in it, for a start. That's fairly unusual for a portrait, wouldn't you say?'

'It depends on your frame of reference.'

'All right. Fair enough. I don't profess to be an expert on art. But I can tell the time well enough: eighteen minutes and forty-one seconds. That's how long it took you to complete it. And you showed no obvious anxiety behaviours as you were painting it. So, I'm left wondering if it's the act of painting that's been causing all your apprehensions, like we discussed, or if it's something else.'

'Like what?'

'I'm not sure yet. We need to talk that through a bit more, but I'm confident we'll get there,' he said. 'And I think it's probably wise to keep you on the Tofranil for now. It appears to be helping. Unless you've any objections?'

For once, I had no answer.

'Good then.' Victor leaned to make one last scribble on his notepad. 'I think we've made terrific strides today already.'

Staying away from the Roxborough in January proved difficult. I managed not to be there for the hanging of my paintings, letting Dulcie and her deputies ascribe the order to the turgid mess I handed them. When the private viewing came around on the 14th, I stayed home, knowing they would make me stand beside my wretched work for photo opportunities and give interviews all night about the (lack of) thought behind them. Still, there

were so many quiet afternoons in the weeks after, when I was
tempted to drop into the gallery to see the paintings *in situ*, hoping the sight of them in this context might somehow redeem
them.

In the lead-up to the opening, Dulcie had posted me the text
for the show's catalogue, seeking my approval. She had commis-
sioned a foreword from a writer called Ken Muirhead, a fellow
Scot who had commended my previous show in the *Telegraph*.
Of my new paintings, he wrote this:

[. . .] these muted, reflective compositions mark a departure
from her bracing early work and show the clear maturation of
her talent. Building on studies of the city from one fixed vantage point, Conroy presents New York as a constellation of
tiny human acts occurring in slow motion. In her hands, what
should be scattershot and frenzied becomes reposed, serene. A
view of life as though from the stars.

I was almost hypnotised by the language in this paragraph,
but I resisted it. Clearly, Muirhead had failed to notice the sheer
apathy that underpinned the paintings, how poorly I had gone
about the task of executing them, how knowingly I had let them
be carried from my studio, one after the next, like meat leaving
an abattoir. And then it struck me that Ken Muirhead and I were
one and the same: factotums, glad to dash off work for the cost
of our subsistence. I agreed to the text and sent it back to Dulcie
without comment, thinking nobody would ever take such drivel
seriously. She called me after the private viewing to tell me, 'Ken
was rather sad not to see you there. He said he'd never wanted to

meet an artist so much in his life. And he doesn't even know how pretty you are yet. We ought to set the two of you up. I don't think he's married any more.'

What I did not expect was the commotion that followed. The reviewers were even more fulsome in their praise of my paintings than Muirhead—'staggering', they said; 'exceptional', 'dazzling', 'ambitious, affecting'—and the public seemed to mistake the ignorance of these critiques for testimonials. The Roxborough attracted so many visitors in the show's run that it had to extend its opening hours to accommodate them. Had I ventured there on any of those quiet afternoons in January, I would have found myself queuing at the door. I learned all of this from Dulcie, when she came by the studio at the close of the show with Max Eversholt and a bottle of champagne already opened. 'Well, *somebody's* got to celebrate your success,' she said, 'even if you won't.'

I was obliged to get three glasses from the kitchen cabinet and sit with them, toasting my so-called achievements in the bedlam of my flat. Max toed a bundle of rags from my sofa and sat down. He had lost more hair since I had seen him last, but he was no less prone to fussing with it. 'Doesn't matter who the artist is—after a while, all these places look the same to me,' he said, regarding my studio. 'Shouldn't you be looking for a bigger space now?'

'I'm fine where I am,' I told him, pretending to drink.

'She's fine where she is,' Dulcie said. 'Stop trying to spend her money.' She dragged a stool all the way from the other side of the room and dusted it off with her coat-sleeve.

We clinked our dirty glasses and I just sat there, letting them assume the yoke of conversation, as always. They went on for some time about the show, how quickly all the pieces had been sold, talking figures and 'next steps', and soon they got round to more interesting matters. 'That little project for the observatory could be worth doing in the interim,' Max said, tossing his hair back. 'Before we start planning too much overseas, I mean.' I was not quite sure how much of my earnings Max Eversholt still had a stake in, but he never stopped speaking as though his involvement in my affairs was paramount.

Dulcie explained that three of the paintings in my show had been bought by an architect named Paul Christopher. They had talked for a while at the private viewing: 'He's good pals with Ken, actually. That's how we got on to the subject . . . Ken asked him where he was planning on hanging all the paintings, and he said, "They're going in my office, if I can find the space." So I said, "It's a shame you don't have a bigger practice—you could've bought another three," and he said, "Well, that doesn't stop me commissioning more."' According to Dulcie, the architect had been hired to build a new planetary observatory in the Lake District. 'I think it's linked to one of the universities up there— Durham, I think he said—but it's all privately funded. You know how these things go: some rich idiot messed around with a telescope when he was a lad and now he gets his name on an observatory. Whatever the reasons, it's more or less built already, and our friend Christopher wants you to do a mural for the science centre.'

'Only problem is,' Max added, 'who the bloody hell's going to see it, all the way up there?'

'I don't know. Scientists and students, I'd expect. I'm sure they wouldn't have built it otherwise.' Dulcie went on talking in the manner she knew I hated: studying her fingernails when she ought to have been addressing me. 'Christopher says he wants to make a real feature of the entrance, and he was knocked out by your show. I asked him what kind of budget he had in mind and he told me there was plenty in the pot. It might be worth considering.'

It seemed to me that anyone whose taste in art was so undiscerning as to appreciate my New York paintings could not be a very good architect. So I dismissed the suggestion of meeting him offhand. 'All right,' Dulcie said. 'Just thought I should mention it.' But as the days went by, the idea of working on a mural grew more appealing. I thought a lot about the intensity of my student work on the top floor of the Glasgow School, the fearlessness of those images I once made for Henry Holden, and I wanted to see if I could restore some of that spirit. When I called Dulcie to tell her of my change of heart, she did not seem surprised.

Five

The drawings for the mural at the Willard Observatory were submitted in April 1961 and approved that same month. I met just once with the architects at their offices in Montague Street. They showed me their original concepts for the science centre and how their blueprints had evolved, and, referring mostly to photographs and scale models, they talked me through their various stipulations for the interior—'the brief', as they insisted on calling it. The dimensions of the entrance hall were not as vast as I had hoped, but, discussing the project further with Paul Christopher, I sensed that we had similar perceptions of what a mural in that space should do. He was a waifish, softly-spoken man who had a very clumsy and unthinking manner: clattering his hips on table corners as he escorted me through the office, picking a clod of earwax from the dip of his right lobe during our meeting. Despite the fact that he had bought three of my weakest paintings from Dulcie, he had a good sensibility for art, and we seemed to share opinions on most aesthetic matters: he had his misgivings about the ideals of Le Corbusier, preferred the sculptures of Brancusi to Modigliani, and had also liked the purely abstract works in the recent RBA show. Everything about the project felt right to me. I had just one condition for accepting the job and Paul Christopher agreed to it: I would paint the mural on a set of canvases in my own studio and install it in pieces when the deadline came. 'Yes, however you see it working best,' was what he said. 'I didn't expect you'd want to do a fresco, and I'm not thrilled with the plastering job anyway—you'd be doing us a favour.' He had thought of me for the mural because of what he called 'the starriness' of my recent work, and I did not care to press him for a fuller explanation.

My initial ideas lacked verve. I knew very little about astronomy and did not want to paint something that failed to reference its surroundings, or that referenced them too bluntly. So I took to visiting the Planetarium for their evening shows to develop my understanding of the cosmos, and took membership of the Royal Astronomical Society, pulling texts from their library in the afternoons. During that spell of research at Burlington House, I was exposed to so much inspiring work: rare celestial charts by Andreas Cellarius from the seventeenth century, ornate star maps from Bayer's *Uranometria*, and Galileo's remarkable moon drawings. I found myself compelled by the mythologies that supported these early visions of the stars, making detailed studies of Pegasus, Ophiuchus, Hercules, Orion and other featured characters, thinking I might incorporate them into the mural somehow. In John Flamsteed's *Atlas Coelestis*, and all the great celestial atlases of the Georgian era, I found the same constellations appearing as mythical creatures, symbolic animals (the serpent, the eagle, the owl), and objects of war (the shield, the spear, the bow and arrow). It seemed strange to me that such precise works of science could be cloaked in so much allegory.

I kept returning to one particular atlas. The archivist said it was compiled by a schoolteacher called Alexander Jamieson in 1822. 'Another great Scot,' I said, but he did not answer me. These celestial charts of Jamieson's were just as meticulous as the others, but the renditions of the animal forms—Cygnus, Leo, and Aries, especially—were better expressed and proportioned. I was taken with the thought of reimagining a section of his atlas in my mural. For a few days, I developed sketches from Jamieson's originals, depicting Centaurus—half man, half horse— skewering the constellation of Lupus, the wolf, with a spear. Each figure was badged with tiny stars, showing the framework of the constellations. But something about this concept failed to convince me. It addressed the subject too directly. The image was too oppressive for the space. I abandoned it.

My brain was not geared to understand the complexities of the science, but I delighted in reading more about the history of astronomy. I grew fascinated by its importance as a means of navigation. In the age of sail, accurate maps of the stars were vital to aid the passage of ships at sea (I read somewhere that this was the sole reason for the appointment of John Flamsteed as Britain's first Astronomer Royal). This relationship between the stars and the oceans reverberated with me. In spite of my experiences aboard the *Queen Elizabeth*, I had not lost any affection for Melville and Stevenson or the cheap pirate adventure novels I remembered from my youth.

I moved my research to the National Maritime Museum and

taught myself about the early instruments of navigation: the astrolabe, the sextant, the back staff, the nocturnal. It seemed for a time that I would include data from old nautical almanacs in my drawings, too, but I could not bring these ideas to a resolution. Then, one afternoon, I chanced upon a compendium of sail-plans and diagrams for merchant sailing ships in the museum bookshop. They were not from the same period as the Jamieson atlas, but there was a clear similarity between these precise designs (made by naval architects to determine the structure and placement of ships' sails) and the star charts I had studied at Burlington House. In the sail-plans, key points of the ship's rigging were numbered and connected by solid or broken lines, in much the same way that the gridlines of the celestial sphere were drawn out by Jamieson. I noticed clear parallels and overlaps. When I traced the sail-plans in the studio and laid them directly on top of my copied star charts, the natural cohesion of the images excited me.

I completed the drawings for Paul Christopher over the next few days. I proposed a mural eight feet high by fourteen wide, depicting a scrapyard for old sailing vessels, seen from various perspectives—a junkpile of merchant sailing ships arranged at curious angles, filling the entire space. I plotted these ships against a chart expanded from Jamieson's atlas so that the junctures of their sails and rigging correlated with the patterns of the stars. I posted the drawings to Christopher & Partners, expecting I would not hear back for at least a fortnight, but he called the very next morning to tell me how much he admired them. The commission was finalised, and I was set a deadline of late September to complete the work, with an extra week for installation and final touches.

I went about the task of painting the mural so methodically. First, I divided my master drawing into one-inch squares with construction lines. Then I made a cartoon—a kind of knitting pattern, drawn on paper to enlarge the master sketch. This was organised into corresponding one-foot squares, helping me retain the proportions of the original. Transferring the design from the cartoon involved puncturing its drawn outlines with my roulette—a small spiked wheel on a wooden handle—and then dusting the perforations with dry poster paint, leaving behind a dotted imprint on the stretched cotton canvas that I could firm up with ink. I underpainted each square using oil pigments thinned right down with turpentine, building thicker coats upon it as the days progressed. It was important to graduate from light to dark so that the image would retain its punch and definition.

My aim was to finish most of the work by July to give the paint and resin enough time to settle, as I was going to have to roll the canvas up and transport it to the observatory in a cardboard tube—it was a five-hour drive, north to Windermere, and the longer the painting stayed on the roll, the harder it would be to install. I planned to affix the final image to the wall with lead adhesive in three separate sections, using the techniques I had learned from Henry Holden. Everything seemed to be in place.

But I was barely halfway into painting when I noticed a problem with the master drawing I was working from. In all of Jamieson's celestial charts, two elements were persistently shown in the form of solid, candy-striped lines. The first of these represented the equator. The second was marked: ECLIPTIC. I intended to present these lines as frayed lengths of rope, arcing from right to left. But, just as I was about to start committing them to paint, I hesitated. It occurred to me that, in my great rush to finish the mural plans, I had not stopped to query the significance of these lines in Jamieson's originals. So I went to get my dictionary (I kept it in my bedside drawer in place of a Bible).

equator / ih-kway-ter / noun
an imaginary line around the earth at equal distances from the poles, dividing the earth into northern and southern hemispheres.

This just confirmed what I already knew. It was school-level astronomy.

ecliptic / ih-klip-tick / noun
a great circle on the celestial sphere representing the sun's apparent path among the stars during the year.

I was more curious about this definition. 'Representing' and 'apparent' seemed like oddly vague descriptors, and left me feeling quite unsatisfied. The next day, I went back to Burlington House to consult their reference books.

The ecliptic is an imaginary great circle on the celestial sphere along which the sun appears to move over the course of the year. (In actuality, it is the earth's orbit around the sun that causes the change in the sun's apparent direction.) The ecliptic is inclined from the celestial equator by 23.5 degrees, and crosses it at two points, known as equinoxes. The constellations of the zodiac are positioned along the ecliptic.

I went to see if the librarian could expound on this for me. She did not understand the definition herself ('I'm part-time here,' she said, 'and I only studied Classics'), but advised me to speak to the archivist, who would be coming back shortly from lunch. And so I sat patiently in the reading room for over an hour until the man appeared. He had helped me on several occasions before, and I always thought that he looked much too young to be an archivist; it seemed that wearing a lot of tweed and brilliantine was his strategy for disguising it. He went to find himself a text from the shelves. As I approached him, he took off his round wire frames and gently closed his fist over them. Raising one corner of his mouth, he said, 'Who told you?'

'Pardon me?'

'Who told you I could help?'

'I'm sorry. The librarian thought— '

'She *knows*. I told her fifty times. It's my day off.'

'Oh. Then why are you here?'

'Because I'm trying to do some research of my own.'

'Snap,' I said. 'I didn't mean to disturb you.'

'It's all right, it's all right.' He sighed. 'You might as well have a seat. I can take a few minutes out of the tedium, I suppose.'

'You're very kind,' I said. 'Thank you.'

There was an uncomfortable moment in which I thought he sniffed my hair as I sat down at the nearest table, but it was only his peculiar way of breathing. 'Excuse my hay fever,' he said, standing over me. 'Tell me what you need.'

I laid out the reference book, pointing to the extract I wanted him to clarify. He leaned in, placing a hand at the back of my chair. 'What I don't understand,' I said, shifting away, 'is how the line is imaginary.'

'It's imaginary in the same sense as the equator and the celestial sphere,' he replied. 'Simple.'

I blinked back at him.

'Oh dear. You'd better shift over.' Wearily hooking his glasses back on his ears, he sat down in the space beside me. He turned back his sleeves. 'All right. Astronomy for naïfs, lesson one. The celestial sphere.' He talked very quickly and flatly, as though dictating a letter: 'The way we envision the stars is by imagining they're attached to a giant invisible sphere surrounding the earth. It's a total fiction, really—just a construction we came up with to help us get our heads around the complexity of it all. And, of course, we can only see half of this sphere at any given time. So, you could say it's more like a dome, or a semi-sphere, but we prefer not to call it that. Our prerogative. Anyway—' He tapped the page: one heavy clop of his index finger to get my attention. 'The ecliptic, put simply, is the plane of the earth's orbit around the sun. But since we all live here on earth, we observe the sun to be moving along this plane instead. Why? Because what would be the point of looking at things from the perspective of the sun? That's no use to anyone. And it's important to have a governing system.' He nudged closer, wetting his lips. 'Ergo, it's an *imaginary* circle, as it's only a part of our human construction of the cosmos. To call it a genuine circle would be quite incorrect. But to avoid confusion, we say that the sun moves in a circular path through the stars over the course of the year. We can observe it going east-

wards through the constellations along a sort of line. That line is
what we call the ecliptic. It's not actually there, of course. In fact,
it's a complete inversion, because it's really the earth that's moving,
not the sun. But to all intents and purposes, it's a bloody great
circular line in the sky made by the sun throughout the year.' His
brow was crumpled now. 'It seems I'm quite incapable of explaining this succinctly. Shall I draw you a picture?'

Perhaps the only way to describe the cosmos was by analogy.
The archivist took out a notebook and a pencil. 'Imagine the sun
is on top of this maypole, here.' He made a line with a head like
a matchstick. 'And you're the earth, dancing round it. For the
sake of time, let's forget about the fact that you're tilted at twenty-
three and a bit degrees to the pole—it only complicates things.'
He drew a wobbly circle and marked it with a cross, then added
a dotted line to show my viewpoint with a smaller cross on the
opposite side.

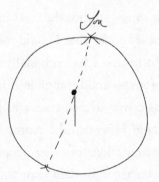

He moved the pencil slowly in a clockwise loop. 'So, from your
point of view, keeping your eyes on the tip of the maypole as you
go round, it seems to track out a circle against the celestial sky.

That circle would be your ecliptic. It's not actually there; it's just the way you perceive it. Really, it's *you* that's going in circles. The maypole stays where it is. Understand now?'

'Yes,' I said. 'The picture helped.'

'Oh good. Welcome to basic astronomy,' he replied. 'Now you'd better let me get on with wasting my day off.'

'What are you researching, if you don't mind my asking?'

'I've been trying to write a biography of Eddington for a while now.'

'Edison?'

'*No.* Good gracious, why does everybody say that?' He closed my reference book. 'One day, people are going to stop asking me that question. They'll say, "Ah yes, Eddington, of course." And I shall have a good old laugh about it. Until then—' He slid the book to me under the tow of his middle finger. 'Best of luck.'

I never got the chance to thank him properly. He was already on his feet, browsing the shelves.

When I got back to my studio, the stars in my mural seemed dimmer. I could not see a way that I could include the ecliptic or the equator in the form that I had originally devised. To present imaginary lines as ropes—solid, tangible things—felt insincere. But to show them as candy-striped tracks, as Jamieson had done, seemed equally wrong. How could I represent things that were themselves just representations of other people's representations? And how could I make them fit the themes of my design without contriving them? I could not continue with the painting until I had resolved these issues in my mind. And so it stayed on the stretchers, half-made.

For a time, the telephone did not ring at all—nobody cared

where I was or what I was doing. But, after a week or so, the calls became more frequent and more difficult to ignore. I left the phone unhooked and, when the bellyaching noise started to bother me, I cut the wire.

The problem seemed to be in the materials themselves: oil paints were versatile, but they could not give me the illusory qualities I wanted. Graphite on paper was so categorical, ink so permanent. Gouache was flat, acrylic like toothpaste. I was aiming to show lines that were not really there, and felt limited by the tools at my disposal. There were tricks of perspective I attempted: re-ordering my scrapyard of ships so that the arc of their upturned hulls, the shadows of their masts, the limits of their sails were subtly aligned and, from a certain angle, alluded to an arcing line. But doing this ruined the balance of the image: what had been an ordered jumble became a clot of pieces, too conveniently manoeuvred into position.

I thought of masking certain areas of the painting, using vacancies in the drawing to suggest a lurking presence. This worked fine on paper, but when I came to transfer it to the canvas, the image looked skeletal, dead. I needed to find some method of getting the paint to vary with the light or decay over the course of time. Ripolin might well have worked, but I did not know where to acquire it or if it was still being manufactured. I mixed various types of glue into the paints I had—no luck; it hardened them or glossed them or turned them lumpy. My telephone was broken so I could not ring around to ask the dealers for their suggestions. And what would I have said? 'I want something to make my lines look more imaginary.' *Ah, yes—I've got just the thing. When can you come and collect it?'* 'Don't you deliver? I can't go outside.' *'No, you'll have to come and get it. Our delivery boy is sick.'* 'But, I can't leave the flat.' *'Why not? What's wrong with you?'* 'I can't leave my work, that's all.' Going outside was simply not possible. It was foggy out there. Full of noises. I had stapled the curtains. Nothing could get in. The water was brown when it came from the taps, but I was still drinking it. So what? Work my way through it—that was the best thing. Just like my parents. Get my head down. No complaining.

The phone rang.

Paul Christopher.

No.

Someone was buzzing. Down there, on the street, at my door.

A startling racket. *Bzz-bzz, bzz-bzz-bzz.* I could not see out the window. *Bzz-bzz-bzz-bzz, bzz-bzz.* It did not go away until I pressed the button.

Different feet this time, not Dulcie's. The thumping on the stairs was deeper. A man's. I looked through the spyhole.

Victor Yail. He was in a cricket jumper, but he still had his briefcase. As he leaned in to knock, his face bent and swelled. I undid the latch.

He stood on the landing, peering into the flat. 'Thought you'd like some fresh air.'

I shook my head.

'Just a quick walk to the corner and back. We shan't go far.'

I did not move.

'OK. Then would you please let me in?'

I held the door open for him.

'You missed your last few appointments,' he said, surveying the room with tightened eyes.

I closed all the locks.

'Is this the mural? It's enormous.'

'Don't touch it,' I said.

He turned sharply, looking for a clean spot on the floor to set his case down, and settled for the milk crate near the kitchen counter. 'Is it all right if I look around a bit? I promise I won't move anything.'

'What are you doing here, Victor?' I asked.

'Well,' he said, piloting a route between the obstacles around him. Boxes, jam-jars, soup cans. 'If you drop off the radar for several weeks without a word, people get concerned.' Bottles, paper, tin foil. Clods of paint and drips of ink. 'Dulcie got in touch. She said she'd tried to phone but you weren't answering.' Dishes, plates, and parcel tape. Paint rags, clothing, bits of wire. 'Happened a few times now, she said. So I thought I'd come over.' Knives and forks and spoons and spatulas. 'I'm very glad I did. What's *this*?' He pointed to the bench where I had been working on my pigments.

'A mortar and pestle,' I told him.

'I can see that. What's inside?'

'An experiment.'

'Did it work?'

'Not yet.'

'Uh-huh,' Victor said. And, when he turned back to me, he was holding something in his hand: a brown glass bottle with a torn-off label. In a kind of pantomime, he turned it upside down to show me it was empty. 'Where are they?' he asked.

I shrugged. I was not exactly sure I could account for all of them. Some were skinned over in the cans about his feet, some congealed on scraps of paper, some had made it to the small test canvases in stacks under the window—the firewood pile, I liked to think of it. The rest could have been anywhere.

'Ellie, how long have you been grinding up your tablets like this?'

Again, I was not sure. But I answered, 'A week or so.'

'I gave you a month's supply. Are they all gone?'

I shrugged again.

Looking earnestly into my eyes, he said, 'Well, this is quite a setback, Ellie, I won't lie to you.' He tossed the bottle onto the couch. It made an oddly noiseless landing. 'We need to get you back on those right away. You can't just suddenly stop. It'll shock your system.' He went to his briefcase, treading without care. A rag stuck to his shoe. In the top compartment, he found his prescription pad and filled out a sheet. 'As soon as the pharmacy opens tomorrow, take this, do you hear me?'

I sat down. The muscles in my legs felt hard as metal.

'In fact, here—' He drew something from a different pocket of the case. Another bottle: plastic, rattling. He made to throw it, then decided not to. 'These are Jonathan's. He takes them for his bedwetting. It's Tofranil, the same as yours but a very low dosage.' He pressed them into my hand. 'I keep them with me for emergencies. Take them. They'll tide you over till tomorrow.'

'What for?' I asked. I was so tired.

'Don't worry what for. You'd better have something in your stomach first,' he said. 'How long has it been since you ate?' He went rummaging in my kitchen. The fridge door opened, the fridge door closed. 'Crikey,' he said. 'Fish paste and sweetcorn. No wonder you look malnourished.' And he rolled up his sleeves to muck out my sink. 'Is there someone who could stay with you tonight? A friend, a neighbour? I don't think you should be alone at the moment.'

'No.' I looked down at the bottle. 'No one else.'

'What about the people downstairs?'

'I don't know them very well.'

'Your parents?'

'Miles away.'

'Dulcie, then.'

'You must be joking.'

Victor heaved out a sigh. He wiped his forehead with the crook of his wrist, soapsuds clinging to his arm-hairs. 'I've a spare room at home,' he said. 'I don't want to insist, but I can't let you stay here alone. It'll just be for the night.'

'No,' I said. 'I can't leave my work.'

And he repeated the words back to me, slower. 'You can't leave your work. All right.' He surveyed the room, nodding. 'I'll stay here tonight then. As a friend. I just need to use your phone.' But when he got to the wall, he found the wire had been snipped. 'Actually, there's a phone box down the road. Why don't I bring us back some fish and chips, eh? My treat.' He took my door keys from the kitchen counter. 'Won't be long.'

He came back a while later in a different set of clothes and without his briefcase. Instead, he had a leather overnight bag and a box of groceries. 'The chip shops were all closed, so I've brought you some provisions from home.' Unpacking the box, he showed me everything he had: sardines and mackerel in tins, bread rolls, canned tomatoes, rice, Oxo cubes, an onion, a pint of milk, some parcelled meat. 'I'll get cooking,' he said, 'once

I've cleaned this place up a bit. Why don't you come and keep me company?'

I told him I was not hungry, but Victor Yail was not the sort of man who could be persuaded from a path once he had started on it. While he sorted through the clutter of my kitchen, changing the bins and clearing the surfaces, I lay down on my couch and allowed myself to sleep.

- - - - - -

The meal was nothing fancy—just minced beef and tomatoes with rice—but it was one of the finest I ever ate in my life. Victor let me finish it in silence, while he leaned on the cooker, reading through the newspaper. It was either very late or very early. The kitchen was gleaming and spare. There was a stillness behind the curtains and the peak-time blaring of the television set downstairs could not be heard. I was already feeling much better. Victor took my plate and I thanked him. He came back with a small glass of milk and two tablets. 'Just those for now, but we're going to start upping your dosage.' I swallowed them down and he gave me a pat on the shoulder. It was strange to be looked after in this way, as though I were a child again. I had not known closeness like this for years.

Victor lit the stove and put the kettle on. He stroked his beard as though trying to remove it with one hand. 'I was looking at your work, while you were sleeping. Hope you don't mind.' And he gestured to the mural that was bracketed to my studio wall, unfinished.

I twisted round to glare at it. The flaws were still so obvious.

'I don't care,' I said. 'There's nothing to look at.'

'I wouldn't say that.'

'Well, your taste is questionable. I've seen your office.'

'What's wrong with my office?'

'Nothing,' I said. 'If you like that academic sort of look.'

'I happen to *adore* that academic sort of look. That academic sort of look is exactly what I was striving for. So I'll take that back-handed compliment and return it to you, forehand.' He acted out the shot, and I could not help but laugh at his ludicrous expression. I was still winding in my smile when he said, 'I'd like to ask about the ships, though.'

'It's just a design,' I told him. 'And not a very good one, it turns out.'

'Yes, but *ships*. I thought it was an observatory you were painting it for.'

'It is. It was.'

I started to recount all the ways in which astronomy was linked to seafaring, and Victor raised his finger, wagged it at me. 'That's not what I was getting at,' he said. 'It just seems curious that the first piece of work you've been excited about for a while contains so many ships—even when it's meant to be about the stars.' He folded his arms. 'It's also interesting that you failed to bring this up when we last spoke.'

'What difference does it make?' I did not understand why he was pressing this point quite so forcefully.

'We could have talked about the significance of those ships, for starters, and stopped you getting yourself into such a state again.' He angled his body to address me. 'There's only so long we can go on dancing round what happened on the *Queen Elizabeth*, you know.'

I ruffled my hair in frustration. 'You see, this is the problem with psychiatry. Everything has to be connected to something else. I just liked the idea—that's all. It got me excited. It's not even the same kind of ship!'

'So what happened?' Victor said, blank-faced. 'Why haven't you finished it?'

'*Because*. It stopped making sense to me.' In through the nose, out through the mouth. 'There's a fault in it. In my design.' I tried to justify it, but it did not seem to register.

Victor stepped to the sink. He began to rinse the meat-flecks off my plate under the tap. 'That doesn't explain why you've been holed up in this place again with your curtains stapled and your telephone cut off. Shall I tell you what *I* think?'

'No. I'd rather you just left.'

'Tough luck. I'm here for the night.'

'Nobody asked you to be.'

'Yes, I'm here out of the goodness of my strange little heart. Please sit down.'

'I don't have to.'

'Ellie, sit down. We're not having an argument. We're just talking.' He was staring at my reflection in the kitchen window. I could see myself framed in it, too, inside a sallow block of light. My face had the greyness of decomposing fruit, the kind that is put out on a still-life table and forgotten. I went to sit down on the couch. Victor had not tidied anything in the studio—he knew better than to move the things that mattered to me.

His theory was that I had chosen to paint ships as a way of expressing what I could not previously evoke in the caldarium pieces. I did not understand how this could be the case, but he

seemed quite certain of it: 'See, it's not a choice you made consciously. Genuine creativity, as you always tell me, doesn't come
from any conscious thought. It's an agglomeration of things. A
happy accident. And there's no doubt that your head is predis-
posed to certain types of imagery. Of course you're painting
ships. You lost a baby, Ellie—that's a terribly traumatic thing
for anyone to go through alone—and it happened while you
were sailing on an enormous passenger ship thousands of miles
from home. Are you trying to tell me that you can't see the connection? That you don't still feel adrift from things? Lost at sea?
All of those clichés you use in our sessions and think I don't
pick up on.'

I found it difficult to answer him. He was barrelling on as
though I was not there.

'And as soon as you come off your medication—as soon as you
consciously take note of what it is you're actually painting—you
find some way to stop yourself completing work. There's this
fault with it here, that problem there. You can't finish anything.
The tablets help, because they keep you from thinking too much
about what you're doing. Isn't that how you got the work done
last time for Dulcie?—"*Knocking them out*," you said. That's when
you were taking your pills regularly. You can finish things when
you're medicated. But when you come off it—' He paused, letting the point resound. 'You get anxious again. You start worrying. You see ships and think of everything you've lost. I don't just
mean the baby—I mean the ships your father built. Clydebank.
Glasgow. Your mother. Home. Jim Culvers. You see paintings
and you think of all the ones you made before, when you were
happier. In that attic room you had. Before you spent the night

with that man. Before you got pregnant. You don't need me to go on listing things, Ellie. I know you get all this. You're as sharp as they come. What we have to do is find some way for you to cope with it that doesn't involve me writing you a prescription. Because, at the moment, you do *not* have a grip on it. And I'm here to help you get one, if you'll let me.'

- - - - - -

Paul Christopher was disappointed that I had to default on the commission and did not understand my reasons. I found it difficult to broach the matter of my real anxieties with him, so tried to convince him of the flaws in my design instead—I used the word 'insurmountable' a few times too often. From his perspective, the drawings we agreed on were still faultless. He said he doubted that another artist would be able to envision something quite so perfect for the space. I told him painters like me were ten a penny, that he should consider approaching someone from the RBA show. *'I'm not sure about that,'* he said. *'I've half a mind to leave it blank for you, until you come to your senses.'* Over the telephone, his voice had even less substance. *'Of course, we won't be able to pay you for the work you've done so far. I'm sorry if that's going to land you in any trouble.'* I told him I would not have blamed him if he'd wanted to besmirch my reputation with everyone in town. *'Never,'* he said, chuckling. *'That would only devalue the paintings I've already bought.'* He thanked me for my time and cheerfully hung up.

Dulcie cared very little about my withdrawal from the project. While I had been worrying about imaginary lines, she and Max had been in negotiations with galleries overseas. They had already recruited the Galerie Rive Droite in Paris and the Galerie Gasser in Zurich to my cause, with exhibitions of my New York paintings organised for the spring. The work was set to tour Italy like some wayfaring stage act, starting at L'Obelisco in Rome and moving on to Milan and Turin before the end of 1962. In her own way, Dulcie was doing her best for me, and I did not want to seem ungrateful for her efforts. It was through her links at the British Council that *Godfearing* was accepted for a group show in Athens that summer, alongside pieces by Matthew Smith and other painters I revered. She professed to have a 'seven-year plan' that would see my work shown in a Tate retrospective before I turned thirty-two. In truth, I was glad to have someone like Dulcie championing my paintings, as I could barely muster a positive thought for them.

After my recent leave of absence, as Dulcie liked to describe it, she did not let a week go by without making contact. We talked regularly on the phone over the summer, and I would sometimes get an impromptu telegram inviting me to lunch at her new favourite restaurant in town. We met in September at the Rib Room in Cadogan Place, where the sirloin was particularly to her liking. 'Look, this European stuff is all very exciting, but it's time we started thinking about your next show in London,' she advised me, mopping up the blood from her steak with a crust of bread. 'Max thinks we can't afford to let all the interest wane— and he's not entirely wrong. It's such a fickle market at the moment. But, in my judgement, a little yearning tends to go a long way. I think we can hold off until next autumn. Unless that's putting you under too much stress?' Somewhere between dessert and coffee I was finagled into it. An exhibition of new paintings was scheduled at the Roxborough for November 1962.

That gave me a full year to compile the work, but I was so securely tranquillised by Tofranil that I was able to complete ten of the paintings before Christmas. I followed the method that had helped me to produce the New York pieces: filling sketchbooks with a raft of street scenes, choosing any that sustained my interest, and transferring them bluntly onto six-by-six-foot canvases. I felt so detached from the process. The images I painted were striking but meaningless. It was as though someone had crept into my studio to make them while I was sleeping.

I drew all of the sketches on the top deck of the number 142 bus. For six straight days, I rode it back and forth from Kilburn Park Station to Edgware, studying the pavements underneath me every time the bus stood still. I hoped to present something of London life from an overhead perspective—an approach that had been so widely praised in my New York paintings that I reasoned nobody would mind if I kept on dumbly replicating it. The only piece that I could say possessed a flicker of artistic value was *Off at the Next One*, a picture that showed two smeared figures in trench coats on Watling Avenue struggling to keep their dogs from scrapping in the street. The men were posed within the frame obliquely, like two bullfighters viewed from above, their Alsatians reared up on hind legs, baying and straining at their leads. ('All these dogs going berserk,' the woman behind me remarked as I was sketching. 'I'll wait and get off at the next one.')

Throughout this period, I met once a week with Victor Yail in Harley Street. We spent a long time weeding through my thoughts, trying to define the exact point at which the mural work had started to elude me. It was not necessarily his recommendation that I withdraw from the project: 'But my inkling is, if you finish it while you're medicated, you're always going to view it as a compromise. What we want is for you to reach a stage where you can finish it to your satisfaction, without the need for drugs at all.' He was right. The mural had to mean something. I did not want it to be another piece of work that I could not be proud to stand beside. There had to be one painting I refused to sacrifice, even if I never found the strength to complete it.

Victor's way of helping me was to get me to address the issues he believed were causing my anxiety. We spent several sessions talking through the episode in the caldarium, my night with Wilfred Searle, my feelings about Jim Culvers, and my childhood in Clydebank—all with no particular outcome, apart from the vague guilt that comes from sharing secrets with a stranger. There were some days when I knew Victor was just grasping at the ether, trying to make associations between things that had no reason to be linked. At other times, he seemed able to locate thoughts inside my head that I did not even realise were hiding there. 'What about Searle?' he asked me, during one of our first sessions back. 'Do you think he would've been relieved?'

'I'm sure he would've thrown himself a party.'

'But you didn't tell him.'

'No.'

'Was that fair, do you think?'

'I couldn't care less.'

Victor gave a little hum. 'And how about you? Were *you* relieved?'

'I don't know.' There was a very long silence. I picked the paint from the creases of my knuckles. 'I can't say I wasn't at the time. But I don't feel that way about it now.'

'Where did you get the pennyroyal?'

'From Dulcie.'

'Yes, but where did she get it?'

'She said from a Chinese woman somewhere. Portobello, I think.'

'I see.' Victor inched forward, setting down his notepad. 'Do you think you'd like to have children in the future?'

I shrugged. 'I can live without them. I've lived without other things.'

'Such as?'

'Love, I suppose. Intimacy. Affection.'

'It's not too late for that. You're young.'

'Yes, but I've chosen this instead.'

'Therapy?'

'*No*,' I said. 'Art.'

Session after session, we talked this way. Every Tuesday afternoon, I would put down my paintbrush, throw on my coat, and hail a cab to Harley Street. I would traipse up the stairs to Victor's office, nod hello to his secretary, and wait for him to come and wave me in. And he would sit me down in my regular chair with my regular blue cushion to pick up our discussion from the session before. We talked a great deal about my apathy towards the new paintings. He wanted to know about every stage of their creation. For a time, it almost seemed that we were painting them together.

Then, one day, I arrived at Victor's practice to find it adorned in Christmas tinsel. He was standing at the apex of a ladder in the waiting area, hanging a white paper snowflake from the light fixture. 'Afternoon,' he said. 'What do you think of the decorations?'

'They'll do.'

'Jonathan made this one at school.' The snowflake swung and hit his cheek. 'Good to know they aren't wasting any class time on algebra and elocution.'

'It might help his geometry a bit,' I said.

Victor laughed. He stepped down from the ladder and passed his secretary the roll of tape he had been using. Looking up at the snowflake, he said, 'That should just about hold, I think.' And he turned to me, patting his sides. 'All right, Miss Conroy. Shall we?'

As soon as we got settled in the consulting room, I began to tell him all about the painting I had started working on that morning—how I knew that Dulcie was going to think it was the best piece in the show. 'It's just three old women sitting on a bench with a few pigeons streaking past them in a blur,' I said. 'It's about the most boring thing I've ever done, but obviously that means Dulcie's going to love it.'

'I wonder sometimes if you're being a little hard on her.'

This surprised me. 'Hmm.' I pretended to scribble a note on the armrest. 'Would you care to qualify that for me, Victor?'

His face twitched in acknowledgement of my clever-cleverness, but he did not smile. 'You know I'm not Dulcie's biggest supporter, but she's really come through for you in the last few years. Don't forget that.'

I stayed quiet, heeding his sermon.

Victor got up and went to his bookshelves. 'What are your plans for Christmas?' he asked, his back to me. 'Will you be visiting your parents?'

'They want me to,' I said. 'But I'm not sure I can face the journey.'

'How long is it on the train?'

'About six hours.'

'Well, if you can't put yourself out for your parents, then who can you do it for? I'd like to think Jonathan will make the effort for me when I'm in my dotage.'

'I take it you'll be visiting your folks this year, then?'

'I'll put some flowers on their graves, no doubt.'

'Oh, I'm—sorry about that.'

He did not give this any further credence. Instead, he came and stood beside my chair with a set of magazines. As he dropped them on the coffee table, the pieces on his fancy chessboard rattled. 'We're going to start you on an exercise today,' he said, peering down at me. 'It's something I'd like you to keep working on over the holidays, until I get back.'

The thought of him leaving brought me a jolt of panic. 'You're going somewhere?'

'Just for a couple of weeks. Seeing relatives in Kent, then back to the States again. I'm delivering a paper.'

'So I won't see you until the new year?'

He shook his head. 'Let's not worry about that for now. This exercise will help. You'll hardly miss me.' On the coffee table, he fanned out the magazines. The covers were marigold-yellow with decorated borders: *National Geographic.* 'Every time I'm in the

States, they have these in my hotel room. I must have a full set by
now. Take a look.'

I picked up a copy. *June 1957.* The inside pages were mostly
colour photographs of strange foreign landscapes: the Grand
Canal in Venice; tourists camping in the Black Forest; rhododen-
dron pastures in Roan Mountain, Tennessee. The November
1958 issue featured illustrated articles—*The Booming Sport of
Water Skiing, The Emperor's Private Garden: Kashmir*—and maps
with accompanying images: *The Arab World: A Story in Pictures.*
I had seen a magazine just like it in the first-class lounge when I
was sailing to New York.

'The pictures are wonderful, aren't they?' Victor said.

I nodded.

'My favourite is January '57—an expedition through the fjords
in Norway. The stillness is incredible. I find myself going back to
that one now and again, when things get hectic. Helps me relax.'

'You should go and see it for yourself,' I said. 'Take a trip.'

'I almost went with Mandy a few years ago. But, quite honestly, I prefer to look at the pictures. If I actually went there, I
think I would spoil it.' He moved back to his armchair, leaving
me to browse the covers of other editions. There were so many
articles, so many places I had never seen before:

Year of Discovery Opens in Antarctica
Across the Frozen Desert to Byrd Station
The Heart of the Princes' Islands
Lafayette's Homeland, Auvergne
Jerusalem, the Divided City
Seychelles: Tropic Isles of Eden

'Choosing one is really the challenge,' he said. 'I want you to take a few away with you and really have a proper look. Study the photographs. Find a place that does for you what the fjords do for me.'

I was not sure that a photograph could ever calm me. 'I don't know, Victor. That seems a bit pointless.'

There was an expression he always brought out when I was not taking him seriously—lips pulled in, eyes rounded—and he was showing it to me now. 'We've been at this for quite a while, haven't we?' he said. 'I've sat here listening to you for months and, honestly, I'm not sure that we're any further forward than we were the day I met you. Aside from you being on a lot of tricyclics and getting more paintings done—most of which you seem to detest. We've reached a point where we have to find a strategy for you to cope with your anxieties or they're going to seriously affect your future. Eventually, you're going to work yourself into a depression I can't help you with. That's why you need to try your best with this exercise. It's just a visualisation technique—not a cure—but I think it will benefit you.'

At once, the spread of magazines on the table began to seem further away. 'I will,' I said. 'I'll try.'

'Good.' He took off his glasses and breathed on the lenses. 'We all need a place that's ours and ours alone. The fjords are mine—you have to choose somewhere else.'

I flicked through the pages of the topmost issue.

Skiers in Alta, Utah.

Oxen in Schneeburg, Austria.

'It can't be anywhere you've been before—nowhere with memories,' Victor went on. 'How you imagine the place is what's important. That's the only way it can belong to you.'

Boulder Peak, Idaho.

Mount Lafayette, New Hampshire.

Diamond Rock, Martinique.

'Do you understand the exercise?'

'I think so. But— '

'No buts. No evasions. Just do your best.'

Perhaps it would be like the first time I left Clydebank as a child after the Blitz. My mother took me on a coach to see my great-aunt in Coldstream. I was not told what to expect, apart from a lot of countryside, so I imagined it as any five-year-old would have: a small town of grey-bricked cottages beside a river that was permanently frozen, happy people skating on the ice in special wooden clogs and drinking hot chocolate. We arrived into something greener and less magical. The Coldstream I had pictured dropped away, no longer mine.

'I don't need to know which place you've chosen,' Victor said, 'but when I come back in January, I want you to be ready to start calling it to mind. If you can visualise this place when you start feeling anxious, centre yourself there when you need to, then we might be able to bring your dosage down, over time.' And he reclined, scraping the dull leather caps of his shoes together. 'I'll bet that journey up to Scotland isn't so bad if you can go first-class, you know. Six hours on a train won't kill you.'

S i x

The news came in an envelope from my mother. She had written to me with her usual gossip about the happenings in her building and reports of my father's foul mood, with one last paragraph pleading for my company at Christmas time. And, clipped to the last page, was a cutting from the newspaper, on which she had written in the margin: *Saw this in the Herald yesterday. Sorry, love xx*

> HOLDEN—HENRY. Peacefully, at Glasgow Royal Infirmary, on Monday 11th December 1961, Henry Mackintosh Holden (artist and lecturer at the Glasgow School of Art), aged 78 years. A generous and loving man who will be sadly missed. Funeral service at Luss Parish Church, Dumbartonshire, his family's village, on 18th December at 10.30 a.m. No flowers, please.

The funeral was three days away. I called my mother to tell her I would be coming home for a spell. Her delight was tempered by the fact that I would not arrive until after I had paid my respects to Henry. She managed to hide the disappointment in her voice. 'All right, love. You do what you feel's best,' she said. 'We'll have the place ready for you.'

It was a very long journey to Luss. I booked myself onto the earliest train to Glasgow, first-class, reasoning that I would need the comfort and the quiet of the roomier carriages. On the way, I read most of a novel and looked through the images in the *National Geographic* issues I had packed for the trip. It had been a few days since I had seen Victor, and I had still not decided on a photograph to call my own—in truth, they had barely left more than a fleeting impression on me, the sort of wonderment you glean from browsing a jeweller's window. But I vowed to keep trying.

From Glasgow, I took a connecting train to Balloch, at the foot of Loch Lomond. My suitcase was so heavy that, after a few minutes lugging it, the joints of my elbows crackled with pain. The train was crowded with families and I had to walk through several carriages just to find a seat. The stolid darkness of the Clyde and its surrounds went by the windows, familiar and yet not. It was so late when I arrived at the station that I missed the last bus out of Balloch. I stayed the night at a nearby inn, and, waking early, traipsed along the road with my suitcase to catch the rusting single-decker that would carry me into Luss.

Still, I managed to be late. The service had already started when I got to the church. I stowed my case in the antechamber behind a stack of hassocks and crept down the aisle as quietly as I could. Two young girls were playing 'Nearer My God to Thee' on recorders by the altar. Half the pews were empty. A shining casket rested on a plinth with a single wreath of heather. I found a space beside an old man in a faded suit adorned with medals. He nodded at me soberly, and I shared my hymnal with him when it came time to sing. After Henry's widow read out a poem by Yeats, the old man offered me his handkerchief, but we both sat through the prayers unmoved.

Four strong lads carried the coffin down the aisle to the grave-yard, where a fresh cleft in the ground was waiting to receive it, just beyond the hedgerows. People arced around it with the breeze whipping their hair. I clustered with the mourners, hanging back. And when the Reverend gave his words of committal and the formalities were done, I threw a fist of soil into the grave and whispered thank you to a box of wood, wondering what Henry might have thought about it all.

Walking back, I saw his widow linking arms with a man I recognised from art school: a thickset fellow named Kerr whom Henry used to tease for painting cats in every mural, regardless of its subject matter ('Did you never think to ask yourself, Kerr,' he once said in our weekly crit, 'whether those wee calicos have any business at a crucifixion?'). Kerr escorted Mrs Holden to one of the black cars near the church gates before I got a chance to introduce myself. Later, in the vestibule, he came to speak with me as I was waiting to sign the condolence book. We smiled at the remembrance of the calicos, and chatted for a while about my new life in London. He seemed only half-interested in my career as a painter but was extremely curious to know how word of the funeral had reached me. 'Big news, is it, down there?' he said, smirking. This led us into reminiscing about Henry and his feel-ings about London—he used to say that it was a city 'without compassion for the individual' but encouraged us to experience it if we were serious about becoming artists. 'Aye, you don't forget a fella like him,' Kerr said, with an air of finality. 'He gave us a job at the School after. Life-modelling. Ha! I was skint at the time, so I couldn't say no. Haven't really painted much since those days.' Kerr had inherited his father's hardware shop in Bishopbriggs and now ran it with his sister. I told him that sounded like a very nice life, and he said, 'Pssh. It's about ten different kinds of hell rolled into one. But it's a living.' He offered me a lift to the pub for the wake, and I accepted. 'Did you sign that yet?' he asked, pointing to the condolence book. 'I never know what to write. Maybe you can think of something for us.'

Kerr went off to fetch his car, leaving me in the hush of the vestibule with my suitcase at my heels. Before I wrote my message in the book, I turned back through the pages to check the tenor of the comments—I had never written a condolence before and did not want to draw too much attention to myself. There were a lot of platitudes: *Deepest sympathies. Always in our hearts. So many memories.* I wanted mine to be more personal. As I searched for a clear space to write, I saw that a page had been turned inwards—creased so that one stumpy half jutted outwards from the spine. I unpicked it. There was another short message there, and a signature:

> Paint what you believe.
> Thanks for everything you taught me.
> Rest in peace, old man.
>   James Culvers

'Are we all set then?' said Kerr.

I did not even realise he was behind me.

He jangled his car keys. 'We could walk it, mind, but seeing as you've got your case . . .' And he stooped to lift it for me. 'You all right, love? You're shivering.'

It was definitely Jim's handwriting. My heart was shuddering and so was my jaw, but I managed to get the words out: 'Do you know if Jim was here earlier?'

'Who?' Kerr said.

I showed him the page.

'Never heard of him,' he said. 'Who is he?'

I held the book tight. 'A friend of mine.'

Kerr nodded. He eyed the tome of condolences vised against my chest. 'You bringing that along for Mrs H? Good thinking.'

- - - - - -

The Colquhoun Arms was less than half a mile from the church, back on the road where the bus had dropped me. Beyond the windscreen of Kerr's Cortina, the outlying hills were yellowed by sunshine. Low clouds seeped across the birdless sky. The treetops softly stirred. We drove in silence. The squat grey cottages of Luss smudged beside Kerr's head. When he wheeled into the parking space, I jumped out of the car so fast I almost left my case on the back seat. 'Steady, love,' he said. 'It's open bar.'

I hauled my suitcase across the car park and dumped it by the coat racks. One corner of the pub had been roped off for the function. A huddle of glum-faced men in black were sitting at a long table with sandwiches, supping pints and rolling whisky in short glasses. There was no sign of Jim Culvers. I checked the corridors, the snug, the dark ends of the place. I peered into the

Gents, but there was just a bald old fellow standing at the urinal. The barmaid saw me coming out and said, 'It's the other one, hen. We need to change that sign. I keep telling 'em.'

Mrs Holden was in a wingback near the fireplace, clutching a tissue. A grey-haired lady was crouched beside her. Approaching them, it occurred to me that they must have been twins. They had equally flat noses and high foreheads, and they both turned to me with the same mannequin expressions as I hovered near them, waiting to speak. 'Mrs Holden,' I said. 'You probably don't know me, but I knew your husband. He was my favourite teacher. I'm just so sad to lose him.' It came out as ingenuously as I hoped it would. The sister stood up and said, 'I'll get you that brandy, Mags, OK?' She left us alone.

Mrs Holden hung a stare on me, lids twitching. 'So good of you to come,' she said. And she had to bite on her lip to keep from crying. 'Were you in—' She cleared her throat. 'I'm sorry. Were you in his mural class?'

'I was. I came up from London as soon as I heard.'

'Oh, that's really good of you.' She gulped something down. 'And what is it you do now?'

'I'm an artist,' I told her.

'You make a living that way, do you?'

'Yes.'

'A good one?'

I did not know if it was right to smile, but I did. 'Yes.'

'Oh, how lovely. He was always so proud of his students. Did you know Geoff Kerr? He's here somewhere, I think.'

'Yes, I just got a lift with him.'

'A good lad, Geoff. He's been such a help.' Mrs Holden sniffed in a long breath. And, seeing the condolence book under my arm, she said, 'Is that for me?'

'Yes. I'm sorry—of course.' I gave it to her. 'I was wondering if you knew where I could find an old friend of mine. Jim Culvers. He was at the service, but I can't see him here.'

Idly turning through the book, she said, 'Who?'

'He's another student of Henry's.' I showed her the page with Jim's message.

She moved her eyes over the words, but there was no glint of recognition in them. 'James Culvers. No. I'm sorry. I don't know who that is.' And she paused, considering the empty fireplace. 'There was an old student of Henry's renting the cottage last summer, but I don't recognise the name. Culvers—I'd remember that. This fella's name began with a B. Bailey, or Bradley, or something like that. Henry never got me involved.'

'The cottage?'

'Aye,' she said. 'His father's place. He liked to come out and paint there sometimes. Then his hands got too sore, and he preferred having the money in his pocket. We planned on selling, but it wouldn't be worth a lot now.' When I asked for the address, she wafted her hand. 'Ach, it's not far. Get to the pier and turn left. It's the only house on the water that's not been looked after—you can't miss it. What was your name again, love, did you say?'

'Elspeth.'

'Elspeth what?'

'Conroy.'

'I'll keep an eye out for it,' she said. 'In the papers.'

I touched her hand. The skin felt thin as a cobweb. 'Take care, Mrs Holden.'

'Aye, you too. Thanks for coming.'

- - - - - -

It was one harsh winter away from a wreck—a simple stone cottage with a pitched slate roof, so bearded with moss it was already bowing. There was a pale craquelure on the window frames, hay-coloured, moulting. The gutters were shot. The door glass was patched up with tape. A trampled path meandered up to the house, away from the brow of the loch, where the steel-blue water roiled quietly and a clutch of white sloops lilted on their moorings. I walked up the slope, skimming the waist-high grass with my palm, until I came to a doorstep, half painted black. There were old net curtains at the windows, dishes on the outer sill with food scraps: brown-bread crusts and pickle, a saucer ringed with coffee. But there was no sign of movement inside. I knocked several times and nobody answered.

There was no letterbox to peer through, and the windowpanes were coated in a sooty grime that made it difficult to see beyond the nets. I put my case down and side-stepped through the weeds. At the back of the house was a small garden, overrun with nettles, and a dank wooden outhouse. Behind it, a bank of firs, and two great hummocks pushing at the clouds. There was just one downstairs window, looking into the kitchen—a newspaper was on the table, but I could not read the headlines or the date. If the place was lived in, it was lived in sparely. The tap was dripping, a dried-up dishcloth spread over it. I could not think what I should do.

Soon, I found my hand was reaching for the door. The handle turned, the latch came away. It was easy. The hinges squealed as the door opened. I waited, pondering the bareness of the kitchen. The tiles were scuffed by chair legs. The newsprint seemed bright, recent. I decided to go in.

But I was barely past the threshold when I heard his voice: 'Never would've picked you for a burglar, Ellie.' It came from directly behind me: slow, amused, admonishing. Spinning round, my knuckles grazed the doorframe, but I did not feel the pain until later.

Jim was standing there in a black woollen jacket. He was holding a small basket of flowers. His face was tanned and shaven. I could see his breath steaming out. It was close enough to gather, to bottle, to keep. 'Why d'you look so afraid?' he asked. 'I'm not going to turn you in.'

'Oh my God—*Jim.*' It was all I could get out of me. '*Jim.*' I stepped forward to hug him, and he did not move, accepting the embrace without returning it. He held the basket aloft, protecting his flowers. Then, giving me one soft tap on the back, he said, 'All right, all right, enough.' He smiled at me apologetically, those familiar big teeth still as gapped as ever. But there was such a newness about him, too. His hair was cut neatly and combed into runnels—it seemed hard as wicker. The skin was smooth about his cheeks and it gave off a limey scent. He looked as sober as a child. 'Go on inside,' he said. 'I've got to get these into brine.' When I did not budge, he said again, 'Go on. I can't stand about all day. And you seem to 've cut yourself a bad one, look.' My knuckles were streaking blood.

He followed me into the kitchen, got the iodine from the

cupboard. I sat down at the table. My head was in a daze, and I was shivering again. I could not tell if I was relieved to see him or frightened of him leaving me. Dabbing a cloth into the iodine, he came and pressed it on my wound. 'It'll sting,' he said, but I did not care. 'Just let me take these flowers in. I'll only be a moment.'

The through-door from the kitchen was just a wall of beads like you might find at the back of a dreary restaurant. As he pushed through them, they swung and clattered, and I could see into the room beyond. It was a bare shell with no carpet and only a wooden rocking chair for furniture. He had made it into a studio. Two narrow tables were arranged beside an easel with a board set up to paint on.

I trailed after him. He was unscrewing the lid of a tall jar filled with cloudy water. The painting beyond him was only part-finished, but it appeared to show the dying blossoms of a cherry tree scattered over flagstones. He tipped the flowers from his basket into the jar. 'How're the fingers?' he asked, not turning to face me. When the lid was screwed tight, he shook the jar vigorously, side to side.

'Fine,' I said. 'What are you doing?'

'It's a process. Helps with the yield.' And he stopped quaking the jar and put it on the table. He took a metal colander and a bucket from underneath its legs. Removing the lid again, he poured the contents of the jar into the bucket, straining out the sodden flowers. He picked up the colander and began sorting through the petals, selecting only the pinkest, which he placed on a wad of fabric to dry.

I said, 'Can't you stop all that for a second and talk to me?'

'Sorry, it's really quite time-sensitive. I just need another moment.' He patted the flowers and folded them into the fabric, as though wrapping a parcel. 'You might want to close your ears.' With the base of his fist, he thumped down several times on the parcel, and all of the brushes and tube paints on the table rattled like fine china. Then he scraped the flowers into a mortar and started grinding. He turned to me, working the pestle, and looked over at the clock above the hearth. 'Twenty minutes until this lot needs to come out,' he said. 'That's all the time I have for talking.'

I sensed that Jim's account of things had been rehearsed so many times in his head over the years that he had learned how to hesitate at just the right moments in the telling of it; when to stutter and stumble over details, which gaps to skim over and which joins to show. But I was simply glad to hear him speak. Too much time had elapsed without the sound of his voice near me. I did not try to interrupt or scrutinise. I just sat in the rocking chair, watching the motions of his mouth as he formed the words. How much of what he told me was a falsehood I could not tell, but if it hurt me less than the truth, I was willing to bear it.

His story went that he had left London on a pilgrimage. One by one, he had revisited all of the towns where he had been stationed in the war. 'Looking for what, I don't quite know,' he said. 'I just knew I had to get back there.' A doctor had put the notion in his mind. He had awoken on the floor of his old studio, feeling raw from three days' drinking, and could not feel his fingers. There was no sensation in his lower arms at all, he said, but he had managed to get dressed—'Don't ask me how'—and taken himself to a doctor's surgery near Abbey Road. The doctor had knocked his elbows with a reflex hammer and listened to his heart, told him everything was fine. If the feeling did not return by tomorrow, he should come back again, but it was likely just a temporary side-effect of the alcohol—he should really think about cutting back. Jim had told him he would sooner cut back on breathing. Then, on the wall above the doctor's typewriter, he had noticed a framed print. 'It was a reproduction of a Stanley Spencer. Horses pulling wounded soldiers into a hospital tent on—what are they called? Travois. You know, those big long stretchers? Anyway, it's an incredible painting. One of his best.' The doctor had said it was there to remind him of his days as a medic in the Great War—not that he would ever forget his experiences, of course, just that the picture inspired him to keep practising through the more difficult moments. On the way home, Jim could not get the image from his mind. It had made him think of his own picture of his friend at the Prince Alfred. 'And I thought, *that's* what my painting has to do to people. *That's* what I have to communicate.' So he had cleared everything from his studio that afternoon, headed to the bank to withdraw his savings, and set off.

The only things he took with him were a clean set of clothes, a blank sketchbook with a few coloured pencils, an old journal from his days with the regiment, and a bottle of Glenlivet, which he poured over the side of the ferry on the way to Calais. 'I knew I couldn't go back there drunk. I had to stand up and face it all or the whole trip would be pointless. I felt rough as dogs those first few days, but I got through it.' He rode a bus down to Arras, where he had first been stationed with his unit: 'The place had changed a lot, naturally, but the noise of the town was the same as I remembered—there used to be an airstrip there, and planes would come in and go out all the time, but in the quiet spots, you know, there was always an alarming quiet. The way the wind shakes up the fields over there—it's peculiar. Something I won't forget in a hurry.' It was here that he had fired his service weapon in anger for the very first time: 'Shot an unarmed German there from seven feet away: total panic job, coming round the blindside of him.' After several months in Arras, he caught a train north to Dunkirk, which he said had changed unnervingly. 'I was glad I went back. It's important to see a city how it ought to be, you know, not clothed in all the miseries of war. Not with tanks and sandbags and all that screaming chaos. But seeing it again, so quiet, left me feeling quite disturbed, if that makes sense. There was a part of me that I knew would always be stuck there. I lost a lot of friends on that patch of land.' Still, he was not satisfied with any of the sketches he made on his return to these places—the work did not resound as brightly as his memories of them.

One night in Dunkirk, he started drinking again. 'I thought if I just stuck to the local brew, I'd be able to handle it. Well, I'm not a particularly smart fella when it comes to drink, as you know.' He got into a brawl with a young French poet who had been reading his work aloud in the bar. 'I wasn't in the mood to hear poems. It was that awful, dismal sort of French stuff—just a roll of sounds without any meaning—so I started hassling him about it and he didn't much like it. I ended up losing a tooth—' He paused here to show me the gap. '—and the lad fractured his thumb. The both of us got thrown into the locker at the police station overnight. Adjoining cells. We didn't speak to each other for a bit, but then he came over and started apologising—he was in tears. I thought, Hang on, this lad's got problems. And it turns out he did. His parents had just died, two weeks ago, so he said, and he hadn't been coping with it very well. That's what his poems had been about. And he'd been run out of the last town he was in because he'd slapped some poor bloke for goading him, too. That makes him sound like a terrible lad—he wasn't at all. Just troubled.' They became friends (this was the only part of Jim's story I did not need to question, knowing how men like to find compassion for each other after they have traded punches, never before) and the poet invited Jim to stay with him and his sister in his family's house in Giverny for the summer. 'I heard "Giverny" and remembered it was where Monet used to have his garden with the lilies—so I thought it couldn't be that bad. And it wasn't. It was bliss. His parents had left him this beautiful old house. Wildflowers everywhere, hibiscus and pear trees. Glorious sunshine all summer. I didn't want to leave.'

He stayed in Giverny for a full year, in fact, trying to make sense of the sketches in his book, painting with gouache on board. 'The French have a wonderful word: *vaurien*. It means "good-for-nothing". That's what all of those paintings were like. I couldn't seem to get the tone right, no matter what I tried.' Because the poet and his sister drank so little, and with Jim living off their charity and provisions, he was forced to become reacquainted with sobriety. 'For a while, I was living off whatever was in the cupboards—I had a lot of stale cognac, and some disgusting old Dutch advocaat. But that ran out soon enough, and I had no money, so it was either I went and stole it, or—well, I didn't want to come back to France after all that time just to start looting the place like a bloody Nazi. It took me until the spring to really get my act together.'

The spring was when the Judas trees in the village came into bloom. He had gone walking one day with the poet's sister and, suddenly, the winding avenues of Giverny had blushed with so many shades of pink. 'To begin with, I thought they were just like the cherry trees and magnolias back home, but she told me they were Judas trees. When she was a little girl, her mother used to collect all the petals to make potpourri. There was so much of the stuff.'

As the weeks passed, Jim had noticed how the Judas blossoms separated from the branches so quickly, how they dusted the ground in endless configurations, every one of them unique. 'The wind gathered them all up and scattered them however it wanted—like it was painting the scenery all by itself. Some of them would just sit there on the ground, stuck on the gravel, on the soil, or they'd get caught between long blades of grass. They'd just sit there for weeks, fading, shrivelling, turning brown. Then the wind would finally brush them away. They reminded me of the war. The transience of it all. On patrols, it always used to get to me, thinking about the future. Your life always felt so inconsequential, you know, but at the same time you'd try and savour every last moment of it, while you still had it. Anyway, the thought occurred to me, What am I just looking at all these petals for? I need to paint them.' He set up a board in his room at the house and started work. 'And right away I got that glorious feeling in my chest again—you know the one I mean. That swell in your heart when a painting takes over you.

I knew I had something to say. There was nothing else that mattered—I had to paint that and nothing else. Just Judas blossoms on the ground, in as many shapes and patterns as I could think of, forever, until I die.'

By the end of the summer, he had filled the farmhouse with boards. Most of them he gave to the poet and his sister as presents, and they lined the walls of every room. Some of them he kept and carried back with him. He came to understand that he did not need to stay in Giverny any longer. The Judas blossoms did not have to be on his own doorstep for him to paint them. He needed no clear view of them from his window, no sketches, no photographs, just his own memories and speculations. That was the only way he could express their real meaning. And so he begged one last favour from the poet and his sister—just a few more francs to get him back to Calais and to England. 'They were sad to see me go, I think, and I was sad to say goodbye to them. But you know how it is: the work is always more important. Art and happiness won't stand each other's company for long. It's hard to explain that to people who aren't artists. I mean, the lad wrote poetry, but it wasn't his life—I got the impression it was just a hobby for him until he found a job in a bank some day, you know?'

Once Jim had landed back in Dover, he had thought about coming to find me. 'I knew that if anyone would understand, it'd be you. But I can't remember why I didn't—the timing just felt wrong. And, honestly, I couldn't face you yet. Not until the work was done. I had visions of putting on a show again in London and you seeing it by chance.' (It would have been the autumn, when I was still working on my mural. If he had only knocked on my door then, just once . . .) Instead, he took a room for a few weeks above a Chinese restaurant in Soho, and worked there, scrubbing vats, until he had earned enough to take a night coach up to Glasgow. 'The only other person who believed in me was Henry. I thought he might be able to find me an attic some-where, like I used to have as a student, or let me sleep for a while in his office. I didn't really have a plan. But that's what made Henry Henry, wasn't it? If he believed in your work, he'd go out of his way to help you, even if it cost him. That's how I heard about this place. He said he wasn't using it any more, but some bloke had been renting it and left it in a state. Bailey or something, his name was—Henry didn't speak well of him.' The agreement was that Jim could have the cottage, rent free, in exchange for light repairs. 'He only wanted me to do a little gardening and sprucing up—no big overhaul. I admit, I haven't got round to it yet. But I've only been here since September.'

The twenty minutes were almost up and Jim was still standing at his work table, grinding away at the flowers in the mortar. Each turn of his pestle gave a biting sound—he had been using these noises to punctuate and dislocate his sentences, as though he assumed we had been apart so long that I could not read the language of his movements any more. He was disguising some-thing, but I was not going to risk the consequences of making him admit it. And, really, there was only one question I cared for him to answer.

He looked at me, then at the clock. 'You haven't said much. I can't tell what you're thinking about any of this.' His pestle kept on circling. 'It's the God's honest truth, I promise you. Look at me—' He stood tall. 'I'm a year sober. Not touched a drop since I got back, and I don't bother with the races any more. I've just been doing *this*.' And, gesturing with his bowl of ruined flowers, he said, 'This is what's important to me now. Nothing else. I thought you'd understand that.'

'I do,' I said, and stopped the rocking motion of the chair with my heels. 'I do.'

'Then why are you so quiet all of a sudden?' His eyes shifted, left and right. 'I thought you wanted to talk about it. You don't believe me, is that it?'

'You're very defensive, Jim,' I said, 'for a man telling the truth.'

'Well, I need you to believe me.'

'Why?'

'So I can get on with my work.' He sniffed. 'I can't have all this guilt hanging over me.'

'What's there to feel guilty about? You just explained yourself.'

'You *know* what,' he said, and gave a shake of his head. 'Don't make me say it.'

'Apologise, you mean?'

He stayed quiet.

'Are you actually sorry?' I said.

'No.' The pestle was working harder now. 'Not for leaving. Not for doing what I had to do. But I feel guilty for not getting in touch.'

'I was out of my mind with worry about you,' I said. 'You could've phoned, or sent a letter. A telegram would've done. Just something to let me know you were safe.'

'Yes. I wanted to. I really wanted to.' And he put the mortar down on the table weightily. 'This lot has to get onto the slab right now or it won't give out much colour.' He turned his back to me, a shield from my voice.

'You couldn't have spared a thought for me just *once* in all that time?'

'I didn't know that I was supposed to,' he said. The pulped flowers dropped down onto the slab—a lumpy pink cement. 'I didn't know that you *wanted* me to think about you. Not in that way.'

'Well, I did.' There seemed little point in hiding the fact any more.

'If you'd told me that before you moved out, it might have been different. But I don't see there's much I can do to change anything now. And I needed to do it for myself. I needed that trip.' He glugged about a tablespoon of linseed oil upon the paste of flowers. Taking the muller from the table, he began to slide it up and over the paste and the oil. It was a large glass object like a flat iron and it sent drips careening everywhere. 'Oh, for crying out loud—another dud batch. It's not giving me *anything*. Hand me that trowel, would you? I need to scrape it off and start again.'

I got up and passed him what he wanted. 'You didn't mention her name,' I said.

'Huh?'

'The sister.'

'Oh. Helène. Ana Helène.' He took the trowel, laughing quietly. 'There was nothing between us, if that's what you're thinking. She was young enough to be my daughter. And engaged to someone else.'

'Young and unavailable. Yes, I hear that's quite a turn-off.'

'It wasn't like that, Ellie.'

'She must've been beautiful, though. From the way you talk about her.'

'I'm really not going to listen to this. I told you: it wasn't like that.'

'So you didn't even look at her? Not once?'

'Stop it now. You're better than this, Ellie.' He slammed down the trowel, throwing a shock of oiled pigment over the table, onto my funeral dress. 'That was an accident,' he said, walking off. I just rubbed the stain into the fabric, but he came back with a wet tea towel, the bead curtain clattering behind him. 'Fine, ruin it. Who cares?' He tossed it aside. 'I really thought you and I were above this sort of nonsense. Jealousies and petty suspicions. You're the only woman I've ever thought about in that way.'

'In *what* way, Jim?'

'Christ. This is ridiculous. This is why I prefer painting to talking.' He went and dumped himself into the rocking chair. 'I suppose I'm trying to say you're the only woman I've ever really cared for. Not because of how you look, which God knows is fine enough to stun any idiot with two working eyes in his head, but because of what you are, how you think. Actually, it's how you paint. That's what makes you who you are.'

'Then you might as well go back to France,' I said, 'because I don't paint the way you think I do. Not any more.'

He squinted at me, arms folded. 'Two solo shows at the Roxborough—that's what I heard. Can't be bad.'

'Now you're sounding like Max.' I looked away. 'Who told you that, anyway? About the shows?'

'Henry. He showed me the press clippings.'

'Did you see any pictures?'

'A few. But they were only from the newspaper. Black-and-white.'

I pushed my thumb into the scabbing wounds of my knuckles. 'And what did you think?' The pain was sharp but not unbearable.

'Like I said, the images weren't the best . . .' Jim gave the slightest cough.

'First impressions will do.'

'All right.' He inhaled deeply, casting his eyes to the floor. It seemed that he was reluctant to voice the thought, but then he just let it escape: '*Vaurien*,' he said. 'A long way from your best.'

And my heart lost its rhythm for the tiniest moment. I felt tears brimming. 'Don't you ever disappear on me again, Jim Culvers,' I said. 'You're the only one who's ever seen the difference.'

He did not take my head against his chest to try to console me. He did not even tell me he was sorry. Instead, he rose from the chair and started unscrewing the lid on an empty jar. And he said, 'I think the problem is I agitated them a bit too much. They need to bruise in the brine but not bleed out. Have you ever made pigments this way? It's fussy work but the paint really sings if you do it right. I could use some help perfecting it. You were always better at this kind of stuff than I was.'

'Show me,' I said, and I stood beside him.

It was later in the day, as the sun was dropping into the loch, that I walked down to the phone box in the village and telephoned my mother. She made me swear that I would travel up again to be with her at Easter, and I promised I would write to her and call on Christmas morning.

- - - - -

At first, we slept in separate rooms. It was almost like things used to be. Jim hauled in his single mattress and made a bed for me in the lounge beside the fireplace, saying he was happy on the floor. There were not enough pillows or blankets to share, so he relinquished the ones he had and told me, 'I'll make do.' He took down the heavy curtains from the bedroom and sewed them together with twine to make a sleeping bag, used a rolled-up jumper to cushion his head, and woke up trying to hide the cricks in his neck. In the days, we painted. In the evenings, we bathed and washed our clothes. I finished the novel I had brought and read it time and again by candlelight: the story of an unnamed girl whose thoughts only became more comforting by familiarity. Before I went to sleep, I leafed through *National Geographic* and savoured the pictures and articles.

Jim had no doubts as to the virtue of his work. He had a very set regimen. Each morning, he went out with his tattered picnic basket to forage plants—sometimes venturing no further than the beanstalk weeds in the back garden or the fringes of the surrounding trees, other times going much further, beyond the scree of the hills to their summits, or right across to the other side of the loch. He could be gone for an hour; he could be gone for five. It depended on his needs and what was out there to be found. No matter what, he always came back with a full basket of pickings: local flora he did not know the botanical terms for, and gave what I assumed were pet-names of his own. Skullcap. Redshank. Horsemint. Muck-button. The only plants that ever caught his eye were those with pinkish flowers or stems. Because I could not bear for him to go anywhere without me in those first few weeks, I accompanied him on all of his 'scouting missions', as he liked to call them. But I soon grew tired of hunting around in ditches and thickets, and began to suspect that Jim would prefer to do his scouting alone. One morning, as we were heading back to the cottage through the neighbouring firs, he said to me, 'You really don't have to come with me any more—I can tell you hate it.'

'It's nature,' I said. 'I don't hate it.'

'But you could do without the pissing rain and cold.'

I shrugged. 'You might run off on me again.'

'I've got a shilling to my name. It'd get me into Balloch, but then I reckon I'd be stuck. I'm too old to be scrubbing pots again for bus fare.'

Every second day, he started a new painting. His process was fixed but unusual: first, he coated all of his boards with a black primer then underpainted thickly with Cremnitz White, a very stiff material that he could spread across the board like stucco. 'My only extravagance,' he told me. 'You can use it if you want, but sparingly—I find it helps to think of it as diamond paste.' He would then add definition to the background in regular tube-oils. Next, he would dip a fat round brush into a batch of his home-made pigment (it was thin like syrup) and, holding it firmly in his left hand, he would thump his right fist hard against the base of the brush, spiking beads of paint against the board to form the Judas blossoms. They would hold there fuzzily on the surface, pink and dazzling, and he would spend the next few hours fine-detailing them with a very slim sable.

For a week or so, I slipped back into a role as Jim's assistant. I believed in the work he was doing and felt it worthier than

my own. Together, we refined the pigmentation of the plants he
brought home. I made some adjustments to his timings and suggested a change from brine to icy water; I showed him a different
mullering technique and altered his mix ratios, all of which
helped to yield much brighter hues and more stable paints. He
was grateful, I knew, but also reluctant to accept too much of my
help. 'This is starting to feel like a collaboration,' he said, at the
end of one particularly long day's painting. We were both exhausted. Our meal of boiled rice and tinned carrots had not
satisfied us and we had finished the last of the coffee that morning. We were living off what little cash I had brought with me
and the few pennies Jim had left. There had been some dreamy
talk about me blowing the whole lot on ingredients for a chocolate cake tomorrow, and we had tiredly reviewed the day's progress as I cleared the table. He was pleased with how the work was
developing, but twitchy about my involvement. 'You know I've
loved having you here,' he went on, 'but you've got a life to get
back to. They'll all be wondering where you are.'

'Who will?'

'Dulcie and Max.' He gave a weak smile. 'You need to get
home.'

'I'll write and say I'm on a research trip somewhere. They
won't care. I'm not in any rush.'

'I can see that,' he said, a scratch of irritation in his voice.

'Are you saying you don't want me around? Is that it?'

'Well, it'd be nice to know what your plan is, that's all. While
I'm here alone, I can make the rations last. Gas meter times out
quicker with you here. Hot water runs out faster. This kind of
thing should not be weighing on my mind.'

I folded my arms.

'Look, don't be offended,' he said. 'All this piddling domestic stuff just slows me down. I resent having to think about it.'

'Fine,' I said. 'I'll call Dulcie today and see if she'll send me some money.'

'No, no, no—you aren't listening. I'm not asking for that. That's the *last* thing I want.'

'You're the one talking about gas meters, Jim. I don't know what you want me to say.'

He pleated his hands on the table. 'I'm telling you, if you're going to be here, then you're here to bloody well *paint*. Not to be my assistant. Not to clear up after me. I'm happy to go hungry for the sake of your art, but not so you can be my housekeeper.'

'It's not that easy.'

'It's as easy as you want it to be, Ellie.'

'I don't have anything to paint. A subject, I mean. I'm just—' And I breathed, realising I was about to say *adrift*.

'Find one,' he said. 'You've done it before. I did it myself.'

'Of course. You're right. I should just punch someone and see where it leads me.'

He smirked. 'Might not be such a bad idea, you know. You're only ever ten yards from a bar fight in Scotland.'

I said, 'Actually, it's what Henry used to tell me—pick a fight, disturb the peace.'

'Yeah, he gave the same advice to everyone.'

'Really?'

'Course he did. Only difference is, *you* listened to it.'

'Oh, thanks.'

He waved away my soreness. *'Paint what you believe.* That was

Henry's way of telling you to stop moping and get on with it. If he were here now, he'd be telling you again.'

Over the past few weeks, there had been plenty of time for me to explain the plight of my recent work to Jim. He had, of course, been understanding of my difficulties in finishing paintings ('You saw my On High pile before it was a mountain,' he said. 'Christ, what a mess I made of things!') and was glad to hear that I had withdrawn from the mural project to retain 'a little integrity'. I expected he would be much less accepting of my capitulation to the Roxborough's chequebook. 'Look, it's certainly a pity to show work you aren't proud of,' was all he said, 'but I suppose you must've had your reasons. And it doesn't seem to have dinted your reputation any. Pressure does funny things to people—I know that better than anyone.' His muted disapproval was almost disappointing. I wanted him to lecture me, put me straight.

It was hard to find an appropriate moment to confess to him that I was taking medication. How was I supposed to broach it? Over rice and carrots at the dinner table? While we were climbing up a hummock in search of weeds? Perhaps I should have introduced the topic one night while the two of us were in the bathroom, twisting the dingy water from our laundry? I was afraid that he would think less of me. I feared that telling him about my sessions with Victor Yail would make me seem weak and incapable: just another foolish girl sent reeling by a man. And I could not rake back over my mistakes again like that: Wilfred Searle, the pennyroyal, the caldarium and what came after. I just wanted to be close to Jim, to be around the music of his footsteps in the house each day, to touch and smell the fabric of him.

Until that evening in the kitchen, he had afforded me the

courtesy of not asking about my plans. I had carried on with-out a purpose, hidden my lack of inspiration just by helping him with his. But it seemed he had finally noticed my aimlessness. 'Don't think I was joking, by the way,' he said. 'The more you help me, the better these paintings are getting—that's not a prob-lem for me yet, but it's going to be soon. I don't want to look at them one day and see your handiwork. They're all I've got. So I've got to draw a line under all this. If you want to stay, you have to stop helping me and help yourself instead. Clear that back room out and *paint* something.'

But I had nothing in me—not the remotest, flittering trace of an idea. All my thoughts were *vaurien*. When I told him I could not paint because I felt no thrill in it any longer, Jim stared me down. 'Rubbish. You're just in a slump.' When I told him I had issues with anxiety that required weekly therapy, he gave an in-dignant shake of the head. When I told him I could only finish work on 100mg a day and showed him the bottles of Tofranil from my overnight bag to prove it, he grew angry—not with me, but at the world that had allowed it. 'What kind of idiotic—I mean, who the hell *put* you on these?' He pushed through the kitchen beads to view the label under brighter light. 'They tried to fob me off with these things after the war. Anti-whatevers. I told them, listen, if I'm going to kill myself, I'll be doing it nice and slow with a cask of single malt, thank you very much.' Open-ing a bottle, sniffing its innards, he emptied out a handful of tablets and moved them around on his palm. Then he tipped them back in. Coming in to place them on the kitchen table, he said, 'It's no wonder you can't paint, Ellie. You won't feel a thing while you're dosed up on those.'

'How do you know I feel anything when I'm *off* them?' I said. 'They've been helping me a lot.'

'Helping you?'

'Yes.'

'With what?'

'With keeping my head above water.'

'Well, you'd be better off with a snorkel.' He had already stacked the three short bottles into a pyramid, and now he was standing over them, hands on hips, like some broken-down motorist examining his engine. 'I know one thing: the girl who used to live up in my attic was the most natural painter I ever saw—you'd never have found her avoiding work, or moaning about having no ideas. She went out and found them. She didn't care about pleasing anyone but herself. That was the real you, Ellie. Not this. Not *those*. You need to take it from someone who's been there.' He looked at me now, brow raised. 'How many times did you watch me painting, pissed as a rat, and how much good ever came of it? None. It's taken me this long to get sober, and this long to start making work I'm proud of again.' Turning away, he went to fill a glass under the tap, and came back, slugging it. I was stuck under the dim yellow bulb light, staring at the pills. What a chore it had been in the past few weeks, sneaking off to take them while Jim was occupied elsewhere, keeping half an eye on the mantel clock all day in case I missed a dose. I did not think I was resilient enough to function without medication. But I was not alone any more, and the prospect did not frighten me the way it did when Victor used to suggest it.

Jim put a hand on the small of my back and held it there. 'I just never imagined you needing that kind of help. You always seemed to pour everything into your work. It was like you had another life up there in that attic—your own little sanctuary.' His thumb was rubbing now at the cotton of my blouse. It made my pulse accelerate. 'What's he like, this shrink of yours, anyway? You trust him?'

I nodded. 'He's been good to me.'

'I suppose all those qualifications have to count for something.' Jim paused. I could almost feel his roving eyes upon me. 'You should probably do what he says, then. Don't take medical advice from me. I never even got my Leaving Certificate.'

'Me neither,' I said.

'See. We're the same, you and me.'

'*Jim.*'

'What? What did I say?' But I was not dissenting from his words, only his fingers: they had loosened the blouse from my skirt and were walking up my bare spine. His eyes were tightened, searching. He turned me slowly, brushed my clavicle with his knuckle.

I had to arch up on my tiptoes just to kiss him. His face was coarse with stubble, but his lips had a pleasing gentleness.

'There,' he said. 'Now we can both stop imagining it.'

For the very first time, we slept in the same bed. Beside the fire on the single mattress. Huddled together like stowaways. His hands seemed to know where to go. They knew me in the way that Wilfred Searle's had not even tried to. I wanted to be kept inside Jim's skinny arms forever, wanted to hold my lips against the scuffed skin of his neck and breathe it every morning as I woke up, wanted to feel him lift and hook the trailing hair behind my ear and stroke it, nimbly and repeatedly, just as he would

approach the painting of a Judas blossom. But there was no pattern or rhyme to our being together. There were nights when he
lay restless and went off to be alone, and nights when he tempted
me from sleep with kisses on the cheek and climbed in, undress-
ing me, only to steal away again before the daylight broke.

We lived this way for months, as intermittent partners, lovers,
individuals. We were bonded in our isolation and invested in each
other's purpose. Occasionally, we quarrelled. We spent hours—
full days sometimes—apart, in protest. And neither one of us
could work without listening for the noises of the other, so came
to recognise the creaks and thuds and hums of one another's
practice the way that a piano-tuner can discern a slackened string
from corridors away. But we shared the few rooms of that tum-
bledown cottage as happily as any two people could. Our connection felt immutable.

Jim even helped me clear the junk from the back room, and we
found a trove of objects that we could sell: Henry's old fishing
gear and tackle, a roll of boat upholstery fabric, a box of earthen-
ware crockery, and five reels of soldering wire. It was agreed that
Jim should take them to the weekend market in Balloch. 'Henry
would be telling us to flog the bleedin' lot if it keeps us fed and
watered,' Jim said. 'You should hang on to that cloth for painting, though. It's proper marine canvas.' He left that Saturday
with everything loaded on his body like a pack-mule and came
back with a crate of groceries, including flour and cooking chocolate. 'For the celebration cake,' he said, pecking my forehead.

I started thinking again about my mural, and tentatively tri-
alled a new white pigment made from thistles Jim discarded; but
these experiments came to nothing. Mostly, I worked on sketches

of myself: the grimy cottage windows reflected my face strangely, ruffled and distorted it. I found this spectacle curious enough to occupy me. The drawings came out less like studies of myself than Pathé newsreel stills of strangers. And, through all of this, Jim remained committed to his Judas blossom paintings. They grew steadily more arresting. It was difficult to glean the meaning of them when each piece was seen in isolation, but soon the lounge grew cluttered with his boards—each scattering of pink blossoms different from the last, the colours in them shifting, layers deepening—and I could feel the strength of the work as a collection. I was proud to have made a contribution to it, however incidental.

But then, one morning, I got up to find Jim already gone. The coals were pallid in the hearth. A pot of tea was stewing on the kitchen table, still warm. Outside, a gauzy rain was teeming. I lit the fire and made a pan of porridge, knowing he would come home cold and hungry, and sat by the fireplace eating most of it until he returned. When he stepped in through the back door, he was drenched and broody. His basket was very short of pickings. He went straight into the bathroom to towel off, saying nothing. His quietness seemed very determined, so I asked him what was wrong. 'Just counting all the things I've got to do today,' he said. Then, later, when he went to light the stove under the kettle after lunch, he found the matchbox empty and it left him quietly incensed. For most of the day, I could hear him huffing and sighing from the back room, where I had begun inking some of my sketches (a mere gesture to convince him I was working). Around three, he called me into the lounge. 'Ellie, get in here.' His voice grew increasingly desperate. 'Ellie—I need you!' I expected to find him mullering another batch of pigment. In fact, he was over by the window with several of his paintings laid across the floor on bedsheets. His easel and his workbenches were pushed against the walls. He was stooping over the paintings with a camera, twisting at the aperture. 'How the heck do you work the light gauge on this thing?' he said. 'I've got two rolls of film and I don't want to waste them.'

'Where'd you get that from?' I asked.

He handed me the camera—shoved it at me. 'It's the same one I've always had. I'm not sure the light is good enough. Might have to wait until the morning.'

I peered through the viewfinder, focused the shot. The gauge was unresponsive. 'I think it needs a new battery,' I told him. 'What's your film speed?'

'Don't know.'

'You've got it on 400.'

'Sounds about right.'

'Well, I can try to set the f-stop where I think it should be, but I'm no good without a light meter. I can't promise it'll be perfect.'

'You might as well just do it,' he said. 'Set it up however you think's best. I don't know where I'd get a battery from round here, and I don't want to waste time.'

'What are the photos for, anyway?' I asked.

'Portability,' he said.

In the viewfinder, his paintings were much less vivid. 'I don't get it.'

'You don't have to. Here—give it back. I can manage the rest.'

I had not even clicked the shutter yet. 'It's difficult to get the whole thing in the frame. You'll need to stand up on a table.'

And then his meaning finally landed. 'Are you taking these to show someone?'

His cheek stayed pressed to the camera. 'You're right—I need to get up much higher.' He slid one of the workbenches closer to the paintings and leapt onto it, the legs buckling slightly under his weight. 'Better,' he said, focusing. 'A tripod would be nice, but you can't have it all.' He clicked, and loaded the next frame, his thumb jabbing hard at the lever.

Jim had deflected so much attention onto *my* plans and *my* lack of purpose in the past few months that I had not paused to consider where his own ambitions were steering him. The daily accretion of Judas blossom paintings had been his priority for so long that I assumed he would go on forever. *Until I die*—they were his words. *Until I die.* The thought that he might suddenly stop making them had not once entered my mind. 'What are you planning to do with these, Jim? I don't see what the rush is.'

He jumped down from the table and squared his eyes at me. 'Look, first things first, I need to get them onto film. Can't do much until that's sorted.' Nudging the table further along, he climbed back onto it. 'Then I've got to sell the camera. I reckon I could get fifteen, twenty quid for it, if I can take it to a proper shop in Glasgow—that'll be enough to get the prints done and pay for the train down.'

'Down where?'

'London.' He said it so nonchalantly. 'I want these paintings to be *seen*.'

I went very quiet.

Jim clicked the shutter, reloaded, clicked again. 'Don't get all upset. I'll be back in a few days.'

'You've told me that before.'

'Well, you're just going to have to trust me this time, aren't you?'

I was not sure that I could, and he read this in my attitude before I could voice it.

He widened his stance on the tabletop. 'Look, you could come with me. I mean, if I can get a decent price for the camera, we'll have enough for two returns. But then I'd have to leave all my paintings here, and I don't want to risk it. You can think of them as a deposit—if I don't come back inside a week, flog them, burn them, do what you like with them.'

This was all the encouragement I needed. In London, there was Dulcie and the Roxborough and a tranche of worthless canvases to finish. In London, there was Victor Yail and the endless recitation of my problems and mistakes. In London, there was nothing. 'Can't you just stay a few more days—at least until you can find a battery?'

He shook his head, wincing.

'You're not doing the paintings any justice like that. All the exposures will be off.'

'We'll see how they come out,' he replied. 'People only need to get the gist of what I'm up to. And I can carry a few boards down with me. I was thinking of getting a suitcase to put them in. The others I'll come back for.'

'Are you showing them to Max?'

'No, I've had my fill of him for one lifetime, thanks very much.' He let the camera hang from his neck like an old gas mask in a box. 'Thought I'd start with Bernie, actually. He can get my foot in a door or two. Everyone likes Bernie, and everyone who doesn't like him owes him a favour.'

'Bernie Cale?'

'Yup.' He hopped down. And, placing the cap back on the lens, he said, 'Come on, don't be getting yourself so worked up. I've known Bernie for ages. I knew him before I knew *you*. We used to go to the track together.'

'I don't care about *that*. I don't care about Bernie, for God's sake.'

He tried to embrace me but I turned away. 'Then what's the matter? You've got a terrible frown on you.'

'I just—' I said. 'I can't believe that you're abandoning me all over again.'

'Woah, steady on. I'm coming straight back. I *told* you that.' He gathered the lapels of my blouse and drew me in close. 'Four or five days, that's all it'll be. You won't even have time to miss me.' And he kissed the tip of my nose. 'Nobody's getting abandoned. Come on, don't chew on your lip like that—you'll make it sore.'

I was biting it to keep from crying.

'In any case,' he went on, 'I don't think Bernie would let me bunk with him longer than a week.'

I should have waited for a moment to let the bright idea that came to me cloud over and extinguish itself. But I did not. I said, 'Why don't you just use the flat?'

'Whose flat?'

'Mine.'

Jim's eyelids quivered. 'Oh, I wouldn't want to—I mean, that wouldn't be—no, I'd feel terrible. I couldn't do it.'

'Well, I'm not having you sleeping on Bernie's floor. He takes all-comers in that place of his. Pays for most of them, from what I've heard.' I had no real evidence for this, of course, just bits of gossip. But Bernie was the sort of man it was easy to envision staggering from a Soho doorway in the small hours with his shirt-tails untucked. So I did not feel too sore about accusing him.

'Only if you're sure,' Jim said. 'Only if you're *certain*.' He kissed me in that way he favoured most: dead centre of my forehead, the first spot I had been taught to reach for when I blessed myself in church. But as he moved his lips away, he did not look at me.

Seven

The heavy heartbeat of the mantel clock, the noiseless turning of its hands; another second lost to waiting, another hour without Jim. And where was I? Alone again, sleepless, the summer running down, new ochre leaves fringing the loch and so much rain. Steam lifting on the hills. Rare sprays of traffic. A flavour to the air: bonfires, boat fuel, cold wet pasture. I slammed the clock against the kitchen wall repeatedly—the glass smashed but the mechanism purred, continued, no complaints. With my bare hands, I dug a shallow grave out in the garden. I buried it alive. Now I did not have to worry about the hours ticking by. There were no hours. Just the slow spread of aloneness and a quickly fading hope. But at least I had the work to occupy me. At least I had the work.

Except the work itself was hopeless. I had tried so very hard with it. At first, I did not bother. I lay in bed, reading that same novel and my magazines, and wondered what Jim was doing in London. Not just silly speculations: good day, bad day, which? I mapped his whereabouts precisely in my head. He was at the barber's shop on Allitsen Road getting a shave; he was in a meeting with the Leicester Gallery; he was eating chips and saveloy with Bernie Cale by the canal; he was standing with me at the bathroom mirror; then he was gone. And I was standing at the bathroom mirror alone, looking sinewy and shucked. My hair was like pulled thistles. My face had dark abrasions. I was decaying. Whose skin was this? I could not remember bathing yesterday or the day before. And I grew very anxious about Jim coming back—he would be coming back any day now—to find me stewing in my idleness—not sure exactly when—and he would spin right on his heels and run. Leave me for a third time. The last. So I ran a hot bath—I had done this before—and lowered myself in.

Next morning, the day was drier, brighter. I took a sketchbook, took a satchel, took Jim's coat. I found some pickings of my own. Lavender, petunias, geraniums. Brought them back to the cottage and mulched them. I did the same thing Jim used to do, or what I used to do for Jim. I worked the muller, smoothed it, left the paint so nice and thick. A dash of Cremnitz in it—*sparingly*. Such a pleasant paint to load onto the brush, upon the knife-edge. But it was much too sunny in that room to concentrate. Shrieking crows and gulls outside, cats stalking the tall grass. Things flashing: glints of chrome on distant boats, wobbling on the loch. Strange how metal sharpened beams of sunlight into needles. The hulls rocked gently, side to side. One moment, there they were—those bright white shards—the next thing, gone. But what if I could capture them somehow? What if I could paint them all in Cremnitz? Everything except those tiny spikes of light. Render the scene so thickly that from ten feet away you would see a formless blur—*pure abstraction*—and from an arm's length you would see the definition. Detail. Clarity. It was possible to achieve a feat like that. But who had tried before? Someone, definitely someone. *Men of soaring talent.*

I made the stretcher frame myself from planks—from left-overs in the outhouse, paintings of Henry's, never started, never finished—and I hammered every brass tack through the fabric with the blunt end of a pestle. Good strong boat upholstery, tightly fibred. Quick to prime. And I hung a swathe of it over the window, tacked that too, holding the light at bay. It stopped me trying for a glimpse of Jim out there. Removed all distractions. Focused.

But no, but no, but nothing.

Accept the flaws or fix them. Someone had told me that once. Over the phone: *Accept the flaws or fix them. That's what I always say.* Like something from a textbook. A very gentle voice. Meek and insubstantial.

And then I ground up all the lavender and geraniums. The petunias would not give.

Blue paste in the mortar. A smidge of oil, then mix.

There was plenty to eat, but nothing I wanted.

I was fine for a while.

A bit light-headed.

I thought the mantel clock was ticking in the ground beneath me. I felt the tremors in my feet. But it was just the crunch of glass under my shoes.

Still, a candy-striped line did not seem right.

I had to show it in the paint.

Try the lavender with geraniums. More linseed oil. A good dose of that Cremnitz White would do it. Except nothing would appear. No—it had to *ache* more. The paint. It had to *ache*. Not shine, not glisten, not hum. There had to be one painting I refused to sacrifice. *Straight for the jugular.* Possible, if I kept on going. There were no hours any more. The clock was missing. And where was I supposed to go exactly? What was I supposed to do?

Outside again and sketching. Strange how metal sharpened sunlight into needles but so difficult to draw. The masts were easier. Flick of the pencil—he would be back any day now—and that was it. Those simple boats. A lot more people on the pier. Pickings in the basket from the verges of the hills. Mostly weeds. Yes, he would come back any day now. He told me so. I trusted him. And I could throw his paintings in the loch if he did not.

Crushed another tablet in the mortar and went straight in with Cremnitz. Smearing the paint, it seemed to ache a fraction more. There were sixty-four tablets when Jim left and now just fifty-two. Coral-coloured things, made white under the pestle. Powdered just like salt. A pinch of it did not go far. That night, for dinner: soda bread, the way my mother used to bake it. Jim made sure to leave me with some matches. He put them in the drawer: two boxes. Some of them were blackened, struck already. When he got back, we would need more. We could exhume the clock or get another. We could get back what we lost.

Night-time and barely a light on. Trees a dense black cluster up ahead. The whispering boat ropes straining with the tide. And

everywhere so quiet and cool. The smells of night so sheer and
fulsome. I was carrying two of his best Judas boards above my
head, pall-bearing.

It had taken all day to work up the courage—his messages
must not have reached me; the last train must have left without
him—but I had waited and waited and waited too long.

They were heavy and rough at the sides. Took them down to
the rim of the loch. Silt and sand beneath me, the water bracing,
ankle-high. I threw them forwards and they splashed. They hardly
flew at all. But still the water doused me. The boards drifted away
like rafts and vanished in the dark. The boat ropes tightened,
gave.

He had gone to look for Ana Helène. It was foolish to think
otherwise. There were plenty more boards in the cottage. I had
stacked them up in the back room. The kitchen light ahead of
me, a woozy yellow star to guide me back. I had his permission
for this, I had his approval. But no more for tonight.

The boat ropes were still tightening when I opened my eyes, but
they were nowhere to be seen. I was lying in Jim's sleeping bag of
curtains, amongst his clothes, the musk of them, and day was
falling onto me. The ropes were very close by, the creak of them
prolonged, repeating. I stood up in the sleeping bag until it
peeled right off me. I followed the sound, along the hallway—
creaking—to the lounge. And Jim was in the rocking chair, arms
folded. A fierce look about his face: all tensed. His boots were
new and glassy. He wore a hefty opal ring. 'Where are they?' he

said, letting the words hang. 'The best two are missing. Where are they?' Those steady creaking rockers, back and forth.

'In the loch,' I said. 'You told me I could do it.'

He nodded. 'After a week, I told you. It's been six days.' But his words could not be trusted any more. Standing now, dusting his hands. Sizing me up, as though for a portrait. Head down and to the side. No pencil to measure me. The proportions would be wrong. 'Ellie,' he said, 'how concerned should I be?'

I did not understand his question. The room was much too bright. He was wearing a fine set of clothes, the kind for impressing: serge blazer, a well-ironed shirt. His hair was no shorter, no longer, but the remnants of his tan still shaded his cheekbones. And that big opal ring. 'Not at all. I've been painting,' I said.

He glared at me. 'Yes, I can see that.' A note of contempt in the voice. 'But you don't look well,' he said. 'Just awful, in fact. Have you been eating?'

I shrugged. 'A bit of soda bread.'

'Soda bread. That's all you've had?'

'Well, just a few bites. I made it too salty.'

'In the whole six days?'

'My mother used to bake it.'

'Uh-huh. All right, I see.' He stepped forward, softening. 'I think you'd better lie down.'

'When did you get back?' I said.

'I don't know. Early.'

'You missed your train.'

'Not exactly. Come on—bed now.' He walked me backwards. 'I'll make you some hot milk and then you've got to eat something.'

- - - - -

Warm milk in our stomachs and half a pack of biscuits. Things were better after that. We sat in the kitchen with the back door open, letting in the dregs of summer, all the giddy bugs. The brightness hard to bear. But Jim was home now. Head of the table, watching me chew. His chin resting on his fists. Slack-faced, sighing. 'I should cook you something proper,' he said. 'Have another.' Raisins in the biscuits were shrivelled and delicious. I kept on eating, drank more milk. 'That's a fair-size canvas in the back room,' he said. 'You stretched that on your own?'

I said, 'No one else around to help me, was there?'

'Well, the painting is—' Head to one side.

'Not finished.'

'More like you can't stop working on it.'

'It won't come together.' No more biscuits.

'It reminds me of something.'

'A very bad Turner.'

'No, I don't mean it's derivative.'

'Your eyes need testing.'

'Ellie—you're worrying me.'

'I'm eating, aren't I? What more do you want?'

He bit on his knuckle, considering the answer. His eyes did not leave mine. I could see the gap in his teeth from fighting. He said, 'Actually, it reminds me of the work I did when I was drinking—*heavily* drinking. Your thoughts are leaking out of so many different places you can't hold them. There's no control, no discipline. Everything's just streaming out of you and you can't stop it. I understand what that feels like, believe me I do. Feels like

freedom but all you're really doing is shutting things out. It leads
you nowhere good.'

'You shouldn't have left me here,' I told him.

'Yes, I think you're probably right.'

'Then why did you?'

'Because I had to.' Staring at the tabletop. 'I've been in the
state you're in now, Ellie, and I can't go back to it. As much as I
care for you, I won't.'

He did not say *love*. He did not even think it. 'I'm hopeless on
my own,' I said.

'That isn't true. You've always been alone. You thrive that way.'

'Well, I don't feel it.' And I pushed myself upright. 'I can't
paint any more. I'm done with it all.'

The chair legs scraped. Jim grabbed for my arm. He took my
wrist. I scowled at him. 'Ellie, please, sit down.' A kindly flutter
of his hand. 'I need to tell you something. It's important.' Such
levelness to his expression: he gave nothing away. (Petunias.) So I
did as he asked.

Inhaling once, sharply. His palms pressed together. 'I wore
this for the trip,' he said. The opal ring slipped off. It wobbled on
the table. 'It's not the subtlest bit of jewellery in the world, but it
has sentimental value.' I did not pick it up. My mouth was dry.

'Sentimental why?' I said.

'It belongs to someone dear to me.'

'Ana Helène.' Only a fool would assume otherwise.

'No.' He smiled. 'A man from my regiment.'

'Oh.'

'I know it's an ugly old thing, but it makes me proud to wear it.'

'Is there any water left?' I said.

Slitting his eyes. 'Of course. I'll get you some.'

Filled a glass from the tap. Studied the birds in the garden. The daylight made me sore, but not Jim Culvers. He admired the afternoon for what it was. He passed me the water and sat down again. 'Listen now, I want you to hear this. It might just stop you doing something stupid.' I took very slow gulps. 'I lied to you, months ago. When you asked me where I'd been, I lied to you. And I'm sorry, but I had to.'

'I know you weren't in London,' I said. 'I'm not an idiot.'

'Ellie, listen to me now. It's important that you hear me.'

'You don't have to pretend. You care for me, that's all. And yes, I care for you. Now we just have to get on with it. We don't need to get married.'

He reached across the table. For the ring, I thought. But no—for my hand. He gripped it tightly. 'Ana Helène is just a name,' he said. 'I made her up—I had to think of something on the spot. Please listen.'

His words could not be trusted.

My mouth felt worse for the water. Pasty thick.

'Everything I told you about the doctor and the trip to France—that was true. I *did* go back to Arras. The bar fight part was true, except it happened in Paris not Dunkirk. I hit a poet in the mouth. The rest was just a story. I don't know if he had a sister but I didn't go to Giverny with him or anywhere else. I got arrested that day and my friend came to get me. He lives in Paris with his wife. He's a playwright now, quite a famous one, actually—doing lots of script work for the films. And this ring, I promise you, it genuinely belongs to him. I need you to know I'm telling you the truth.'

'What does it matter?' I said. 'You're here now. And you care for me. That's all.'

He slipped it back on his finger, twisted it round. 'I don't even know if there are Judas trees in Giverny. That isn't the place I saw them. Ellie, keep listening to me, please. You're not even—all right, let's do this later. You rest a bit. You rest, and I'll see if I can get us something that's worth eating. How would you like some—'

- - - - - -

Fried eggs and beans. The only time Jim ever cooked me anything. The sight of it was sickening. And how long had I slept? The kitchen beads were taped against the frame. Just embers in the hearth. He made me eat again. Some of the beans and most of the eggs. And then we carried on. The ring belonged to his playwright friend—he had told me this before—and his wife who lived in Paris—yes, I knew all this, I said.

'We served together. He was my sergeant. I'd seen him just a few times since the war, but we wrote to each other a lot. Anyway, that day he came to bail me out at the station—well, I could tell how concerned he was about me, you know? I was in an awful state. Worse than in the Army. It was him and his wife who helped me get sober. To begin with, at least.'

Jim made the tea too strong. I could not drink it.

'Listen, Ellie, listen.'

I still felt a bit light-headed.

'So I was in a bad way, I'd given up on painting—he could see that I was struggling just to get out of bed in the morning. I was always the one who used to keep his spirits up, you know—I'd draw him pictures to cheer him up when we got stationed

anywhere new. Just sketches of the fellas in the regiment. And he
knew how much it meant to me, to be painting well. We used to
talk about it all the time in our letters.'

He was telling the truth. His eyes were bright and clear. Nothing evasive, nothing shifting. Finally, Jim Culvers was telling me
the truth.

'Anyway. One day, his wife goes out to meet someone, and
we're alone. And he tells me all about this time when he was
younger, how he'd been through a similar thing to what was
happening to me now—drinking a lot, and hardly writing. Even
though his plays were being put on every year, he said he'd felt
this despair inside, eating away at him. Something just wasn't
right. He'd tried to kill himself a few times, he said, and I was—
well, I didn't know what to think. Got your attention now,
though, I see.'

I was staring at him—at his mouth.

'Well, he'd clearly managed to get himself straightened out, so
I asked him how he'd done it. And he starts talking very fast
about everything he'd been through, hitting rock bottom, all of
that. I don't know if he was worried about his wife coming back
and hearing, or what, but he really did talk quickly. And, next
thing, he's telling me all about this place he knows in Turkey.
Some island off the coast of Istanbul. There was a set-up there,
he said, a kind of sanatorium. A place only for artists—not a
colony, not a resort or anything like that. A refuge. He claimed it
turned his life around, this place, just being there. Gave him
back his sense of purpose. Completely cleared his mind.'

It sounded like a perfect spot to disappear.

'So I just looked at him, you know—same way you're looking

at me now—and my heart was thumping in my chest. I knew I had to get there, wherever it was. No matter what, I needed to get there. I asked him how to find it, and he said, "It's not that simple. There are rules you have to follow." I said, "I'll do anything. Just tell me how to get there." So he did. He told me everything. And I want you to hear this now, Ellie, and really listen, *really listen*, because I won't have a chance to repeat it.'

- - - - - -

Waiting at the phone box on a street somewhere in Luss. Expecting it to ring. Jim said I should stay in bed, but I could not sleep a moment longer. The food had strengthened me a bit. I could stand up straight without faltering. We were half under the streetlamp. No cars on the road. Grey smoke shuffling in the darkness, a line of cottages turned in for the night. Already Jim had dialled a number and spoken to his contact. 'All right,' he had said, 'we'll stand by,' and he had read aloud the number of the phone box. 'Doesn't matter when. However long it takes. If we don't hear in a few hours, we'll have to—all right, thank you.' That seemed like forever ago.

We sat on the kerb, throwing stones, like two kids playing in the lane. 'You don't have to worry about anything,' Jim said. 'It's going to be difficult at first, but, trust me, it gets easier. My first season there, I hardly painted anything. I just tried to get used to the surroundings. That's OK, by the way—you can't be afraid of losing time. Just let your mind absorb things, let it settle. And, eventually, you'll work yourself out. My advice is, go up to the mansion roof a lot. That's where you'll see things clearest. All the Judas trees come out on the islands in the spring—it's like nothing else on earth. You can see them from across the water. And when you see them, think of me, remember this moment, OK? Because the main thing out there is not to get lonely. There'll be people who you'll get along with, and people who you won't, but it's important not to get lonely. It happened to a few people I—' Phone was ringing. 'This is it,' Jim said. He patted the dirt from his hands. Swinging the rusted door open, stepping in. He looked at me, smiling. Picked up the receiver. 'Yes?' A nod, a nod, another. 'Thank you, sir, yes. I'm keeping well. The work is flowing. Things are selling, too, which helps.' Pause. Nod. 'I've no doubt that it did, sir, yes.' A genteel laugh I had never heard him give before. An odd formality to it all. 'Of course, of course. Well, I won't keep you. I'll pass on the good news. And thank you so much again for—no, but I really do appreciate it.' That laugh again. 'I will, sir, yes. *Hoşçakal.*'

One

The boat was nine heaves out of the bay and getting smaller. From the escarpment, we could just make out Ender straining at the oars, his back hunched like a dune against the drizzle, the grey sea swaying all around him. With each stroke, the bow seemed to move only a fraction. If we had been near enough, we might have heard the old man complain about his aching bones to Ardak in the stern. The two of them had spent all afternoon preparing the boy's body: wrapping it, weighting it, hauling it down the forest slope on their shoulders. But whatever thoughts were shared between them in that boat, whatever they felt about performing this dire duty on our behalf, nobody could tell from so far away. We could only gauge it from the respectful indolence of the old man's rowing motions, and the straightforwardness with which Ardak went about the job of lowering the boy into the water.

It happened like this:

Twenty more heaves and Ender let the boat drift, pulling the oars in from the rowlocks. Ardak came forwards, his feet straddling the thwarts. He took one end of the body and the old man took the other. The boat teetered and swung. They seemed to give themselves a count of three, and then they hove the body sideways, scraping it along the boards and resting it a moment on the gunwale. The body was wedged against the frame of the boat—a limp shape bundled in black plastic and a cheap Turkish rug, all strung up like a boxing glove. Ardak had to lean his weight backwards to prevent them from capsizing. They had a short consultation, hands on hips, and then they tried again, pushing the body overboard. It was so loaded with cinderblocks that it sunk fast, and the boat wobbled suddenly underneath them, causing the old man to stumble; Ardak grabbed his sleeve to keep him from lurching into the water. They steadied themselves and sat down on the thwarts again. For a moment, they just waited there, drifting on the Marmara for no reason.

Then the provost began to eulogise. 'I have no words of inspiration for you today,' he called out over the breeze. 'I had hoped that I could compose a few lines that might capture the significance of the life that we have lost, but I have failed to do so, and I feel some shame about that. Yesterday, we had a great young talent in our midst, and today we've buried him. Nothing I say can match the depth of our sorrow. That such a tragedy should happen on my watch as provost is a regret I will take to my own grave.' He paused here, rucking the ground with his cane.

Every last guest at Portmantle was standing on the southeastern bluff with their eyes towards the sea. The provost had angled himself to address the whole crowd, but we knew his speech was meant only for the four of us. There was a reverential distance in his tone, a suggestion of apology. 'Nothing good can be salvaged from a day as dark as this,' he went on, 'but there is—it only strikes me now, in fact—there *is* a lesson to be taken from it.'

He was sermonising from a mound of shingly soil and wore a long black overcoat that shimmied in the wind. The short-termers were huddled in a crescent alongside him, but we stood further back: MacKinney with her arm around me, Quickman squatting to ruffle the fur on Nazar's chest, and Pettifer hovering over them with an umbrella like some awkward hand-servant. My toes skimmed the frill of weeds on the escarpment's edge, and I focused on the sea washing below, until it became so metronomic I could sense each breaking wave without having to listen.

'Because, at times like these, it is artists like you whom we consult for solace—' *Wash.* 'The poets and writers in our libraries—' *Wash.* 'The paintings on our walls, the music.' *Wash.* 'Death is something only art can qualify. And that is all—' *Wash.* '—the encouragement I can take from this unhappy mess.' *Wash.* 'Because surely all great art is made for people left behind. For those—' *Wash.* '—who suffer death and cannot fathom it. And so what else is there to say, except—' *Wash.* 'To Fullerton! May he rest in peace and live on through his work.'

'To Fullerton!' everyone called.

'To the boy,' I said.

Wash.

I tried to imagine what it would be like to jump, to fall, to be devoured by the sea. It did not give me much relief to think of it, or bring me any deeper sense of understanding.

MacKinney tugged at my shoulder. 'Come on, let's move back from the edge, eh? The wind's picking up.' I was tucked inside her wing. We were flanked by pines and scrub, but still a fair breeze swirled about our ankles, moving tiny pebbles underfoot. I stepped back. 'That's better. That's it.'

The short-termers were dispersing and heading for the trees. Out on the water, Ender had already turned the boat for home. He rowed with the same tired action as before, yet he seemed to glide much faster. 'What are we supposed to do now?' I said.

'I'm not sure.'

'Gülcan's made a special supper,' said Pettifer. 'Everyone's going back up to the house.'

'I don't see what's so special about any of this,' Quickman said.

'It's out of the ordinary, that's all I meant.'

'I'll say.'

'They're holding a wake,' Mac cut in. 'The provost's idea.'

Quickman scruffed the dog's head. 'What the hell's the point of that?'

'Well, they've got to do *something* for the lad, haven't they?'

'They didn't do anything for him before. No reason to start now.' Quickman seemed to say this to the dog. She had not left his heels all afternoon, and, in turn, he had been patting and cajoling her when she made the slightest plea. 'They didn't even know him. What are they going to do, stand around making up anecdotes?'

'Knell knew him better than anyone. And if she wants to go—'

'I don't. Q's right,' I said. 'It's a sham. The provost couldn't care less.'

I could still feel the boy's wet body in my arms, a phantom ache. The day had passed with agonising slowness and I just wanted to see it out. I had spent most of the morning by the fire in the day room, watching the fight of the flames, hoping that if

I stared for long enough into the blurry heat it might tranquillise me, blank my memory. But I could not stop myself from thinking of the duct tape on the boy's mouth—the very stuff that I had given him—or the leather belt around his neck, the simple weave of it. He had won it from Tif in their backgammon game. Such small details plagued me. They lured me into a trail of senseless speculations on what might have been: if the four of us had only done *x*, if I had just said *y* to the boy, if the provost had done *z*. I was searching for logic where none existed.

At the provost's instruction, the boy had been carried out of his lodging on a hammock made of bedsheets, Ender and Ardak providing the muscle. Quickman had stayed with me in the day room, surveying every movement from the window, until they had taken the body too deep into the woods for us to see. Q had gone to the couch, where the dog was lying, and towelled her belly until her hind legs kicked. There was a homely dampness in the air. 'It'll be all right, you know,' he had said. 'In a few days, we're going to feel better.' After a while, Gülcan had brought in cups of hot *salep* and pastries left over from breakfast; I had drunk two cups and eaten as much as I could stomach, but Quickman had fed his own share to the dog.

I had told him, 'Someone's got to let his family know. I don't care what the provost says.'

'And how are we supposed to do that exactly?'

'By getting out of here.'

'Don't talk silly.'

'I'll write a letter, sneak it in the outgoing post somehow.'

'You don't even know if he *has* a family. You don't even know his real name.'

'So what are you saying, Q? Forget about him?'

I had thought, of all people, Quickman would try to reassure me.

'There's a bigger picture, you know,' was his response. 'Think about what you're suggesting.' He had brought the pipe out of his pocket, slotting it into his teeth. 'You have to remember that he did this to himself. He made his choice. That might sound very cold-hearted, but, I'm sorry, that's just how I see it. The provost has a point.'

'So you're caving in now, too. Terrific.'

'Think about it, Knell. He's one boy. One out of God knows how many. You're really going to let him run this place into the ground? That isn't what he wanted.'

My mind would not be changed as easily as Quickman's, but I could not blame him for his second thoughts. He was the one who had found the boy in the bathtub, after all, and he had earned the right to view things however he wished. It was the provost whom I could not forgive. There had been an eerie calmness about his behaviour that morning, in the height of our emergency. Both he and Ardak had followed me out of the mansion, running back to the boy's lodging; Ardak had sprinted ahead of me, but the provost had lagged behind, barely jogging, his old doctor's bag gripped under one arm. In the bathroom, he had genuflected at the sight of Fullerton on the tiles. He had removed a stethoscope from the bag and placed the metal cup against the boy's chest, allowing an empty moment to go by.

'Anything?' Q had asked, though he must have known the answer.

The provost had shaken his head. He had checked Fullerton's

distended eyes with a torch and closed the boy's lids in the thoughtless way you might shut the clasps on a briefcase. 'I'm afraid he's gone,' he had said. 'We'll have to bury him right away.' He had turned to give Ardak some instructions in Turkish. *'Adamı denize atabilir misin?'*

'Karanlık olmadan atmalıyız,' Ardak had replied, shrugging. *'Ben botu hazırlarım.'*

'What are you going to do with him?' Quickman had said.

'Well, we can't keep him on the grounds, that's for certain. It's much too risky.' The provost had stuffed the instruments back inside his doctor's bag. 'Ardak thinks we ought to put him out to sea. I'll have to check with the trustees, but I think that's probably safest.'

'You can't just dump him in the Marmara.'

The provost had stood up, towering over me. 'Knell, we have to be pragmatic about this.' He had rolled his good eye downwards. 'It wouldn't be the first funeral we've held here—people get sick, and we can't always treat them if they refuse to go to hospital. There's a procedure.' He had spoken to Ardak again. *'Yaşlı adamdan yardım al.'* Then he had dusted off his hands and said to us, 'I have to make some calls. Excuse me.'

'Are you going to talk to his sponsor?' My voice had sounded so puny. 'His family needs to be told.'

The provost had inhaled deeply. 'I'm not sure that's in anyone's best interest.'

'Of course it is.'

'You can't honestly be suggesting that we go on as normal,' Quickman had said.

The provost had slung his bag over his shoulder. 'I know you two were friends of his. But what do you think would happen if I told his sponsor? The news is bound to leak—we can't control what sponsors say or do—and we'd have a thousand people banging on these gates, asking all kinds of questions. We'd be shut down before the season's out. I'm sorry, I won't put the refuge in jeopardy like that, for anyone.'

Quickman had looked bewildered, even sickened, and I had thought he would share my anger towards the provost forever. 'So what do you propose we do, sir?' he had asked.

'Follow procedure. That's all there is to it.'

Ardak had called from the doorway: '*Bunin için ekstra ödeme gerekir beyefendi.*'

The provost had nodded back at him emphatically. Then, shuffling towards us with an air of appeasement, he had said, 'Nobody wants it to happen this way. But it's one of the eventualities we all have to prepare for. You understood the risks when you both came here.'

And so, at the end of the miserable afternoon, the boy was tossed into the sea like fish guts, and I was left with a deadness in my belly, a shame that I feared might never subside. The provost's eulogy had rung hollow. I wished that I could have spoken in his place, but I was not invited to, and what exactly would I have said? Aside from a few personal things the boy had shared with me—about recurring dreams, and Japanese scribblings, and listening to old records at his grandfather's house—I had no great insight into his life. He was not someone who deserved to be spoken about in half measures.

The dour sky was darkening still. I held on to the crook of Mac's elbow and she steered us off the escarpment. The mansion surfaced above the treeline: what an ugly grey hulk it was in the drizzle, what a mangy old dump. Nazar scurried by us, bounding through the scrub. 'I guess it's feeding time,' Pettifer said from behind. 'At least some of us are thinking clearly, eh?'

'Shut up, Tif,' Mac said.

'Just trying to raise a smile.'

We were only yards from the clearing where my mushrooms grew—they were just beyond the coppice to my left, and my chest tightened at the thought of them.

As we came through the pines, I saw the provost waiting in the mulch by the studio huts. I did not want to speak to him, but he was loitering in an official way, as though he had some form awaiting a signature. Nazar ran to him, circled his feet, sniffing. He was without an umbrella. 'Go around him,' I told Mac.

'You sure?'

She tried to veer away, but he moved to intercept us. 'Can you spare a moment?' he said. 'Both of you.'

Tif and Quickman were just a few strides behind.

'What's going on over at the house right now?' Q asked.

'I've asked Gülcan to make her special *köfte*,' the provost replied, 'in honour of the boy. You don't have to join us if you aren't feeling up to it. It's been a very long day.'

'His appetite's taken a hit,' Tif said. 'But I'm keen.'

'As you wish.' There was an awkward pause. 'Well, if I might borrow the ladies for a moment?'

'They're not ours to lend,' said Quickman.

'It's all right,' I said.

They left us alone, and Nazar hurried after.

The provost waited for them to be out of earshot. He folded

his arms. 'You know, I was beginning to wonder if the trustees really understand how this place functions. But, in your case, MacKinney, they've proven me wrong.'

'I'm not following you, sir.'

'It seems our appeals have been heard, after all. They're going to let you stay.'

'Are you serious? Oh, that's—oh, my goodness, thank you,' she said.

'I'm just glad they came to their senses.' He scraped the mulch off his shoe. 'I've taken the liberty of cancelling tonight's reading. Hope you don't mind.'

'We would've cancelled it anyway,' Mac said. 'Given the circumstances. But, really, sir—thank you.'

'I knew you'd understand.'

'Can I keep the same room?'

'I don't see why not.' He peered towards the mansion. 'Unless you'd prefer to change. I wouldn't want to hold you there against your will.'

'No, no, I'm happy where I am.' She managed to quell the jubilation in her voice, but it seeped out onto her face, tugging at the corners of her mouth, mottling her skin. 'This is going to make all the difference to my work, sir—I can't tell you. It won't be long before I've finished it.'

'I have no doubt you'll use the time productively.' The provost reached for his pocket watch, shielding it as he flicked it open. 'You haven't said anything, Knell. I thought you'd be grateful for a bit of good news today.'

After the pitiless way he had dispatched Fullerton, I could only feel sceptical. It seemed that this sudden backpedalling was intended to placate us—to quiet any impulsions we might have had to scream the boy's name from the mansion roof, or, in Mac's case, to confess what she had witnessed to her friends back on the mainland. 'I'm pleased Mac gets to stay,' I said. 'If that's what you need to hear.'

'She's a bit exhausted,' MacKinney said contritely. 'I ought to take her back now.'

'Yes, she does look quite run down.'

'I'm fine,' I said. She tried to walk me forwards, but I resisted. There was plenty enough strength in me yet. 'I'm sure their sudden change of heart has nothing to do with dumping the boy out there.'

'*Knell*,' Mac said.

A wen of rain dripped from the provost's brow. 'The trustees aren't infallible. They've acknowledged their mistake, and I don't think we should be asking questions if the outcome is the right one in the end, do you?'

I felt Mac pulling at my elbow again.

The provost turned his back on us, resting his cane upon his shoulder. 'I suggest you try to get some rest now, *both* of you,' he called, treading the path. 'Provost's orders.'

- - - - - -

There was little sense in sleeping. But, with everyone convening in the mess hall under the pretence of mourning, I did not want to be around the mansion until lights-out. So I took a shower and changed my clothes again (everything I wore seemed to be possessed by memories) and then I cleared my studio, washed up my equipment and organised my materials. Afterwards, I made a cup of tea and sat down on the couch to take the weight off, and I must have leaned my head back a degree too far, because I woke up in lamplight with the teacup full and cold. I was out of kindling for the stove and could not light it. There was plenty in the mansion stores, I knew, and Ender would replenish my stocks come morning. But the rain had left the evening damp and rheumy on the lungs; I needed to stay warm.

Ender had a room on the ground floor—not much more than a storage space with a single bed and bathroom fixtures screened off behind muslin. His door was closed when I got there, and he did not respond when I knocked. Upstairs, there was movement on the landing, and I went up to see if he was in the mess hall or the kitchen. But there was only Lindo, the Spaniard, and a few of his short-term friends. They were playing shove ha'penny on our table and making quite a din. When Lindo spotted me, he gestured for the group to quieten. 'Is everything OK?' he asked. The other heads turned. I barely recognised their faces: gormless, spongy, self-amused.

'Looking for Ender,' I said. 'What are you doing on our table?'

The Spaniard shrugged. 'The game requires it.' He held my gaze, unflinching. 'Ender is not here. We have not seen him. Should I tell him you were looking?'

The serving pass was shuttered and the kitchen door was closed. 'No, that's all right,' I said. Lindo nodded and returned to his shove ha'penny. For a short while, I dawdled on the landing, expecting Ender to emerge from a stairwell or a corridor, but he did not. In fact, the mansion was curiously still, as though Gülcan's special supper had left everyone so sedated they had all retired to bed.

Quickman's room was at the near end of the hallway, separated from MacKinney's by the landing and the library. I rarely
disturbed him in his own space. Of the four of us, he was the
most guarded about his lodging and it was simpler just to wait
for his appearance every mealtime than try to lure him out—if
he was absent at lunch or dinner, we assumed that he was in a
solitary mood. But I was feeling less in thrall to Quickman's need
for privacy than usual. I went to knock for him.

It took no time at all for him to answer. My knuckles were
hardly off the wood. He peeked out through the gap, lifting his
chin at me. 'Thought it might be you,' he said, and let the door
hang open. His room had changed since my last visit: generally
less cluttered, but something else, too. Quickman must have
sensed me trying to work it out, because he thumbed towards his
desk and said, 'Used to be under the window, if that's what's
bothering you.'

'Tired of the scenery already?' I said.

'It helps to change your view every now and again, I've found.'
He went to sit down in his swivel-chair, a high-backed rosewood
thing with metal casters and a few turned spindles missing (his
hands reached back into the space where they should have been).
'And I get distracted by the birds. If you stare at them for long
enough, they develop personalities. Now I can't look up in case I
see myself in the mirror. One glimpse of this face is like a dose of
salts.'

'Yes, I've often thought so.'

He almost smiled. There was subdued light about the place,
like some rare-book shop. A lamp was poised over the empty surface of his desk. 'You're not working?' I asked.

'I never write and entertain at once,' he said. 'I'm not Gertrude bloody Stein.'

The last time I had ventured into Quickman's room, seasons before, I had seen a stack of pages on his bedside cabinet: hand-written, curling, weighed down by some dull brass ornament. The stack had been thick as a breezeblock. The same papers were still there, except the ream was just a quarter of the size, and a pot of *ayran* rested on it with its cap peeled back. 'I was trying to find Ender,' I said. 'Didn't want to interrupt you.'

'Well, I don't know where the old man is, but I'm glad you stopped by.' Using his heels, he swung the chair round and shuf-fled to a set of drawers. From the topmost, he pulled out a bundle of cloth. 'I've not been able to concentrate all day. I tried to sleep but I don't think I've been this restless since the war.'

'You were in the war?' It surprised me that Q had volunteered this information, though I had always assumed he would have served in some capacity. There was a forlorn silence that belonged to men his age, in which you could detect reverberations of expe-riences too bewildering to relay.

He inhaled, nodding. 'I was indeed. The Sappers. Saw a bit of action out in Nijmegen, and then got shot in the foot. Shot *myself* in the foot, quite literally. So don't be staring at me all misty-eyed or anything. I'm no war hero.' Wheeling himself back to the desk, he set the bundle down and unfolded the fabric. It was a T-shirt, pale blue, with crusted marks about the armpits. And, inside it, were the boy's index cards. The entire block of them, jointed with tape. Some of the ink was smudged here and there, but the Japanese was still legible.

'Where'd you get those?' I said, stepping forward.

Quickman stared down at them. 'I took them from his table before you brought the provost.'

'Why?'

'I've been wondering that myself. A sense of duty, I suppose. Even though—' He broke off, drawing his pipe out of his pocket, biting on it. 'Even though I hardly knew the lad. But, God, I don't know, Knell. Once you've held somebody in your arms like that, someone as young as him, so dead, you just—it does things to you. I had this awful feeling, as if I'd failed him somehow. And then I saw the cards and that was it. I took them.'

Under Quickman's desk light, the boy's scrawled notes seemed like preserved exhibits. I still did not know what they meant. 'Did you translate them yet?' I asked.

'Some of them,' Q said.

'And?'

'They're extremely odd. Not dissimilar to the boy himself, in all honesty.' He picked up the cards and turned back through them. 'These ones, for example. They read like advertising copy. Some sort of public health notice from the United Fruit Company—I'm not joking. I've translated to the best of my ability, but still, there's something awkward about the language. See what you make of it.' He slid open the drawer of his desk and brought out a yellow notepad with his own writings in pencil. And removing his pipe, he read:

'*How to add life to your years*—dot, dot, dot—*and years to your life*—exclamation mark. *You've probably noticed it among your own acquaintances. Some people at sixty or even seventy seem to be doing more, and having more fun at it, than others who are fifty, or even forty*—exclamation mark. *Chances are, if you could look closer into their lives, you'd learn a few things. They chose the right parents.* Open bracket: *Heredity—possibly lineage,* that word, not sure—*has something to do with it.* Close bracket. *They find joy in their work.* Open bracket: *That has a lot to do with it.* Close bracket. *You might discover that the people who live longest and enjoy life most are people who eat enough of the right kind of foods. For a properly balanced diet, medical scientists—possibly just doctors* there, but *medical scientists* seems more correct—*medical scientists can literally slow up the ageing process.* Slow up. Sounds very American, doesn't it? Hang on. Lost my place now . . . *That means plenty of proteins—the building blocks that keep your body in a state of good repair. Vitamins and minerals—the protective foods that keep your eyes shining, your hair and skin in good condition—* dot, dot, dot—*and your whole outlook on life brighter. Energy foods—the fuels your body has to burn to give you vigour and enthusiasm.'* Q widened his eyes. 'I'm not sure you need to hear the rest.'

'Is that all of it?' I said.

'No, there's more. Plenty more.' He leafed through his notepad, clearing his throat. *'That is not to say you have to eat a lot. In fact, as we grow older, we need less food. The important thing is to eat a wide variety of the right foods. For instance, take a banana. Take it—* exclamation mark—*peel it, eat it—*exclamation mark. *It's satisfying and nourishing. Vitamins and minerals are there in well-balanced supply and wholesome natural sugars to give you energy. Slice a banana into a bowl and pour milk on it—*dot, dot, dot—*you're adding proteins to keep your body in good repair, as well as consuming—* don't know what that word is—*and bone-building—*possibly *bone-growing,* there—*calcium. Easy to fix.* Again, that's quite

American. *Easy to fix. Easy to eat. Easy to digest. In fact, doctors often recommend bananas in cases of severe digestive disturbances. And you don't have to feel very hungry*—open bracket—*or even be very old*—close bracket—*to enjoy this simple treat*—exclamation mark. And then the tagline: *United Fruit Company. For health, eat and enjoy a plentiful variety of the right foods.'* Quickman tossed the notepad aside and clamped down on his pipe again. 'If you can tell me what any of this relates to, I'd be very glad to know. Because I've spent the past few hours working on all that and it still baffles me. I mean, who the heck *was* this lad, anyway, if this was the nonsense filling his head?'

I did not have the answers for him. 'All I know is that we didn't do enough for him while he was here.'

Q said nothing.

'Have you translated any more?'

He sighed. 'About half of them. There's an ad for Cadillac and the *Encyclopaedia Britannica*, and one for Zenith hearing aids. I'm officially bemused.'

'Please keep at it,' I said. 'They're all that's left.'

'I will.' He scratched his beard, leaning back. 'Any distraction at the moment is a welcome one. Except—' He straightened up, swivelling to catch my eye. 'They're not quite *all* that's left. I mean, he came here with a bagful, didn't he? There must be other things in his lodging we can save.'

- - - - - -

Fullerton's window was boarded with plywood. 'Just for now,' Ender said. 'I can order tomorrow some glass.' He unlocked the door for me, flipped on the wall-switch. A stark fluorescent haze brightened the studio. I tried not to look towards the threshold of the bathroom, where my last sighting of the boy was still imprinted in the space like some trick of the light. There was a stink of Ajax in the air. The concrete floor had been mopped dry and the boy's bed had been stripped. His guitar was stored above the wardrobe. 'What's wrong with the lamps?' I asked, seeing they were all unplugged.

'For safeness,' Ender said. 'We have to test.'

The boy had a large drafting table, similar to Pettifer's, though his was tilted at a sharper angle against the wall. There were no sentimental images from home tacked up on the plaster behind it, no inspiring prints or clippings, as you might have found in other studios. The materials on his workbench were quite meagre: a few coloured pens and pencils; a pot of red ink, a pot of blue; a graphite stick and blotting tissues. 'I will come back soon, yes?' Ender said.

I nodded. 'Thank you.' But it struck me that I should not let the old man leave without pressing him for answers. 'Hang on. Ender?'

He was halfway out the door. '*Evet.*'

'Did you come across a note at all? When you were cleaning up the place?'

'Excuse me. My English . . .'

'A *note*—' I made the action: left hand paper, right hand pen. 'Did the boy leave a note?'

'Foolertin?'

'Yes,' I said. 'Fullerton.'

The old man shrugged. 'There was nothing like this, I don't think.'

'You're sure?'

'Yes. Very sure.'

'The provost doesn't have it?'

He shook his head. 'No. No. There was nothing like this.'

I had been thinking all day about the circumstances of the boy's death, and I had concluded that nothing ought to be assumed. Everyone was behaving as though Fullerton had killed himself—even Quickman had swept to judgement on the matter, though he seemed to be wavering on it now—and I still had misgivings. I had seen the odd effects of the boy's sleepwalking, after all, the full influence of his dreams, and I reasoned that his drowning in the bathtub might well have been its consequence. Accidents like these were possible.

'I can go now?' the old man said.

'Yes. I won't be long.'

'I will come back for you soon. To lock it. The wood I leave outside your door, OK?'

I nodded.

The neatness of the room was troubling—it had been forced back into order after cleaning, and the placement of the boy's possessions was too overtly conscientious. I dragged the desk-chair to the wardrobe and brought down the guitar. Its wooden hips were damp at the edges, watermarked. As I thumbed the strings, it made the most unmusical sound. The thinnest strings were missing, in fact, and so were the little white pegs that secured them. When I laid it on the bed, I heard something clattering inside the body of the instrument. I had to shake it upside down, expecting the pegs would drop out, but a *jeton* fell onto the mattress instead.

Everything about it was familiar—the groove in the metal, the phoney gold lacquer worn away in all the same places—but, turning it over in my fingers, I saw that it was not a ferry token. Its faces had no markings. This must have been what the boy had flashed at me that day, when I had confronted him about the broken window. I felt strangely disapproving of him, then disappointed in myself for not expecting he would lie to me.

The drafting table seemed out of place, moved in from someone else's studio. When I connected the desk lamp, it cast a doomy light over the surface: there were handprints on the laminate, pencil marks and skids from an eraser. An array of papers rested on the table's narrow ledge: finely textured sheets, a heavy gauge, expensive. Apart from the foremost page, which showed a rectangle sketched in freehand, they looked unused. I checked them against the lamplight, hoping I might find the indentations of the boy's handwriting; but, instead, I saw the fault lines of a picture in the paper, fading through each sheaf.

I took the graphite stick and rubbed it sidelong over the page with the heaviest depressions. Bit by bit, the faint white furrows left in the graphite began to form an illustration. It was made of four thin panels, about an inch across and several high. Each box contained a line drawing of one man's face in close-up. They showed his dawning expression: (i) gasping anger; (ii) recognition; (iii) a softening of the brow; (iv) tears.

Even as a rough negative like this, it was a spectacular drawing: an assembly of simple lines, some feathered, some solid, that seemed to lift the man's whole character from the blankness. I had seen this exaggerated style somewhere before, but could not think where. There was a darkness to it, an acuteness of detail. The character's face was ageless and muscular, the sinews of his neck implied through subtle cross-hatching. He looked hewn from a block of lumber—superhuman—but also jaded, fragile. At the bottom of the page were the makings of a signature I could not read: an L, perhaps an N, and a thatch of jagged squiggle.

I put the drawing to one side and searched the cupboard by the table. There was nothing in it but a pine cone and a pencil sharpener and three red guitar picks. In the boy's closet, I found his cagoule and a canvas bag half stuffed with clothes: his bee-striped sweatshirt was in there with the rest of his dank laundry. I checked the pockets of all the jeans and discovered only lint. There was a fountain pen and a Roman coin in the boy's sock drawer, along with a few seashells and Pettifer's camphor-wood turtle, which I could not resist winding up and letting spin across the floor. It scuttled underneath the chest of drawers; I could not retrieve it. On the bedside table was a paperback of *Huckleberry Finn*, loaned from the mansion library; it bore the provost's stamp on the back cover and a strip of dental floss was serving as a bookmark three hundred pages in.

I checked every recess of the place, from the gap under the bedframe to the shelf above the roller blinds, and even the boy's stove (I saw the grate was resting slightly off its latch). There was barely a mote of ash inside and the coke-scuttle below it was almost empty. On the blindside of the fluepipe, though, I noticed Quickman's lighter. I spent a moment trying to make it flame. It would not even spark—perhaps it never had.

The bathroom was the only place left to inspect, but I could not bring myself to search it. Instead, I put the boy's drawing and the trinkets into my satchel and left. The wooden crate that he had sat upon to make his scribblings was still out on the walkway. I rested there awhile, trying to view things from the boy's perspective. That marshy, weathered lawn. The bare bones of the pomegranate trees. This little patch of ground was such a wondrous place to be in springtime, when oleanders bloomed between the pines and all the fading purples of the sunset seemed brand new, uncharted. It was the best spot to put down a chair and watch the sky for herons. Now the winter had corrupted it.

I leaned the crate against the wall and headed for my lodging. Even at its borders, the grass was swampy, so I kept to the trail of grit and sawdust Ardak had laid down. It cut a line in the wrong direction—towards the mansion and away from my studio, where it joined the regular footpath. But I could already hear warbles of laughter up ahead, from short-termers on the portico, and the sound of them revolted me.

So I broke off the path and went straight across the grass. The clay soil underneath was thick and tacky, and I remembered how it cleaved to Fullerton's skin on his first night. He had dug through it with his hands when he could not find his matches. It had rung against the innards of the oil drum like loose change. And then—

I stopped.

I turned so fast I nearly left my shoes behind me in the clay.

The rusty drum was still standing on the open ground ahead,

but tilted now, subsiding. It was skirted by a pool of water that I had to hurdle. My heels went skiing on the other side and I grabbed the can to keep from falling on my face. I tried to heave it up, but the dirt inside had been compacted by the rainfall and it would not budge. It did not even wobble. The only thing to do was scoop the soil out by the fistful, until the can was light enough to tip over.

I clawed at the dirt, tossing debris over my shoulder.

When my fingers were too sore to carry on digging, I gave up. I kicked hard at the drum and it shifted in the mud. It was just light enough for me to haul into the trees, ploughing a runnel through the grass behind me.

Under the pines, the ground was not so wet. I pushed the drum on its side, spilling its contents. Amid the clods of soil there was a soggy mass of colour. A saturated pile of magazines the size of *Reader's Digests*. I had to gently excavate them.

The first one I pulled out was flecked with mud, congealed, but the cover was still glossy underneath, a little oily to the touch. I brushed off the muck from its middle. It was not a magazine at all.

A shirtless young man with plaited hair snarled back at me, meticulously drawn. His wrists were cuffed with iron shackles and crossed beneath his chin. Thin strings of saliva hung from his blunt teeth like guy-ropes, and, on the crest of his tongue, was a black key small enough to fit a music box.

It was a comic book.

The draughtsmanship was faultless and familiar, bearing the same jagged signature as I had noticed on the drawing in the studio. I had to rub away more dirt to see the title clearly. My heart seized at the sight of it.

's

THE ECLIPTIC

It was as though I was staring at my own face in someone else's family portrait.

The lettering was designed to look held on by rivets, and the author's name—the boy's name?—had been sliced out with a blade. It was a sodden mess of paper, but I felt the oddest kind of intimacy with it. Whoever Fullerton had been, he was contained inside those pages. Not just his talent and his labour, but every last peculiar shape that ever lurked in his imagination. I was overwhelmed by a responsibility to preserve it. This and every other comic in the pile.

There were footfalls now in the distance, and a tuneful hum. Ender was tramping down the pathway from the mansion, singing quietly: '*Hey goo-loo, helleh helleh goo-loo . . .*' I could not let him see me.

I lifted out as many comics from the soil as I could and tucked them in my coat. Three of them. Four. Five. Just when I was running out of room, I found another in the mud. That was all of them. I kicked through the rest of the dirt, levelling it off. And in that scattered mess, a square of burgundy showed through. The boy's passport was there upon the mulch.

'*Kiz goo-loo, helleh helleh goo-loo . . .*'

It was in a decent state, soggy but not ruined. The photo page fell open in my hand. There he was again: the real Fullerton. British citizen. He did not seem any younger in the photo. His lank hair was the same but his face was studded with acne. Surname: ~~scratched out~~. Given names: ~~scratched out~~. Date of birth: ~~deep laceration~~. I dropped him in my satchel and withdrew into the trees.

Two

Preserving *The Ecliptic* was a wearying endeavour. Each issue had to be unpicked from its staples, hand-squeezed of moisture with a rubber print-roller on a cotton towel, then hung on a string across my studio. I did not know a simpler way of doing it. Many of the pages were too damaged to rescue. They stuck and tore as I tried to part them, or bled most of their ink into the towel as I dried them. I lost whole sections to careless mistakes with the roller: too much pressure buckled the paper, shards of grit got caught up in the rubber and shredded several panels, front and back. Issues 2, 4, and 6 were too warped to read, their pictures washed out or occluded. Most of Issue 5 ripped in my hands as I unpicked it. By the time I had finished all this conservation work, I felt sapped of energy. At least a hundred pages hung on the lines above my head, stretched from every corner of my studio. I fell onto my bed, into the deepest sleep I ever earned.

Daylight brought no change to the foul weather. I rose cold and stiff, and stood drinking weak tea in my thermals until the shower ran hot enough to bathe. The fragrance of damp ground was all about the studio, and the stove-smoke only seemed to worsen it. I had the urge to put on the boy's striped sweater—it looked so worn and comfortable—but kept to my normal painting clothes instead. Who knew what time it was? I had not heard the breakfast bell or any distant calls to prayer, but I had woken with a queasy sense of urgency.

Bringing down the boy's pages from the lines, reassembling the issues, I was overtaken with excitement. The moody covers lured me in. I could not remember the last time I had been so absorbed by someone else's work.

I had managed to save just two complete issues—#1 and #3—but most of the front covers were still intact. They were logoed with a kind of origami swan at the top right of the page: CYGNUS COMICS. In each of the cover illustrations, the main character grew a fraction older, shown in various states of distress: submerged in a petrol tank, crawling through an air duct, trapped behind a porthole, clutching sticks of dynamite and other weapons.

The cover of #1 showed the character in half-light, dangling from a gantry. He was hanging over a vast metallic chasm by the fingers of one hand and it seemed certain he would drop. I was transfixed by the determination in his face, the glint of vengeance in his eyes. I felt just like him: about to plunge into a world of the boy's making. And I did—I fell. I devoured the whole issue and the next.

Issue 1—G Deck

AT COORDINATES UNKNOWN . . . (They all seemed to open with these words, top left). Inside the dank and rusted chamber of what appears to be a ship, a young man is slumped, unconscious, shackled by the wrists to a steel pillar. A voice fizzes out from a loudspeaker above his head (in spiky word balloons): *Passenger announcement! Children on B Deck must be accompanied by their guardians at all times.* His eyes slowly creak open, and he seems woozy and disoriented. *Repeat: all children on B Deck must be accompanied*—He feels a sudden pain in his mouth. A tiny key is lodged underneath his tongue and he spits it out into his hand, unlocks the cuffs. His wrists are chafed and raw.

The angle widens. He is alone and naked in a room containing two generators, oxidised and derelict. There is a smoky auburn light, a metal locker, and a steel hatchway with a reinforced door. He goes to the locker and removes a leather suitcase containing personal effects: a Bible, a hipflask, a Bowie knife, a wristwatch. Hanging in the locker is a set of blue overalls, streaked with oil. The name-badge on the breast says: IRFAN TOL, 4TH ENGINEER, and stencilled on the back in white is the phrase: DV-ECLIPTIC.

Cut to a dark corridor. The man finds his way into a cargo hold where hundreds of giant wooden crates are stacked. He crowbars the lids from three of them, discovering a hoard of taxidermy, furniture, paintings, boxes of cigarettes (he pockets several packs) and tins of crabmeat (he stabs one open and drains the juice). The announcements continue on the loudspeakers: *This is a notice for all passengers in first-class. The totaliser on the ship's run will be announced at 11.00 hours on the Promenade Deck Square. The totaliser will be announced at 11.00 hours on the Promenade Deck Square. Thank you.* But his watch says it is 3.15 already—a.m. or p.m.? He is not sure.

The man believes he is alone (he says so aloud, in a word balloon). There is no daylight, just flickering bulbs (a greenish hue to the panels throughout this section) and he climbs the crates to get a view of what is below him, reaching a gantry. His thoughts are shown to us in slanting words: he thinks the ship is moving, but he cannot hear the engines (his words: *the powertrain*). There are no doors. The space below is dark. The walls are gently leaking. He slips and, dangling from the railing of the gantry (reprise of the cover image here), notices something: a sway of shadows in the hold below. Dropping down onto a crate and leaping to another, he follows the shadow, but it recoils. He loses it.

Descending to the floor, he side-steps between a maze of crates. At the far end of the hold, there is a line of candelabras, coiled with Christmas lights, that leads into a sort of glade amongst the cargo. He is surprised to find an old woman sitting in an armchair, playing chess with nobody. She holds a finger to her lips and shushes him, moves her queen upon the board. The Christmas lights are wired up to a cable conduit on the wall behind her.

The woman has made quite a life for herself in the cargo hold, living off the salvage. She is adorned in a fur coat with a collar of mink-heads, and wears so much jewellery that she gives the impression of a Pharaoh on a throne. 'I knew somebody would come for me,' she says. 'I knew it would happen eventually.' And she offers the man a cup of vinegar. He raises his hipflask and she says, 'Oh, even better.' But, as he leans down to pour the liquor into her cup, she points a pistol at him. 'I'm not going to let you take me,' she says. 'I have it too good here.' There is a tussle—the man lunges forwards; she shoots and misses; he overpowers her.

And now holding the pistol at the woman, he forces her back against a crate. All he wants to know, he says, is where he is, and how to get out.

And so she explains it all to him (in that way that villains do in films, always wanting to reveal the lengths of their true evil). 'This,' she tells him, 'is what they call a dead vessel. You're on a ship that's been retired from navigation, sonny. Listen—' She points to the air. 'No engine noise. But what's funny about that is you can feel it moving, can't you? And you'd be right, because we are. We're going somewhere all right. So if you want to know where in the world the two of us are standing at this moment, my answer is: anywhere, everywhere. Who the hell can say? You're on the *Ecliptic* and there's no way off it, not that I've ever found. So I'd get used to this place, shipmate, if I were you—' (squinting) '—Irfan.'

'That's not my name,' he says.

'Your badge says otherwise.'

'Irfan Tol is not my name.'

'What makes you so sure?'

'Because I feel it in here.' (Tapping his heart.)

He insists that there has to be a way to escape the ship. The woman tells him that the furthest she has ever reached is F Deck, and she has no intention of ever going back there. 'I'm richer here than I ever was on land,' she says. 'Look at this garb. It's best Russian mink.' The air between decks, she warns, is poisonous and cannot be breathed. 'But I can show you a good way to get to F Deck, if you'll put the gun down.' In a trunk, she has some breathing apparatus: a deep-sea diving mask attached to an oxygen tank, marked: ST ANA'S HOSPITAL. She leads him to a hatchway, sealed with candlewax. He thanks her, gives her back the pistol. 'Oh, I think you're going to need that more than I will,' she says. 'Godspeed to you. But don't ever come back here.' She lets him go and shuts the door behind him.

The hatchway opens to a narrow metal stairwell. The climb is sheer and he withers after the first flight, slouching, crumpling. There are more steps than he has ever seen (this thought shown in **bold for emphasis**). He breaks through the F Deck hatch and collapses, hitting his head. The loudspeaker again: *Notice for stewards in cabin class: the purser's office is now closed. Thank you.*

Issue 3—E Deck

AT COORDINATES UNKNOWN . . . A leap ahead in the narrative. Irfan Tol, fourth engineer, is still in his overalls. He is straddling the steel-mesh walls of a baggage lift. He cannot put his feet down because there is no floor beneath him—it appears to have eroded and there is nothing but a very deep shaft underneath. The lift is going nowhere. His face is knotted and tense. He scrambles to the other side, falling into a room crammed with suitcases (replicas of the one he found in the first issue). Hurriedly, he empties them, gathering provisions: a first aid kit, a torch, a carpetbag, a tape recorder, a bottle of gin. He encounters a trunk with a military emblem, tries to open it with a little key (from Issue 1?) and it comes loose. Inside: sticks of dynamite, a gas mask, and a thermos flask. He opens it and dry ice steams out. *Goddamn.* Everything is stowed inside the holdall, and he keeps on going, through the next hatch. Now where is he? Behind a pane of window glass, looking down upon a swimming pool. The water is stagnant and brown. He sniffs, getting an acrid stench, so puts the gas mask on.

Coming down the steps, he treads carefully on the poolside. Flies buzz all around him. The tiles are dabbed with animal excrement. He sees a bootprint in it—not his own—and feels a presence near by. (In slanted letters: *Something's here . . .* and then a full page of wide panels showing various aspects of the room, but no people.) Crouching by the diving board, he spots a shape quivering at the bottom of the pool. The water is too rotten to see through (shown as though from the gaze of his steamed-up gas mask). Excrement floats on the surface. Getting up from his haunches, he is startled. *What the—?* Alsatian dogs are running for him in a pack. He cannot move quickly enough, and they send him toppling into the filthy dark pool with a *splash!* that takes up half a page.

(Dark brown colouring to the panels in this section.) Irfan Tol is underwater, gas mask on, carpetbag strapped to him, almost like a parachute. Bubbles rushing upwards. And the deeper he plunges, the more is revealed of what is resting at the bottom of the pool: a junkheap of motorbikes. He notices a child playing amongst the engine parts. A young girl wearing goggles. But, as his buoyancy lifts him back to the surface, he loses her. (Brighter panels here.) The dogs are baying on the poolside. He is gasping for air. Something pulls him under. He is dragged beneath the water again: a slender hand upon his ankle. And down he goes, clambering, towards the rusty motorbikes. He sees the girl's pale face is staring up at him. She is breathing through a snorkel. Her hair is in a very long braid that whips up from her back. And she pulls him further and further, down past the wheels and handlebars. There is a kind of submarine hatch on the pool-bed. She turns the lever, opens it, and they squirm through. They drop into a dim metal chamber, filling with grungy water. She asks for his help to shut the hatch and they put their shoulders into it. The water stops gushing. They stand there, drenched. He tears off his gas mask. 'Where are we?' he asks her. 'Sewage tanks,' she says. *H Deck*, he thinks. *Going backwards.*

— — — — — —

I could glean some of the rest of Irfan's story from the scraps of comics that were left. But there were few complete pages to reckon by. In these later issues, the panels were laid out in more inventive ways: oblique shapes that intercut at curious angles, text and word balloons that branched out from the frames of drawings and encroached on those adjacent. The covers hinted at Irfan's ascent up the decks of the dead vessel, and some of the torn images revealed more serene environments than previously encountered: a gymnasium with stewards lifting dumb-bells, a cocktail bar serving dry ice in champagne flutes, and a cinema playing what looked like *Gone With the Wind* or a pastiche of it. It was the most dissatisfying feeling: to have only a quarter of a story, and no way to ever find out the ending.

I reassembled as much of #5 as I could. Its cover showed Irfan Tol armed with fizzling dynamite and a harpoon. There was desperation in his eyes and obvious pain. The title was drawn to look burned onto the tarnished innards of the ship where Irfan was leaning. Again, the author's name was cut away, as it was from every other issue I had found. I studied the inside page, reading through the credits. Story: ~~name redacted~~. Art: ~~redacted~~. Lettering: ~~redacted~~. Colours: ~~redacted~~. The publisher's information was scratched right off. Except, there was something in the small print there, at the foot of the page, that was not quite scrubbed clean. It was faded, and difficult to make out with the naked eye. I had no magnifying glass, so I took my glass muller and held it up against the print like a lens. The words bleared and then sharpened, amplified:

Text and illustrations © Jo Nathaniel

- - - - - -

In the mess hall, Nazar was sitting patiently beside Quickman's feet. He had saved her a few strips of *sucuk* and a small mound of scrambled eggs and was decanting everything into a napkin. We were not supposed to feed the dog—it was one of the unspoken tenets that we knew the provost took seriously—and so, when I came to the table, Quickman flinched at the sound of my footsteps, hiding the bundle of food on his lap. 'Oh,' he said, seeing it was me. 'You frightened me half to death.' He brought the napkin out and added a few walnuts from Mac's bowl. 'I know the rules, but sod them—it makes me feel better.'

'I'd be more worried about how that spicy meat's going to come out of her,' said Pettifer, invigilating from across the table. 'Someone's going to smell your crime eventually.'

'I'd like to see how they'd prove it was me.'

'She'd buckle under questioning. All they'd have to do is rub her belly.'

I sat down, as always, beside MacKinney. 'Did you not sleep?' she asked. 'You're much too pale. I'm getting you some fruit.'

'Mac, we all look pale to you,' Tif replied on my behalf. 'Give it a rest. Let the woman eat what she wants.'

I poured myself a glass of milk.

'That won't be enough,' Mac said.

'I'll have another then,' I said.

'Steady,' Tif said, wobbling his gut. 'That's how it starts, you know.'

Quickman was now leaning down with the napkin held out for Nazar under the tabletop. She guzzled the food right from his hand. 'I do realise,' he said, 'this means she's never going to leave me alone ever again. But I've rather got used to her following me around.' When the dog was done, he straightened up, looking for a spot to dump the slobber-stained napkin, deciding on Pettifer's plate. 'Oi!' Tif said. 'That's revolting.' And this set Quickman off laughing, then Mac. But the impulse for laughter made me feel so guilty that I had to gulp down some milk just to smother it.

Then Q got up and started gathering his empty dishes. 'Knell, would you mind helping me take these over?'

I stared back at him.

'The woman just sat down,' Tif said. 'You can manage all that on your own.'

'I'll help you,' Mac said.

But I could tell from Q's pointed expression that clearing the table was just an excuse to speak to me. 'It's fine,' I told them, standing up to take their dishes. 'I'm in the mood for some tea, anyway.'

Pettifer bunched up his eyes. 'You two aren't—?' He leaned back, crossing his arms. 'My God, I knew it—you *are*.'

Q said, 'Are *what* exactly?'

'You know what I'm getting at.'

'No, Tif. Enlighten us.'

'Together, he means,' Mac said apathetically. 'He thinks you're an item. I've already told him he's being ridiculous.'

At this, Quickman sniggered. Then he turned to them and said, 'I should think Knell could do a fair sight better than me, don't you?'

'I'll say,' Tif replied. 'But you don't have to sneak around, you know. I'm fine with it.'

'Thrilled that we have your permission,' Q said. 'To walk from one side of the room to the other.'

'I'm just letting you know: I'd be hurt, but it wouldn't kill me. The two of you getting together would make sense in an odd sort of way.'

'Well, that's really touching, Tif, thank you. Completely misguided, as ever, but touching.'

'It's straight from the heart.' He grinned. 'Knell's staying quiet on the subject, I notice.'

'Best not to engage with you in this mood, in my experience,' I said.

'Hmm.' He made a face I could not read: nostrils tightening, tongue rolling across his teeth. 'Go on then, lovebirds. Off with you.'

I went with Quickman to the ledge by the kitchen, where we left the plates for Gülcan, and then trailed him to the serving pass where Ender handed us both hot glasses of *çay* on saucers.

Nazar was never far behind. At the condiments table, Quickman took three sugar cubes and dropped them in my tea without asking. 'Keep your strength up,' he said, then put four into his own. Stirring it, he leaned in and said, 'Did you find much in his lodging?'

'All kinds. Your lighter for one thing.'

'Oh good.'

'And—' I whispered it: 'Comic books. That's what he was here for. He wrote them.'

Quickman puffed out his cheeks.

'You've got to see them, Q. They're so well done.'

'How d'you know for sure that he wr—?' He pretended to smile at a short-termer passing by us on the way to the serving pass. 'How'd you know he wrote them?'

'If you come over, I can show you.'

'There's a difference between drawing them and writing them. The stories aren't always done by the same person.'

'Well, I'm sure you're right, but I'm certain he did both.'

He was waving now, affectedly, at Pettifer, who was turned on his chair gawping at us. 'I need to shake off hawk-eyes over there before we do anything. How long has he been this way? Did I miss something?' Peering down at Nazar, he said, 'At least the dog knows when to be quiet.'

'He's always been Pettifer, if that's what you mean.'

'Well, perhaps I'm just losing my patience for his uglier side, I don't know.' Q lifted his *çay* glass, blew across it. 'Listen, I finished the translation. Took me all bloody night, and I'm still none the wiser.'

'What does it say?'

'More adverts,' he said. 'But the last few are the strangest.'

'In what way?'

'I can't explain it all now—Tif's already making me feel guilty just for standing here. We should get back to the table.' He paced alongside me, Nazar trundling behind. 'Let me leave first, OK?' he muttered. 'Finish your breakfast, then come to my room when you can. I'll be waiting.'

I had often wondered what possessed women to have romantic affairs, and now I could understand exactly what it was: operating in the margins brought out the most attractive qualities in men (decisiveness, attentiveness, mystery) and, somehow, all the sly manoeuvrings gave each brief connection more significance. But I had already chosen the man I loved, and Quickman—good friend though he was—would never be a suitable replacement.

'It took me a while to work out the tone of the language, but my best judgement is, they're photograph captions. From a travel brochure, perhaps. I'm not one hundred per cent on that yet. Have a listen—'

Quickman was perched on the edge of his desk, one hand in his pocket, the other clutching a legal pad. His pipe was laid on the windowsill. The curtains were open, but the gloom of the afternoon offered scant reading light, so his lamp was turned on, angled upwards. It gave him the backlit quality of the rocks in a fish tank.

'*Goats wait to be milked by the village cheese-maker.* And then, in brackets: *Norwegian Office of Travel.*' He smirked at me. 'Any idea what that is?'

'No,' I said.

'Me neither.'

'Keep going.'

Quickman read on: *'Norway's horses are experts in farming on sheer slopes. As the markings on this fine animal's legs show, it is a Norwegian*—no idea what the next word is, so I've left it blank—*an ancient breed, highly prized amongst the locals.* It goes on and on like this. Meaningless, really.' He flipped the page. *'At fifteen hundred feet, the waterfall of the Seven Sisters cascades into the*—I believe it says *fjord*, not creek or stream; it's more specific than that—*into the fjord at the village of Geiranger*—that bit's just written out in English, well, Norwegian, I suppose—*almost four times the height of the Statue of Liberty. There is a permanent worry about landslides in this region. During the ice age, tumbling glaciers from the mountains widened the gorges into giant canyons. The Norwegian coast is a long sawblade of fjords, spanning thousands of miles. Pictured centre, local villagers eat a picnic of bread and curd with—'*

'Wait,' I said. 'Wait.'

Quickman lowered the notepad. 'I'm fairly certain it says "curd" there, and not "jam". But I can triple check it if you think it's necessary.'

I needed a moment to think.

'Knell, are you all right?'

I needed a moment.

'What is it?'

The Norwegian fjords, I thought.

Skiers in Alta, Utah.

Oxen in Schneeburg, Austria.

Diamond Rock, Martinique.

'They're not from a brochure,' I said. 'They're from a magazine.'

The realisation left me woozy. I had to rest my hand on the bedframe.

'How the hell did you get that—from bread and curd?' Quickman said.

I could hardly explain it. My head was awash. 'It's *National Geographic*.'

'If you say so.' He stepped back. 'You seem very certain about things all of a sudden. What am I missing here?'

'I knew the boy, Q.'

'Of course you did, but still I— '

'No, you're not hearing me. I *knew* him.' I lowered myself to the bed. The linen was fresh and creaseless. 'Before I got here. I knew him from London.'

'But he'd have been a kid back then, surely.'

I nodded. 'He was seven or eight when I saw him last.'

'I still don't understand how you can get all that from *this*.' Quickman struck the notepad with his knuckles. 'Unless it's some sort of code.'

'It's not a code. It's more than that, it's—something else.' I had to write it down, to spell it out. 'Lend me that pad and a pencil, would you?'

Quickman did as I asked. He stood across the bed, head slanted, while I wrote it out in capitals: JO NATHANIEL

'Who's that?'

'It's the name I found on his comics.'

'Oh.' He sniffed. 'Well, I suppose that's fairly concrete.'

'It matches the signature on all of the covers,' I said. 'So I know that he drew them.'

JONATHANIEL

JONATHAN IEL

I turned the paper round. 'What does that say to you?'

He read it aloud: '*Jonathan Ee-ell. Jonathan Ay-ell?*'

'Could be,' I said. 'Or— '

J O N A T H A N   Y A I L

'Now you've lost me,' Quickman said.

'I'm telling you I knew the boy.'

'Yes, but you haven't said how.'

'You really want my life story, Q? I'm telling you, that was his name.'

'I don't doubt it was,' he said. And he went pacing to the windowsill to retrieve his pipe—the comforter, the thing that made him think clearly. 'But you're going to have to give me something more, Knell. I don't see what difference it makes if you knew him or not.'

'Because now I can't ignore it,' I said. 'For his father's sake, I have to do something.'

'Don't do anything rash—give it some time.'

'No, this changes things, Q. It's bigger than this place. Bigger than you or Mac or anyone else.'

'You're going to have to give me more than that. I'm trying my best to understand you here, but—' He gestured to his desk. 'Write it down if it's easier. Just help me understand what's going on, before you go and do something you'll regret.'

I told him as much as I was willing to admit—about sailing to

New York but not the caldarium; about therapy but not my anxieties; about the mural and the ecliptic but not about Jim Culvers. And Quickman did not judge me. He just chewed on his
pipe while I talked and, at the end of it all, he said, 'I see. All
right. I get it.'

'Then you'll help me?'

'I didn't say that. This isn't my fight.'

'But you aren't going to stop me.'

'I don't think I could. You've got that look about you.' He
slumped into his desk chair, swivelling. I could see that something was rolling over in his mind that he wanted to release. 'Did
I ever tell you about my old passphrase?'

'I thought you couldn't remember it.'

'Well, I lied.'

'Why?'

'I don't know. I'm superstitious.' Q pinched at his beard. 'It's
from a Dickinson poem. *One need not be a chamber to be haunted,
one need not be a house; the brain has corridors surpassing material
place.*'

'That's beautiful.'

'It is. But I can never decide what she meant by it.'

'I suppose she's saying everyone's got problems.'

'But there's another side to it, don't you think? She's saying, no
matter where you are, you're doomed. You can't close off all those
corridors in your brain; there are just too many of them. You'll be
haunted wherever you go.'

'Maybe.'

He turned to face the window. 'I'm not going to try to talk you
out of anything you need to do, Knell. And I won't stand in your

way. But you have to seriously think about whether it's all worth it. I mean: consider every angle. If that raging feeling doesn't go away tomorrow—fine. Do what you think's best, and don't worry about the rest of us. We'll land where we land. All I'm asking is for you to wait awhile.'

- - - - - -

The mansion roof was studded with moss and a trench of slimy rainwater ran all along the parapet. I did not venture far. Gripping the tiles, I sidled out until I had a view into the bay, where Fullerton's body—*Jonathan's* body—rested somewhere underneath the roiling waves. The afternoon was no less dismal from this height. A flat discolouration to the sky, like dirty turps, and the air so cut with damp that everything seemed glimpsed through a smeared windowpane. I wanted to follow Quickman's advice and deliberate on things before I acted. But being on the roof amidst the countless swaying pines, with the nearest family house a mere grey shape in the distance, I could only think how far the boy had come to die. And I could not let the world continue so indifferently.

Because when I thought of Fullerton now, I saw the prom deck of the *Queen Elizabeth* and a child with a Superman comic, and the sweet 'Get Well' card he had drawn for me: *Your super friend, Jonathan.* Every word that he had spoken in the past few days was loaded with a new significance: those awkward lies about Green Lanes (he could not tell the truth about his upbringing in case it alerted me to his real identity), the talk of his father not taking him camping (Victor was not an outdoorsman), the constant mention of those weekends at his granddad's flat (Victor being so frequently abroad for conferences, Amanda so routinely at her squash club, that it made sense for the boy to form a bond with the only grandparent he had left). And something about cycling 'all the way to Hampstead' one night in his sleep? (The Yails had a home in Primrose Hill, not far from there.)

There were so many inferences that now seemed blatant. Of course, the *DV-Ecliptic* was an extrapolation of the *Queen Elizabeth* and other ocean liners the boy had sailed on. Irfan Tol likely represented some inherent fear of being alone (given how much time the boy claimed to spend with his granddad, this seemed reasonable to assume). And what were those comics if not just a way to express the terror of his nightmares? The provost had said as much himself: *The dreams are part of his creative process. That's all I can tell you.* It was not unfeasible to picture Jonathan reading through his father's session notes and seeing THE ECLIPTIC scribbled down and underlined. Easy to imagine how it might be overheard through the door of the consultation room, or dropped into a no-name-basis conversation at the family dinner table. Perhaps Victor had discussed his patients' cases brazenly on the telephone with other doctors as the boy listened on the upstairs line—who could say? I had never believed much in coincidence, and it seemed unlikely that the two of us would converge on the same point of fascination without some guiding hand. Now he was gone. And Victor—poor Victor—was out there somewhere, wondering, oblivious. I had to get word to him.

Down on the front lawn, the Frenchman in his yellow poncho was walking in large circles with another guest—I could not see who it was. I had not bothered to study them too closely, but as they started yet another lap, I realised that the other man was not a guest at all. The Frenchman had made a scarecrow out of a broomstick, an old peacoat, and what looked like thatches of dry leaves. He was dancing this strange manikin around the boggy grass as part of some performance. With every circuit, it seemed that he dismantled a piece of the dummy, and, the longer it went on, the more of its guts and fibres lay strewn upon the lawn. He was calling out now in French, but I could not understand what he was saying.

After a moment, guests started to emerge from their lodgings to watch. An audience of short-termers gathered on the portico steps. Ender looked on from the path, his arms stocked with firewood. Even Ardak was tempted from the outhouse to see what was going on, and leaned there, pulling off his work gloves while the Frenchman kept on calling out his nonsense. And when I heard the provost's voice below—that murmuring tenor with all its affectations—I sensed an opportunity. The fuss about the Frenchman's piece grew louder, fuller. Everyone was preoccupied with it. And so, as fast as I could manage, I edged along the parapet and climbed back down the ladder, through the roof beams, until I reached the empty hallway.

The provost's study was in the other wing of the building, across the upper landing, and the parquet floor resounded with my every step. I lifted off my shoes and left them in the corridor, striding past the staircase and the mess hall underneath me. The floor was oddly warm against my feet. I expected the door would be locked—and it was—but I was able to scrutinise the keyhole. It was a warded lock that required a short, fat key, most likely of the same dull brass as all the door fixtures.

I hurried down two flights to the lobby, where Ender's door

was still ajar at the back end of the house. There was a cheery rumble of voices out on the portico, and I tried not to be seen, stepping quietly along the hall. The Frenchman kept on crying out his garbled script. I pushed inside the old man's room, unsure where to look. A fleet of leather slippers was neatly lined under his bed, his pyjamas folded on the pillow. The muslin curtains were tied back with ribbon, and I could see right into the old man's bathroom: a clot of foam left on his shaving brush, a rim of whiskers in the sink. There was no time to feel ashamed. I searched his desktop and the bending bookshelves, rifled through his cupboards, finding nothing. My blood began to cool. In the drawers of his writing table, I discovered only envelopes, boxes of *baklava* (his private stash), and a mound of typewritten pages in Turkish.

I could hear boot soles on the floor outside, amusement in the corridor. The old man was coming back—I felt sure of it—and I stole into his closet, holding my breath. My head grazed a row of hooks behind me on the wall. All manner of things hung from them: bales of twigs, a whistle on a lanyard, large blue beads with painted eyeballs, and keys on metal loops. When Ender did not appear, I snatched two of the stumpiest—one brass key, one silver—and fled back to the hall. Heading for the portico, I was certain I would feel a meaty hand upon my shoulder, hear a chiding *tsk* from another guest behind me. But it never came. I was able to break out onto the steps and merge with all the short-termers, while the Frenchman carried on his strange performance. He was calling: '*Adieu! Adieu! Adieu!*'

Gluck seemed more bemused by it than interested. His tufty eyebrows were pushed into a point over his nose. I went to him and said, 'Do you know what all this gibberish is about?' And he gestured to a sign that hung around the scarecrow's neck that said: DOUX ET NÉGLIGEABLE. 'It's very polemical,' Gluck said, 'but I don't really know the motivation. From an aesthetic standpoint, though, I'd say it's quite successful.'

— — — — — —

Something else you will not learn at art school: real inspiration turns up only when your invitation has expired. There is no preparation you can put in place for it and no provision you can make that will entice it to your door. It will find you either sleeping, occupied with chores, or entertaining the dumb neighbours you allowed in as a compromise. And when it finally shows, you will have to wake up fast, abandon everything, turf out the pretenders just to make it welcome, because it will take less time to disappear than you spent waiting for it. There is no finer company than inspiration, but its very goodness will leave you heartsick when it goes. So do not waste time asking it to wipe its feet. Embrace it at the threshold.

— — — — — —

The boy's comics were exactly where I left them: spread out on the workbench with the muller rested on the inner page of Issue 5. I went to light my stove and filled the kettle. My nerves were still fidgeting and I needed some weak tea to calm myself. Lying on the couch, I gazed at the paint-spattered ceiling and thought of Victor Yail. His face all shapeless with grief. His lenses fogged by tears. Cracks in his voice. I tried to think how I was going to break the news to him, but every sentence I conceived was banal:

Your boy is dead—I'm sorry . . . He took his own life . . . We threw him in the sea . . . How else could I say it? The facts would not change.

As the fire burned rosily in the stove, I grew so absorbed in looking at the flames that my head began to haze and drift. I made the tea and took it to the window. No promise of sunshine outside. Clouds like sooty thumbprints on a chimney breast. Turning round, my hip knocked against the workbench and the muller slipped slightly off the page. Something caught my attention: the grain of the image underneath the glass. Blurry discs of colour.

Standing over it, I held my eye up to the muller as if it were a gem loupe. And through the glass I saw the printed substance of the illustrations. Their colours were made up of tiny dots in rows: magenta, cyan, yellow and black. Some overlapped, some were spaced apart, the rest were tightly packed. A galaxy that could not be seen from far away. A thing that was there, and yet not.

- - - - - -

When the lunch bell rang, I did not leave my studio. I pulled out the timbers I had been keeping underneath my bed, wiped off the heavy film of dust, cut all the angles with a mitre-saw, and screwed them into place to make a stretcher. I rolled out all the canvas I had on the studio floor and pulled it taut across the frame, hammering in the tacks. Before long, I had a four-by-nine-foot rectangle of blankness staring back at me. It spread across the full width of my studio and there was not one inch of it I feared. The primer coat still had to dry, and I stood near, projecting the image onto it in my mind. There seemed no point in making a cartoon: the mural I had conceived was very simple—pure abstraction—and it was best to let the idea express itself without too many constraints. First of all, I needed darkness.

The boy had ruined all but one of the mushroom garlands in my closet. There was the tobacco tin of pigment stowed behind the bathroom cabinet—not quite enough to get me through the night. I could grind up what was left, but I would have to harvest more.

My muller and the mixing slab were already clean. Still, I gave them another rinse for procedure's sake and organised my workbench as normal. I drew the shutters, stapled the roller blind against the window frame, and then—with a sadness that twinged the length of my spine—I went to fetch a new roll of tape from the cupboard and left it on the tabletop for later.

When the dinner bell sounded, I ignored it. It struck me that I did not have to wait for dark to harvest what I needed. I knew the route into the woods so well that I could walk it blindfold. And with all the other guests now gone to the mansion for their evening meal, I did not have to worry about being noticed. So I stuffed a roll of tin foil into my satchel, edged lightly down the path, and slipped into the apron of the trees.

In the vapid daylight, the woods became a different place, cloistered but not as menacing. The pines had a crisp, fulsome scent, flushed out by the rain. I looked for the notches I had knifed into the trunks—the four short lines upon the bark that I used to help me navigate at night—and followed them, one notch at a time, until the air turned dank and the ground felt more elastic underfoot. Up ahead, I saw the enclave with the leaning trees, and then the narrow clearing with its nest of rotting logs.

And there they were: the mushrooms, so ordinary before sunset. Plain brown clusters of fungus with brims almost translucent. I dropped to my knees and sliced every last fruithead from the bark, until the tin-foil sheet was covered by them. I wrapped and taped them inside, putting the packet in my satchel. Dashing back between the pines, I got the feeling I had left something behind—my knife, perhaps my scarf.

I stopped.

There was nothing on the ground that I could see. But the clearing had a plundered look, the logs all stripped, forsaken. And I sensed that I would not return to these deepest woods again, that there was no more pigment after this. Because I would be gone before another cluster had grown fat enough to harvest.

Three

When at last the old man came to snuff the candles in the portico, I closed my door and sealed its frame with the tape. The tacky lengths of it came off the roll so noisily, and I tried not to think of Fullerton or the sounds he must have heard when he had used it. I was responsible for that, I knew, and I would say as much to Victor on the phone. But there was nothing to be done about the boy till morning. The only time I knew for sure the provost left his study was just after sunrise, when he liked to take his *Türk kahvesi* on the front steps with Nazar. I would have to plant myself inside the mansion before then, but there was no sense in wasting the darkness.

My samples gleamed upon the wall: a chequerboard of blues. They were my guide in every way: not just because they gave me a small amount of light to paint by, but because they helped me judge my mixes and my tones. All that work I had done in the past few seasons—getting the pigment right, learning all its facets and refining my technique—came to fruition that night. For the first time I could remember, I knew exactly what I had to paint and how to achieve it. I could not tell if this was clarity or just the prelude to it, but I hoped it would never leave me.

I emptied all the mushrooms from my satchel, cutting through the liners. A spume of blue rushed from the punctured plastic, as though I had unearthed some underground lagoon. It did not take me long to garland them—eight strings of fungus in total, densely packed—and I hung them from the crossbar of my closet to dry out. I retrieved the one remaining garland from the depths where I had hidden it; its glow was that bit fainter than the rest, but it yielded plenty in the mortar when I ground it down. Loading all the powder on the slab, I went to consult my samples, checking the dosages of oil and fruithead sizes that were noted in the margins of the squares. Choosing the right tone and gleam, I made the measurements, added the linseed to the powder, slid the muller over it until I had a good consistency: thin enough to coat the bristles of a medium sable, thick enough to rest upon the blade-edge of a palette knife. And, loading up the largest, roundest brush I owned, I made the first commitment of the paint to canvas.

I had considered using a compass to put chalk lines on the nap that I could follow, thinking it would look cleaner if the circles were precise. But I changed my mind. Although I wanted it to be a purely abstract image, I had to do more than simply colour in blank spaces. Better to paint the overlapping circles freehand. If they were imperfect, fine. I needed them to look man-made. So I swept the brush around, using the natural roll of my shoulder— fast, flowing strokes that came from the whole arm, not just the wrist. And when the paint began to scuff out, I loaded up the brush again, and kept on going with the same circling motions, over and over, working from the outside in, using up the whole batch of paint until I had made a complete disc. It rested on the left side of the canvas, neatly within the limits of the frame—the lighter of the three I planned to paint. A hue so radiant it soothed me like a nightlight, so lucent I could see the trails of brush marks and the nap of the primed fabric underneath.

The mortar and the pestle, the muller and the slab, the brushes and the knife, the workbench—all of them had to be washed and dried again before I could start the next phase. I went about the task quite hurriedly, impatient to begin again, and wary of the failing darkness. When everything was clean, I lifted the bathroom cabinet from its brackets, got out the tobacco tin and brought it to the slab. More tape to unpick and peel away—I thought again of Fullerton—and as the lid hinged open, there was a powder-puff of blue that almost made me sneeze. I scooped it all onto the marble, checked my samples for the apt mix ratio, table-spooned the linseed on and worked it with the muller. This paint had to be a little thinner, with a deeper tone, a richer glare. When it was ready, I applied it to the canvas with the same sweeping gestures. This circle was supposed to be exactly the same size, and I needed to judge its scale by instinct. Its left-hand side was meant to overlap the other circle at the halfway mark. So, as the two discs overlaid, both tones merged, forming a segment with a hue all of its own.

I did not stop working until all the paint was spent and the mural showed two beaming discs of blue, one fractionally weaker than the other. I had no pigment left to make the final circle. Birds were chirruping outside and I was running out of darkness. The paint would need to dry but I could not leave it for the

world to see, so I covered it with bedsheets, fixing brushes to the
top edge of the frame to keep the linen off the surface. I scrubbed
my hands with soap. And, checking that the old man's keys were
still in my pocket, I pulled my door until the tape tore off and it
swung back. The sun was not quite up yet. There was a rinse
of dew upon the lawns that smelled familiar. I slatted my eyes
against the light and sprinted for the mansion, still in my painting
clothes, with pigment on my boot caps and my hair part-streaked
with oil.

The fatigue hit me when I reached the hallway. My muscles
burned and pinched. But I kept going, quietly up the stairs, trying to mute my every footstep. The floorboards gave off cawing
sounds until I reached the landing, where the mess hall door was
fully agape and I could hear the clatterings of Gülcan in the
kitchen. She worked ten times as hard as anyone: the last to bed,
the first to rise. I could not say what made her do it, but she always did it smiling.

I went bounding up another flight—the highest stairs were
carpeted and dampened my footfalls. There were empty lodgings
in the east wing, but I did not know which doors would open
onto them. I had to guess. I pressed my ear to the wood and
heard the sounds of snoring. I chose another door: silence. Twisting the handle steadily, as though a single squeak from it would
wake up all of Heybeliada, I pushed at it and stole inside. The
mattress was bare and mapped with stains. Day was dawning in
the window. I was alone.

It was impossible to stop my heart from jouncing; slow breaths
in and out did very little. My bones were lagging. I kept the door
ajar a tiny crack and peered along the hall. For a good while,

nothing stirred. I wondered what would happen if the provost shunned his Turkish coffee. How long would I wait for him? Until the breakfast bell? Till lunch? I thought about my mural, feeling a pride so copious it warmed my cheeks. It occurred to me that even if the provost caught me I would soon be leaving. I could deliver my message to Victor in person. And this notion made me anxious. I started reasoning myself into a knot: Did I even need to make the call? Was it not safer just to finish off my work and leave with all my documents in order? How important was it, really, for Victor to be told?

Suddenly, there came a scrape of claws in the corridor. Nazar was hurtling for the stairs. I watched the provost edge out from his room, locking the door. Such languidness about his movements. He trailed his bamboo cane along the skirting boards and yawned. Reaching the landing, he leaned upon the balustrade. I thought he might have seen me. But then Nazar whimpered from the flight below and he spun round. 'Ah, there you are,' the provost said. 'I thought we agreed you wouldn't do that any more?' And he went downstairs and out of sight, saying, 'Get on with it, scamp, or you're going to get trampled.'

I allowed a few moments to pass before stepping out. A sediment of dust teemed in the angling sunshine halfway down the hall, and I passed through it with the sureness of a child rushing at garden sprinklers. I had to tread softly while going at pace, and I felt certain that every time my boot soles clapped the parquet someone underneath was taking note. But I made it to the provost's door. The brass key did not fit the lock. The other went in snugly, and it turned.

I did not expect to find the curtains drawn inside. The air was bitter with the stench of stubbed-out cigarettes: unmistakable. It was one of the broadest rooms in the mansion and the most ornate. The green velvet settees had been arranged to face each other, as though to host some tournament of conversation, and dangly crystal light fixtures were mounted on each wall. The provost had a hulking antique desk made out of cherry wood. The wallpaper was floral and intense. The rugs were vast and plush with mazy patterns, and cream upholstered chairs were placed in every corner (it was not quite clear what for). On the side-table was a silver tray of *çay* glasses with silver rims on silver saucers. The leather headrest of the provost's desk-chair was dinted and worn down. (Seasons back, I had been shown this room during my introduction to the refuge—it had been a matter of some pride for him to explain the strange paperweight on his desk, a cast-iron seagull once owned by his favourite author: 'I've been assured that it once sat on manuscripts of Gürpinar's. The photographic evidence exists, I promise you.' It had still been on the desk, several days ago, when the four of us had perched upon those green settees and heard him talk about some boy named Fullerton. How far away that afternoon now seemed. The paperweight was missing, too.) I was wasting time just standing there, gawking at the provost's things. But the room was so luxurious in comparison to my lodging, and the urge to sleep on the soft cushions of the couch took some resisting. Every joint inside me ached. My brain felt panel-beaten.

I moved to the teak cabinet behind his desk. And there it was: the only telephone on the grounds. Its stand was fancy, golden, engraved with minute fretwork. The jade handset was so heavy that my elbow sank a little as I picked it up.

I heard a pigeon-cooing in the earpiece. The line was working.

I dialled zero for the operator. Nothing happened. After a moment, the crackling line scratched out. I tried again and got the same response. It had to be zero. Zero for the operator. Or had they changed it to 100? I dialled that instead.

'*Hello. Operator. How may I help you?*'

I had assumed she would be Turkish.

'*Hello? Did you need me to assist you?*'

I must have reached the international operator.

'I need to place a call to London.' It came out in a flurry.

'*Can you speak up, please? I can't hear you very well.*'

'No, I can't, I'm sorry.' But I whispered it more plainly: 'I need—to place—a call—to London.'

'*Do you know the number, madam?*'

'Only the name and the address.'

'*I'll need to take those down.*'

'It's Yail.' I spelled it out, and she spoke it back to me using the phonetic alphabet. 'His first name's Victor. He's a doctor, if that helps you find it.' And I told her the address. 'Please hurry.'

'*I have the number for you now. It should only take a moment to connect.*'

A trilling noise, a trilling noise, a trilling noise. And then—

'*Hello, you have reached the answering machine of Dr Yail and Dr Fleishmann, Harley Street Practice.*' A man's voice, but not Victor's, very strained. '*Office hours are 10 a.m. to 7 p.m., Monday to Thursday. If you are calling outside these hours and wish to make an appointment, please leave your name and the number where we might contact you. Listen for the tone and speak as clearly as you can. Thank you.*'

'Yes, this is an urgent message for Dr Yail,' I said. 'It's very important, that I speak to— '

A long beep in my ear.

'Hello? Is someone there?'

Just a fuzz of static.

I started again: 'This is an urgent message, please, for Dr Yail. I have some very sad news about his son.' I paused, tweaking the language in my head. 'I'm afraid I have to let him know that Jonathan is dead. It happened early yesterday.' It sounded so cold, so final. 'I'm sorry I've had to leave it in a message like this. I really wish I didn't have to be the one to tell you—I really am so sorry . . . It's Elspeth Conroy—Dr Yail knows who I am. *You* know who I am, Victor. It's terrible, having to say all this to a machine. I suppose it must be early where you are. It's early *here*. The sun has only just come up . . . Victor, I really am sorry. I just had to let you know. Poor Amanda must be going mad with worry. But there was nothing we could do. He drowned himself— it was the dreams. They made his life such hell, but he . . . He didn't suffer . . . It's difficult to say exactly where I am. How well do you know Istanbul? If you can get a ferry out to Heybeliada, it's—' Another long beep. 'Victor, are you there?'

But the line had cut off. I pressed the hook and pressed the hook, trying to get it back. There was nothing, just the dial tone. I hung up the receiver, thinking I would have to call again, but when? The provost hardly left his room. My only chance was gone.

I needed to get out.

The door seemed very distant now. I could not run. My chest

was tight. I turned the handle, checked the hallway. Bright out
there. All clear. But, coming out, I struggled with the lock. The
brass key—so smooth before—would not go in. I fumbled with
it, and I realised: the silver key, the *silver*. When I finally had it
locked, I rushed away. Then someone stepped up to the landing.
I grabbed at the dado rail to stop myself. My boots squealed on
the floor. I almost knocked a picture off the wall: it swung
around and settled.

Gülcan had the provost's breakfast on a tray: orange juice, a
rack of toast, and two boiled eggs. When she saw me, her arms
flinched. The juice wobbled in the glass.

We did not speak. Her eyes were like a rabbit's, darting, blinking. I put my palms together, mouthing 'Please'. And, after a moment, she exhaled and nodded gravely. I carried on along the
hall, straight past her, down the stairs, with the feeling in my gut
that I had swallowed turpentine and chased it with a flame.

- - - - - -

Breakfast was the third meal in a row that I had missed, and it
prompted MacKinney to come knocking at the studio. She woke
me from the darkest trenches of my sleep: dreams the like of
which you only get from sheer exhaustion, that drag your fears
out from the roots and shake their dirt off in your conscience. A
butcher's shop, a bloody floor, a mop and bucket—things that I
was very glad to get away from. 'Knell, it's almost lunchtime. Are
you in there?' My window was still shuttered and the blinds still
stapled back. Tape clung to the door in strips. 'I'm coming in.'
She pushed inside.

I was on my couch under a pile of blankets. The tiredness had been too much—I had not lit the stove when I got back, just shivered into sleep.

Mac looked at me: 'You have a bed, you know. I recommend you try it.' Then at the mess: 'Crikey. You've been painting.'

'I'm as shocked as you are.' I sat up, squinting at the room. The mural was propped up on the wall, covered by linens. 'It's not finished yet, though.'

She was already filling up a jug with water. 'We thought you'd been ignoring us, but I suppose you've had your head in all of this. It didn't even occur to me that, well, you know what I mean.' There were no clean cups for her to pour the water into, so she passed me the whole jug. I glugged from the spout, soaking my chin and the front of my shirt. 'So, what was it—a lightning bolt?' she said. 'Or total accident?'

'I'm not sure. A bit of both.'

'Well, if you've really got your muse back, don't keep her to yourself. We're all in need of her company.' She searched the ceiling. 'Where is she? Can I borrow her for just an afternoon. I swear I'll bring her back.'

'What happened to *Oh, thank you, sir. I'll have it done in no time, sir!*'

She folded her arms, peering down. 'I don't remember sounding quite that sycophantic.' And, nudging my feet aside, she lowered herself onto the couch next to me. 'Anyway, from the looks of things, I don't have to worry about being the first one out of here. How long until we see your name up on the bulletin board?'

I shrugged. 'I need one more night of painting, maybe two.'

'That soon? Wow. This is serious.' She lifted her brow. 'I suppose you'd better make an appointment with the prov, then. Give him a head start on your paperwork.'

'It might not be that simple.'

'Course it is. Just go straight up and ask him.' Patting my calves, she turned to me and smiled. I could see the oily smears of fingers on her glasses. It seemed pointless to tell her about my stolen phone call in the provost's study. The less she knew of my behaviour, the less she was incriminated by association. 'I always thought you'd be the first of us to crack it, you know,' she said. 'Pettifer's going to be wrecked, poor sod, and we might even see a tear from Q when you go. I'm sure he won't cry in front of you, though. Retain a bit of dignity. As for me—' She gripped my leg. 'They'll have to cut me off you with a hacksaw.' We laughed together. In that moment, I felt glad and desolate at once. Then an idea came to her. I could see it brightening her eyes. 'Will you do me a favour when you're back in the motherland?' she said.

'Of course,' I told her. 'Anything.'

'If you could get a letter to my kids for me, I'd be so grateful.'

'Don't let me leave without it.'

'You might find that they've moved, so best to put your return address on the envelope, just in case, eh?'

'Done. I'll walk it to them, if I have to.'

She took my hand and kissed it. 'You're a great friend, Knell—you know that? I always knew you'd find a way out of here.' The crusted white paint on my fingernails drew her attention. 'Look how bony you're getting, though. You'd better have a decent lunch today.'

'I'll think about it.'

'Long trip home, you know. Important to stay healthy.'

'I'm fine.'

'Just promise me you'll eat. A bowl of rice, a bit of fruit—that's all I'm asking.'

'If I'm hungry, Mac, I'll eat. Don't worry.'

I went to start the shower running in the bathroom. My painting shirt was curiously ripe. I stripped off and put a gown on while the water heated up. When I came back into the studio, Mac had lit the stove and was standing at my workbench with one of Jonathan's comics. 'Are these yours?' she said. 'They're incredibly dark.'

'Fullerton drew them.'

'You're kidding.' She sat down with the comic, putting her feet up. 'I thought you said he was a musician.'

'That's just what we assumed.'

'I don't remember giving it much thought.'

'All right, *I* assumed.'

She nodded distractedly. 'Well, his dialogue needs work,' she said, 'but you've got to admire the drama of it all—and the drawings are something else. You know for certain that he did them?'

'I got them from his lodging.'

'Doesn't mean they're his, per se.'

'I know. But trust me.'

'Uh-huh,' she said, so immersed in Issue 1 she did not seem to care that I was dodging her. 'Go on, have your shower. I'm at the part with the old woman in the mink. It's just started to get frightening.'

Later, washed and more awake, I explained it all to her. About my connection to the boy and Quickman's translations, what they signified. She did not seem surprised. Using the muller, I showed her Jo Nathaniel's name in print, and let her see the rows of dots up close. She gave a little gasp of fascination. I talked vaguely—mentioning no names—about my issues with the mural commission, and how seeing all these tiny circles on the page had helped me find a new approach. 'No lightning bolts,' I said, 'more like a very slow earthquake.'

She listened closely, engaged and sympathetic, as though heeding the advice of a director in her ear. But she responded only in the past tense: 'That sort of thing used to happen to me all the time,' she said. 'The number of dead-ends I used to wriggle out of that way,' she said. 'You wouldn't believe how fast I used to work,' she said. I told her I would wait for her in London, that she would always be welcome in my home, that I would go and watch her plays wherever they were staged—all the platitudes you give to friends when, privately, you fear that what exists between you in that moment will abate in separation.

- - - - - -

Not only were the residents confounded by the sight of Ardak doling out great dollops of moussaka at the serving pass, but his slowness left them queuing all the way back to the mess hall door. And, waiting in line, I could hear them gossiping in broken English about what must have happened to Gülcan. Mac got talking with Lindo in Spanish, and I did not know where to put my eyes. Q and Tif were at our table, napkins tucked into their collars; great ugly mounds of food lay in front of them, and they were not quite tucking in with their customary enthusiasm.

When I reached the pass, I held out my plate to Ardak, and he grabbed it from me, huffing. He slopped out such a loaded spoonful of brown sludge that it dripped over the sides. As I took the plate from him, he held on to it, and scowled.

'What was all that about?' Mac asked, as we headed away. 'Did you forget to say please?'

I tried to keep quiet, but Pettifer was already adding up the twos of Gülcan's absence when we got to the table. He moved aside to let Mac sit, saying, 'Yes, but it has to be more than that, Q, or they'd have put the old man on the pass instead, wouldn't they? I think they've given her the boot, and Ender's up there pleading her case.'

'It amazes me,' Mac said, 'the speed at which you construct these fairy tales of yours. The poor girl's probably got a stomach bug. She probably thought it best not to contaminate our food.'

'I hope you're right.' He ran his spoon through the mush on his plate. 'I can't bear much more of this gruel.'

'Lindo says he heard somebody vomiting earlier,' Mac said. 'I hope she's OK.'

Tif stayed silent for a moment. 'Morning sickness, maybe.'

'Christ, Tif, put a sock in it,' Quickman said.

'Well, I don't see why we're taking Lindo's word on things ahead of mine.'

'I can't help it if he speaks more sense,' Mac said.

'You don't have to quote him, though. As if he's the Spanish bloody oracle.'

And I lost my patience with them all. 'Could everyone, for once, just try saying nothing? How about that?' I had been allowing them to speculate as long as it deflected from the truth of Gülcan's absence. But I could not stand to hear aspersions being

cast on the woman. She had done nothing wrong except for carrying up the provost's breakfast a fraction too soon, and I could
not resent her if she decided to confess. 'You're making my head
spin, the lot of you.' I pushed my plate away.

'You promised me you'd eat,' Mac said.

'Sorry. It's completely inedible.'

'There's plenty of bread and yoghurt over there. Even Ardak
can't mess that up.'

'I'll have something at dinner.'

'I knew you'd find an excuse.'

'Is everything all right?' Q asked.

'Perfect,' I said, and smiled. In truth, the instant I saw Gülcan
missing from the serving pass, my pulse had started thrumming.
I was expecting the provost to come down at any moment, to
command the attention of the mess hall with a clap of his hands.
Eat up, everyone, he was going to say. *Knell has some important
information . . .*

But all that happened was Mac leaned into Tif's ear and said,
'Knell's getting out.'

'Huh?'

'She's painting again. I just came from her studio. In a few
days, she'll be off.'

'Mac, *don't,*' I said.

'Come on, I'm proud of you.' And, glancing at Q, she said,
'There's a canvas at her place the size of a billboard. I haven't seen
what's on it yet, but if we ask her nicely, we might get a little preview.'

'Are you serious?' Q said.

'It's true that I've been painting again,' I said. 'I don't know about the preview.'

'That's wonderful!'

'We'll see. I'm not quite done.'

'You *will* let us see it when you are, though, right?' Mac said.

'Possibly. Probably. I haven't decided.'

Pettifer stood up from the table, rattling dishes. 'Excuse me. I'm not having any more of this slop. I'm going to see what else there is.' He carried off his plate towards the kitchen, walking as fast as I had ever seen him manage. The back of his shirt was striped with sweat. The balding crown of his head was pink and sore-looking.

'What's bitten him?' Mac asked.

'You could've been a little gentler with his ego,' Quickman said. 'He's only just got used to the thought of *you* leaving. Now you're staying put—although, I'm still not a hundred per cent certain why that is yet—and suddenly it's Knell who's off. Tough on the system, all this being glad for other people.'

Mac laughed softly. 'I told you: I'm not satisfied with the play yet. A thousand plot holes to work out. You know how it is.'

'Ah, yes, I remember. Plot holes. The council fixes those, eventually.'

She grinned.

'Well, spare a thought for Tif and me, when you get home.' Quickman brought his pipe out of his pocket. 'Because the only way we're getting out of here is if somebody comes back to collect our ashes. Which, I can assure you, is not halfway as romantic an ending as it sounds.'

- - - - -

The mushrooms were not dry enough to powder. A full day next to the boiler had left them white and shrunken, but I needed them to desiccate. Still, when darkness came, I unhooked two of the driest garlands and stripped them clean. I had to try, at least, to make one batch of paint. And there was a sample on my wall, still gleaming blue, that I knew had been made in the earliest stage of my experiments with the pigment, when I had used much damper fruitheads. Those first few nights, spent keenly testing out the possibilities of the stuff, toying with mixtures of emulsions and pastes, had yielded one daub of shining paint that I hoped I could now replicate. The hardest part was deciphering my handwriting in the margins of the little canvas square: some of the 7s looked like 1s, some of the 9s looked like 8s. But I was thankful to my father for instilling such a methodical streak in me that I could always bank on the lees of my work to be accounted for. *Never bin your scraps*, he used to say, if I stood watching him repair a table leg or fit a new U-bend in the kitchen. *One day that bit of junk you threw away will be the only thing that does the job.*

Ground up in the mortar, the damp mushrooms formed a viscid blue cement. I was light-handed with the oil, following the measurements on the sample, and after some persuasion with the muller, it became more pliable, until I had a paint as thick as clotted cream. I had the instinct to thin it out with turps, but held off, knowing one mistake would spoil the entire batch.

The radiance of the paint was a good start. And the tone

seemed rich enough for what I needed. It did not take so naturally to the brush head, falling off in tiny clumps—I had to hold my free hand underneath to catch them—but once I put the first stroke on the canvas, it cooperated. The smooth opacity of the stuff gave off the most resplendent sheen. If anything, the moister pigment helped me realise a better outcome than I ever could have planned.

I worked it in the same way as the other paints, in sweeping, fluid gestures, and, although it sputtered out towards the end of every brush load, there was an easy slide to it across the nap in the first motions—I could sculpt it, add textures and inflections as I dragged and shoved the bristles.

The two circles I had left to dry the night before were still vibrant, slightly shivering on the canvas. The final, thickest circle overlaid them in the middle section, creating an effect that I had never seen before in ordinary paint: an ache that I could see and feel at once, as though it were not solely in the fabric of the thing itself but somehow part of me. I had made a simple thing so resonant with sadness, so pure in its substance, that looking at it made me grieve. Tears rushed from my eyes and I could not wipe them fast enough: they putted on the workbench, oozed along my neck. I felt ready to collapse with tiredness and relief. The picture showed glimmering blue circles in a void, growing in intensity as the eye passed left to right. An abstraction of a complicated truth. A way to comprehend it. *The Ecliptic*, I would call it. The only painting I refused to sacrifice. The one real thing I ever brought into the world.

Four

Ender was sent to get me. He must have been watching for some sign that I was up and moving, because no sooner had I got the kindling lit and fuming in the stove, he came thumping on the door. I was in my dressing gown and halfway to the shower. He did not even wait for me to let him in. The door ripped open and he stood at the threshold with the bright afternoon behind his back, snatching a hang-down strip of tape from the frame above him, as though it were a party streamer. When he saw that I was barely dressed, he did not apologise, just turned his head away, covered his eyes. 'The provoss asks for you to speak with him,' he said. 'He has told me to make certain you will come. So you will come now, yes?'

'In a moment,' I said resolutely. 'Let me put something on.' I took a bundle of clean clothing to the bathroom and got dressed, washing at the sink, taking more time about it than I would usually have done. The creases of my eyes were streaked with hard white paint. My fringe was greased and gungy. After I had washed myself, a sediment of dirt clung all around the basin.

Ender was still on the threshold when I emerged. He gave me

a dismayed look and tucked his pocket watch inside his waist-coat. 'You are too late now for lunch,' he said. 'But there is *salep* and *ayran* and fruit, if you want it.'

I shook my head.

He gestured to the covered canvas leaning on my wall. 'You are working?' he said, lifting an eyebrow.

I replied, 'I *was*. How cold is it out there?'

'Excuse me?'

'Do I need a coat or not?'

'No. There is sunshine, lots of sunshine.'

I put it on anyway. Ender huffed.

'Let's get this over with,' I said.

The old man led me along the curving path instead of cutting straight across the grass as normal. He walked just a stride ahead of me and kept craning his head back, as if to check that I was still in grasping distance. From behind, his silver hair looked impossibly dense. Sprigs of it splayed out from the pleats of his long ears and almost twinkled in the sunlight. He had a lurching gait that seemed to pain him. As we went up the portico steps, he stopped to hold the door for me. And then, all at once, I was leading him instead, through the hall and up the stairs. I passed Crozier and Gluck on the landing. They both said quiet hellos to me, raising their coffee cups. It was the first time I had ever been glad of the sight of them. I smiled and wished them both good afternoon, and Gluck was so surprised that his response got caught up in his throat. 'Yy—er, ya,' he said. 'You too.' The old man was still in my wake, his nostrils wheezing. We went up another flight, over soft carpet (I wondered how many guests before me had made this same walk of condemnation) and clipped along the corridor together until we reached the provost's study. 'You wait,' he said, rapping the wood three times.

The door drew back abruptly and we were met by Ardak. He flicked a nod at the old man but did not acknowledge me. They exchanged a few words in Turkish, then Ardak brushed past us and went off down the hall. Inside, the provost was preparing a drink for himself at the hostess trolley by the fireplace. 'Have a seat there, won't you, Knell,' he said, motioning to the settees. 'I'm making what I like to call an Afternoon Refresher. Can I get you one? It's just lemonade, a dash of grenadine, crushed ice, and pomegranate seeds. If you can get fresh mint, that makes it better, but I don't have any.'

'No, thank you,' I said.

'You're missing out.'

The old man shut the door and loomed there like a warden. As I sat down, I noticed Gülcan in an armchair near the provost's desk—she had been partly obscured by his gaunt frame at the hostess trolley, but I could see her now, reclining deep into the cushions with her head back and her fingers worrying her hair. She did not look at me. Nazar was the only one who did, in fact; lazing in a hot-bright shank of sunshine underneath the window, she rolled her pupils round to meet mine, perked up her snout, and then came stepping over. I petted her head and she settled at my feet.

Drink in hand, the provost lowered himself onto the settee opposite. He stirred the ice with a straw. 'I am troubled, Knell,' he said. 'I never thought that I would need to sit you down for a conversation quite like this, but here we are. It's hugely disappointing.' He took a liberal swig of juice and gave a little noise of satisfaction. 'Do I presume, from your lack of an expression, that you understand where this is headed?'

'It's never wise to presume anything,' I said. 'I heard you wanted to speak to me, that's all.'

The provost pursed his lips and nodded, though I was not sure at what. 'All right,' he said. 'Then let's discuss the facts. *Onus probandi*—' He leaned to put his drink down on the strange glass table between us. And, just when I expected he would lean straight back, he reached into his breast pocket and removed two keys—one brass, one silver—and snapped them on the tabletop. 'Ender discovered these amongst your things last night at dinnertime. I apologise for the intrusion on your privacy, but these were special circumstances.'

Nazar put her chin on my toes and whined. My heart was skittering; I could not quell it. I decided it was best to say nothing at all.

'Obviously, I don't need to tell you where they were missing from, or whose doors they belong to— '

Staying silent was the best strategy. Until the thing was proven beyond doubt.

'Add to this the information I received from Gülcan yesterday,' he went on. 'You mustn't blame her—she's been so twisted up about this whole matter she's been quite unwell. In the end, it's her own livelihood at stake, so you can understand why she would come to me. And then—' The provost paused to slip a coaster underneath his sweating glass. 'Then there is the matter of my telephone, which I found slightly off the hook last night and could not for the life of me think why—I mean, I have to be very precise about such things, as you know, with my eyes being the way they are, and if the receiver isn't put back firmly, no calls can get through, which rather puts us all at risk. Anyway, you know about all this—' He reclined again, crossing his legs.

I tried my best to look dispassionate. 'I didn't even know you had a telephone,' I said.

'Knell, please. You have been in this room a number of times. You have seen it. You have heard it. I have spoken of it. Let's not make this conversation any more uncomfortable than it has to be.' He looked down at Nazar, twitching his brow. She did not stir. 'I have contacted the telephone company. They're sending me a log of all my outgoing calls. It takes a bit of time, of course, but I should have them by tomorrow. And if I see that you have made connection with anybody using this phone line, and given any details about your whereabouts to anyone—well, that would be a serious breach, a serious breach.'

'A serious breach of what?' I said.

He glowered at me. 'Of the fundamental purpose of this place. Of the honour code. Of the privacy of every artist under this roof and all the others gone before. It will not be taken lightly by the trustees, I assure you.'

I was feeling the same cold helplessness that had come over me at art school, when I was asked to justify the 'profane' content of my *Deputation* mural by the board of governors. I had not conceded my position then, so why now? 'I think we'll just have to wait and see what those phone records show. Because I promise you I haven't spoken to a soul.' Technically this was true: I had only talked to a machine.

'Oh dear, I really hoped you wouldn't take this line with me,' the provost said. He spread an arm over the back of the settee.

'Whether the records show anything or not, you have still broken into my study, which is a clear contravention of the rules. So, as far as I can see, you have two choices. One: that you stay with us, work here, carry on as normal. Try to come to terms with what has happened to your friend and find that sense of purpose you've been searching for. Everything as it used to be.'

He lingered here to give me time to understand the gravity of my circumstance. I did not trust a single word that passed his lips.

'If that isn't acceptable, then I will have no option but to impose much stricter measures.'

Again, he stopped, as though anticipating a reaction. But I simply folded my arms.

'That means you'll be escorted off the grounds without documentation,' he said, 'without support to secure your route home, or any acknowledgement from this office whatsoever. Any work you've made here will remain in our possession and you will forfeit any protection you might have otherwise received. In short, you'll be entirely disowned. And, who knows? Perhaps the police will see to it that you're arrested for trespassing on private property. We have some very useful friends in the local force. I understand they can be quite unforgiving on such matters in these parts. Am I being clear enough for you?' He pitched forward for his glass and sipped at it.

I managed to still my heart enough to say, 'And what if I've already finished my work. What then?'

'Last I heard, you weren't producing much.' The provost shot a look beyond me—to Ender, I assumed, for clarification.

'*Last you heard.*' I glared at him. 'As it happens, I finished my mural last night. I'm done. I was actually going to arrange an appointment with you today to see about getting out of here.'

At this, he sniffed. It almost seemed to amuse him. He took another sip of his Afternoon Refresher. 'Well, I'm very pleased about that, Knell, but the choices stay the same. I cannot let you leave knowing you pose a threat to this establishment.'

'I'm just supposed to stay here till you throw me in the sea, is that it?'

'Not exactly.' He swirled the ice round in his glass. 'My hope is that you'll come to see the value of what's here eventually. You have three good friends in residence whom you've disrespected in your haste to use my telephone. What will happen to them and their work if you insist on blabbering to outsiders? You are jeopardising more than just yourself.' And, dredging the last of his juice until the grenadine bled against the tip of his nose, he said, 'In any case, people usually find ways to occupy themselves—ask Ender. He writes a letter to his sister in Armenia every day, and not a single one of them has ever been sent without my reading it first. They're full of fictions of his own. You wouldn't believe the things Ender gets up to in his imagination, the things that he takes credit for. But ask him if he's happier with what he has here or with the alternative—he'll tell you.'

I snapped my head round to look at the old man. He had one hand on the doorframe, one upon his hip, and he was gazing at the patterns on the rug. I could not tell if he was listening impassively or just pretending not to understand. 'What Ender chooses to accept is up to him,' I said. 'I wouldn't allow you to censor me like that.'

'We all need this place for different reasons, is my point.' The provost dabbed his nose. 'Gülcan is distraught: she's sacrificed a lot for her position here. There are people who rely on her. Ardak, too; myself, *everyone*. There is an honour code on which this refuge operates, and you have shown us just how dimly you regard it. Which, as I've said, is a tremendous disappointment to us all.' He waved the old man over: two inward jabs of his fingertips. 'Ender will take you down now. I'm giving you until dinnertime to think it over. But there really isn't a choice to make here, as you know.'

– – – – – –

Ender stayed with me the whole way. I was escorted through the empty corridors and down the stairs, until we found ourselves outside again in the sunshine on a slow walk back towards my lodging. I felt, in that moment, like some old zoo animal, captured on the brink of her escape, being paraded to her cage as an example to the others. The closeness of the old man's steps behind me was pressuring and measured. I tried to see goodness in the sky and beauty in my surroundings—the neighbouring islands were so verdant with evergreens, the sea chalk-lined by ferry crossings, the apartment blocks of Heybeliada clustered far below, awaiting families to shelter through the coming summer. But where I used to look upon these things with reverence, they now filled me with anxiety.

The old man accompanied me as far as my door. 'At the dinnerble,' he said, 'I will come back for you.'

'Is this how it's going to be now?' I said.

He peered back vacantly.

'A chaperone to every meal? Because I can tell you, it's already getting tedious.'

'Dinnerble. I will come back again.'

'All right. But if you're going to make a habit of this, you can knock for me and wait on the doorstep like everyone else.' I let myself inside and he walked off, heading straight across the grass.

The studio was dark but I did not pull up the blinds or turn the shutters back. The warmth outside was yet to permeate the cinderblocks and the floor was cool against my stockinged feet. I did not light the stove. I went and fell upon my bed, front first, and smelled the stale mattress. Its linens had been stripped to cover up the mural and the bare fabric had a curious musk—the fetid body odour of a hundred sleepless nights, not all of them my own. I felt the need to get up, but I stayed exactly where I was, my cheek pressing against the springs until it tingled and went cold. I thought about lying there forever. And I realised that if I settled there, doing nothing, seeing out my days inside the studio with no purpose left at all, then I might as well go and throw myself onto the rocks. The boy would stay lost and so would my mural. But if I went now—if I cut the painting off the stretcher *now*—I could carry it with me. I could circumvent the gates before the dinner bell and try to get home. And even if I had no papers, at least I would have my work. At least I would have the truth. This thought lifted me up.

I ran to the bathroom, got out the jewellery box, collected the *jetons* and my opal ring.

I took as many garlands as I could see in the back of my closet.

The mushrooms came off with the slightest push. I scooped them from the table, onto a sheet of tin foil, enfolding it with tape to keep the light out. On the shelf below, I found my suitcase. The parcel of mushrooms fitted in the front pouch. Next thing, I was pulling clothes from their hangers and tipping out my bedside drawers and throwing in the boy's comics. I was unpicking all the samples from the wall, baling them with string, jamming them inside the case wherever they would fit. I was clearing a space on the floor for the canvas, shoving the workbenches into the doorway, spreading out the linens to protect it, lowering it face-down to the concrete. I was on my haunches with my knife, and cutting along the line of the brass tacks, pressing firmly, surgically, so the fabric separated from the wood. And then I was hauling the stretcher frame away—an empty rectangle, cumbersome but light—and I was standing over the blankness of that canvas once again, right back where I had started.

When I flipped it over, I could just make out three white circles of texture. I had no time to worry if the paint would crack in transit, or if the final layer was dry enough. The canvas was four feet tall and twice as wide, so it took some rolling up—I had no carpet tube or dowelling to guide it with. Planning ahead, I ran a loop of string along the edge, then bunched up the lip of the canvas into my fists, folding inwards, inwards, inwards, until the weave of the cloth found a natural curl. I rolled until I had a bulky cigarette shape with a string running through it, and taped along its join to hold it all together. I waterproofed it with black plastic sheeting and more tape, more tape, more tape, more, then tied the ends of the string to form a strap. I stood up to test it, holding the roll across my back like a quiver of arrows. The string dug into my breast, but it was secure and it was portable. I just hoped that it was strong enough to last.

- - - - - -

His windowpane was dappled with the silhouettes of pines and skewed with the reflections of the mansion gables. But I could still see enough of Pettifer's head above the top edge of his drafting board to read the glumness in his expression. He was gazing out into the trees so absently that he did not even notice me approaching. When I reached the sloping path down to his doorstep, my hurried movements seemed to startle him. He called to me: 'Knell? What the heck—?' Then he undid the latch to let me in. 'Are you leaving already?'

'Shshhh,' I said, pushing past him. I threw my suitcase on his bed. 'Close the door.'

'What?'

'Just do it.'

He did. 'Oh, sure, fine. Don't worry about the interruption or anything. I mean, it's not as though I could possibly be— '

'Shshhh.'

I went to draw the blind. There was just a single sheet of paper on his drafting table: a sketch of a vaulted doorway with a sort of fish-scaled covering. 'I've been trying to invent a new type of awning,' he said. 'Collapsible but solid. Pointless, as it transpires. But I don't suppose there's any good reason why we're standing in darkness now, either . . . At least put a lamp on.'

'*Don't.*'

'What's going on?' he said. 'I'm starting to sweat.' He dabbed his forehead with his sleeve.

'I need your help, Tif. It's really important.'

'Of course,' he said, straightening his face. 'What is it?'

His stove was hot behind my calves. 'I can't go to the mansion myself—don't ask me why, just trust me.'

'All right.' Some hesitation in his voice. 'All right.'

'I need you to go and get Mac for me. Tell her if she's got anything to give me, then she'd better bring it now.'

'You seem a bit panicked. Is everything OK?'

'Please, Tif. Please just do what I ask.'

'All right, but I'm—' He stopped himself. 'What about Q? Should I bring him, too?'

'Yes. If he's there.'

'Where else would he be?'

'Just get him, Tif.'

'OK, OK, I'll put my shoes on.' And he rushed to retrieve them from under his bed and clumsily tied up the laces. With one hand on the door latch, he turned. 'Do you need me to run? Because, honestly, I might not make it up there in this shape.'

'I don't care. Just go as quickly as you can.'

'Well, anything above third gear might flatten me.' He smiled. 'Listen, I don't need to know what's going on exactly, or whatever that thing is you've got there—' He gestured at the bagged-up canvas strapped to my back. 'But please swear this isn't going to land me in any bother.'

'You're going to be fine,' I said. 'It's not you they have a problem with.'

A bouncing nod. 'You're like that pretty girl at school who made me steal things from the tuck shop.'

'I don't have time for memory lane now, Tif.'

'Just an observation. Want this closed behind me?'

'Yes. Go. Bring them.'

There was a rush of sunlight as the door opened and shut. Through the gap in the blind, I watched Pettifer head up the slope and trundle out of sight. He gave a cheery whistle of a tune I did not know. Then I was alone again, inside the partial darkness of his lodging. The place was dogged by small noises: the tick-tack-tick of the water pipes somewhere in the walls, the crackle of the coals in the stove, the restless yattering of the songbirds in the forest, the gulls and the crows on the roof. I could not relax. My fingers twitched. My spine was tensed like a cable. I needed to sit down but I did not want to have to take the canvas off my back, so I paced around in little circuits.

Up on the wall were masonry sketches and designs for quaint fenestrations. Tweed blazers hung on a rack near Tif's bedside and his plan chest was dotted with trinkets. The model ship he had built was all painted and varnished, and stood now inside a glass dome on his plan chest—I thought that some huge insect had settled on it, but in fact there was a fracture in the glass that Tif had crossed with sticking plasters. I lifted off the cover to get a closer look. The model was so expertly built that it would probably have floated, but the colourwork was drab and sloppily applied. Wens of varnish cloyed to all its joints, drips had hardened on the stern. It looked like something a man had assembled and a child had been allowed to decorate. As I put it back, the wooden stand collapsed and a piece of it fell down, landing in the partly open drawer by my ankles. Bending to get it, I noticed the drawer was crammed with drafting paper, tattered at the edges, and could not help but pull the top sheet out, expecting to find an elevation or a floor plan, part of some visionary design for a cathedral. But no. It was more like an artist's rendering. A carpeted room with a sweeping tiled shelf and ornamented pillars, skinny pencilled women lying frontwise on towels, bathing at a font. I recognised the room at once. The label said: CALDARIUM (PRELIMINARY). I rifled through the plan chest, searching all the drawings, but the same image repeated through them: varying drafts with tiny details changed, or inked in slightly different hues. Caldarium after caldarium after caldarium after—

I tore the last of them in half and balled it up inside my fist. And, rattled now, unthinking, I opened the grate of the stove and threw it on the flames. I was not satisfied with that. The drawers were full of them. I scrunched as many of the drawings as I could gather and fed them all into the fire, jamming them in, smoke thickening around me, glutting the room. The stove could not contain it all. My throat was dry and scorched. I had to run outside to get some air, feeling the closure of my lungs. And, stooping into the sunshine with great reefs of smoke draining out from the doorway, I saw Quickman, Mac, and Pettifer coming back along the slope. When they saw the fumes, they came jogging down and nearly skidded off the path. Mac rushed to me, saying, 'Are you all right? What happened?' But Pettifer went straight by me, calling: 'Christ almighty, Knell, what have you done? You fucking lunatic.' I turned to see the stove grate open and flecks of singed grey paper dancing in the room like dust motes. He was grabbing at his hair. 'Is that—oh, for Christ's sake, *everything.*

She's burned *everything*. That's years—*years* of my life! You mad fucking woman! What did I ever do to *you*?' His face was flushed so red I thought that he might choke.

'Calm down,' Q said. 'There's a few over here. They're fine, look. All isn't lost.' He was lifting sheets of paper from the floor, from the chairs, from wherever they had landed.

'Don't tell me to calm down! She gets me to fetch you, I come back to *this*.' Tif was pacing between the walls. 'I will—I'll bloody kill her.'

MacKinney grabbed my arm. 'What the hell's got into you?'

I did not answer. I flung off her arm and went back in.

'Knell,' she said. '*Knell.*'

I dragged the suitcase from the bed.

Quickman stared at me, talking very fast: 'Don't do it. Don't leave like this. It's not going to fix anything.' He stepped forward with an arm out, trying to take my case. 'Tif'll be fine. Won't you, Tif? We'll be fine. If we all stick together, we'll be fine.' I let him get a little closer. 'All right, now, come on. Sit down. We'll clear up this mess now, OK? It's going to be fine. I promise you.'

But I bolted.

'*Shit*,' Quickman said. 'She's not listening.'

Mac tried to block me as I came through the door, but she had no conviction—she backed against the cinderblocks as though afraid of being burned, and reached out for my shoulder, grabbing my canvas. The strap tightened on my throat for an instant, and then she lost her grip. 'Knell—please! My letter!' I stopped, turning on the slope, the ground giving under me, sliding. She came quickly to me, lifting up a square of paper in surrender. I held out my hand for it, splinters of sunlight in my eyes. 'Whatever you do from this point on, keep going,' she said, pressing it into my palm. No disappointment in her voice. Approval. Good wishes. I pushed it into my pocket. 'Do not stop again, you hear me?' she said. 'If you've got to get out of here, then run and don't look back.' So I did.

I sprinted up the slope, the canvas roll smacking my legs, the suitcase light but awkward. Leaping over tree roots, I made it to the path, and did not turn, did not even wave goodbye to Mac or anyone, just ran as hard as I could go, the pebbles spitting out from under me. The blur of the boy's lodging waned to my left, the mansion reared up to my right. I kept going, aiming for the woods beyond my studio, and then to the escarpment. But, coming round the east side of the mansion, I saw Ardak hastening towards me with a fire extinguisher. I looked back over my shoulder and the smoke was dark above the trees. When Ardak noticed me, he paused, nearly tripping. He was caught between two emergencies. I went flailing on, already out of breath. He swivelled like a weathervane as I sped by, and then I heard him shouting after me in Turkish. '*Dur! Hey! Nereye gidiyorsun!*' And, glancing back, I saw him coming after me, the extinguisher toppling on the grass. I did not stop but I was slowing. '*Hey! Dur!*' The case was dragging on the draught. Now Ender was hurtling across the lawn to my right and I could not see another way that I would make it. So I let the case go. It went tumbling in my wake, and, suddenly, I had some impetus. '*Dur! Hey! Dur!*' I went past my studio, past another and another, and through the fringe of the pines, Ender and Ardak still in pursuit. The scrub nicked my hands and ankles. The trees narrowed and spread, and I kept looking for the notches I had made in them, but I was too starved of breath to see straight and my strides were all so jarring. If I held to this course I was sure that I would end up by the mushroom patch, but that would be too far—I needed to bear east before I reached the clearing.

The old man was gaining ground. I could not separate my own noises from his. The woods rustled with footfalls, cracking branches, panting tongues. I could not feel my body. It was just a moving husk. And then somebody stepped in front of me from nowhere, and I clattered hard into his chest, skittling him backwards. I fell onto him, rolling, my knees in his ribs. He grabbed for my boot, but I slipped away.

I was bruised and winded, scratched and muddied. I did not glance back. The trees started thinning. I could smell the sea. It loomed in my view. And I came to the edge of the ridge at some pace, just managing to halt, with dirt and shingle and pine cones spilling forwards and down.

It was not a sheer drop. The steep beginnings levelled out into a beach of rocks, washed by the Marmara. I had nowhere else to go. There was down or there was backwards. '*Dur!*' Ardak was behind me. Ender, too. Their faces were glossed with so much sweat. Shirts torn and bloodied. The old man had no shoes on. He was holding one in each hand. 'Where can you go?' he said, gasping for air. 'Why? Why run?' He hacked up some mucus and spat. 'Is OK. Is OK. You be still.' And the two of them inched closer: dog-catchers in the park. Ardak clutched his ribs. 'Where can you go?' the old man said. Backwards would not help me. Only down.

I darted left.

'*Ugh. Sen delisin.*'

They did not rush after me.

Evergreens lined the escarpment ahead: a twist of overhanging trunks that would help me get down. I kneeled, the roll of canvas bending, scuffing on the ground, and groped over the edge, grasping for a branch. The sea buffeted the rocks below. It hissed and it churned. I was not sure the branch would hold me. But Ardak and the old man were now strutting towards me. I let it take my weight, planting my feet on brittle stone and moss. I winched myself down, branch by root by branch, until there was nothing left to grip and I had to just release my hands and pray for a good foothold. Letting go, my boots pinched at the rock and then collapsed.

I skated down the escarpment, turning, twisting, and I felt a quick, hot pain in my shoulder. It was more like a very long scrape than a fall and it happened so fast. Settling at the bottom, shaken, beaten, wounded, I had an overwhelming sense that I had not survived, that my soul had left my body somewhere on the slope. Then came a rush of victory. The deepest relief. The searing, knifing realisation of the pain in my right shoulder. I wanted to pass out, but my heart would not let me. It was shuddering with adrenaline and shock. And somehow I knew that I needed to get up, because the old man and Ardak would be standing on the bluff, searching the rubble for my body. Soon they would be coming down the slope with the rowing boat on their shoulders. They would heave me into it. And what then? I would not let my injuries count for nothing. I forced myself back to my feet.

The canvas had snapped off me. I panicked, scanned the breaking waves, the rocks. I nearly buckled at the thought of losing it. My knees started to give. But then I saw it hanging by a string, a few yards up the shore. It had snagged in the jutting weeds upon the scree. One layer of plastic was shredded, the tape was scruffed at the edges—overall, a decent state. Better than mine.

I peered up: no Ender, no Ardak, no anything. Just the ghost-thin sunshine and trees against the sky. I could hear nothing but the wash of the sea behind me. Every movement of my head drove the pain in deeper. I had shattered my shoulder or dislocated it. My arm was limp and useless. I trudged in the direction I assumed was south, cleaving to the shoreline until the waves quietened, lapped, and I reached the chain-link fence and the warning posters: DIKKAT KÖPEK VAR. There was no other way across the bay. I had to swim for it.

The water took me, a step at a time. It was not as cold as I expected. The salt stung my wounds. I tried to swim with the canvas raised aloft in my good arm, but I did not have the power in my legs. The pain was so bracing, so endless. Coiling the string around my wrist, I let it trail behind me, not quite floating, not quite sinking. I knew I could not hold my head above the water for too long, so I kicked until the strength went out of me. Soon, I felt the current grasp me, flip me, seize me. It was not as sudden as I thought.

- - - - - -

Then I blinked and I was face-down on the gravel in the dark. My mouth was parched, agape. There was so much brine inside my throat I had to sick it up. I gulped in air and it jolted me. The barbs of pain returned, but so much worse. I crawled forwards on one arm. The canvas roll was gone from my wrist: burning where the string had been. I could hardly see my own hand before me. The only light came from the moon, a row of houses in the distance, and a clutch of yellow spots across the sea. I was drenched and cold. It seemed that I had washed up in the bay. I was on a sort of beach—mostly rubble underneath me, broken shells and flotsam. It grazed my knees as I crawled through it. I was praying. For my canvas roll to rear up in the dark, to brush against me. But nothing did. I lay upon my side and hoped the pain would snuff me out.

Only the wind was gusting stronger; it bullied at my ears till I sat up. I heaved myself onto my feet again, getting my bearings. The black outline of a jetty to my right. High banks of trees on both sides. The shore a perfect crescent in between. And, behind me—I swivelled to look. Behind me a pale dirt road. Level ground. I staggered to reach it. There were chunks of concrete to step over, driftwood. What I thought was a bare pine tree in the blackness was, in fact, a telephone pole—I followed the bellying wires above my head.

The far side of the road was skirted by a wall. I ran my hand along it, scraping through the dark. I kept on going, like Mac-Kinney told me to. The agony in my shoulder was enough to bear; I could not grieve now for the mural. In the morning, I would search for it. The sea could not take everything.

I hustled on. The road curved right—north-east? It was hard to orient myself. Then, born from the darkness, I saw a low white building and a vacant lot with chain-link fencing. Getting closer, I saw decimated palm trees. I saw another jetty, ladders and stairways leading into solemn water. I saw a hundred or more deck-chairs and sun-loungers stacked up into columns, parasols folded and propped in a huddle. I saw a payphone with a hooded cubicle outside the fence, a tiny light glinting above it.

My shoulder stung as I limped over. I leaned myself against the payphone hood. The receiver was intact. The wire was attached. The line was operational. I dialled 100 and waited. Clouds shuffled across the moon.

'Hello. Operator. How can I assist you?'

'I need Victor Yail. It's 46 Harley Street, London.'

'Do you have the number, madam?'

'You'll have to look it up.'

'There's no call to be rude.'

'I'm sorry I hurt your feelings. Just connect me, please.'

'Huh!'

Soon, the trilling noise. My arm was dead. I could not keep from shivering.

'Hello. Dr Fleishmann's office.'

'Victor Yail, please. Hurry.'

'I'm afraid it's Dr Fleishmann's clinic this evening. Can I ask what it's concerning?'

A frantic bleating sound rose in my ear. I realised it was asking me for money. So I let the phone hang while I rummaged in my pocket for a coin. I found the boy's *jeton*. It seemed to slot in perfectly, rattling in the guts of the machine. But it did not stop the bleating.

'Hello? Miss?'

'Please, just put me through to Victor. It's about his son. I called yester— '

'Hello? Are you still there?'

Three more blips and it cut off. I smashed down the receiver and the mouthpiece broke.

I was too cold, too tired, in too much pain. I had to get some shelter.

There was a faded sign upon the fence: HEYBELIADA PLAJI. The gate had no padlock; I slid out the bolt. The hinges wailed as I went in. But the main building was shut, the doors chained up. Metal shutters at the windows. It was all that I could do to crawl into the stacks of chairs and loungers. I knocked a column of them and they landed in the parasols, which toppled to the ground before me. I thought their canopies looked warm and shielding. Hobbling on my knees, I went to nestle under them. I lay beneath their musty awnings and their ribs and springs and poles. The stars were jewels in the small gaps above me, and I was nothing any more, and nobody.

- - - - - -

Daylight tinted blue by parasols. The cosy dampness of a tent. I woke up feeling more exhausted than before I had passed out. Ceaseless pain around my collarbone, zipping through my legs. I rested on the concrete, eyes shut, counting down the seconds. Things almost went to black. I nearly let it happen. But then I heard the clopping of a horse near by and the jangle of its tack. Fear kept me awake. There was a noise of cart wheels on the road and a far-off voice called softly: 'Woe, woe, ayy.' And suddenly, another voice, much closer, right beside my head. I winced, holding my breath. His feet scratched the ground—so near to me. He carried on in Turkish: a dead-end conversation. I thought I could smell smoke again, but no. His feet scuttled up close to me and there were movements from above. Rustling and murmurs. The parasols were being lifted from me, one by one. There was nothing I could do. I lay there, waiting like a louse under a rock. The daylight greyed. I was exposed. He spread his shadow over me. His hands stayed on his hips. A cigarette fuming at his mouth. I got to my knees, squinting back at him. And I could see he wore a pale blue shirt with an embroidered crest: POLIS. He said something meaningless. He repeated it louder, flapping his arms. I took too long to react: he stepped to me, grabbing my hand, pulling me up by my elbow. He might as well have shot me. I screamed so loud the crows dashed from the palm trees. Everything went white.

Then I was looking at the glossy backside of a horse. A man in a black cap was at the reins, facing the road. I was propped up in an open *fayton* with the POLIS man beside me. The horse was hoofing slowly down the track. We were curving back around the bay, the sea to our left, the scrabbly beach made clearer by the light of morning. A sloop was moored out in the shallows, tilting on the waves. *'Adiniz ne?'* said the POLIS man. I looked at him, afraid. He offered me a cigarette. I shook my head. *'Anliyor musunuz?'* His arms were sprawled along the back seat of the carriage. The horse clopped on. I did not speak. I gazed towards the sea. I watched the listing of the sloop at anchor. Upturned dinghies by the jetty. A bluff of trees across the bay. And then I caught a glimpse of something in the jumble of the beach: a long black shape upon the gravel. My canvas roll, still in its plastic. The sea had brought it to me.

I stood up in the *fayton*. The wheels were rolling quickly, but I jumped. *'Hayir! Hayir!'* called the POLIS man. The pain of the landing tore me in half. I fell upon the road and hit my head. The last thing I heard was the *fayton* skidding to a stop. All the dismal voices I had pushed back in my mind escaped me then, as I lay bleeding. They said that I should stay down in the dirt where I belonged.

A familiar kind of ceiling, low and speckled. I found myself in a magnolia room with the pain muted out, fluids going into me through a tube. Right arm in a sling and thirsting. In the corner stood a dark-haired man in uniform, pure white and steam-pressed. He had three gold pips on his epaulettes and a face of consternation. 'Do you know where you are?' he said, watching me stir.

I shook my head.

I was not in a bed but on a padded trolley. They had dressed me up in pale blue fatigues. 'This is the Naval Academy, the hospital bay,' he said. 'You were brought by the police.' I tried to clear my throat but nothing would come out. 'Would you like some water?' He filled a paper cup from a cooler by the wall and handed it to me. 'Your clavicle is broken. It will get better in a month or maybe two. There are some stitches in your head, but the scar I think will be OK. I can say that you are very lucky.' The water was so cold I could not taste it. 'More?' he said.

I gulped and hummed.

There was a youthful slouch about his step as he went to the cooler. But he was much too old to be a cadet. He must have been an officer. Passing me the cup again, he smiled. 'What is your name?'

I croaked it out: 'Elspeth.'

'Ah. You can speak,' he said with a grin. He had teeth as bright and straight as his trouser seams. '*Elspess*. That is good. I like this name.'

I blinked at him.

He went to get a cardboard folder from a stand on the wall. Through the wire-glass in the door, I could see into the hallway. Framed photographs of sea cadets in dress regalia were hung from floor to ceiling. 'The police bring you here and tell me: she does not have any identifications. She has no name. They think you have no business here and so you do not deserve help from anyone, but they do not want your blood to spill on their nice shoes, so they get me to look at you. There are some people in this life who do not have God's kindness in them. Do you know what I am saying to you?'

I blinked at him.

He flipped through the folder, reviewing his notes. 'But now you have a name. *Elspess*. So, you see—you are a person now, like me and them. You are the same as everyone else.' He removed a clear plastic wallet from the folder. My ferry tokens weighted down the bottom corner. There was a sheet of creased-up paper in there, too. He held it out for me to scrutinise. 'I did not show this to them,' he said, 'but maybe I will have to, for my own sake.'

It was MacKinney's letter. Badly water-damaged. There was none of her usual cursive. Just the remnants of typewritten words, blotted out and paling:

PROPERTY OF PORTMANTLE
PLEASE RETURN (TL REWARD)

It winded me. 'Where did you get this?'

'From your clothes. You are lucky that I found it before the police.'

I went quiet. I could not understand why Mac would give it to me. She must have handed me the wrong letter.

'You know, I have treated some people like you here before,' the doctor went on. 'Coming down from that big house when they get sick. I cannot say that I am happy about this arrangement, and I do not like those people up there very much, or their policeman friends. But I am a doctor—I will not say no to people needing care. And maybe you did not know this yet, but being in the Navy does not make you rich.' He half smiled, closing the letter back inside his folder. 'So maybe I have to show it to the police so we can share that cash reward. That is what they would like. Take the money and ask no questions. We can all buy nice big houses of our own. For our retirement.' Returning the folder to the stand, he lingered by the door with his back to me. His right arm reached down for the handle, not quite turning it. 'But I think I have always liked ships more than houses. I am a Navy man. So what the police say is not important.'

He spun round.

'That line will come out, very easy, I can show you. Then I think you can get back to your feet.' There was compassion in his voice, candour to his expression. 'Because, you know, strange things happen here when I am on duty. Cadets do not like staying in the hospital. They enjoy to be outside with their friends. And there is no locks on the doors here, so I cannot make them stay.' He stepped forward and began to disconnect the tube from my forearm. 'Yes, they go down the steps and out of the gate. Nobody tries to stop them. It is crazy.'

Lifting out the sharp little butterfly from my vein, he padded the bloodspot with cotton wool and tossed everything into the waste bin. 'Thank you,' I said, but he did not acknowledge it.

'I gave you codeine for your clavicle. The rest you must do by yourself. Good luck.' He shut the door behind him and it did not lock. His feet went silently along the hall.

I got up. The floor seemed to wobble. There was a tightness in my breastbone. If I could make it to the beach again, I thought. If I could find my mural on the shore. If I could make it to the ferry. If I could make it to the mainland. If I could make it home.

I rifled through the doctor's folder to get my ferry tokens back. I hugged the walls, passing frames of posed cadets out in the hallway. My arm was strapped but I flinched with every stride. There was no exit sign, only a set of steel doors to my left. I ran for them and broke into a stairwell, bounding down the concrete steps and out into the afternoon. Boys in deep-blue uniforms were on the parade ground. Their heads turned as I hurried by. They were mumbling, pointing with their eyes. Five of them. Smokers. Sailor boys with nothing to do but suck on cigarettes and gawp at injured women. A vast white building of too many windows stood beyond them. I could smell the Marmara but could not see it. Gulls were hustling in the sky.

I kept going.

Twenty, thirty yards until I reached the gate. An older cadet in full regalia was standing guard inside a wooden sentry box. The barrier was down, but I could hurdle it if I needed to. I knew that

I could. I carried on, blanking the soreness, pushing it back. There was a hopeful feeling in me. The guard would let me through, I knew it. But the other cadets were taunting me now, shouting: *'Allez! Allez!'* When I glanced back, they were gone. Only cars in the parade ground. Parking spaces. I began to slow.

Ahead of me, the guard had stepped out of his sentry box. He was raising the barrier. He was waving his gloved hand to hurry me through. But behind me, the shouts were getting louder, brighter. They were coming from the sky. 'Ellie!' they said. 'Ellie!'

Whatever you do, Mac had warned me, *keep going.* So I did.

But then I saw a sign was screwed upon the middle of the barrier, slowly lifting, arcing through the sky. No Parking. No Admittance. No, something else. Its dotted lines grew sharper and more definite.

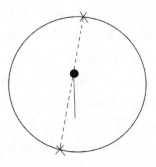

I stopped.

The whole afternoon appeared to dim around me.

Those shouts were echoing still. 'Ellie! Ellie!'

I turned back, gazing up at the roof of the building. No one was there. Just a row of blackened flues. A metal winch. But all the bright paintwork had now tarnished grey. There was a foreign mizzle on my face.

'Ellie, wait right there! Don't move one inch! I'm coming down!'

I saw him. He was high up in the very top window, flailing his arms.

A studious fellow.

Victor Yail, 46 Harley Street, London.

The operator must have found him.

Four of Four

- - - - - - - - - - - -

Clarity

One

The road was flanked by leafless trees and ordinary grass verges. Every so often, we would pass under an empty footbridge and the lane-markings would curve slightly to the left or right, but we seemed to have been driving in one straight line since leaving the hospital. Cars that were just dabs on the horizon closed in fast and thumped right past us. The day had not yet ceded to the darkness, but it was readying itself. All the streetlamps had the bleary orange makings of a fuller light in their glass hoods. Victor kept an even speed: not more than fifty and not less than forty-five. He drove with one loose set of fingers on the steering column and his elbow on the windowsill. His other hand stayed poised on his left knee, occasionally reaching up to flick the indicator with the sedateness of a man collecting tickets at a kiosk. Soon, the hummocks began to rise in the narrows of the road ahead. And then the soot-dark loch was spreading in the windscreen and I followed it with my eyes, round to the driver's side, till Victor's profile fuzzed out in the window, and it all bled into an open stretch of sea.

'How are you holding up?' he said.

I looked away, worrying the glove box. 'It's difficult to say.' I let my eyes recalibrate. There was plenty between me and the water out there—hedgerows, pasture, thickets of trees—but it was hard to reconcile it all. Every time I saw a cluster of pines I felt both homesick and at home. Being in a car, flashing over land without questioning its sureness beneath the wheels, following the road back to a place that I felt certain I had left years ago—all of these things were not easy to accept or comprehend, and yet they seemed to be the smallest of my problems. 'I'm trying not to think about it till we get there. How much further is it?'

'Oh, not far now,' said Victor. 'Five or ten minutes. We'll pick up a sign in a moment, I should think.'

He was driving me back at my own insistence. It had taken a while to convince him. He had tried to deflect me with excuses. But now we were just five or ten minutes from Luss. Five or ten minutes from knowing.

— — — — — —

A staff nurse and a porter had run out to fetch me. Blood was trailing in a chute all down my arm. I had an oozing hole where the butterfly had torn the skin, and I was standing in a car park in blue hospital pyjamas and a sling. 'Come on, lovey, let's get you inside,' said the nurse, her kindly hand on my good shoulder. She steered me back to the entrance, under the annexe, past the waiting ambulances. The porter held the bay doors open for us, asking if I needed a wheelchair. I said no, I could walk. But voices kept sputtering in and out like mistuned radio. I was still seeing cadets in uniforms: the corridor was teeming with them. They parted for us, shaking their heads as we slow-marched through, muttering their insults in Turkish, spitting on the floor. 'Here you go, pet—let's put you in here,' said the nurse, and she sat me down near the lifts between potted plants. The soil in them was dry and strewn with bent cigarette stubs. When the lift doors parted, cadets loitered in the strip-lit cavities, mouthing words at me I did not understand. The walls still seemed to be covered with pictures: old vessels in gilt frames, tall ships and steel frigates. I got lost in them for a while. I thought I smelled fresh *salep*. The nurse wiped my arm with a stinging wet tissue. Then Victor Yail came hurtling out of the lift, right past us. The nurse called: 'Doctor, she's here!' and the porter whistled after him.

Victor's shoes went sliding as he tried to change direction; he teetered and regained his balance. Seeing me between the plants, he held a palm to his chest and said, 'Oh, thank goodness. You've got her. Well done.'

'Where d'you want her?' said the porter.

'Back in the ward,' said the nurse. 'She needs that drip put back in her.'

'Yes, she's got to have that,' said Victor. 'But let's put her in a chair this time.'

'She didn't want the wheelchair,' said the porter.

'No, I mean a normal chair.'

'Aye, that'll be fine,' said the nurse.

They were talking about me as though I were a truant child caught stealing.

'All right then. Up you get, love.'

Then Victor said, 'Hang on. Let me check her over first.'

The nurse said, 'Right. I'll go up and sort that drip out then.'

'Thank you. Yes.'

The porter lingered. 'D'you want us to help you take her back?'

'No, I can handle it from here.' Victor crouched. 'But, thanks—I'll shout if I need you.'

'Aye, all right.' The porter wandered away, towards the bunched cadets playing dice games in the corridor. They did not seem to pay him any mind.

I felt Victor's hands upon my knees. He was on his haunches in front of me, leaning in to get my attention. 'Ellie? You remember me, don't you?' he said. 'It's Dr Yail. *Victor.* Can you hear me?'

I stayed quiet. The lift pinged, but when the doors slid back, the cabinet was bare.

'Elspeth,' he said, 'look at me now. Look at me.'

So I did. I stared right into his face. There was a flaky ridge upon his nose from the chafing of his glasses. His beard was dense but neatly clipped. He had a waxy quality to the skin below his eyelids, and rich green irises, like two halves of an olive. These were things that I had noticed many times before. He had not changed much in ten years. Hardly at all. 'I can hear you, Victor,' I said.

There was a visible release in his expression. 'Good girl. I knew you could.' He patted my knees and stood up. 'I'm very glad to see you in one piece.' He helped me to my feet. 'You've had a lot of people fretting after you.'

'Did you get my messages?' I said.

'Mm-hm. Don't worry about that for now. The registrar was showing me your bloodwork. Your liver enzymes are still elevated slightly. We've got to sort that out before we do anything.'

'I'm so sorry about Jonathan,' I said.

'Yes. I know you are. But we don't need to talk about that

now.' He guided me by the elbow, jabbing at the lift button. 'I want you resting and I want you getting fluids—nothing else for the moment.' The lighted numbers were not moving. 'Where the heck *is* this thing, Jupiter?' And when it finally reached our level, doors sliding back, a sea cadet was waiting for us in civilian clothing. 'Can you hit three for me, please?' Victor asked him. The cadet rolled his eyes but still pushed the button.

I was cleaned up, given a dressing gown, and put into a day room on the ward. Victor made them turn my armchair towards the window. 'Let's see how much of this you can register, eh?' he said to me. 'I'm not sure what you've been used to recently, but there are worse places to be.' He sat near me on a plastic chair, reading quietly through the notes in my folder, while a pouch of clear medicine seeped through me. Now and again, he looked up to check on my progress, smiling when I caught him looking, or getting up to fuss with my drip-stand.

I still could not understand how I had got there. For a while, I studied the movements of the cars below. I watched them reverse parking. I saw a man climb out of a little Ford Anglia, place his fedora on the roof to get a bouquet from the back seat, and walk off hatless. I even saw an ambulance crawl by with VALE OF LEVEN HOSPITAL painted on its flank, noticed the same words stencilled on the backs of wheelchairs and on signs outside the annexed buildings. But I could not trace the path from where I was to where I used to be. I could not see the joins between the mornings and the afternoons, from one month to the next. And my mind kept painting things that I could not be sure were there.

Coiled ropes left on the kerbside. Lifebuoys hung along the railings. Naval uniforms. So I just listened to the forward-ticking of the wall clock behind me and studied the drips as they came down the tube in perfect synchrony. I found that counting off the minutes soothed me. I sat there for sixteen more of them, Portmantle getting further from my mind, the bay of Heybeliada drifting away, and the mural escaping my reach. I got up and tried to point my chair in the other direction. 'Woah, hold on there,' Victor said, 'let me do it. Are you sure you don't want to look at the view?

'I want to see the clock,' I said.

He slatted his eyes. 'All right.' And he swivelled me round and moved my drip-stand.

I watched the thin red second hand circuiting the clock face, marvelling at it, feeling more and more secure with each shift of its mechanism.

After a moment, Victor folded his notes under his arm. My drip was finished and he went to tell the nurse. When he came back, he had taken his blazer off, and was scrolling up the sleeves of his shirt. He dragged his plastic chair very close to me. 'They're going to take some more bloods from you now, I think. We've got a good dose of thiamine in you, though, and that should make things a bit less foggy. You're still quite undernourished. We need to start building your strength up again—so it's a therapeutic diet for today. Once you're eating properly, they'll let me sign you out of here. OK?'

I shrugged, wincing.

'The collarbone's going to hurt you for another month or so. But that's the least of your concerns.' He smiled consolingly.

'Your bloodwork's telling us you've had some toxins in your system—we think it's a reaction to your tablets, but the tests have been a little inconclusive. So they've been trying to see how you'll respond after some fluids. You're starting to look a little better. A healthier colour, at least.'

I watched the second hand complete another lap. 'Is Jonathan all right?' I said, addressing it to the clock.

'He is,' said Victor matter-of-factly. 'My secretary, on the other hand, you almost gave a coronary. She's on a fortnight's leave to make up for it.'

'I really did think— '

'I know,' he said.

Victor reached to throw my notes onto the bank of chairs beside him. 'The police aren't sure how you injured yourself. Do you remember anything?'

'I fell,' I said.

'From what? The sky?'

I had forgotten how much he liked his little jokes. 'An escarpment,' I said. 'And then I hit my head. On the ground, I think.'

'Well, that would certainly make sense.' He inhaled, folded his arms. 'They had to drag you out from under a pier. Did you know that?'

'No.'

'All true, I'm afraid. You were in quite a state.'

'Where?' I said.

'Hm?'

'Where did they find me?'

'A village down the road. I forget the name.'

'Where?'

'Hang on, I've got it written down.' He arched his back to re-trieve his notes, flipping through them. 'Luss,' he said. 'Luss pier. L-U-S-S.'

The breath went out of me.

Victor was nodding at his page of scrawl. 'The police said you were camped out under there. And it says here you stole the tar-paulin off a boat to wrap yourself in. They weren't sure how long you'd been there. Any light to shed on that?'

I could not even muster a noise.

'Well, they tried to get you in the squad car, but you blacked out. So they put you in an ambulance instead and took you here. You're lucky you were close to a good hospital. They got you on an IV right away.'

Luss, I thought. *L-U-S-S.*

'They got my name from a prescription in your pocket,' Victor went on. 'I told them to hold you here till I could get a train up. But they've been doing lots of engineering works—delays across the board. I had to drive up. It took me a while to arrange things. And by the time I got here, well, you'd already discharged your-self, so to speak. I wish I could have come sooner.'

'Does Jim know I'm here?' I said.

'I'm sorry.' His brow bent. 'Jim?'

I told him that I had been in Luss for Henry Holden's fu-neral, and found Jim Culvers living there in the old cottage. I told him I had stayed with him for several months. He absorbed the news without much change in his expression. 'So do I take it that's where you've been holed up since I saw you last? With Jim Culvers?'

'Not the whole time.'

'Where else?'

'I don't think I can explain it,' I said.

'Try.'

'It's hard to separate the truth from the rest of it.'

'Well, I can work on that with you.'

'Part of me still feels as if I'm there. I know I'm not—I know I can't be. But it hurts to think I never was. Does that make sense?' I could not tell where it was coming from, but a great swell of sadness came over me then. Tears hung fat in my eyelids and spilled.

Victor put the notes down. 'Shshhh, it's all right,' he said. 'It's going to take some time for things to level out. I shouldn't have pushed you so hard.' He offered me his handkerchief. 'Go on. It's clean.'

I took it and dabbed my eyes. I could not take them off the clock.

'I've got something that might help you,' he said. Standing up, he took the leather wallet from his trouser pocket and sifted through it, lowering himself down again. 'It was in here last I looked. Gah, where is it?—all right, phew. It's here.' He lifted out an oblong photograph, folded up to wallet-size. Passing it to me, he said, 'We took that last summer. At our place in Norfolk. He didn't want to pose for it, but Mandy got her way—I'm glad she did. Not so much of a pipsqueak any more, but you just try and get that costume off him.'

In the photo, Jonathan Yail was no older than eleven. He was standing high up on a drystone wall, his arms outstretched and fists closed tight. The wind was surging through his hair. A clouded sky behind him. Sunlight on his face. He was dressed in a snug blue jersey with a sinuous cape. Across his breast, the yellow-red emblem of Superman, stitched on by hand. He had a look of purest focus. I was very glad to see his face.

'The things I have to put up with, eh?' Victor said. He turned the photo round in my hands, pointing at the caption he had written: *Whooshing to the Broads, Aug. '62.* 'He's just about to start big school now. Still a bloody great pain in the neck, but I should think the world would lose all meaning if I ever lost him. I could never find a way to cope with anything like that. So whatever you think happened, just be happy that it didn't. And keep thinking about that happiness until the rest of it gets easier.'

– – – – – –

The friendship I had worked on with MacKinney over time, the admiration I had felt for Quickman, the baiting closeness I once shared with Pettifer: such things are not easy to release when you have nothing to replace them with. But speaking about them was not denying their existence. I could accept the truth and still be grateful for my fabrications. And I knew that Victor would not belittle them.

That afternoon in the day room—with the next infusion draining through me and another chalky therapeutic milkshake not quite finished in my cup—I felt clearer-headed but no less conflicted in my heart. 'I understand that where I've been is not really where I've been,' I found myself saying. It came so abruptly from the silence that Victor flinched. 'But I can't decide what's worse: keeping that place to myself so nobody can share it, or letting it all out so it just disappears.'

Victor had been mostly occupying himself with paperwork,

and had now started on a crossword in the newspaper. He looked up. 'Well, you don't have to share anything that you don't want to. But I would think it's always better to talk about experiences than repress them. And you know how much respect I have for your imagination.' He did not try to write notes. 'I'm your doctor,' he said, 'but I'm also your friend. I'm here to listen when you feel ready. I won't force it out of you.' I nearly revealed it all to him in a rush, as Jonathan had once explained to me the world of Superman. Except I could not bring myself to voice it. I felt that if I spoke the word 'Portmantle' I would diminish it, and I was not prepared to let it go yet.

Victor went back to his crossword. 'Naturally, I'd like to bring you off the Tofranil,' he said, not looking at me. 'It might have been a huge mistake to put you on it in the first place. But you weren't exactly sticking to the dosage.'

'No one's blaming you for this, Victor.'

'I blame myself on everyone's behalf.'

'You did what you thought best.'

'Perhaps that's how I failed you—by not listening. I've made plenty of blunders in treating you. I'll be reviewing all your notes when I get back, and seeing what I could've done better. But for now, I'm just glad you're OK.' He unscrewed his pen lid and sighed. 'Fourteen down. *Atavistic*. Seven letters. What is that, "primeval"? Does that fit?'

'Jim could still be there, you know,' I said. 'In Luss. At the cottage.'

'Yes, the thought had occurred.' He peered up at me. 'But I'm not sure you've quite reasoned that one out in your head, Ellie. Keep resting. Let that thiamine do its job.'

'I need to get back to that pier,' I said. 'I left something there. It's important.'

He ignored me. '"Primeval" seems to work. Seven down: *Whittles*. Six letters.'

'Victor, I need to go back.'

'Yes, I heard you,' he said, filling in the blank spaces. '"Carves" seems to be right, but that means I've got the other letters wrong.'

'*Victor.*'

He crossed his legs, eyeing me over his lenses. 'I really don't think going back there will help you. It's better you keep thinking ahead. Rest now and we'll be driving home by tomorrow morning, all being well.'

'It's important to me—I need to find it.'

'You aren't listening now, Ellie.'

'Please. If you come with me, you'll understand why.'

'Sit back and relax. We aren't going anywhere.'

'But I was painting again,' I said. 'I really was *painting*.'

'You never had a problem painting, as I recall,' he said. 'Stopping was the issue.'

'Well, I finished my mural.'

This loosened something in him. 'When?'

'Yesterday.'

'Yesterday you were under a pier.'

'Before then. Please, Victor. You have to drive me back there.'

He pulled at the grey of his sideburn. 'I don't know.'

'I left it on the beach somewhere. It's the best work I've ever done in my life. I can't just leave it there.'

'What's it of, this finished picture?'

'It's abstract. You just have to see it. I can't put it into words.'

'Would there be ships in it at all?'

'No, not a single one,' I said. 'It's pure abstraction.'

'And how exactly did you get it down there? If it's half as big as the mural I saw in your studio, it's—'

'I cut it off the frame and rolled it up.'

'Why?'

'So I could carry it.' I stared at him, pleading. 'What does it matter, Victor? If you don't take me there, I'll find some other way. I'll take the bus. I'll walk. Isn't it better you come with me?'

He shifted in his seat, folding his newspaper, casting it aside. 'The ward doctor wants you here till morning. I can't sign you out without his agreement.'

I could sense that he was wilting, so I kept on at him. 'Just take me when they say it's all right.'

He huffed. 'I really must get back to London by the afternoon. I've appointments, other patients to see.'

'*Please*, Victor. It's important.'

'I only planned on being here for one night.'

'Then take me on the way home.'

'You're just like Jonathan, you know,' he said. 'I don't respond well to this sort of pestering. It's not how I prefer to do things.'

But I could tell that he had already decided.

- - - - - -

The road took a dip and we were passing by the loch almost at the level of the shore. Boats and bright red buoys were moored out there in fitful patterns. Dinghies, sloops, and cruising yachts, tarpaulined. I did not want to ask Victor if he could see them, too. I just let them smear out behind the thickening treeline.

One more turn and we approached a sign that welcomed us to Luss. 'You'd better direct me from here,' he said.

We went on, past low stone cottages, slate roofs, farm walls shaped like pommel horses, barbed-wire fences. We left grassland behind us, firs and oaks and chestnuts, ivy-coated monsters. The hummocks bulged in the dimness, patchy brown and misted under clouds. 'It's strange,' I said. 'Everything's how I remember it.'

'Why wouldn't it be?'

'It's not the place I thought it was, that's all.'

'I don't get what you mean.'

'I know you don't, Victor. It's OK that you don't.'

The stuccoed barns of the Colquhoun Arms were on our left now. I told Victor to go right, and, braking quickly, turning, we came along the road that Geoff Kerr had brought me down after the funeral. Quaint beige cottages with steaming chimneys on both sides and so much green. Up ahead of us: the pier. A shingle beach and placid water. A vast sky darkening above the frosted hills on the far side of the loch. It was familiar and yet somehow meaningless to me, this scenery. A backdrop to a play I had not seen.

'You ought to park up,' I said.

Victor rolled us slowly to a stop. We were right beside the pier now and I still felt so removed from what lay beyond the windscreen. I tried to think back to the night that I had left this place for Portmantle—when Jim had walked me to the bus that would carry me to Balloch. The way I still imagined it, I had travelled on to Glasgow, taken the train to catch a ferry at Dover, on to Calais, on to Paris, on to Milan, through Belgrade and Sofia, and into Istanbul. I could remember everything about that jour-

ney: from the noises of the Gare de Lyon to all the speckled china
in the train carriages and the brief conversations I had held with
other travellers. But the winter gloom of Luss was somehow less
substantial in my memory.

I left the car and Victor trundled behind me. There was a
wood-panelled building at the nearside of the pier and a hard-
worn boardwalk ranging out into the loch. The water was clear
enough in the shallows to see the pebble-bed and, further out, it
creased and eddied as though stirred by something deep beneath.
I came sideways down the steps and onto the shingle. There was
a hollow underneath the pier's stilts, and I got to my knees to
search around in all the sand and grit and goose muck, one-
handed. My sling pulled at my neck. 'Can you tell me what I
should be looking for?' called Victor from behind me.

'It's like a tube, about eight or nine feet long. Wrapped up in
black plastic sheeting.'

'That shouldn't be hard to miss.'

I scoured the damp and shadowed ground on both sides of the
stilts. 'Well, it isn't here,' I said.

Victor's hands were in the pockets of his coat. He was staring
left and right along the shore. 'This beach runs all the way round.
It's miles.'

'It can't be far from here.'

'Let's try that way.' He pointed south.

'The cottage is the other way. It's more likely to be north.'

'If you say so.'

'No, you're right. The current might have washed it further
out.'

I went south, combing the shoreline with my eyes, until the

beach thinned out and there was nowhere left to walk. Nothing
was floating on the loch that I wanted to see. 'Let's head back,' I
said, and Victor tracked my footsteps quietly. He walked a few
yards behind, observing my behaviour, only partially invested in
my search. 'How long?' he called.

'Huh?' I was looking north along the beach towards the pier
again.

'How long until you give this up?'

'You could help me, you know, instead of hoping I'll fail.'

'Is that what you think I'm doing?' he said.

'I'm not sure.'

'Let's speed this up, Ellie. It's getting late.'

But Victor did not understand that darkness was our ally. If
the plastic had ripped back from the roll, the gleam of the paint
would vent out. We might catch a glimpse of blue somewhere in
the pitch-black night and follow it.

I peered down at the shingle, looking for a knoll or a raised
edge where the mural might have been covered over, buried.
There was nothing. I zigzagged up and down, checking the pavement side of the beach, walled off by cobbles. Nothing.

We reached the pier again and I checked through the windows
of the wooden outhouse to see if it had been found and left there,
leaned up in a corner as lost property. But no. It was only a closet
of boxes.

Victor had stayed on the bank, propped against the bonnet of
his car. He looked at his watch. 'You haven't checked up there,'
he said, thumbing north. 'I'll wait for you. My shoes are full of
stones.'

I went down the slope, along the strip of shingle. A few small dinghies were moored in the shallows. There were four of them, differently coloured and named, with mainsails scrolled around their willow masts, tied off. All but one of them was tarpaulined at the stern.

Beside me, a partition of green hedgerows ran most of the way along the beach. Above that, a hummock bristling with tall trees. Cottages dotted the lip of the shore. I knew that Jim Culvers was not waiting for me in any of them. I understood that he had left me. I did not know precisely when, but he was gone. And there was nothing on the waterline for me to salvage, nothing that I hoped to see. So I turned back. Each dragging footstep on the shingle seemed to drain the spirit from me.

Victor was already in the car. The windows were fogging and I could hear the throbbing voices of the radio news. He wound down the window as I approached. 'Forecast is for thunder and lightning this evening,' he said. 'I'd like to be off the motorway by then, if I can help it.'

I nodded, traipsing over. I did not want to think about the journey back to London or returning to my empty flat.

He turned the engine on. My shoulder was aching. But then, coming up the slope, I took one last glance towards the pier and I noticed something bobbing and scraping underneath the stilts, halfway along it. A bulky cigarette shape.

I went rushing for the boardwalk, forgetting the pain.

'Ellie!'

Reaching the middle of the pier, I lay on my good side, got on my back.

'Ellie!'

I slid under the railing.

Victor caught up with me. 'You're going to do yourself another injury like that. Get away from there.'

The peaceful loch was rippling under me. My legs were dangling over the boards.

Victor must have seen it in my eyes then, because he came lurching forwards with his arms to grapple me. But I was already dropping.

Two

Victor waded to the shore, flinging water from his arms, peeling off his coat. His shirt was rinsed, translucent, and I could see the matted hairs of his torso underneath it. He had taken off his glasses to protect them, and was spitting the loch from his mouth, wringing his eyelids clear. I was on the gravel with my canvas roll beside me. I was soaked and tender, slingless. The pain was stabbing through my side, but I had enough relief in me to smother it. Victor had no such consolation—only the sight of me, safe and unharmed. 'One of these days,' he said, dripping at my feet, 'I'm finding you a different therapist.' He stooped to get his breath back, wheezing. 'What the hell are you trying to do to me? I'm fifty years old, for crying out loud. I'm not cut out for this.'

I was panting too much to hold my smile. 'You didn't have to come in after me.'

'I bloody well slipped trying to reach you.'

'I told you I was fine.'

'How was I supposed to know that? I thought you were crying out for help.' He lowered himself to the gravel next to me, shivering. The mangy roll of tape and plastic lay between us. He glanced down at it. 'So that's it, is it? Doesn't seem like much from here.'

My hand was still gripping it. 'It's what's on the inside that counts.'

'Well, that's not always true, believe me. That thing better be worth all the trouble. There aren't many paintings I'd jump into a freezing lake for.'

'I thought you slipped.'

He cornered his eyes at me.

'Sorry,' I said.

'Well, about bloody time.' He patted his hands clean of stones, hooked on his glasses. 'My kingdom for a towel.'

'We can dry off by the fire,' I said.

'Where?'

'In Henry's cottage. It's five minutes that way.'

He looked north. 'That might not be such a bad idea. My teeth are chattering.'

'I can hear them.'

He gripped his jaw to quell it.

'It'll be worth it when you see it,' I said. 'I'll show you.'

'I just want to get dry and get home.'

'It's yours—the painting. I'm giving it to you.'

He rubbed his knees. 'That's all very sweet. But I don't want it. Even if it's worth a fortune, I'm not taking your work.'

'You kept that portrait I did of you.'

'That had diagnostic value.'

'So does this, probably. I wouldn't have found it without you.'

'Well, I've already diagnosed you once, and that didn't turn out very well, did it? We're not great adverts for the wonders of psychiatry.' He stood up, extending his arm to me. 'Come on. Let's find somewhere to dry off and then we'll hit the road.'

I let him haul me up.

We walked along the shore, the pair of us doused and shuddering. The canvas sagged and drooped in my clutches. 'You'd better check that's actually what you think it is,' Victor said. 'People dump all kinds of stuff in lakes, you know.'

But I could tell from the configurations of the tape around it, from the way that I had tucked and joined the pieces over its ends, that my mural was inside. The outer plastic was torn up; the inner layers still seemed to be intact. 'I just hope it isn't ruined,' I said. 'If the water's really got to it, I might as well throw it back in.'

'It's probably more soaked than we are.'

'I knew you'd find a way to cheer me up, Victor.'

'You're lucky I'm still talking to you. I've not been this drenched since I set the hotel sprinklers off on my honeymoon.' He snorted a laugh from his nostrils. 'One cigar. I've had one cigar in my life and I nearly set fire to the whole bloody building.'

And the thought of this did cheer me up somehow. We trudged along the beach, with the dregs of the daylight waning above us, and the silhouettes of dinghy-masts scratched darkly on the sky.

When we reached the nettled pathway to the cottage, Victor hung back. There were no lights on inside and the mossy roof was sagging ominously in the middle. The chimney had crumbled off. One of the windows had a brick-sized hole in it. The general impression of the place amidst the gloom was of a ship-wreck. I pushed on, through the high weeds and grass. Part of me was still hoping to find Jim coming through the woods with a basket of fresh pickings. Part of me was thinking of Portmantle.

The front-door fixtures were corroded shut, so I led Victor round the side, into the thicket of the garden. There was a rusted oil drum lying in the nettles. The back door was unlocked and there must have been a shilling or two still left in the meter, because the bulb blinked yellow as I turned on the switch. The kitchen sink was stacked with unwashed crockery, and all across the table there were stale food scraps, tea left mouldering inside cups. It was colder in than out. The room had the upsetting reek of sour milk and Victor covered his mouth. 'Blimey,' he said. 'All the medication in the world couldn't make me put up with this mess. You'd have to hold me here at knifepoint.'

But this was not where I had really been. This was just the place my body had been ghosting.

I laid the mural across two of the kitchen chairs and went to find the matches in the drawers—there were none. Victor had already parted the beads in the doorway and was looking through into the lounge. He turned the lights on and, going through, said, 'Well, this is one way to live, I suppose.'

I followed after him.

A mattress was spread out by the fire, covered in dirty blankets that looked more like decorator's dustsheets. The fireplace was crammed with singed paper and splinters of pine cones. The curtains were taped around the window frame. A fold-up table was loaded with rags and hardened tubes of paint, jars of briny water and murky bottles of linseed oil. There was a scattering of flora all across it and the floor, and a bucket of mulched pink petals, soaking. 'That's all Jim's stuff,' I said. 'Or it was Henry's. I can't tell the difference any more.'

I found matches by the hearth and crouched to light some of the kindling scraps I found left in the scuttle. 'Is there any paper over there that I can burn?' I said.

But Victor's mind was on something else. He was standing, cross-armed, by the wall at the far end of the room. 'Ellie,' he said. 'Come and see this.'

'I thought you wanted to get dry,' I said.

'Just come and look.'

I left the kindling fizzling out and went to him. 'Honestly, we're going to catch pneumonia if I don't get this lit.' And, when I gazed towards the aspect of the wall that so fascinated him, I saw that it was pasted with images—they were glued right onto the plasterwork. Vivid colour photographs showing lush greenery, white houses glinting on a summer waterfront, men driving horses and carriages, two enormous buildings nestled in dense pines. I stepped closer, near enough to read their printed captions in the borders:

The only cars allowed on the islands are police and utility vehicles. Instead, there are horse-drawn carriages known as phaetons ('faytons' in Turkish). . .

'*National Geographic*, if I'm not mistaken,' Victor said. He walked towards the window, where there was another workbench of materials. I could not take my eyes from the wall. 'You seem to have given my exercise some thought. Perhaps too much so.'

Heybeliada's most visited attraction is the nineteenth-century Aya Triada Manastiri, a Greek Orthodox school of theology, which looks down over the island from its northernmost peak . . .

'At least now I understand what you were trying to tell me in that message. My secretary couldn't figure out what you were saying. She thought she heard "Istanbul", but it wasn't the best of connections. You were rather garbled at the end.' Victor was a blur now in the fringes of my vision. 'I thought you said able something, table something, maple something. I should probably get my hearing tested.'

On the south side of the island is Heybeliada Sanatorium, a refuge for TB sufferers at the farthest point of Çam Limani Yolu.

I felt so numbed. There must have been ten or twenty of these images, cut from the magazine and glued down flat. And, surrounding them, I could see lines of my own handwriting in pencil. Ribbons and ribbons of scrawled text curving and bending all along the wall. I had copied it straight from the magazine, verbatim.

'The Heart of the Princes' Islands' by ~~scratched out of the wall with a blade~~. We know little about the island before we step off the ferry, but there are some things we have researched. This is as much a scouting mission as it is a relief exercise. Heybeliada lies twelve miles off the coast of Istanbul, the second largest of the islands that the locals know as Adalar. It is crowned by two steep forested hills to the north and south and its middle section bows into a plane of settlements where the natives live and ply their trades. Much of the work is seasonal. In the winter, the squat apartment

blocks and rangy wooden houses stand vacant and unlit,
but when the bright weather comes again they fill up with
summering Istanbullus, who sit out on their fretwork
balconies, sunbathe on the rocky beaches, flock upon the
shining Marmara like gulls, and drink merrily on their
roof-decks until dark. The Turkish meaning of its name—
Saddlebag Island—evokes its shape at sea level. It is far up
on the south-eastern peak, amidst the dense umbrella pines
and pomegranate trees, that the Heybeliada Sanatorium is
positioned. And we are—

I heard a noise like buttons rattling in a jar. Victor was holding a glass medicine bottle with the label ripped off. He shook it and shook it and the tablets clattered weakly inside. 'I don't know how many were in here to begin with—maybe sixty or so,' he said, and tipped out a mound of them into his palm, 'but this suggests our toxicology's been off the mark.' He picked up a tablet and examined it. 'It's Tofranil, no question. Looks to me like you stopped taking them. So, whatever's been showing in your bloodwork, I wouldn't think it's necessarily from these.'

'Then what?'

'You tell me.' He brushed past me. 'Could be the oil paints. They're full of chemicals. Or the turps, maybe.'

'I don't know.'

My eyes turned back to the wall, picking up a section further down:

We have been advised to chart a horse-drawn fayton when
we leave the ferry port. The best way to reach the sanatorium

is from the east, via a dirt road that leads up to a spear-top
fence, cordoning off the property. On the way up, we pass
warning posters stapled to the trees along the slope: DIKKAT
KÖPEK VAR /BEWARE OF THE DOG. *But we are not worried.*

   The sea view from the promontory affords tuberculosis
patients an abundance of fresh air and serenity, removed
from the hustle and the noises of the city. Built when the
disease was at its most widespread and fatal, the sanatorium
was opened in 1923, a year after the founding of the Turkish
Republic. Previously under the ownership of Greek
authorities, the building was revamped under the aegis of
Mustafa Kemal Atatürk, the founder of modern Turkey—

It was a complete transcription of the entire article, scribbled
from the ceiling to the skirting boards. On and on it went in
detail:

   Most of the patients are students from all over Anatolia who
came to Istanbul for their education at the city's universities.
They take in the sea air in the daytime and engage in debates
at night over çay *and* salep. *Friendships boost morale*
amongst the patients and so do activities—

Victor was busy at the hearth. He tore something, and struck
a match, and then I heard the sudden puff of an ignition.

   Concerts are organized and films are projected for the
residents in the day room twice a week. The sanatorium
is also equipped with a rehabilitation centre, where local

craftsmen such as Ardak Yilmaz (pictured right) are brought in to teach woodworking skills to patients. Although it has established a fine reputation over the years as a centre for thoracic surgery, the facility is now extremely underfunded and the chief doctor is concerned that a—

'Come and get warm,' Victor said. 'It's really getting going now.' He was kneeling at the fireplace with both hands extended to the flames. The orange light dappled his face. He looked so entrenched in the glow of it, and I felt so cold and jittery, that I could not resist.

Kneeling beside him, I saw that he had ripped the topmost pages of another magazine and fed them to the fire. The uncomfortable dampness of my clothes began to bother me. We stayed there on our knees together for a while, saying nothing, letting our bodies gently warm through. And then I said, 'I don't know if I'll get over this, Victor.'

He kept his eyes upon the flames. 'You'll be all right. We'll work through it together.'

'I'm not sure I can go back with you. Not yet. I always thought that I could live without anything as long as I had painting. Now look at me—I'd be better off in a factory, doing something useful. I think I'd be much happier that way.'

Quite unexpectedly, he placed his arm around me. 'Elspeth,' he said, 'you are twenty-six years old and you are still alive. And the sun will rise tomorrow, as it always does. That's all you have to think about for now.' I wanted to lean my head on his shoulder, but I could not get past the pain. 'What happened to your sling?'

'It came off in the loch.'

'Then I'd better make you another.' He reached onto the bed and removed the grubby slip from the pillow. He ripped along the seam, folded a triangle, and put my arm inside it, knotting it at the back of my neck. 'You have people who care for you. Remember that,' he said. 'I've never known Dulcie Fenton to get sentimental about anyone. But she is genuinely fond of you—and not just because she has a vested interest.'

'Well, she tries to make it seem that way, at least.'

'No, I think it's quite sincere. She must have called me twenty times, asking if I'd heard from you.'

'Worried about the show, most likely.'

'At first, maybe. She said that you'd written to her. Gave me an earful about it, actually—I told her you would be OK travelling on your own, that we shouldn't be alarmed. But even after your show went on, she was still calling about you. I think she even phoned your mother a few times. Everyone said the same thing. *Travelling*. None of us knew where to look for you.'

He tore off another page of *National Geographic*, balled it up, and threw it on the fire. I could not tell what time it was. The mantel clock was smashed and buried outside. But it did not matter. We were drying out, slowly and steadily, and soon we would get back to the car and he would drive me all the way to Kilburn, where nobody was awaiting my return.

'So what do we do now? Go back to having sessions once a week?' I said. 'Pretend this didn't happen?'

'If you feel that'll help.'

'I doubt I could afford you any more.'

'Nobody can. After this, my fees are tripling. I'm pricing myself out of the psychiatry game entirely.'

'That's probably for the best,' I said. 'You're a bad influence on people.'

'Precisely. The world is better off. I'm going into show business.' He grinned. 'Jazz clarinet has always been my calling. There has to be a career in it for me.'

I smirked.

'You think I'm joking. I've actually got—' The bulb went off above us, and the kitchen light had blinked out, too. 'I suppose that's the last of the meter,' Victor said. 'We ought to be making tracks. Are you dry yet?'

The hospital had given me back my wretched painting clothes: a paint-smattered flannelette blouse and stiff cotton trousers. They were grimy and still damp, but I felt much warmer now. 'Not quite,' I said.

'We'll put the blowers on in the car.'

He helped me up. The flames gave off the last remaining light inside the cottage. It quavered on the floor and our moving bodies flashed and dulled it. Victor reached down for the bucket of mulched petals. Lifting it, he sniffed the liquid to make sure it was not flammable, and, when he was satisfied, he came and threw it on the flames. They spat and sizzled into blackness, and gave off the smothered scent of a dud firework. For a second, it was so dark that I could not see where Victor was standing. 'Hang on,' he said, 'I've got the matches in my pocket.' And I heard him get them out and fumble with them. But before he could strike one, the far end of the room brightened, swelling with a pale blue light. I could see Victor's outline now before me, burnished like the moon. 'What *is* that?' he said.

He went after it, walking into the blue glow on instinct: a moth in the tow of a porch light. I trailed after him. Beyond the hallway was the storeroom that I had once cleared out with Jim. The door was shut but there was a clear blue eking out from the gaps around the frame, between the hinges. Victor looked at me, slightly fearful. 'It's OK,' I said. 'Nothing can harm you.'

'What can't?'

He was dithering now, so I twisted the handle and showed him inside.

All he said was: 'Jesus, Ellie.'

The walls were banked with wooden painting boards, turned inwards—there must have been over a hundred. Victor hardly paid them any mind. He was staring at the gleaming garland by the water boiler. It was hanging from the clothes-rail at the back end of the room. As he approached it, the radiance of the mushrooms was so strong that his whole body seemed floodlit. He moved even closer, shielding his eyes. 'What are they?' he said, clasping one of them in his fingers. 'They're unbelievable.' But I did not answer. I was moving for the door, breaking through the hallway, through the lounge, and swinging back the kitchen beads. Victor did not call after me. He was transfixed by the shine.

Now the kitchen sink was faintly humming blue as well. Drips of the pigment had hardened on the edges of the mixing slab that lay inside the basin; flecks of it were on the handle of the muller, drying on the rack beside it. I felt a prickling elation, scoring along my spine.

With my good arm, I cleared everything from the table, sending food and dishes careening, smashing. I picked up the mural
and laid it there, dropping it to the surface like a cut of meat.
With my sore nails I picked at all the tape along the corners and
the seam. I pulled at the plastic and lifted it away. There was a
blush of pallid light. The canvas unfurled. It spread across the
table, moist in my grip. It spilled over the edges, kissed my boot
caps.

Victor clattered through the beads. He stood at the threshold,
dazed. Three blue circles bloomed upon his lenses and I could
not see his eyes behind them. I thought he was about to speak,
but he stopped himself. He moved slowly to the canvas, knitting
his hands behind his head. It was a gesture of surrender. He did
not ask me any questions. All the darkness in the room was
painted out.

Acknowledgements

- - - - - - - - - - - - - - - -

This book could not have surfaced from my imagination without the generosity and support of a number of people. First, a special thank you to my former editor Jessica Leeke, who afforded me the time and space I needed to chase down these ideas and whose confidence in me was so important throughout. Thanks to everyone at Simon & Schuster, most particularly Rowan Cope, Jo Dickinson, and Carla Josephson. Thanks as ever to my agent Judith Murray and the team at Greene & Heaton, to Grainne Fox at Fletcher & Co., and Ed Park at Penguin Press. I am greatly indebted to Jonathan Lee, Karen Brodie, and the British Council for giving me the chance to live and write in Istanbul; to November Paynter, Anlam Arslanoglu, and the teams at SALT and Noa Apartments for hosting me so warmly while I was there. My eternal gratitude to Cansu Ataman, Caroline Hesz, and Machiko Weston for the various translations featured herein. Thanks to Shumon Basar, Robert Weston, Simon Johnson, Ellis Woodman, Funda Kucukyilmaz, Sema Kaygusuz, Sam Alder, Jack Cocker, Derek Dunfield, Peter Irving, Alistair Windsor, and the fine comforts of Galata Kitchen; enormous thanks to Professor Ian Crawford and Dr David Lloyd for assistance with research matters; to Birkbeck College and all of my supportive colleagues in creative writing. Thanks to the Hesz family, to my brother Nicholas for help with *everything* (NaCW!), to Katy Haldenby, and my family, especially my granddad for steering me on course when I most needed it. To JB and RH for inspiration. Above all, thank you to my wife Stephanie, whose love and understanding of me is the most extraordinary thing: every day with her is clarity.

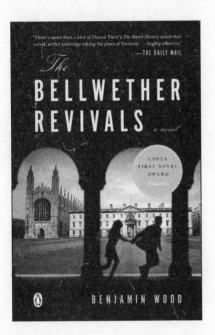